W

—*Vows*—

JUST MARRIED

NANCY WARREN
KIMBERLY LANG
LESLIE KELLY

WEDDING
Vows
COLLECTION

April 2015

May 2015

June 2015

July 2015

WEDDING
Vows
JUST MARRIED

NANCY WARREN
KIMBERLY LANG
LESLIE KELLY

Published in Great Britain 2015
by Mills & Boon, an imprint of Harlequin (UK) Limited,
Eton House, 18-24 Paradise Road, Richmond, Surrey, TW9 1SR

WEDDING VOWS: JUST MARRIED © 2015 Harlequin Books S.A.

The Ex Factor © 2010 Nancy Warren
What Happens in Vegas… © 2010 Kimberly Lang
Another Wild Wedding Night © 2007 Leslie A. Kelly

ISBN: 978-0-263-25371-9

011-0315

Harlequin (UK) Limited's policy is to use papers that are natural, renewable and recyclable products and made from wood grown in sustainable forests. The logging and manufacturing processes conform to the legal environmental regulations of the country of origin.

Printed and bound in Spain
by CPI, Barcelona

THE EX FACTOR
NANCY WARREN

To Sharon Kearney,
for too many years of friendship to count.

USA TODAY bestselling author **Nancy Warren** lives in the Pacific Northwest where her hobbies include skiing, hiking and snow shoeing. She's an author of more than thirty novels and novellas and has won numerous awards. Visit her website at nancywarren.net.

1

"STACY REALLY WANTS the circus theme," Patricia Grange said, a note of appeal in her voice. It was a tone Karen Petersham knew well—the desperate cry of a woman who has spoiled her baby girl for so long she doesn't know how to stop. As one of the top wedding planners in Philadelphia, Karen got her share of spoiled princesses and their bizarre wedding requests, but this was right up there.

"A circus themed wedding is certainly unusual," Karen said smoothly. "You don't get a lot of them."

"It's because of Cirque du Soleil," Patricia explained, throwing her hands out in a gesture of helplessness.

"Cirque du Soleil?" What on earth could a bunch of acrobatically theatrical circus performers have to do with a wedding?

The mother of the bride nodded. "Hudson took Stacy to see the touring production of *Kooza* for their first date. They think it would be romantic to recreate the circus theme for their wedding."

"Well, I guess we can be happy he didn't take her ice fishing for their first date."

The woman smiled weakly. "I suppose so." She straightened the perfectly straight hem on her Gucci skirt. "Cirque is about both clowning and acrobatics, of course."

"Two excellent attributes of a successful marriage."

"Exactly." The woman smiled at her gratefully. "And Cirque did perform at the Academy Awards one time. I remember seeing it on television."

Only a Philadelphia society girl could equate her wedding with the Academy Awards. Already Karen suspected that this ceremony was going to be one of those nightmares. The mother of the bride had shown up for the appointment, but no bride. Always a bad sign. She was conscious of a wish to tell the woman to take her flying circus acrobats and find another wedding planner, but she didn't. As much as she despaired over some of the demands made of her and her company, If You Can Dream It, Karen also got the most juice out of the toughest assignments. Frankly, the challenges stopped her from succumbing to boredom.

Rich October sunshine streamed through the windows of the renovated brick warehouse she'd bought in Old Town to house her growing business, bringing out the rich caramel in the floors she'd had restored.

"Let me see what I can do. I'll put together a proposal for you and we can meet again, shall we say in two weeks? Perhaps with the bride this time."

When the mother left, Karen sat for a few minutes, typing her notes into her computer, then she got up and walked through the office.

"I'm going to see Chelsea," she said to her assistant, Dee, on the way out. The young blonde British girl who was both support staff and her assistant wedding planner nodded, unsurprised, since Karen took the short walk to her caterer and good friend's premises at least once a day. She trekked to Hammond & Co. to discuss jobs with Chelsea Hammond, her exclusive caterer, or simply to chat with the woman who'd become a close friend. And if she walked the two blocks briskly enough, that was as good as fifteen minutes on the treadmill.

Slipping on sunglasses and a light coat, she strode toward the storefront where Chelsea sold takeout gourmet food and coffee while she ran her growing catering business from the huge industrial kitchen in back. Upstairs was a small apartment that she used as her office.

Chelsea was placing a heaping bowl of quinoa salad into the display case when Karen walked in. She only knew it was quinoa because a sign said so. Unlike her friend, food was not her passion but her enemy and she tried to think about it as little as possible. She certainly wasn't one for cookbooks and those endless TV torture shows featuring gorgeous men preparing mouthwatering meals—two things she most wanted and that were so bad for her, with her figure that was both top-heavy and bottom-heavy on a much too short frame.

The caterer—blessed by nature with a long, slim body that was neither top- nor bottom-heavy, but just right—smiled her rich, slightly mischievous smile at Karen as she straightened from her task. "Perfect, you're just in time for coffee."

"Make mine with cream. And I want one of your four-thousand-calorie brownies to go with it."

Since Karen was on a perpetual diet, Chelsea raised her brows. "Bad day?"

"The bride wants a circus theme. Cirque du Soleil, no less."

Chelsea poured two cups of coffee, deftly popped several decadent treats onto a plate and called out to someone out of sight in the back kitchen, "I'm taking a break upstairs. Keep an eye on the front and call me if you need me."

"'Kay," came the reply.

They hiked up the stairs and Karen said, "I wonder if the wedding night will feature trapezes and human pyramids."

"Your cynicism is showing," Chelsea said, as though it were a slip hanging below her skirt hem.

Karen sighed. "I know. Easy for you, with a big rock sparkling on your finger and the world's cutest guy in love with you, but I'm a bitter divorcee. The wedding planner who doesn't believe in marriage."

"Sure you do," Chelsea soothed. "You simply haven't found the right man."

"I'm thirty-five years old. And the brides get younger every year." She gazed longingly at a brownie. "And thinner. I should give up and let myself get fat. It's not like anyone ever sees me naked. If I'm not getting sex, at least I should take pleasure in food."

"You are not fat, what you are is voluptuous." The woman saw where Karen's eyes were straying and said, "I know you. If you eat that brownie you'll only torture yourself." Her brown eyes twinkled. "But that lemon dream bar is low-cal."

"You're too good to me," she sighed, almost snatching the yellow confection off the plate.

"Are you kidding me? I wouldn't have this great location or half the business I have if it wasn't for you. I am so happy you took a chance on me."

It was true, Karen mused as she bit into a lemon-flavored slice of paradise. When they'd first met,

Chelsea Hammond had just returned from cooking school in Paris and was trying to launch her own catering business. When Karen had tasted the woman's food and chatted with her for a few minutes she'd experienced the gut deep excitement of knowing she'd found the missing piece of her wedding planning business. She'd pretty much signed up Chelsea on the spot to be her exclusive caterer. It meant that no other wedding planner could use the services of Hammond & Co., though she was free to cater any other events on her own. In return, Chelsea got all of If You Can Dream It's catering, and there was a lot of that.

Chelsea opened a computer file on her desktop computer. "When is this wedding circus scheduled?"

"Depends on Cirque du Soleil's schedule."

The woman glanced up, her dark brown hair swinging. "Wow."

"Yeah. Apparently somebody on the groom's side knows somebody who might be able to get them to perform at the wedding." She shook her head at the enormity of the task ahead of her. "We will need a huge space, lots of height. The bride thinks she might want an honest-to-God circus tent."

"I'll play with some ideas for food." Chelsea twisted her mouth to one side. "Not that circus exactly screams matching food. I'll have to work on decoration and presentation." She typed a few more words. "Laurel's the one who'll be thrilled."

Laurel Matthews was a cake maker and decorator of such extraordinary talent that her cakes were true works of art and architecture and, equally amazing, they tasted delicious. An If You Can Dream It wedding was notable for meticulous planning, delicious food, and a cake that always surprised and delighted. "You're right. She'll love the challenge. I can't even imagine what she'll dream up," Karen said.

"Which is what's so great about her cakes."

"I've got another prospect coming this morning—she's looking for a May or June wedding next year, is that a problem for you?"

Chelsea glanced up, looking slightly puzzled. "No, why would it be?"

Karen had been trying delicately to find out when this woman who was engaged to the man of her dreams was actually getting married. So far, subtle hadn't worked. "I'm wondering when you and David are getting married. Won't you need some time off?"

Chelsea waved a hand, her engagement ring catching the light and sending out a spray of fireworks. "Don't worry. We'll get around to it. We're just both so busy right now."

"That man needs to stop playing hard to get," she snapped.

Karen still hadn't entirely forgiven David Wolfe for making a deal with Chelsea to pose as his fake fiancée in order for him to snag a promotion at work. Of course he'd fallen in love with Chelsea along the way. Who wouldn't? She was gorgeous, a gourmet cook and one of the sweetest women Karen had ever met. So, had he snapped up this amazing woman when she'd obviously loved him? No, of course not. Being a man, he had no idea when the greatest woman in Philadelphia was right under his nose. Instead, he'd almost lost her.

Karen would never forget the heartbroken woman who had taken refuge in this very space, living in the small suite she now used as her office while she struggled to get her business going and forget David, the man who had broken her heart.

Fortunately, he'd come to his senses just in time and now they were engaged for real, living in his amazing town house in Rittenhouse Square. But Karen would be a lot happier when the engagement ended in marriage.

What was stopping David? Did he really want to lose this woman again?

"He's fine. Really. We're both fine."

She didn't believe it for a minute, but she also knew that Chelsea wasn't one to unburden herself easily. She'd talk to Karen when she was ready.

Deciding she had too much on her plate with circus acts and new business coming in every day to worry about why her best friend wasn't in a hurry to marry the man she was engaged to, she reluctantly drained her coffee cup.

When she returned to her office, Karen felt calmer. The taste of lemon clung to her lips and the idea of a circus for a wedding seemed more ludicrous than annoying.

"The Swensons asked to move their appointment back half an hour," her assistant said. "And two new messages came in. I put them on your desk with your mail."

"Great, thanks."

She stepped into her office. The Hepplewhite desk had nothing on it but her laptop, the big leather-bound day planner she still used in spite of technology, the small stack of mail and the phone messages.

She had ten minutes until her next appointment, a new client, Sophie Vanderhooven, and while she waited she flipped open the newest bridal magazine. It was important to keep up with the latest trends, though after ten years in the business she found trends fairly predictable. Now, for instance, with so much uncertainty in the world, weddings were turning strongly traditional. When the economy boomed and wars were somewhere else, then more couples tended to exchange vows on the beach wearing love beads or shouted their I Do's from hang gliders.

She was skimming an article about nonallergenic bouquets when her assistant beeped her intercom. "Ms. Vanderhooven and her fiancé are here," she said.

"Thanks. I'll be right out."

A quick peek in the mirror she kept in her top drawer confirmed that her mouth was now free of tell-tale lemon dream bar crumbs, her red hair was confined into a smooth bun, her mascara unsmudged. A quick swipe of lip gloss and she stepped back into the towering heels she wore to raise her closer to her dream height of five foot ten from her God-given, stingy five-two.

Her practiced smile on her face, she stepped out to greet her latest clients. She reached the reception area and stalled, her hand already half extended, her mouth open to speak. But nothing came out.

Normally, she gave her initial attention to the bride since she was almost always the true client, while the groom was only peripherally involved. But the man who rose from the plush waiting room seats was not one she could ignore.

He was still commanding, still gorgeous in that careless way of a man who's so used to female attention he barely notices it. Keenly intelligent gray eyes held her gaze, a twinkle of amusement lurking in their depths. His hair was still dark, though a few threads of silver glittered at his temples. Neither of them spoke, then a female voice broke into her trance.

Her hand was taken in a cool clasp. "Hello. I'm

Sophie Vanderhooven, I'm so pleased to meet you. And this is Dexter Crane."

Automatically, Karen pumped her hand up and down, forced her mouth back into some semblance of normality. "Nice to meet you."

She inclined her head at the man still staring at her. "Mr. Crane." There was a slight pause as the three of them stood there before she pulled herself together. "Um, won't you come into my office?"

She turned and began walking.

She felt his eyes on her all the way, and bitterly did she regret every calorie she'd so foolishly imbibed in the five years since she'd last laid eyes on Dexter Crane. A woman had her pride. The last thing she wanted was to look fat in front of her soon-to-be-married ex-husband.

Especially from behind.

2

"WHEN ARE YOU and MR. Crane planning to be married?" she asked in her most professional tone. She'd taken her place behind her desk and motioned for the happy couple to occupy the two pretty chintz chairs opposite.

A well-bred laugh answered her. A finishing school hah-hah, perfectly-modulated and quiet. "I'm not marrying Dexter. He's the best man, but my fiancé is out of the country and he asked Dex to come along with me so I don't get carried away."

Her gaze rose and connected with Dexter's. Yep, that was definitely a glimmer of amusement. Bastard. He was enjoying this.

"I see." In a much lower voice she muttered, "Lucky escape for you."

"Pardon?"

"I said, 'It's a lucky thing you've come early in the season.' Things really book up. Well, what do you have in mind, Ms. Vanderhooven?"

The young woman's ideas were lifted right out of the

current issues of bridal magazines. Clearly, she'd been perusing every one.

"And I thought maybe I should have a non-allergenic bouquet, you know, in case anyone's allergic." There was a moment's pause. Karen took refuge in taking notes so she could think of the questions that might help her discover what this bride really might like, ideas that wouldn't change every month when a new batch of wedding mags hit the newsstands. Then Sophie said, "But I'm very open to suggestions."

Dexter said, "I'm not the one getting married here, but I've always thought something a little less formal would be nice. A garden wedding, let's say."

Her pen slipped, drawing a squiggly line right through the word *bride*. She realized her hands were sweating, that's why her pen had slipped.

She and Dex had married among a garden of roses and irises, her favorite flower of all, and lilies, so the perfumes intermingled. Even as he spoke the words she was transported back to that magical day, the day she'd thought would begin her own personal happily-ever-after.

Fool.

"I'm sure Ms. Vanderhooven has the best ideas for her own wedding."

"Not really," the bride said. "I'm pretty open to ideas. And Andrew always listens to Dexter, so we thought if he came instead it would be almost as good."

"Dexter, that's an unusual name." Karen frowned. "Makes me think of the serial killer on TV."

Dexter shot her an "oh, come on," look and explained that Dexter was his mother's maiden name, as though she didn't know it perfectly well. Then he rose. "I think better on my feet. You see, Ms. Petersham, mind if I call you Karen? It was Karen, wasn't it?" He didn't wait for an answer, naturally, and continued, "You see, Karen, most people want to feel that a marriage is forever, so you want something that's going to mean something in fifty years. You want a wedding you'll look back on with fond memories."

She felt her color heighten as she locked gazes with him. "Do you?"

KAREN HAD A SPLITTING HEADACHE the rest of the day. She knew it wasn't only the stress of seeing Dex again, but the added insult to her body of skipping lunch. Of course she knew that depriving herself of a few calories wouldn't suddenly make her magically thin or grow her half a foot so she could look Ms. Sophie Vanderhooven in the eye—and spit in Dexter's. She'd skipped lunch anyway, which she knew wasn't good for her, all the diet books said so, but sometimes she refused to believe their logic.

And ended up with a headache as well as a cranky, empty stomach.

With no further appointments, she settled in to work on her monthly accounts, not that there was much point in it since she couldn't concentrate. All she could do was relive that moment when Dexter had walked back into her life. Worse, it was clear that he, Sophie and the missing groom had all agreed to appoint him stand-in groom and assistant wedding planner, which had her hauling the large bottle of painkillers out of her emergency drawer and swallowing two of them with the zero calorie water on her desk.

Dee popped her head in the door at a few minutes before five and said, "Is it okay if I head out now?" She grinned. "I've got to get home and change for my date tonight."

Sure, Dee was thin, gorgeous, young and had that British accent going for her, but she seemed to get more than her fair share of dates.

"Where do you meet all these men?"

"Online," the younger woman said, her blue eyes twinkling with excitement. "It's mad fun, you should try it."

"Online dating? It seems so desperate."

"It's not. I do it all the time." Dee didn't bother saying she wasn't desperate. All you had to do was look at her. "Our trouble is that we work in an industry that caters to women, and the only men who come round here are already spoken for. Honestly, you should at least give it a go."

"I don't know."

"Tell you what, I'll set you up a profile tomorrow and show you how to get on. It's really simple and gives you a chance to screen someone first before you waste your time meeting them."

"I guess I should be open-minded," Karen said. Normally she'd have scoffed, but seeing Dexter today was making her feel more than usually single. And vaguely desperate.

"You'll have fun, I promise."

A slight woman with multicolored hair that looked as though Edward Scissorhands was her hairdresser drifted in behind Dee. She blinked big eyes and glanced around as though wondering where she was and what she was doing here.

"Hi, Laurel," Dee said.

"Hello."

"What do you think about Plenty of Phillys?"

"The online dating site?"

"That's right."

Laurel pulled her sketchbook out of her peace-sign-emblazoned bag. "I don't think about it. Why?"

"Honestly, Laurel, how do you manage in the real world? I don't mean do you contemplate the site the way you'd meditate on world peace or whatever you do when you sit around cross-legged and chant aum, I mean what do you think about Karen doing the online dating thing?"

"Oh." The cake decorator turned her huge eyes to Karen. "Do you want to meet men on the Internet?"

"Of course she does, she's desperate," Dee announced. "And you should try it, too." She sent them both a megawatt smile. "Right, then, see you tomorrow."

"Yes. Have fun tonight."

Once Dee had gone, Karen turned to Laurel. "I'm not definitely going to do it, I'm only thinking about it."

"I think you should do whatever makes you happy."

And the amazing thing about Laurel was that when she said wacky things like that, she actually meant them. "I know you do. So, what have you got for me?"

Laurel was in the habit of bringing in her cake designs for Karen to approve. Not that she needed to, everything she baked was incredible, but Karen suspected she liked the reassurance of her approval.

But she really wished the woman didn't bring sketches of the most delectable treats that looked so good even in the sketchbook that Karen's mouth started to water. Especially not at the end of the day when her willpower was at its lowest ebb.

Once she'd approved half a dozen designs and they'd gone over timing and delivery of the cakes for this weekend, Laurel drifted out of the office and Karen got back to her accounts.

After giving in to her hunger and nuking a Lean Cuisine meal, she continued wrestling with her books for another couple of hours. When the muted chime that announced an after-hours caller rang, she wasn't surprised. She supposed on some level she'd expected him.

Ignore the bell or go answer him?

It really wasn't an option. With a sigh, she rose and stepped back into her heels and took her time going to the front door.

In the dim light he looked almost a stranger to her, so tall and elegant and, she reminded herself sternly, no longer hers.

"You look good, Kiki."

In spite of herself she smiled. "No one's called me that in years."

"Good."

It was cold outside and she shivered.

"Can I come in?"

Only now did she realize they were both standing at the entrance.

She stepped back to usher him in. "Of course."

Once more he followed her into her office. He glanced around as though he hadn't been there earlier that very day. "Place looks good. You've done well for yourself."

Not compared to him. After they'd split, he'd become one of the top architects in New York, the go-to guy for bringing faded grandeur back from near death. He was fanatical about reclaiming and modernizing heritage properties and designing new buildings or additions to fit the old neighborhoods. She felt his approval at the way she'd used the best of the old building she occupied while still managing to bring in ultramodern conveniences.

"Do you own the building?"

"Not that it's any of your business, but yes I do."

He nodded. "Smart girl."

"Too smart to be charmed by you." She sighed. "What do you want, Dex?"

"I don't know." He scratched his head and her eyes were drawn to the thick, black hair she remembered so well. "I knew this was your outfit, obviously, but I thought it would be fun to surprise you."

"You certainly did surprise me." But if almost giving her a heart attack was supposed to be fun, she thought she'd pass.

His gray all-seeing eyes locked on hers. "You didn't tell Sophie about our past."

"Didn't seem very good for business to bring up my divorce when the woman's here to plan a wedding." She shot him a glance. "Did you tell her?"

"No." He picked up her gold Montblanc pen off the desk, ran his thumbnail over the monogram. "I decided to leave it to you." He'd given her that pen back in happier times, and now she was annoyed with herself for her sentimentality in using the damn thing every day.

"So, we don't tell the lucky couple that their wedding planner and his best man used to be married?"

"No, I guess not."

"And that we hate each other?"

He put down the pen, straightened to his full six feet and looked down at her. "I never hated you. That's your department."

A moment passed and she pressed her lips together to keep from crying out that she missed him. Instead she said, "Why are you here, Dex? I mean, in the city. You work in New York now."

"I do. But I'm quoting on a project here in Philadelphia. A grand old structure that's been a home, a warehouse and a boardinghouse, to name a few." Enthusiasm lit up his eyes. "She's a tired old girl, but with amazing bone structure. The best of the original architectural features are intact and the client wants to work with them, while bringing the building up to date. It's going to be a boutique hotel and retail combination."

"Sounds amazing, and right up your alley."

"It is. I really want this one. And if it works out, you'll be seeing a lot of me."

She raised one eyebrow.

"Helping Sophie and Andrew plan their wedding."

He looked so sincere, so good, so sexy that for a moment she forgot the reason she'd divorced him. The five-foot-ten blonde goddess she'd found half dressed and wrapped around her husband. The saddest aspect of that fiasco was that on some level she'd noted that Dexter and the former model had looked natural together, two tall, glamorous super-people.

"You're good at planning weddings, not so good at staying faithful once you're in one." Her venom seemed to curdle the air.

"Like I said, hate was always your department."

"Well, I got over it." With a lot of tearful sessions with her girlfriends and some rather expensive ones with a therapist. "Now I've accepted that our marriage was a mistake."

"You sure didn't fight for it."

The old, familiar anger began to surge inside her

but she bit her tongue and counted to ten. Then eleven. Finally twelve before she felt calm enough to speak.

"Why would I fight to keep an unfaithful husband?"

He shook his head. "I don't know why I bother, but I am telling you again that I never had sex with that woman. She was drunk and crazy."

"Didn't look like you were trying very hard to peel her off you."

"Believe me, I was, and I could have used your help that night instead of having you turn tail and abandon me."

Oh, how she wished she could believe him, could have believed him six years ago when it had happened. But she didn't believe him, and couldn't imagine living with a man who thought so little of her that he'd betray her like that.

"I guess maybe we were wrong about each other."

"I guess so."

He shoved his hands in his pockets, leaned against her desk, looking ridiculously masculine against the feminine lines of the furniture; it appeared as though the wood might snap from the weight of him leaning on it. But like her, the piece was stronger than it looked. "You're still the sexiest woman I've ever known."

She snorted. "Oh, please."

"Or maybe it was us together. I miss a lot of things about you, but mostly I miss you in my bed." He looked at her with such intensity that she felt her blood begin to pound. Of course she remembered. When she wasn't cursing the man for his faithlessness she spent more time than she should cursing him for giving her the kind of sex that she'd never found before or since. Soul-scorching, sometimes tender, sometimes dirty but always intimate. She was secretly pleased that he hadn't found that again either. Or so he said. But then maybe that was another line in the player's handbook. How would she know?

She forced herself to meet his gaze coolly. Took a deep breath and uttered the biggest lie of her life. "I don't miss you."

She should have recalled that nothing ignited Dexter's competitive instincts like a challenge. She saw heat flash in his eyes, anger and lust and a mix of emotions she couldn't begin to identify.

One second he stood there before her and the next he was pulling her to him, crushing his mouth against hers so fast that she couldn't have moved away if she'd tried. She uttered a muffled protest, squirmed against him and then as the inevitable tide of heat swamped her, found herself melting into that oh, so familiar embrace.

The initial hardness of his kiss softened and he began to play with her, igniting all her responses until she was crazy with pent-up lust and a need so strong she couldn't begin to stifle it. She was so weak-kneed she clung to him, responding wildly, mindlessly.

Every part of her ached and burned and throbbed. If he threw her down on the Hepplewhite desk now, or even on the reclaimed hardwood floor, she'd let him take her and both of them knew it.

Then, as suddenly as he'd moved on her, he let go and stepped back. His breathing was faster than normal, his mouth wet from hers. Still, he managed to sound cool when he said, "I don't think I believe you."

Then he turned and headed for the door. "Don't work too late."

3

"WHAT ABOUT THIS GUY?" Dee asked as they cruised the single man ads on the online dating site that she insisted had the best success with Philly singles. They were in her office and Dee had just finished setting up her account. Even twenty-four hours ago, Karen knew she wouldn't have put up a profile on something called Plenty of Phillys but since that scorching kiss yesterday, she was determined to get out there and try to find a genuine, decent man who wouldn't screw around the second her back was turned. Wouldn't melt her with his kisses when he came back into her life.

But the man whose photo she was looking at on her computer definitely wasn't that guy.

"I want to correct his spelling," she said.

Dee sighed and moved to the next one. Mohawk, tattoos and a spiked dog collar. "Ick," they said in unison.

The third profile featured a perfectly average-looking man with glasses, a full head of hair, and, perhaps more important, a profile written by someone who'd obviously passed high school English. "He's a CPA, never been married, but looking to find a partner." Dee glanced up at her. "That's good, right?"

"Yes." Karen finished reading his profile. "I like that he mentions taking things slow. I really can't handle fast right now."

"Great, let's send him a wink," Dee said pushing a couple of buttons before Karen could slap her hand away.

"What have you done?"

Dee laughed, the happy trill of a woman who dates regularly and isn't scarred by love. Yet. "You have to let them know you're interested. That's how it works. You send a wink."

"I am so not ready for this."

"You so are." Her assistant danced out of the office. "Call me if you need me."

Dee hadn't made it to the door when a funny noise emanating from her laptop made Karen squeak, "I need you."

Dee peeked over her shoulder. "Hey, he winked back."

"Is that good?"

"That's great. Means he read your profile and he's interested. He's online now, so you can chat. Look, he's sent you a message. Click here."

Hello, Karen. I see you are a virgin.

"A virgin?" she squealed. "What is he, a pervert?"

"Would you relax?" her twenty-three-year-old mentor insisted. "Read on. He means you're new to the site."

"Oh. He says, 'here's a bit more about me.' Um, I think he's included his resume."

"Just give the guy a chance. And remember, there

are lots of guys out there, so don't be afraid to keep looking."

"Okay. Thanks."

She kept reading. He had sent her a profile, obviously prewritten for such an occasion and if he hadn't included his resume, there wasn't much about his schooling and work life she didn't know when she'd finished. In the back of her mind she was thinking how much her business could benefit from a decent CPA, then she remembered she was supposed to be looking for romance, not accounting services.

His name was Ron and he did sound like a nice guy. Nothing flashy, which was good. She was pretty sure, for instance, that he wouldn't shove a woman against her own desk and kiss her senseless. Certainly not without first asking permission. Then she was for damn sure that he wouldn't waltz back out of her office, having made the point that she was still desperately attracted to him, and leave her seething with sexual frustration as well as anger at her own stupidity.

Which made Ron a lot closer to perfect than certain men she could name.

She replied to Ron, telling him a bit about herself.

Then she clicked off and got back to work.

When she checked her e-mail again at the end of the day, she had a few random winks, and Ron had replied. She had to admit it was nice to make "get to know you" conversation with a man, even if it was next door to anonymous.

He ended by inviting her for coffee. I always do coffee as a first date, he explained, obviously catering to her "virgin" status. There's no pressure. It's only an hour of our time and if we don't want to continue that's fine. And if we do, then we go from there. What do you think?

What did she think?

She had no idea, so she decided to lay the entire situation before Chelsea.

"Online dating?" her friend said when she'd walked over to her place to ask for advice. "Wow. I've never tried it, but some of my girlfriends met boyfriends and husbands that way." She shrugged. "And a few use the site to find booty calls."

"Booty calls? Seriously?"

"Hey, different strokes."

Karen bit deeply into a lemon dream bar before saying, "Honestly, I don't even know what I'm doing. I think I'm scared."

"Honey, you book acrobats for weddings, you drag grooms to weddings on time, solve blended family conflicts that would baffle the entire Oprah/Dr. Phil team. I once saw you personally climb a tree to fix twinkle lights. While wearing four-inch heels. I think you can handle a cup of coffee with a CPA."

"I guess you're right." She put a hand to her chest where her heart was beating rapidly.

Chelsea looked at her with concern. "You seem way more bent out of shape than seems appropriate for a coffee date. What's going on?"

"Oh, Chelsea, it's all such a mess," she wailed and promptly shoved the last of the lemon dream into her mouth. Once she'd taken what comfort she could from the food, she told her friend everything, from her first meeting Dexter at a party, to their wedding, the marriage, the betrayal, to him coming back into her life. She ended with the kiss.

"Scumbag!" was Chelsea's succinct response to the

story. For which Karen was enormously grateful. "And now he thinks he can waltz into your business and try to get back in your pants? I don't think so."

"Yeah, I know."

"Getting out and dating new men is a fantastic idea. Really. Get your mind off your ex."

"I suppose you're right."

"I am right. And you know what else you need?"

She thought of some of the other well-meaning advice Dee had dispensed from time to time. "Please don't say sex toys."

Chelsea grinned at her. "I am assuming that you have a good selection, as every woman should. But no, I was referring to a girls' night out."

"Oh, I would love that." A night off from worries and stress with some of her female friends would be sooo good.

"Okay." And as she saw Karen's mouth open Chelsea stopped her, saying, "And, Ms. Planner Extraordinaire, this is one that I'll be planning. You come and have a good time. That's all. Got it?"

Impulsively, she hugged her. "Got it. Thanks."

"WE'RE SEAHORSES," the voice on the phone explained.

She really didn't charge enough for this job. "Seahorses? Maybe you need an aquarium, not a wedding planner," Karen said as gently as she could.

The young woman's laugh was sudden and loud in her ear. "No, I mean me and Steve, the guy I'm marrying, we belong to the Seahorses Scuba Diving club."

"Oh, okay, I get you."

"You must have thought I was nuts," the woman said, with another boisterous laugh.

Karen joined in, hahaha, without admitting she'd assumed the woman was certifiable. Or that she wouldn't be the first crazy person who'd hoped If You Can Dream It was a company designed to make any hallucination come true.

"Before I waste both of our time in a meeting, I want to ask you if you could arrange an undersea wedding."

"An undersea wedding, like *The Little Mermaid?*"

"I guess, sort of. See, we dive the wrecks off the Jersey shore and we were thinking it would be so cool to get married underwater."

"Oh, wouldn't it." Karen rubbed her temple. Surely you couldn't get a headache this fast. "Hard to cut the cake, though."

More laughter greeted her. "I can see we're going to get along fine. No, what I'm thinking is if we could rent a glass-bottomed boat for the guests and then me and Steve could get married underneath. We wouldn't have thought of it, but we met a JP who also dives. He could perform the ceremony from the boat, and we'd be wired for sound. Instead of saying, 'I do,' we'd give the thumbs up sign. Isn't that totally cool?"

"Oh, totally."

"We want to get married next August. We need some ideas. We really want our wedding to stand out as something different."

No problem there.

"So, will you do it?"

"Arrange a wedding on a glass-bottomed boat so two scuba divers can give a thumbs-up?" She shook her head. "Sure, why not?"

"Great, when can we come in to see you?"

She made an appointment for the scuba sweethearts,

and then almost broke down and wept when her next appointment informed her that she wanted a completely traditional wedding. Church, flowers, white gown, bridesmaids, hotel reception, everything simple and staid and normal. How refreshing.

As she was finishing up the proposal, Sophie Vanderhooven called sounding excited. "I heard Melissa Stanhope got the most divine cake for her wedding this Saturday."

"Yes, it's lovely. Laurel, our cake maker has a real gift."

"But Cinderella's coach? That is such an amazing idea." She now recalled that it was the Stanhopes who had recommended her services to the Vanderhoovens.

"Even better, the cake is made with pumpkin."

"I know! She told me. Can I have something like that for my wedding?"

"Of course you can." Did this woman not have any original ideas of her own? "Not the same cake, of course, because Laurel creates a unique design for every event, but you can give her guidelines."

A sigh wafted over the phone. "Mother wants a traditional tiered cake complete with little plastic bride and groom on the top, but I want something more romantic, more me."

"I'm sure we can find something that will make you and your mother both happy," she said diplomatically.

"I hope so. Anyhow, I'll see you Saturday."

"Saturday?"

"At Melissa's wedding."

"Oh, of course. Though I'm not a guest. If I do my job right, you shouldn't even notice me."

Sophie laughed in her elegant way. "No one could miss you."

Before she could ask what that was supposed to mean, in a polite way, the woman was gone.

Puzzled, she got up and walked to the front reception area. "Dee?"

Her assistant glanced up from matching the place cards to the Stanhopes' master guest list. "Mmm-hmm?"

"Do I stand out in a crowd?"

Dee blinked at her. "You have Amy Adams's face and hair and Marilyn Monroe's body, and, I don't know, a sort of commanding way about you. It's what makes you a great wedding planner. Everyone scurries when you tell them to. So yes. Of course you're noticeable."

"Huh. Thought I was being so discreet." She wandered back toward her office.

"Hey, speaking of discreet, when are you meeting that CPA?"

"We're having coffee Sunday afternoon."

"Brilliant. I can't wait to hear about it on Monday."

"What's the weather forecast for tomorrow?"

Dee didn't have to look, she'd already checked. "Low fifties, no precipitation expected."

"Wonderful. A perfect day for a late fall wedding."

And so it was, she realized when she rose the next morning. The day was dry, the sun was shining and there was no snow on the ground. After showering and doing her hair in a restrained bun, she slipped into a navy pencil skirt and white blouse, then pushed her feet into her high-heeled navy pumps. Discreet and professional, that's how she thought a wedding planner should look.

Amy Adams indeed. Dee must be angling for a raise.

4

"WE CAN'T FIND the best man," Mr. Stanhope hissed into Karen's ear.

So far, everything for the Stanhope wedding had been going smoother than a chocolate milkshake. This was her first lump. "Has he answered his cell phone?"

"I don't think so."

"I'll get right on it. In the meantime, Mr. Stanhope, remember, you hired me to take care of problems. I'll stall the bridal party." Her calm manner and soothing smile had their desired effect. The father of the bride's high color receded and he nodded, standing straighter in his tux.

"Glad to have you onboard."

"We may need to call in a stand-in, but I promise, you'll have a best man for your daughter's wedding.

"Keep an eye on things out front," she whispered to Dee, then, without any visible haste, she walked from the front of the church and out into the parking lot. Guests were still arriving but the bridal party was scheduled to pull up in fifteen minutes.

She slipped into her car and reached for the Stanhope

wedding binder. In it was all the information she could possibly need, including home and cell numbers for the missing man.

She called both and was invited twice to leave a message. Which she did. Not good.

She then called the driver of the limousine bringing the bridal party to the church and asked him to take a detour. "I need five extra minutes."

"No problem."

Having stalled the bride, she left her car and slipped into the church through a side entrance. She knew her way around most of the churches and synagogues of the city. She made her way to the anteroom where the groom and his party would be waiting.

The groom looked a little pale, but steady. He glanced up when she entered. "I'm going to kill Brian. He promised he'd be here."

"Does he have issues with punctuality?"

"Not usually."

Her cell phone rang. "Ah." Sure enough, it was the best man. "Flat tire," he panted. "I went to change it, but that is my spare."

"Where are you?"

He named a location that was a good five minutes away. "Are you dressed to go?"

"Yep."

"All right. I'll come and get you."

She turned to the groom. "Appoint a stand-in just in case."

"But the ring?"

She slipped a plain gold band from her right hand. "I always carry a spare." Then she smiled at him. "Good luck."

"Thanks."

She sprinted to her car and made her way out of the parking lot, now quieting as most of the guests had arrived. She was in time to see Sophie Vanderhooven step out of a Lincoln, Dexter behind her. She supposed she should have known Sophie would bring a stand-in for her fiancé who was still working in Italy.

Since she felt it would be rude to drive by a paying client, she drew to a stop and rolled down her window. The autumn day was crisp and cold and tonight the temperature was forecast to dip.

"You look lovely, Sophie," she said. The blue woolen suit was both stylish and classic, rather like Sophie herself.

"Thanks. I can't wait to see Melissa get married."

"Do you drive away before all the ceremonies?" Dex asked her.

Now that he'd addressed her directly, she had to look at him and nothing in the world could stop the warm blush that heated her cheeks as their little tussle in her office roared back to her.

She forced a smile, though no one could have called it cool. "Of course not. Just a little wedding business to take care of. I'll see you later." And with a wave of her hand she drove past.

DEX SQUINTED as he turned to watch Karen drive away. He'd made her blush. Good. It was a start.

"What's going on, Dex?"

He turned back to his date. "What do you mean?"

Sophie scanned his face. "I'm not sure, but you were looking at Karen the way—well, the way Andrew looks at me. I guess that's why I recognized the expression."

"She's a very attractive woman."

"And she was blushing." She grabbed his hand and began walking toward the church. "And there's this sort of energy field when you two are together. I noticed it when we first met her. I wasn't born yesterday, Dex. Something's up with you two. What is it?"

The slim hand in his was friendly, but firm. He suspected he wouldn't get away with anything but the truth. "You're pretty smart for a socialite."

"I know. And I smell a delicious secret. Come on, spill. I won't tell anyone."

"I've never yet met a woman who didn't break that promise."

The patrician nose wrinkled. "Can I tell Andrew if it's good?"

Andrew was the son of a famous wine-making family in Italy. He'd hired Dexter's firm to renovate the family's Park Avenue town house and during the project, the two had become friends. They played squash, moved in similar social circles and, instead of dropping him when Andrew and Sophie got engaged, the couple had tried setting him up with a series of single women.

They knew he'd been married before, but he'd never offered them much in the way of details. Hadn't thought it would matter. Now, he knew that his past did matter.

The past had just caught up with him.

"The truth is that Karen and I used to be married."

If he was into shocking people he'd have been gratified by the way Sophie's mouth fell open so far he could see all her expensive dental work. He'd never seen a mouth with such perfectly straight molars.

When she'd recovered enough to close her mouth,

she said, "But I don't get it. Why? What?" She heaved
a sigh. "What's your plan?"

The pavement seemed to tick under Sophie's heels,
sounding like a clock counting seconds. "I don't know.
Honestly, I didn't have a plan. Don't have one. I thought
it would be cool to surprise Karen, but—"

"The force field got to you." She shook her head.
"That is some powerful chemistry between you two."

She was right. The moment Karen had stepped out
of her office and he'd seen her again, he'd known that
what they'd had wasn't over. Not for him. "Yeah."

"So, what happened between you two?"

"We should go in."

"That's Melissa's dad over there looking all stressed.
Means the bridal party isn't here yet. We've got some
time." She hauled him around the side of the church.
"Spill."

The story was so stupid he felt foolish even repeating it. "This drunk woman came onto me at a party
and Karen flipped out. She got it in her head that I was
cheating on her."

Cool blue eyes stared into his. "Were you?"

"No. I never would have done anything like that to
Karen. I loved my wife."

"Then why would she think it?"

He leaned his back against the brick wall. It seemed
sturdy, solid, the way a good marriage should be. "I've
spent a lot of time asking myself the same question."

"How badly was the drunk woman coming onto
you?"

"Oh, it was bad. She was undressing herself, trying to undress me. When Karen walked in on us she
was plastered to me, and I was trying to stop her unzipping me. Must have looked to Karen like we were

in a big hurry, both trying to get me unzipped." He'd never really looked at it from her point of view before. He'd been too busy being pissed that she didn't believe him.

"Wow. That sucks."

"I know."

"Did you go for counseling?"

"The only counselor she wanted was the kind in a lawyer's office. She started divorce proceedings right after she threw me out of the house."

"Why would she end a marriage without even fighting for it?"

Leaning against the brick of that old church he felt like a little of the wisdom of the aged building was seeping into him. "Her dad really ran around on her mom. For years, with a lot of different women, until her mom finally divorced the jerk. Maybe, on some level, Karen expects a husband to be unfaithful."

"Then you're going to have to figure out how to convince her that some husbands can love a woman faithfully. And that you are one of them."

"We're already divorced. Why would I do that?"

When she shook her head at him, the sun struck her pale blond hair, giving him the impression of a halo. "No wonder you never looked twice at any of those women I introduced you to." She patted his shoulder. "You, my friend, are still in love with your wife."

KAREN FOUND the best man without trouble. He was the only guy in a tux standing on the freeway looking miserable.

She pulled over. "Hop in," she said. Then, before pulling back into traffic, she made contact with her limo driver. "Where are you?"

"Five minutes away."

"Make it ten."

"You got it."

She delivered a very grateful best man to an equally grateful groom and breathed a sigh of relief. Then she dashed to the front of the church to welcome the bridal party. As she'd suspected, they had no idea they'd been stalled.

The bride was as radiant as could be hoped, and after escorting her and the bridesmaids to where her father waited, adjusting her veil and reminding everyone to take a deep breath and smile, to remember to savor the walk down the aisle, she slipped inside to give the organist the heads up.

As the strains of "Here Comes the Bride" boomed through the church, everyone rose. In her head she heard her own personal musical mash-up, the wedding march overlaid with her own version of "Another One Bites the Dust."

Once the wedding was underway, she eased back out of the church and called Chelsea who was already preparing food for the reception. "Heads up. We're running behind about fifteen minutes."

"'Kay, thanks." And the woman was gone.

She then drove to the mansion where the reception was being held. The kitchen was a hive of organized chaos. Chelsea overseeing the sit-down dinner for one hundred and fifty that would take place as soon as the guests arrived.

She walked into the huge ballroom-turned-dining room and was filled with pleasure. It looked beautiful. They'd gone with autumnal colors and the burgundies and golds and greens looked lovely against the rich mahogany wainscoting in the room. Real fires already burned in the two fireplaces and bouquets of autumn leaves, artfully arranged to look casual and natural adorned the space. Fat candles waited to be lit, the crystal shone, the cutlery glittered, and Cinderella's confectionary coach lent a whimsical touch.

Dee called her when the bride and groom were on their way, so she was at the front door to greet them.

"We did it," Melissa cried, holding up her left hand where a brand-new band glittered.

"Congratulations," she said, hugging the happy young woman. "I've got rooms upstairs for both of you so you can freshen up. Once all the guests have arrived, we'll announce you and the reception can begin."

She took the extra ring that the groom pressed secretively into her palm, slipping it onto her right hand once more for safekeeping.

As with most weddings, the guests enjoying the perfect event could have no idea of the infinite number of details handled and the disasters averted that went on behind the scenes. And that was exactly how Karen liked it.

So she was less than pleased when Dexter surprised her at the end of the evening when most of the guests had departed.

"You do good work," he said. "I'm truly impressed."

"I thought you'd gone," she snapped, then could have cursed her tongue for betraying that she'd noticed when Sophie left and assumed Dex was with her.

"I told Sophie I had a ride." He shrugged, looking impossibly gorgeous in a well-cut suit in shale gray.

"Do you?"

"I do if you give me a lift, otherwise I guess I'll call a cab."

"Why didn't you go home with your date?"

"Because she's not a date. She's the fiancée of a good friend. I didn't want anybody thinking there was something going on between me and Sophie when there isn't." He held her gaze. "You know how suspicious people can be."

Refusing to rise to such obvious bait she said, "Well, I guess I can give you a lift but you'll have to wait until I'm finished here."

"No problem. Can I make myself useful?"

"You can help load the supplies into the van." In fact, she hired a company to take care of the cleanup, but she was annoyed with Dexter and half hoped he got something nasty on his pretty suit.

As though he'd read her mind, he slipped off his jacket, and, to her surprise, slipped it over her shoulders. "Take care of that for me." Then he rolled up his sleeves and headed toward the cleanup crew, turning quickly from wedding guest to menial laborer.

The jacket was warm from his body and, weak woman that she was, she slipped her arms into the sleeves and enjoyed the sensation of wearing something of his. She caught an elusive scent of him, something hot and spicy and forbidden.

Then she went into the kitchen to check in with Chelsea. Her caterer was pretty much ready to go, the kitchen cleaner than when she'd arrived and all her food and supplies loaded into her van.

"How you doing?"

"My feet hurt." She grinned. "But we pulled off another miracle."

"I thought the Cinderella coach cake was a bit much, but everyone seemed to like it."

"Seems we're never too old for fairy tales."

"Speaking of fairy tales, who's the Prince Charming out there hauling tables and why are you wearing his jacket?"

"That's no prince, that's my ex-husband." She didn't bother to explain the other part.

"Wow." Chelsea did a double take, and she followed her friend's gaze to the sight of her ex's delectable backside as he bent over, helping lift a heavy table. "That's the scumbag? Too bad he's a wretched human being. He sure looks good."

"Yeah."

They both watched out the window for a few more moments. "He doesn't mind getting his hands dirty, I'll give him that."

"No." She'd always loved that about him, the architect who was only too happy to get down and dirty with the construction aspects of his projects. She was never sure whether he appealed to her more when he was designing and envisioning a finished project, or when he was covered in sweat and sawdust, muscles bulging.

Chelsea pulled herself away from the window first. "Okay, I've got my own eye candy at home. I'd better get back, David's waiting for me."

"Sure. Have a great Sunday." They hugged quickly.

She was, as usual, the last one to leave. Only this time, she wasn't alone. Dexter followed her to her car. The temperature had dropped suddenly and there was a sharp chill in the air.

Once they were settled into her car, the heater humming, she turned to him and said, "So, where can I drop you?"

He gazed at her mouth. "I was hoping we could pick up where we left off the other night."

5

"WHAT?" The word bounced around the inside of her car, even though her shock was only pretense. She'd known the moment Dexter asked her for a ride home that he had more than transportation in mind. You didn't love a man for six years, live with him for five, without knowing a thing or two about how his mind worked.

Or have him know about how yours worked, she realized, as he gazed at her separated by nothing but a couple of feet of cold air, with an expression that suggested he knew she was as aware of him as he was of her. "Come on," he said. "You've been thinking about having sex with me, too. I know you're too honest to pretend you haven't."

Which was exactly what she'd planned to do. Deny, deny, deny. She sighed out a breath of mingled frustration and—no, it was all frustration, both the irritation of a woman dealing with a man she thought was out of her life, and the huge dollop of sexual frustration that being around Dex again was causing. Because she couldn't be near him and not remember how they'd burned up

the sheets together. No matter their problems, their sex
life had always been superb.

"I can't—"

"Whatever else was wrong between us, you can't
deny that when we got naked, everything worked," he
said, oddly echoing her own thoughts on the matter.
Then he reached over, and ran a fingertip under the hem
of her skirt. "Or not even naked," he mused, his eyes
crinkling as memories rose around them. "Remember
that time when we took my first brand-new car out for
a spin?"

"No," she lied.

Which was a huge mistake because then, of course,
he had to remind her of an incident they both knew she
remembered perfectly well.

"I'd only ever driven used beaters, and now suddenly
I had a company car, and it was brand-new. We went to
the dealership to pick it up. A silver GM sedan." It had
been a green Ford, but she refused to rise to the bait no
matter how provocatively he behaved. She shifted an
inch closer to her door, but he shifted, too, so his finger
continued to trace the hem of her skirt which had, naturally, ridden up when she sat down. She could smack
him away, but that would make an issue of something
she preferred to ignore. Besides, what he was doing felt
so good, and it had been so long.

"It was summer and you wore a red sundress." He
was right about the season, but she'd worn a blue cotton
dress. She never wore red with her hair color. His wandering finger had reached the crease of her closed legs
and he paused for a second. "Is any of this familiar?"

"Not ringing any bells yet." Ha.

His voice grew husky. "We took a drive, didn't know

where we were going, didn't care. We found ourselves down by the river. It was quiet, nobody around."

Because he'd obviously carefully done a reconnaissance mission beforehand. When he'd pulled out a bottle of wine from his briefcase along with two glasses, she'd known it.

"Do you remember what happened then?" he asked, his voice so close, so deep and low, that she knew he'd moved closer.

"No," she lied.

"That's too bad. I'll never forget that night as long as I live."

The touch of his finger doing no more than trace her hem, running along her upper thigh, was so erotic it was an act of will not to squirm, not to push his hand higher, where she needed release so desperately, or at least depress the handy button that would recline their seats. Or even better, act as they had that night he was describing, and simply crawl into the backseat where there was more room.

"I'm sure you've made lots of new memories since then," she snapped.

"Don't you want to know what happened?" he asked her, as though she'd never spoken.

"It was a long time ago."

"Not that long."

Maybe she could force her body to remain still while that one finger played at her hem, never going higher or doing anything that would make it necessary for her to slap him down, but she couldn't seem to control her breathing. Even as she tried to pretend she felt nothing, remembered nothing, a combination of his finger stroking her skin, his nearness, and the sweet, painful pull of memory was causing her breathing to speed up along with her pulse.

"We talked about my new job, and a new event you were organizing, and it seemed like we could do anything. We were young, smart, ambitious and we had each other. What an unbeatable team." The finger stalled for a moment and she felt the tension in his hand as though a spasm of emotion had hit him. It felt like anger, but she had to assume it was guilt for throwing everything they'd had away.

Then the moment passed and the back-and-forth exploration of her thigh continued. He tugged her skirt up a full half inch, torturing her again with a slow track back, his finger pad tracing a line of heat across her skin.

"All the while we talked, I did this. Played at your hem, and you pretended you didn't notice, like now."

"I think your memory's playing tricks."

"And then, suddenly, you parted your legs and turned toward me." He swallowed. So did she. Heat flooded her body as she remembered what came next.

"I thought I was so in control, touching you, turning us both on, but you were the one in control, weren't you? You were the one with the secret."

"No," she whispered, but she wasn't telling him she hadn't had a secret, she was trying to stop the flood of memory that was as warm and thick as desire.

"When I got up to touch your panties, you weren't wearing any."

Oh, how she remembered. The feel of the air wafting up her skirt, the wanton knowledge that she'd stood by while he'd finalized paperwork at a car dealership, while they'd driven public highways, and all the time, underneath her cotton sundress, she'd been bare-assed.

"We were in the backseat so fast I ended up with bruised elbows and knees. We never did take off our clothes, did we? I ended up flipping that skirt up, pulling down the top of your dress to reach your breasts. You were always so sensitive there." He laughed softly. "We were like a pair of kids going at it." He sighed, obviously realizing that this little trip down memory lane wasn't working. Her thighs didn't ease open, though he couldn't possibly know what torture it was to hold them closed against him. "God, I loved you."

"But not enough," she said, her voice so soft she wasn't sure if he'd heard her.

"Do you think we rushed into marriage too fast?"

She turned her head, wondering where he was going with this train of thought. "We knew each other a year. I guess I wish we'd waited. Long enough for me to realize you weren't the kind of guy to stick with one woman."

He pulled his hand back into his own lap and she fought the urge to grab it and put it where she needed, so urgently, to be touched.

"I wish I'd waited long enough to get a handle on those demons you carry around with you."

"What demons?" she snapped. How like a man to cheat on her and then try and pretend she was the one with the problem.

"The demons that stopped you being able to trust."

She was not going to have this conversation again. She'd moved on. "If I'm so full of demons, what are you doing still trying to get into my pants?"

A sigh of pure frustration rolled through him. "Hell if I know."

6

THE READING TERMINAL MARKET was crazy. Naturally. It was a Sunday afternoon and every yuppie with a craving for organic arugula or some fresh monkfish had made tracks down here. Karen had a love/hate relationship with the market. While she loved this place simply for the fun of people-watching, she also suffered as only a woman who loves food and tries to live on fifteen hundred calories a day can suffer.

Since she'd barely slept thanks to Dex and his antics in her car last night, she felt weaker than usual. The worst part had been driving him to his hotel, with all the steamy atmosphere between them churning around with a lot of emotions. Anger, frustration, and a bitter kind of longing that hurt more than all the other feelings put together. How could she still want the man so much?

Dex was her ex. He had to remain that way if she had any chance of hanging on to her hard-won self-esteem.

She'd half thought he'd invite her up to his room and was ready to let him have it when he did. Somehow, the fact that he didn't say any more than, "Thanks for the ride. Night," was an added insult. He didn't even ask her up to his room so she could annihilate the guy with a few well-chosen words that she'd been practicing for blocks.

How unfair was that?

The bakery smells were so good. There were blocks of cheese bigger than house steps and she wanted to buy one and gobble every succulent morsel. She loved cheese, every fat-saturated ounce. Hard cheese, soft cheese, runny cheese, blue cheese. Oh, stop it. She averted her eyes. She really shouldn't be here.

But Ron had suggested the locale for their first coffee date and, under instruction from Dee, she'd agreed without quibbling. Now she was here she wished she'd quibbled big-time. She wanted to turn tail and head home. Apart from being exhausted, cranky and cheese-obsessed, she'd probably dressed all wrong for a first date with a stranger. Her jeans were casual, but she'd pushed her feet into high heels instead of giving them a well-deserved Sunday rest, and she was worried that the green sweater was too low-necked. The last thing she wanted to do was stick her boobs in some poor man's face, so she'd added a scarf at the last moment, and now wished she could go home and start over.

Dee had made her promise to let her hair down, which she'd first assumed was some kind of veiled allusion to being open for sex with a stranger until Dee had clarified that she actually meant she should leave her hair unpinned and unconfined. "You have such great hair, that gorgeous red color and the natural curls." And since Dee seemed to know what she was doing in the online dating world, Karen had been persuaded.

Now she suddenly felt like a country-and-western

singer with too much of everything. Big hair, big heels, big breasts, big butt.

She was a few minutes early, because it was her way, and stopped to stare unseeing at a booth selling nothing but spices. She never should have agreed to this date with Ron the CPA.

Somehow, this was all Dexter's fault. If he hadn't got her so riled up she never would have agreed to a date with some guy she met over the Internet.

However, she realized that whatever her reasons for being here, she wasn't about to stand this man up. It wasn't his fault she was an idiot. So, they'd have coffee. An hour of her life would be wasted, and then she could get back to attempting to make something of the years left to her.

On that optimistic thought, she made her way to the busy coffee shop and immediately spotted Ron, who was standing near the entrance, obviously as punctual as she was.

He looked exactly like his photo. Exactly like a CPA. And suddenly she relaxed. He was reassuringly unassuming, no other women were covertly studying him or overtly drooling. He was the kind of man who wouldn't forever be tempted to stray, which had to be a good thing.

She forced a smile to her face and walked up to him. "Hello, you must be Ron. I'm Karen."

They shook hands. He seemed pleased by her punctuality, insisted on buying her a coffee and they settled at a table.

For a moment, neither spoke. Finally he said, "You're very punctual. It's a quality I admire."

Oh, how old-fashioned he sounded. What was she even doing here? Her mind flashed back to the night before, when she'd been humiliatingly close to parting her thighs and doing her ex-husband in the parking lot. Something had to change, and fast. She smiled at him. "I feel the same way."

Now that she looked at him, she saw that behind his glasses he had warm gray eyes. He was fairly forgettable until you took note of those eyes. He was dressed neatly, in jeans that bore such sharp creases she suspected he ironed them, a polo shirt he'd probably bought at Costco or Sam's Club and a well-worn leather jacket.

Another pause ensued, while they both took refuge in sipping coffee, and finally she blurted, "I have no idea how to do this. I'm so sorry, it's my first time." She sighed, sensing the genuine niceness of this man, and opened up even more. "In fact, it's been a long time since I had any kind of a date. I'm so out of practice I have no idea where to begin."

It was as though her confession took all the awkwardness out of their date. Ron nodded with sweet understanding. "It sucks. Really."

She was surprised into a spurt of laughter by his sad admission.

Then realizing how that must sound, he added, "I don't mean meeting you, but online dating is a new skill you have to learn." He shrugged. "I've been doing this for a few months now and I find the hardest part is that people often, when they write their profiles, put a description of what they wish they were like rather than something that's actually true."

She thought of the way she'd fudged her height, claiming to be five-four, and tried very hard not to blush.

"The worst thing for me was the bad spelling and grammar. I don't think I'm too fussy, but if a man can't spell *relationship,* I really don't think I want to have one with him."

"True. For me the biggest turnoff is women who are so obviously looking for the father of their future children that they all but ask you for a sperm count."

Once again she laughed, sensing that maybe he wasn't quite as dull as he appeared. "I've tried very hard to be honest," he said.

"You told me all about your work," she reminded him, "but very little about yourself."

"There's not much to tell. I'm thirty-seven. Single, I'm a CPA."

"Whoa," she said. "We're getting back to your résumé again."

"Sorry. I'm not one to wear my heart on my sleeve."

"Whereabouts do you live?" she asked, seeking for some topic that they could talk about.

"I'm within walking distance of Independence Hall," he said and she wondered if he was being deliberately vague in case she turned out to be a stalker or crazy person.

"Wow. In Society Hill? That's a nice area."

He paused for a second, then said, "I inherited the house from my mother. It's a Federal-style town house. She recently passed."

"I'm so sorry," she said with ready sympathy. She couldn't imagine life without her mother, who was both nosy and annoying and the person who loved Karen most in all the world.

"Cancer," he said. "It was very hard."

She heard the almost hidden quiver in his voice and impulsively reached over to lay a hand on his. Because she didn't know what to say, she said nothing, merely offered her silent support.

After a second, he said, "My only regret is that she didn't get to see me settled, with grandchildren. It was her dearest wish."

"I'm sure she was very proud of you." She searched for something else to say. "Do you have brothers and sisters?"

"No, I'm an only child." And she received the impression that he'd been his mother's pride and joy. She didn't ask, but she suspected he'd never left home, had nursed his mother through her final illness and now, lost and alone, was trying to find a substitute.

"How about you?" he asked, obviously determined to steer clear of painful subjects.

"I'm divorced." She didn't think he wanted to hear the ugly details. Well, who would? So she merely said, "I've been single for almost five years now. I run my own wedding planning business."

He began asking her precise and intelligent questions about her business and she felt that it was a relief to both of them to discuss something as impersonal as business.

At the end of an hour, she knew two things. One, Ron was a genuinely nice man, she suspected he was an excellent accountant, and two, she felt not the tiniest spark of attraction.

They exchanged business cards and agreed to meet for lunch one day soon. She had no idea whether either of them would follow up, but she was toying with the idea of hiring him for her business.

They shook hands at the end of their coffee date and he headed one way while she turned in the opposite direction.

She was trying to decide whether the coffee date had been a success or a disaster, when a voice hailed her, "Karen."

She glanced up to see Chelsea standing in front of her, a canvas bag of fresh food in her arms. Beside her was her fiancé, David, loaded down with two more bags. She was struck with how good those two looked together, two tall, gorgeous people who were so clearly meant for each other you could feel their bond.

After the greetings were over, Chelsea turned to her lover and said, "David, do you see that fish market way over there?"

He glanced at his woman with slightly raised brows. "You mean the one with the long lineup?"

"That's the one. Can you go buy six spot prawns and a pound of fresh crabmeat?"

He glanced from one woman to the other. "You wouldn't be trying to get rid of me, so you can do the girlfriend gossip thing, would you?"

Chelsea grinned at him. "Do you want what I can whip up with six spot prawns and a pound of crabmeat or don't you?"

With a good-natured shrug, he said, "Goodbye, Karen." And wandered off.

"That was rude. We'll see each other at work tomorrow."

"I can't wait until tomorrow. Believe me, he'll end up happy when his dinner is served. And I have to hear about your date."

She made a wry face. "He was really nice. A truly nice man."

"That sounds very unpromising."

"It's not his fault. I wouldn't even be doing this if it

wasn't for Dee, my darling assistant who seems to think I'm in desperate need of a man."

"She's young, what does she know?"

Karen snorted. "She thinks she knows more than I do. Know what I found on my desk Friday morning?"

"What?"

"A box of condoms and a note from Dee reminding me to always play it safe."

Chelsea had the kind of full-bodied laugh that made strangers stop and grin as though just being around her made them part of the fun. "What did you do with them?"

"I put them in my desk drawer. I have everything in there from hemorrhoid cream, which is good for minimizing puffy eyes on brides and their mothers before a photo shoot, to extra nylons, shoelaces, pins, tape, flower wire, film, batteries, hair spray, you name it."

"And now you've got condoms." She leaned closer so none of the fresh fruit and veggie shoppers would overhear her. "Maybe the CPA will get to sharpen his pencil after all."

She snorted with her own, hardly dainty laughter. "Stop it. I'm thinking of hiring him to do my books. We talked a lot about my business, it was an easy subject for both of us and he asked intelligent questions."

"Oh, poor guy. So the date was a disaster."

She wondered what Chelsea was planning to do with that dark green spiky stuff sticking out of her bag and decided she didn't want to know. "No, I wouldn't say he was a disaster, just there was no big spark, you know?"

"Oh, yeah. I know. But maybe he's worth giving

another chance, seeing as sometimes people we spark off aren't always good for us."

"I so agree."

Her friend drilled her with her gaze. "Speaking of bad news and sparks, how's Dex the Ex?"

7

DEXTER WAS A SUCKER for punishment. He knew it, could curse himself as much as he liked, but all the cursing didn't stop him from pulling up in front of Karen's office for the latest wedding planning meeting. He'd had to cut short an earlier meeting with the developers of the mixed use complex he was designing in order to be here. He'd been far more delighted to bag this project than he should have been and he suspected his level of satisfaction was related to the fact that he'd be spending a lot of time in Philadelphia for the next few months.

In missile range of the redheaded termagant he'd so foolishly married.

It wasn't like his buddy Andrew and Sophie couldn't have a perfectly good wedding without him playing assistant wedding planner.

And yet, here he was.

He pulled in to park in the office lot and there was Karen's car. A surprising shot of lust pummeled him as he recalled their all-too-short time together Saturday night when her mouth had told him *no* even as her body shouted *yes*.

What was he going to do about this very inconvenient thing he still had for his ex-wife?

Until he figured that out, he supposed he was going to play assistant wedding planner.

He was a few minutes early and it didn't look as if Sophie was here yet, but they'd booked the last possible appointment so they could both get in a day's work. Probably she'd be here any minute.

Loosening his tie, he went into the office anyway. He glanced around but the cute British girl wasn't at her station or anywhere in the front area of If You Can Dream It. He walked toward Karen's office and heard her voice. He was conscious of the familiarity of that voice, the slight breathlessness that he doubted she was even aware of. His day had been successful, the client had approved the more expensive option, the one Dexter had hoped they'd go with since it was both greener and preserved the architectural integrity of the building.

There was a time he'd have rushed to tell her the good news and they'd have celebrated. Now they were all but strangers to each other. And yet he knew every timbre of her voice as well as he knew every inch of her body. It was crazy.

When he got to her doorway he paused there, enjoying the view. She was talking on the phone, her bare feet up on the desktop, a sight he suspected not very many clients were privileged to see. Her feet were small, dainty, the toes painted bright pink. Her floral skirt had ridden up revealing a shapely thigh.

He rapped on the door frame and she turned, startled. When she saw him, she yanked her feet off the desktop and he watched, enjoying the sight, as her toes did a version of Riverdance under the desk until she located two high-heeled shoes and attempted to jam her feet into them while simultaneously dragging her skirt back into place.

She continued her conversation, to a florist he presumed, since the words *rose* and *baby's breath* occurred so often.

Once she'd successfully navigated her feet into her shoes, she turned her chair, and thus her back, to him and continued her conversation. "What about the ribbon? Were you able to match the color of the bridesmaids' dresses?" He watched her pick up the pen he'd given her and begin to doodle. "Mmm-hmm. Okay. I know it's a difficult color to match, but the bride is very particular about tone." She made a quick note. "Well, I think you should send over a sample of the ribbon and we can let the bride decide. Yes, I know. Right. See you." And she hung up.

She let him stand there another moment while she made notes. Then she turned her chair so she was facing him.

"Hi," he said.

"Didn't Sophie get hold of you?" his ex-wife asked, rising and coming to stand in front of her desk.

He'd had his cell phone turned off while he was on-site with the client. Had he remembered to turn it back on? He didn't think so. "Why?"

"She got held up at work. She rescheduled our meeting."

"Oh." He pulled out his cell phone and when he turned it on, there was the little voice mail icon. "Guess I forgot to check my messages."

"Guess so."

She didn't move. If there was a posture for "there's

the door, don't let it hit you on your way out," she was demonstrating it. But he'd known this woman for a long time, and during the best of that time, intimately, and he knew she was skittish because she didn't want to be alone with him. Not when they both knew that the fire that had always burned between them hadn't grown fainter from time apart. If anything, it burned fiercer than ever.

Ever since that kiss the other night he'd been thinking that it was inevitable they'd end up back in bed.

He glanced at that sturdy-looking desk. Or not in bed.

"Has your assistant left for the day?"

"Yep, and I'm finished for the day, too, so I'll let you know when the meeting's rescheduled." She stuck out her hand for him to shake.

Maybe if she hadn't done that he would have walked away as she was pretending she wanted him to. But offering her hand like he was a casual business acquaintance?

She might as well have flipped him the bird.

He took her hand. Held it in his for a moment too long, felt the quiver running along her skin, the soft warmth of their palm-to-palm contact. Not letting go of her hand he took a step toward her.

She stepped back.

He took another step toward her.

"Dex, what are you…" Her hips bumped the desk and their gazes locked.

He watched the quick intake of breath, the way it raised her glorious, extravagant breasts against the silk of her blouse. Her mouth opened slightly and he moved in, taking her mouth as though he owned it because on some primitive level he did. Always had. Always would.

The sweet taste of her exploded on his lips and tongue and then he pulled her in all the way, tight against him so her breasts were pressing against his chest, her hips jammed against him, her butt pressed against the edge of her feminine desk.

For a second he felt her go rigid, thought she might push him away, but as quickly as her resistance rose, it receded and with a low moan in the back of her throat, she pushed her hands into his hair, pulled him into her.

He'd always loved her honest passion, the way she let him know what she was feeling and what she wanted. Mindless, they pulled at each other, the years of separation, the anger, the frustration falling away as they clawed at each other.

He had his hands shoved down her top, grabbing at her breasts, pulling them out of her bra so he could see them, feel them, taste them. She'd always been slightly embarrassed about the size of her breasts but he loved them. When he put his tongue to her nipple the flavor took him back to the first time they'd ever been together, when he'd discovered this woman was made for sex. Or, as he secretly liked to think, she was made for sex with him.

Her head dropped back as he curled his tongue around the sensitive point, pushed his knee between her legs until she parted for him. Without taking his mouth from her breast he reached under her hips and hoisted her up until she sat on the desk, her pretty floral skirt sliding up as he pushed it up, up, over her hips. She spread herself wide for him, her arms twined around his neck, her head thrown back as he pleasured her.

The joy of this woman was how well he knew her body, how intimately he could gauge her responses. Beneath his tongue her skin was heating and he could feel her pulse hammering. When he trailed a hand down between her thighs he found her as wet and hot as he'd suspected he would. He cupped her, making her moan and squirm against his fingers.

"It's been so long," he murmured against her plump flesh.

"Too long," she moaned.

Slipping his hands beneath her hips, he peeled the tiny scrap of pale blue silk and lace that passed for underwear off her, bending as he slid the foolish thing down her legs and over the ridiculous heels. He was throbbing with need, so aroused he was in danger of embarrassing himself as he rose and slid open his zipper.

She reached between them, unbuttoning him and sliding her small, capable hands around him which didn't help his self-control.

While she caressed him he returned the favor, cupping her heat, slipping one finger into that glorious wet until she squirmed against him. He knew her so well, he knew that she was as close to exploding as he was.

He looked down into her face, her eyes that clear blue-green, her cheeks flushed with passion, a sprinkle of freckles across her nose and cheeks, her lips parted and eager. He closed the distance between them, kissing her hungrily.

Had he ever wanted her this much? Had he ever wanted anyone or anything this badly? If so, he couldn't remember.

She pulled him closer and as he touched the wet heat he suddenly checked himself as reality intruded. They weren't married anymore. He had no idea if she was on birth control or what she'd been doing since they were last together. With a groan of gut-deep frustration he cursed himself for no longer carrying a condom in his wallet. But he wasn't a kid anymore. The only prophylactics he owned were safely in his bedside drawer at home.

Pulling away slightly, then resting his forehead against hers, he admitted the awful truth. "I don't have protection," he gasped.

"Oh, no…wait, I've got some condoms in my desk drawer."

"Really?"

"Yeah. On top of the hair spray, I think."

He bounded around the desk and flung open the drawer. The oddest assortment of products greeted him. He dug around and found the unopened box wedged between a can of breath spray and a tube of Preparation H.

Whatever.

He didn't let himself think about why his ex-wife kept a box of condoms in her desk drawer, simply decided to be grateful.

He tore into the box and swiftly sheathed himself, then holding his pants up with one hand, made his way back around to where his ex-wife still sat, leaning back, supported by her hands, still open for him.

Waiting.

He didn't keep her waiting for long. Teasing her with his fingers, toying with her until her breathing grew shallow and raspy and she was moving against him, he brought her up and then pulling her hips to the edge of the desk, he stepped between her thighs and slowly eased into her. Oh, it felt so good, so right. He'd forgotten how amazing she was. Snug heat, the sweet slide as she thrust against him, the crazy dance she did with her hips when her excitement began to peak, pumping and corkscrewing around him until he had no resistance left.

Their mouths fused, their hearts pounded in sync and he thrust up and home again and again while she danced and pumped against him.

She lost control, began to pant, to moan and gyrate her hips crazily.

"Yes," he whispered, loving the way she let herself go completely.

"Oh, Dex," she cried, and then he felt the spasms clutch at him even as her head fell back and she cried out in ecstasy.

He stroked in and out of her slowly, easing her through her orgasm and then she opened her eyes, unfocused and huge and with a tiny moan, she grabbed his hips and thrust against him again, driving herself to a second climax and taking him along for the ride.

No way to hold back when she grabbed his ass like that, squeezing and pulling him into paradise even as she continued that crazy corkscrew thing with her hips. He was lost, and when she came the second time, he cried out in unison.

For a few minutes they remained slumped against each other, panting. Sweat dotted her upper chest and her mouth was swollen from their passion.

He didn't want to pull out of her body, loved the feel of all that snug heat wrapped around him, still pulsing with aftershocks, their bodies close and intimate.

At last she leaned back and glanced up at him, a half-embarrassed grin splitting her face. "That wasn't quite the meeting I planned."

"It's always been best between us when it was spontaneous," he reminded her. When he thought of some of the places they'd done it, half-derelict buildings he was working on, a Finnish sauna that time he'd almost passed out, his parents' garden shed. Her office after hours seemed pretty tame.

She gazed at him through slumberous eyes that sent him so many messages he wanted to take her all over again. His breathing wasn't quite steady, his pulse nowhere near slowing.

"Next time," she said.

Oh, yes, if she was talking next time then he hadn't completely blown any chance he might have with her by acting like a Neanderthal.

He liked the sexy half smile on her face.

"Next time? What? Do you have any special requests? Positions, locales, maybe a toy you'd like to try?"

As though she'd made up her mind about something, she leaned back and said, "Who needs toys when I've got you?"

A toy? Shock held him speechless. She was planning to treat him like a battery-operated pleasure tool? The kind he saw in sex shops in a million girlie colors. Oh, wasn't that just great. He'd planned to invite her out for dinner, maybe try to talk to her and instead she was treating him like he had multi-speeds and a rotating head.

She pulled up her legs and swung around and off her desk, as graceful as a dancer. "What I was going to say was, 'next time, maybe you could take your tie off.'"

8

I had a very nice time, the e-mail said. Perhaps we could do it again sometime.

Karen stared at the words and felt ridiculously guilty. She didn't owe Ron anything. All they'd shared was coffee, but the fact that she'd shared completely inappropriate desktop sex with Dexter only a day after her date with the CPA filled her with remorse and that translated into an odd feeling of guilt where Ron was concerned.

Not knowing how to answer or what to say, she closed her computer and did what she too often did in times of stress. She walked over to Chelsea's place.

But it turned out she wasn't the only one acting uncharacteristically crazy. When she got there, before she could open her mouth and wail out her troubles, her caterer and friend put a finger over her lips and beckoned her to follow.

Wondering if her complete lunacy was perhaps catching, she warily followed Chelsea who crept toward the industrial kitchen she shared with Laurel, the cake designer. Stealthily opening the door, she quietly beckoned Karen into the kitchen ahead of her.

And then Karen realized why she'd acted so secretive.

Laurel was in the throes of creation.

Laurel wasn't a woman who worked in a normal way. In fact there was little about Laurel that was exactly mainstream. She was a wraithlike creature who tended to wear gauzy clothes and Indian cottons. She practiced yoga and had spent more time than was probably good for her in an ashram.

She was as insubstantial as gossamer, as unworldly as a nun, as hard to pin down as a cloud.

But her cakes were pure magic.

An artist whose media were devil's food and fondant and royal icing and marzipan and heaven knew what else, she was a joy to watch, though easily distracted, so both women stood quietly watching as she painted food coloring onto whimsical flowers. The cake itself was a child's fantasy of fairies and strangely shaped trees, animals and a pair of dainty children.

They left the kitchen as quietly as they'd entered it. "What's the occasion?" Karen asked.

"It's a fundraiser for a children's shelter. She volunteered the cake."

Karen shook her head fondly. "It's a good thing she has us or she'd never make any money."

"I know. She truly is the most airy-fairy person I've ever met. Can you imagine how she could clean up in New York or L.A. if she had any ambition?"

"I do have ambition," a soft voice said behind them. Laurel moved as quietly as the fairies she loved to create and seemed neither surprised nor offended to find them talking about her. "I want every cake to tell a story." She removed the scarf she'd wrapped around her multicolored hair and shrugged out of the plain white apron that always seemed much too big and heavy for her slight frame. "I'm just not into material success."

"I know, honey," Karen said. "We weren't criticizing you. We love you."

"I know." She turned suddenly, her waifish look vanishing in a mischievous grin. "And it's a lot easier to pay my rent since you two took over my billings." She rolled her neck and then did a few shoulder exercises. "Would you like to see my sketches for the circus wedding cake?"

"Love to."

Laurel dug a well-worn sketchbook from her handwoven bag. She flipped through the book and showed them a watercolor drawing of the cake.

"This is why you are a genius," Chelsea exclaimed when they looked at the drawing. "I'd have gone with a circus tent probably, or tightrope walkers or something to suggest a circus."

Karen nodded.

"Too mundane," the young woman replied.

What she'd created was difficult to describe. She'd drawn a tower of diminishing-sized cake layers that grew narrower as the cake grew taller, so it felt as though the cake might disappear into the clouds. From the top she'd drawn an explosion of multicolored ribbons cascading like fireworks.

"Will these be ribbons?" Karen asked, wondering how she'd get ribbon to contort into those shapes and stay there.

"No. Gum paste. That's sugar with natural gum that feels like Play-Doh but dries hard. It holds its shape so I can get icing ribbons to curl and dance."

"Amazing. And I know that's fondant, right?" Karen added, having worked with Laurel long enough to know how much she liked to cover her cake with the smooth icing which she could paint, often using a special airbrush tool. The cake design was like an abstract painting, with reds and purples, blues and greens, and bright splotches of yellow all clashing and intermingling. Somehow she suggested movement through color. Without including a single circus element, she'd caught the energy of Cirque du Soleil. "It's brilliant," Karen agreed.

"Glad you like it. I'll probably add a few elements, but this is the basic idea." She stuffed the book into her bag. "Well, I've got to go to my Vinyasa flow class. See you later." And she was gone.

"Sometimes I wonder if she's real or a figment of my imagination," Karen said after the door closed silently.

"I know. Nobody should be that quiet. Or serene. It's kind of creepy."

"What's creepy is that she weighs ninety pounds soaking wet and works with cake all day. It's not fair." She stared at the door broodingly. "What is Vinyasa flow anyway?"

"Some kind of yoga, I think."

"Maybe I should take up yoga. Maybe I'd end up as thin as Laurel."

Chelsea shook her head. "Are you back to that again?"

"Did I ever leave it?"

"Someday you will meet a man who adores your curves."

"I should have been born in the era of Mae West and all those tiny, chubby pin-up girls." She put her hands on her ample hips. "Instead, I come of age when the ideal is a ten-foot-tall anorexic. It's not fair."

"I would think a lot of men would prefer a curvy woman to an elongated skeleton."

Karen thought of her and Dex on her desk and felt heat suffuse her face.

Chelsea was quick to pick up on it. "Oh, no. Look at you blushing and staring at the floor. Have you met such a man?"

"No. Not exactly." And she realized that her feelings about Dex were far too confusing to share with anyone. Instead she said, "That CPA e-mailed me. He said he enjoyed our coffee date."

"That's great, right?"

"Yes, I suppose. I didn't think it was a very exciting date though."

"Give the guy a chance. You said yourself he was nice."

"He was. You're right." And maybe a nice man was exactly what she needed to keep her thoughts off a certain architect. "I should suggest dinner or a movie or something."

"That's the spirit. And he's not the only single man in Philly, you know. Who else is out there?"

She glanced up and put a hand over her mouth. "I keep forgetting to check the Web site."

Unfortunately for her, when she got back to her office for her rescheduled meeting with Sophie, Dexter had come along. For some reason she'd assumed he'd have enough tact not to show. Seemed she'd been wrong. She refused to blush when she met Dex's knowing gaze.

"Sophie, it's nice to see you again. What did you think of the bridal salons I suggested?"

"Fantastic. I found my dress. Look, I brought you

a picture," the woman gushed pulling out her digital camera. She'd chosen a perfect dress for her figure. Sleek and simple.

"Very classy," Karen said approvingly. "And for the bridesmaids?"

"I went with blue. It's Andrew's favorite color and he's not here to help choose anything, so at least I'm keeping him in mind."

"That's nice. And it's a good blue for a winter wedding." She consulted her notes. "Let's see, you're getting married at your aunt's house in mid February."

"Closest Saturday to Valentine's Day we could find."

"That's sweet," she said in her professional tone, controlling her gag reflex with an effort. "In my experience the men don't get too involved in the wedding details."

"Except for Dexter here. I don't know what I'd have done without him."

She sent him a thin smile and he responded with a wink. Suddenly he rose. "I've been meaning to tell you how much I like this desk, Karen," he said, walking toward it, standing in the very spot he'd stood when she'd so wantonly let herself be carried away by lust.

Heat suffused every inch of her body from her toes to the roots of her hair. She watched, unable to think of a thing to say as he ran his hands along the edge of the curved wood, caressing the grain the way he'd caressed her skin. "It's a lovely piece. Classy." He leaned against it. "Seems sturdy, too."

He must know it was since it had held up under the strain of them having sex on it.

"I didn't know you were interested in antiques, Dex," Sophie said, thankfully looking at the desk and not at

Karen who was forcing her blush down. The curse of being a redhead.

"I like classics," he said.

"Well, we all do," Karen interjected. "And I think your dress is absolutely classic. Now, I was talking to the florist this morning about you. I know you were keen on a garden theme even though we'll need to be indoors. He's a genius. He's suggesting pots of forced blooms and he wonders if you want to think about a four-seasons garden. His idea is that love is eternal, like an ever-blooming garden."

"Oh, what a fantastic idea. I love that," Sophie exclaimed. "And do you think he could include a few Italian plants since Andrew's family is Italian and he's been spending so much time in Italy?"

"I'll make a note of it," Karen said. "If you like the idea, he'll draw something up for you to look at."

Dexter didn't say much more during the meeting, but he didn't seem able to keep his hands off her desk.

She could barely concentrate. And the fact that Dexter knew exactly what he was doing to her, only made her more furious.

9

CHELSEA CAME INTO Karen's office with the spinach salad she hadn't had time to pick up and a formidable looking woman in a power suit and a riot of black curls framing a face dominated by big blue eyes and a square, "don't make me hit you" jaw.

"Do you have a minute if I bribe you with food?" Chelsea asked.

"Of course. Not that I consider salad food."

"You should have let me pack you a dessert."

"I don't want to talk about it."

Chelsea shot her a frustrated glance that suggested she'd soon be hearing some story about how fat was the new thin. But for now they weren't alone so she figured she was safe.

"This is David's sister, Sarah. She's getting married."

"Congratulations." Karen smiled politely but it was hard to hold herself back from outright laughing. Most brides came in looking excited, or nervous or blissed out on love.

Sarah seemed irritated about her impending bridalhood.

"Thanks. I'll be honest. I don't have a lot of time to plan a wedding, I've got a busy law practice, but I don't want a lot of hearts and flowers. And I won't be wearing white."

Fortunately, Chelsea had warned her about Sarah. The woman was a classic type A, an aggressive up-and-coming divorce lawyer who'd fallen for a school guidance counselor and part-time yoga teacher. Karen loved opposites-attract couples, but she had a feeling this was going to be one of the weirder pairings that made her job so much fun.

"You can wear whatever you want," Karen assured her. "Though popular tradition that wearing white is a symbol of purity isn't correct. The Greeks wore white as a color of celebration."

"Really?"

"Mmm-hmm. But the Western white wedding gown was popularized when Queen Victoria wore white to her wedding. At the time, only rich women could afford a dress they'd never wear again. Now, of course, any bride can wear whatever she wants."

"That's interesting, but I'm still not wearing white."

"That's fine."

She wondered if she really wanted to work with someone whose every sentence sounded like a barked order.

She glanced at Chelsea, wondering how she felt getting stuck with this woman for a sister-in-law. If she and David ever actually got married.

But she was surprised yet again when Chelsea said,

"Sarah's been my best friend since I moved here when I was fourteen."

Sarah's face softened completely when she smiled, Karen noted with relief, which it did now, in an impish grin. "You only hung out with me cause you had the hots for my big brother."

"Not true." She opened the takeout container and handed Karen a fork. "Not completely true. Go ahead and eat, I know you're starving."

"Yeah, please, don't mind me," Sarah said.

"I can't take notes and eat at the same time," Karen argued.

"Look, I don't think you're going to need a lot of notes. You probably won't even agree to plan this crazy wedding."

Once more she sent Chelsea a puzzled glance.

"Why wouldn't I want to plan your wedding?"

Sarah assumed her irritated expression once more. "It was my boyfriend's idea. He wants to recreate our first date."

Now Karen understood the irritation. She was beginning to feel some herself.

"You two went skydiving?"

"No."

"Hang gliding? Spelunking? Snorkeling? Some activity that took place underground, undersea or in the air?"

Sarah's eyes grew round. "Undersea? Are you kidding me?"

"Nope. I'm planning a scuba wedding for next summer as we speak."

"And don't forget the circus wedding," Chelsea reminded her. "I told you, Karen can do anything. She's amazing."

"Well, I never wanted a spectacle. I want to spend my life with the guy and that's it. I must really love him to let him talk me into this."

"Maybe you should tell us what it is?"

Sarah slapped her forehead with her open hand. A modest diamond twinkled on her ring finger. "I'm a serious person. Hardworking. A divorce lawyer. I have a certain reputation around town for toughness and smarts." She put down her hand and stared at Karen. "If news of this gets around, I'll be a laughingstock." She glared.

But Karen was pretty tough, too, and also had a reputation to upkeep. She adopted Sarah's drilling gaze. "Where did you have your first date?"

"I must have been insane," she said, more to herself, Karen thought, than to anyone else in the room. "I must still be insane."

From imagining feats of derring-do, her mind moved to seedier possibilities. If they'd done something sexually kinky or engaged in some illegal activity on their first date then she really didn't want any part of it.

She was a little firmer this time when she asked, "There are some weddings I won't plan. Where did he take you on your first date?"

As though admitting a terrible secret the woman said, "The zoo."

Once again, Karen had to struggle not to laugh at her newest potential client. "The zoo? Here in Philadelphia?"

"Yes," came the sulky reply. "Mike is this weird alternative guy. He adopted a zoo animal as part of their conservation program and he took me to the zoo on our first date to meet little Mikey."

"I'm guessing this is an opposites-attract kind of relationship."

"Oh, you've got that right. I'm a classic Type A." Like Karen might not have figured that out yet. "Mike's all Zen about everything. Doesn't own a microwave, only has one clock in his house. He's a high-school counselor and he teaches yoga."

There was a beat of silence. "I'm guessing he's great in bed," Karen said before she could censor herself.

To her relief Sarah laughed, a husky, earthy laugh. "Oh, he is. It's the only reason I put up with him."

"Huh," her old friend said. "What she means is, he's the only guy who's ever put up with her."

That laugh came again. "True."

"Well, I can tell you that a wedding at the zoo is easy to arrange, it's a popular spot for weddings and if it means something to the two of you then you should do it."

She took a shaky breath that Karen suspected was more about the idea of getting married at all than about the venue. "All right, then. Let's do it."

Karen began to take notes. "And I'm sure you know that Chelsea is the best caterer in town."

"Totally."

"And Laurel will do you an amazing cake."

"I'm not having a cake with zoo animals on it," she protested. "It's bad enough getting married at the zoo without having a wedding cake that should be at a kids' birthday party."

"Laurel would never be so boring as to put a zoo animal on a cake. You can meet with her to discuss your needs."

"No, no. You do it. Honestly, I want to leave everything in your hands."

After that it was easy. Sarah was businesslike, knew how many people were coming, had chosen several possible dates in the summer and very clearly liked to delegate. To Karen, that made her close to a dream client.

"I am so excited," Chelsea said at one point, her eyes shining with emotion.

The usually tough Sarah softened immediately. She leaned over to grip Chelsea's hand. "Me, too. And when you and David get married, we won't only be best friends. We'll be sisters."

Would they? Karen couldn't help but wonder.

Chelsea seemed genuinely excited about seeing her best friend get married before she could drag the woman's older brother to the altar.

Not for the first time, Karen wondered what was wrong with David to keep an amazing woman like Chelsea waiting.

He'd almost lost her once through his own stupidity. Karen was worried he was about to repeat his mistake.

Mistakes. There seemed to be a lot of those in the air.

Chelsea's cell phone rang and, after checking the call display, she backed out of the room. "It's Anton. I'd better get back. Come visit me when you're done with Karen," she said to Sarah, and with a wave she was gone.

It didn't take long for Karen to extract all the information she needed for now. Then, on a hunch, she said, "Can I ask your professional opinion about something?"

"Sure. I can't give free legal advice, but I can give you information if I've got it."

The second Sarah had mentioned being a divorce lawyer, she'd felt the urge to ask her a couple of questions. But now she had the woman's attention, she wasn't sure how to begin. Finally, she plunged in.

"In your experience, how many men who cheat on their wives claim to be innocent?"

Sudden sympathy clouded the clear eyes. "Ninety-five percent. You can catch them with a naked woman in bed and their pants around their ankles and they'll still say—" here she shook her index finger in Karen's direction and lowered her voice "—I did not have sexual relations with that woman."

Karen nodded, sadly. "That's what I thought."

10

Okay, Karen decided, at the end of the day, when, no matter how busy she'd been, she'd always found time to relive the things she and Dexter had done on her desktop.

Enough was enough. Dexter was a player, a Casanova, a Lothario. Of course he was great in bed, he'd had plenty of experience. Some of it, she had to remind herself, while they were married. She'd begun to feel a spark of hope that maybe she'd been wrong about him, but Sarah the divorce lawyer had pretty much killed that notion.

Just because she felt a connection didn't mean there was one.

She was so angry with herself for falling like a ton of bricks the minute he came onto her. She'd assumed that once he'd had her again he'd disappear, but he'd shown up at Sophie's planning meeting, teasing her about that desk. He seemed still to be sniffing around her.

If she didn't care about him even after all this time maybe she could go along with it, have a fling with her ex. She wouldn't be the first woman ever to do so. But she'd worked long and hard to rebuild her self-esteem after it had been shattered by the man she'd loved and she wasn't about to compromise her hard-won peace again. Not for some cheap sex and a few orgasms, intense though they might be.

Gritting her teeth, she made a date with her laptop. She'd spend the evening going through all the listings at Plenty of Phillys. She had some messages to answer, some new profiles to check out.

When she got home that night, after a punishing thirty minutes at Curves, she zapped a low-cal dinner in the microwave which tasted so uninteresting it felt like a complete waste of four hundred calories, then showered and decided that if she was going to do this online dating thing then she'd better put a little effort into it.

Wrapping her towel around her she padded into her bedroom. She'd bought the town house after her marriage ended and she'd gone out of her way to make her bedroom as feminine as possible. Decorated in soft pinks and creams with a raw silk bedspread and white-and-gold French Provincial furniture, the room all but sported a No Boys Allowed sign on the door.

She opened her closet and tried to work out what one wore to go trolling for men using the Internet. She finally decided on a black cashmere V-neck sweater and black stretch exercise pants that were the most comfortable slacks she'd ever owned.

She let her hair dry naturally, curling down her back as it did when she didn't ruthlessly straighten and style it, and then she poured herself a glass of wine and logged onto the dating site.

There were a couple of men who'd sent her expressions of interest but she didn't like the appearance of either of them. Then she decided she'd better look around and see if anyone in her general age range caught her interest. She was clicking listlessly through the offerings when her doorbell rang.

Her video display showed her Dexter waiting at her front door with all the assurance of a man who knows he's welcome.

Wrong.

She ignored him and padded back to her couch.

Her cell phone rang.

She picked it up. "Yes?"

"I know you're home," said the all-too-familiar voice. "I checked. Your car's in your spot."

"Hmm, could there be a reason why I might be home and not answering my door? Oh, wait, there is. I don't want to see you."

"I came to say goodbye."

"Goodbye?" she blurted, much too fast for someone who didn't want to see the man. She couldn't believe he was leaving.

"I have to go back to New York for a couple of weeks, but I'll be back."

"Oh." Fine. It was fine. She'd managed without him for years, she didn't need him now.

"Could I come in? I want to talk to you."

Reluctantly, she let him in. Was he going to try to seduce her? One for the road? She couldn't believe he'd be that crass, and yet she must have a few crass bones in her body too for the idea didn't repel her. Maybe he was bad for her in a whole bunch of ways, but the sex was still so good it wasn't fair.

However, he didn't rush in and jump her. Instead, after he'd come in and removed his coat and shoes, he shoved his hands in the pocket of his jeans and seemed a little unsure of himself. In her feminine space, he seemed more than usually masculine and since she wasn't wearing her heels he towered above her.

"Would you like to sit down?"

"Yeah. Sure."

"Can I get you something? Some wine?"

"If it's open."

She went into her kitchen and poured him a glass.

Her body felt tingly and the scent of her body lotion rose as her skin heated from the images flashing through her brain. Good thing she'd showered and freshened up, she thought even as she tried to remind herself of all the reasons why having sex with the hottie in her living room was a bad, bad idea.

When she'd run out of lecture, she walked back in to find him sitting, not where she'd left him, but in her chair. And, horror of horrors, he was staring at her laptop screen with undisguised fascination.

He glanced up. "Are you kidding me? Online dating?"

"What's wrong with online dating?"

"Nothing, I guess. I thought..." He seemed to run out of steam and she didn't press him to finish his sentence. Instead she handed him the wine.

With a brief word of thanks, he took a sip and then put the glass down so he could devote his full attention to her computer. How could she have been so stupid as to have left the thing open for him to find?

Of course, anyone with any integrity wouldn't have snooped. But as she well knew, integrity wasn't Dexter's strong suit. If she made a big deal about it, he'd only laugh at her, so she decided to humor him. If he wanted to mock her and her efforts to find a nice guy, then that was his problem.

She steeled herself while he continued reading. Until she couldn't stand it anymore. "Why are you reading the profiles of single men in the city?"

"I'm not. I'm reading yours."

She rose. Enough already. She'd get that computer out of his hands if she had to wrestle him to the ground for it.

Finally he glanced up and shook his head. "I can't believe your profile. You missed all the best things about yourself."

That wasn't at all what she'd expected and he didn't appear to be teasing. She faltered. Puzzled. "Why do you say that?"

His expression was impossible to read. "Because no one knows you the way I do."

11

"ARE YOU SUGGESTING I should get you to write my online dating profile?" she asked, wondering if she could have misunderstood him.

"Why not?"

"Because you're my ex-husband. It seems a little unorthodox."

"Like I said, nobody knows you better, or knows all your good qualities better than I do." He grinned at her. "Of course, I know all your not-so-good qualities, too, but I'll keep those to myself."

"This seems like a really bad idea."

"Come on, let me take a crack at it. If you don't like what I write, you can delete it."

Intrigued in spite of her better judgment, she said, "What would you say?"

She had her legs curled under her, sitting in a corner of the couch. He picked up the laptop and brought it over, sitting beside her. His thighs brushed her toes and she felt a zing of connection from nothing more than the denim warmed by his body heat shifting against her foot.

He didn't move away.

And she didn't pull her foot out of the way.

He typed. She was certain he was correcting her height, knocking her down to size, but when she couldn't stand hearing the tap-tap-tap of keys, and watching the concentration on his face as he typed, she finally leaned over to check his progress.

What he wrote was, To know Karen you have to be patient. She's outgoing and funny, has a laugh that makes people join in and the minute you meet her you feel like you've known her forever. His fingers paused and she waited, silent, until they resumed. But to know the real Karen, the one behind the fun-loving social creature, takes work. She doesn't show her true self to many people, but it's worth waiting for. She's gorgeous, with clear blue-green eyes that make you think you're on the bottom of the ocean.

"Oh, Dex," she whispered, but he ignored the interruption.

Her skin's Irish fair, with a few freckles that remind you of the kid inside her. Her skin tastes like rain-washed apples, and she smells like cherry blossoms.

"Do I?" she murmured. It was like reading a love letter while it was being written, both romantic and the sexiest thing she'd ever seen. Those long artistic architect's fingers moved with precision over the keys, barely hesitating, as though all this had been composed in his mind and it was a simple matter to type it all out.

"You do. Stop interrupting." He thought for a moment and continued.

Her hair is a rich red, it's long and curly, thick

enough that you could wrap it around your hands like rope, but when she's making love to you, looking up with those big clear bottom-of-the-ocean eyes, her hair seems to catch fire, sparking flame. Hot and cold. Cold and hot.

"I'm not," she said, feeling breathless.

"You are."

And when she's naked her body is a glory. Breasts so rich and full you can fill your hands with them. But go carefully, for they are sensitive to the touch.

She made a tiny sound in the back of her throat.

He took one hand off the keyboard, as though he were pausing to think, and ran it across her nipples, already pebbled inside her cashmere sweater. She sighed, rippling her body against him like a cat desperate for affection.

He turned his head, looking down at her with lust blazing in his eyes. She didn't even think, simply pushed her computer off his lap and onto the couch, and then threw herself at him.

He caught her against him, crushing his mouth to hers, shoving his hands into the curling mass of hair tumbling around them, and began giving her what she needed.

Off came her sweater. Underneath it, she wore a sexy black camisole and, since she hadn't expected company and had wanted to feel at her sexiest, she wore no bra.

He groaned when he realized this, running his hands over her, squeezing her breasts in the way he knew she liked, firm but not too hard, and never squeezing the nipples, which were exquisitely sensitive.

Instead he kissed them, suckled them, bringing her

close to climax. She used to be embarrassed by how responsive her nipples were, but she'd learned to accept the easy pleasure. She leaned back, loving the feelings coursing through her body and the murmured appreciation from this man.

But she didn't want this to be a quickie, like the desktop escapade. She wanted time to enjoy him, especially if he was going to be gone for a few weeks. This was her chance to savor him, and then she could figure out what she was going to do about her inconvenient passion once he was out of state.

So she rose, took his hand and pulled him toward her bedroom. She flipped on the bedside lamps, which cast a muted pink glow over everything. Except Dex, who somehow still managed to look masculine and commanding.

She wanted to see all of him, enjoy every inch of his body, so she slowly undressed him, pulling off his sweater, the T-shirt he wore beneath it.

"I see you still work out," she murmured, running her lips over the muscular ridges of his belly.

The pale slash of an appendectomy scar, an old and nearly forgotten friend, drew her tongue and he sucked in his breath as she traced the line, something she'd done hundreds of times when he'd belonged to her. Moved by the memory, she suspected, as she was.

He was so familiar to her. His legs with the freckles above the knees, that ridiculous tattoo on his left shoulder he'd got on a drunken college trip to Thailand. He claimed he'd asked for an eagle and somehow either in a bad translation or a lack of artistic talent on the part of the tattoo artist, he'd ended up with a rooster on his back.

Which always made her smile. It was a reminder that

her ex-husband might be competent at business and brilliant at design, but he could be crazy and unpredictable and just as stupid as the next person.

"I see you still have Millie." And who but she would have named a rooster Millie?

He smiled at her, all dark eyes and simmering sexuality. "Do you know how much it costs to get a tattoo removed?"

She laughed at him, running her hands up and down his smooth, muscular back. "You've got lots of money. You're just a weenie about pain."

He grabbed her wrist and pulled her down beside him on the bed until they were in easy kissing distance. "You know me too well." He kissed her. "Which has some advantages."

"Such as?"

He grinned at her wickedly. "You know exactly what I like in bed."

And the truth was he knew the same about her. As he pulled her even closer and began playing with her body, and she began playing with his, she knew precisely what he meant.

Just touching him, feeling his skin warm under her hands, hearing from his whispered encouragement how much he enjoyed her own response got her hot, hotter, and finally too hot to hold. He'd always been able to gauge her response and pace himself accordingly so she had the bone-deep pleasure of feeling orgasm begin to swamp her and then feeling his pleasure double hers. It was the ultimate excitement and she'd never found it before or since.

But once the first round was over, and their urgent need slaked, they began to play, rolling and teasing, laughing and groping until the play turned serious, and they were making love once more.

"I can't keep up with you," he groaned, his body slick with sweat, his breathing ragged. "You are the most insatiable woman I've ever known. But you've worn me out. I need fuel." He slapped her rump playfully and rolled out of bed as gorgeous as she remembered. If anything his body had improved. It was so unfair.

"What have you got to eat?"

"Nothing. I ate earlier."

He yawned, still naked, like it was no big deal and then he headed for her kitchen. "Any leftovers?"

"No." She didn't want to tell him she'd stuck a frozen diet entrée in the microwave. It seemed so lonely somehow.

But Dexter seemed to think he had the right to entertain himself in her kitchen. Maybe he felt like he could still open her cupboards and fridge as though they were still married.

Because she had to find her robe and slip it on, plus find slippers and run a brush through the red tangle that used to be her hair, by the time she got to the kitchen, naked Dex was standing with his head in the freezer section of her fridge.

He turned to her with a look of disgust. "What is all this diet crap?"

"In case you hadn't noticed, I've put on a few pounds."

"No. You haven't." He shook his head and shut the door with the plastic thunk of a freezer that prefers to keep its secrets. "No wonder you're always in a pissy mood. You don't eat." He went for his coat and for a sad, sick moment she thought he was leaving, but he emerged with his BlackBerry. A couple of clicks and he was dialing.

"Who are you calling?"

"Chinese. Found a great delivery place."

"Not Chinese," she almost shouted.

With a puzzled expression he ended the call before it completed. "You always used to love Chinese."

"I still do," she moaned. "But I've used up all my calories today. I cannot watch you eat and not dig in."

"You need to quit this diet craziness, you hear me? You look fantastic. Even better naked than I remember." He grinned at her. "And I've got a very visual memory. It's an architect thing."

The thought of him comparing today's naked body with that of five years ago was enough to send her into the bathroom to slam the door and lock herself in until he was gone. "You're lying."

He shook his head and pressed redial. She heard him ordering all of her favorite foods and wondered if any woman would blame her if she killed the man by plunging chopsticks into his heart. So long as the jury was packed with women on diets, she knew no one would find her guilty.

While they waited for the food to arrive, he poured them another glass of the wine and pulled his jeans on.

They sat together, chatting, almost like old times.

"Tell me about your project," she asked.

"I'm excited about this one. The original building is a perfect example of classical revival architecture. The Stockard was built in the 1920s as the headquarters for a trading company, then converted to a bank and then a law firm. Our challenge is to transform The Stockard into a twenty-four-story mixed-use building with office, retail and luxury residential." He took a sip of wine and she knew he was picturing the project. "They'd already agreed to preserve the exterior façade and mezzanine, where most of the original historic details still exist. But we had to convince them that green building was the way to go. And we did."

"Congratulations," she said, knowing that Dex, with his passion and vision, was hard to resist.

"Thanks. We're mixing smart design with the original architectural detailing. Retail at street level, a couple of floors of offices and a separate entrance leads to top of the line condos. I love mixing old and new."

She smiled at his excitement. "It sounds amazing."

"It will be. I might buy one of the condo units." He shrugged. "See how they turn out."

She was surprised and she knew it showed on her face. "You'd move back to Philly?"

He flicked her a glance. "I don't know. Maybe. Or if I keep doing a lot of work here it might make sense to keep a place. I haven't decided yet."

She didn't know what she'd have said, wasn't even sure what she thought of the idea of him spending enough time in the city to keep a home here, when the doorbell sounded.

"Get the plates, will you?" he said, as he jogged down the stairs to answer the door.

"Plate. One," she muttered, even as she licked her lips in anticipation.

He jogged back in with a shallow box containing far too many takeout containers.

"What did you buy? Everything on the menu?"

"Sex makes me hungry. You know that." He plopped the box on the counter and flipped open a carton. Waved the thing under her nose. "Makes you hungry, too. Don't think I've forgotten."

"Oh, I am a weak, weak woman, and you are an evil, evil man," she said as she reached inside the container for a crispy chunk of ginger beef and popped it in her mouth where the spicy flavor exploded on her tongue.

From that moment she was lost.

They talked, they ate, and when she tried to stop, claiming she'd had enough, he started feeding her little pieces with his own chopsticks. When he dropped a fat, juicy prawn before it reached her mouth, so it slid down her chest, and then he went after it with his mouth, she laughed. "You did that on purpose."

"Maybe." He leaned forward and undid her robe.

"No," she cried, trying to pull the lapels back together.

"Let me look. You are so beautiful."

"After I lose five pounds."

"You're crazy, you know that?"

She shook her head at him.

He got a cunning look in his eye, one she knew well, and that stirred her blood. "What are you planning?"

"Maybe just a little peek."

She laughed, but the light in here was so bright. "You've already seen everything there is to see."

"Come on. I like to look at you."

But she let him ease open one side of her housecoat. Revealing one plump breast, the nipple already as round as a blueberry.

He glanced up at her, then back at her breast. "I haven't had dessert."

"Have a fortune cookie."

He reached for his chopsticks. "I have a better idea."

12

"OH, NO," she said, seeing where he was going. "Not the plum sauce." But she was already giggling.

He opened the little cello pack of prepared plum sauce, squeezed some out and painted her nipple with sauce. It felt sticky and cool and when she glanced down her nipple glistened.

To her shock, Dex took his chopsticks and snagged her nipple between them. "What are you…"

He lifted the plump flesh carefully toward his mouth, lowering his head until he could lick plum sauce off the end of her nipple. The sensation was intense: she felt the pressure of the wooden sticks, not squeezing tight, he'd never hurt her, but holding her, as though she were a morsel of food to be offered to his mouth. And then, beside the rigidity of the wood, clamping lightly, came the warm, wet caress of his tongue on her sensitive skin swirling the slick sauce around until she felt herself beginning to melt.

She didn't even try to protest when he pushed her robe away from her other side and proceeded to squeeze more plum sauce, take her other nipple between chopsticks. Lick and suck her halfway to oblivion.

Her robe was gone. Fallen away, and she didn't care that it was probably going to be ruined. He trailed plum sauce down her body in unpredictable patterns, following with his tongue.

When he hit her belly, she felt herself growing heavy and liquid with desire as she sat, sprawled on one of her designer kitchen stools.

"Now," he murmured, "I wonder where else I could use chopsticks."

"Oh, no, I—"

But he was already slipping her legs apart, and she was offering herself up like a banquet on a Lazy Susan. She watched through heavy lids as he parted her folds, exposing her clit which had no need of plum sauce to glisten.

He came slowly toward her with the chopsticks and she began to tremble.

She could pull away, shut her legs and close up shop, but she didn't. She watched. Everything about her was plump, including her intimate parts and when he took that most sensitive of her parts gently, ensnaring the root with the chopsticks, she thought she might fall onto the floor so wildly did the sensation rock her.

A strange sound, not moan or sigh, but some combination of both slipped from her mouth. He took the plum sauce, squeezed a dab onto her hot, aching clit. Then he began to lick it off, unbelievably gently because he knew how sensitive she was, how close.

Torture. It was torture. The most amazing, incredible, delicious torture. He wouldn't let her come. Controlled her as though her body was his, her response his to order.

Those hard, rigid sticks held her in place and that soft, mobile mouth made love to only that one spot.

Slowly.

Delicately.

Exquisitely.

She had her arms stretched out, hanging on to the cold granite countertop, it was the only way she could remain still. But nothing could stop the crazy sounds coming from her throat.

She thought she'd die of pleasure. It would go on forever and she'd never achieve release.

Then, as though he knew she couldn't take any more, he increased the speed of his movement, upped the pressure slightly and with a wild bucking cry, she exploded in his mouth.

"I need you…in me…NOW!" she yelled, but he was already stepping between her legs, already there, and as he thrust home, she cried out again.

MORNING LIGHT DAPPLED HER BODY as Karen stretched luxuriously, every cell in her body singing the "Hallelujah Chorus." The gesture pushed her breasts up and Dexter leaned over to kiss them, his face all manly with emerging stubble.

"I didn't mean to spend the night," he said.

"I didn't mean to let you." This was all too intimate, too familiar. In a minute, he'd suggest they shower together, or she would, and then they'd drink coffee and share the paper. She'd kiss him goodbye and wish him a good day.

"I'd almost forgotten how good we are together," he murmured.

The memories of the night before made her smile with mingled pleasure mixed with mild embarrassment that she'd been like a sex-crazed maniac last night. "I'll never look at Chinese food the same way."

"I'm having those chopsticks bronzed."

He reached for her breast where the persistent tingling told her her nipples had reacted to the memories. Of course, since he was currently pressed up against her, she could feel that his body had also reacted to the memories of last night.

His mouth closed on her breast. "You still taste like plum sauce. We should take a shower together."

Yep, right on cue. As though they were still the happily married couple who had sex with their takeout and showered together in the morning. But they weren't…

Suddenly a wave of mingled grief and rage swamped her, the likes of which she hadn't experienced since they'd first split up.

If they were so bloody good together, why weren't they still married?

"Why?" she whispered, knowing he could hear the anguish in her voice.

He raised his head and leaning on one elbow, gazed down at her. "Why what?" She suspected he knew exactly what her question referred to, but she obliged him anyway by expanding her question.

"Why did you cheat on me if we were so good together?"

His fingers traced a pattern down her chest.

A rueful half smile lit his face. "It always comes back to that, doesn't it? Here's a question for you. Why were you so quick to jump to a conclusion that was insulting to both of us?"

An inarticulate squeal formed in her throat. She felt the hot wash of betrayal sting her skin. "I saw you. She was half naked in your arms."

"I know what you saw, I was there. What you didn't see was me having sex with another woman because it never happened. I had no idea how to handle a nightmare embarrassing situation. She was messed up and needy and drunk or high. What you saw wasn't me undressing her, it was my trying to get her dressed so I could find you and we could take her home."

But the image of betrayal was burned on her retina. She could describe every part of the image as though she were describing a scene as it unfolded. "She was kissing you. You had your arms around her and were unzipping her dress." The anger felt so fresh and raw she wanted to smack him. Wanted to reverse time to the moment he'd arrived yesterday so she could tell him to go away.

"I was trying to zip it up! I've told you a hundred times. And she plastered her mouth on mine while I was doing it. Believe me, I wasn't kissing her back."

"How can I believe you?" she cried, knowing with all her heart that she wished his words were true, but she'd been cheated on before. So had her mom and her sister. In her experience and that of most women in her life, men weren't to be trusted.

She remembered her father, how good-looking he'd been and how special she'd felt in his company. He'd traveled a lot on business and the house used to be kind of empty and depressing when he wasn't there. Her mother always seemed to be in a bad mood. It wasn't until she'd grown older, and he'd finally left the family for good, that she understood that there was a lot of pleasure mixed in with his business trips.

Men couldn't help it, her mother hypothesized after the divorce when Karen pelted her with questions. It was part of their genetic makeup to spread their seed as far and wide as possible. Nature or nurture, Karen had sworn to herself that no man would make a fool of her that way, and she'd stuck to her principles.

If she'd been stupid to marry a man who was as good-looking and charming as her father, at least she hadn't put up with years of lying and cheating like her mother had.

As much as it had hurt her, she'd dumped the lying, cheating scumbag as soon as he showed his true colors.

But oh, she'd had no idea that part of her would be destroyed.

She thought he looked a little sad as he said, "No one can answer that question but you."

"I even tried to talk to her, you know. After."

"Who?"

"The model."

"How did you find her? She didn't even have a last name."

"I can be very persistent." And in some still naive, hopeful part of her she'd wanted the woman to corroborate her husband's story.

"Wow. I can't believe you tracked her down."

Her eyes narrowed. "I don't hear you getting all excited about how she backed up your story."

"Because I'm not stupid. If she had, we wouldn't be here now. We'd still be married." He shook his head. "Actually, we probably wouldn't. Some other shadow would have frightened you away."

"You're right about one thing. She didn't corroborate your story."

He snorted. "So, you'd believe a drunk woman without a last name before you'd believe me."

"All she told me was that she couldn't remember

anything about that night. By the time I tracked her down she was in rehab."

"Great. Just great," he said. "That father of yours sure did a number on you."

"Don't you blame my father. He had nothing to do with this. The only mistake I made was in marrying a man just like him." She pulled the covers up so her breasts were no longer exposed.

He rolled to his back, putting distance between them. She felt cold without his arms around her. "The mistake you made was not believing you hadn't. It all comes down to trust."

"You hurt me."

"You hurt me, too." He'd never said those words to her before and as she turned to him, she saw that it was true. Whatever he'd done, at least he felt the loss of their marriage. She supposed that was something.

"Some days I wish I'd never met you."

"I should have made you go to marriage counseling with me," he said at the same moment.

"There was no point," she insisted.

He jabbed a finger toward the living room. "Do you think there's a perfect man in that computer storehouse out there? Some guy who won't ever come home late or go on business trips with attractive women? What are you going to do? Spend your life savings on private dicks and all your energy on suspicion?"

"No. No, I'm not. I believe there's a nice man out there who can be faithful."

"Do you?"

"Mmm-hmm. I won't set my sights so high this time."

He rolled over and got back up on his elbow so he could stare down into her face. "Come again?"

"I've done a lot of reading since we broke up. There are theories about what makes a successful relationship and one of them is that you should match up with people who are similar status to you." She shrugged. "So, really good-looking people should stick together and more homely people should go with homely ones. I was always so flattered when you took an interest in me, but I think in the end you're too good-looking. Too successful."

He blinked at her, his face darkening with anger. "That is the biggest load of bullshit I've ever heard," he argued, pulling himself up to sitting. "Setting aside the fact that I think you're beautiful, what does that say about me? In ten years, when you start to age, do I turn you in for a younger model? What about love? What about the old-fashioned idea of sticking together through thick and thin? Better and worse and all that?"

"I don't know."

"I don't know, either." He rolled out of bed, unconcerned that he was naked. Even though she was angry and confused she couldn't help but drink in her fill of that tall, buff body and wish things could have turned out differently.

He pulled on his clothes swiftly and efficiently and then walked over to where she sat in bed, watching him.

"Is this really about me being unfaithful or is it about you being insecure?"

"I'm not insecure, I'm realistic."

He made a dismissive sound. "Tell that to your mirror."

"I—"

"I didn't fall in love with a status symbol. I never thought you did, either. I think you're gorgeous, and successful. I like your curves. Did it ever occur to you that I wasn't the one who betrayed our marriage?"

"I don't have any idea what you're talking about. You can't make this my fault."

"I can't make you see reason." She thought he'd say more, then he clamped his mouth shut.

"I'll be back in a couple of weeks. Take care of yourself."

"You, too."

He kissed her swiftly. Rose and as he reached the door of her bedroom turned back. "Oh, and you might want to edit that profile before you post it."

13

DEX WAS GORGEOUS, sexy, dangerously good in bed and completely bad for her. Forget sex with Dex. She had to start over.

So after that fiasco she renewed her online efforts. Thursday she had a lunch date with a guy named Larry who spent the entire time talking about his ex-wife and what a bitch she was. It was so depressing she had a headache when she returned to the office.

Saturday evening she had drinks with Steve who admitted over his second martini that while his profile claimed he was divorced, he wasn't completely divorced.

"How close are you?" she asked.

Larry ran a hand through rapidly receding hair. "I can't upset her right now, she's moody. But as soon as I find my soul mate, I'm telling my wife right away."

She declined to stay for dinner.

When she reviewed her latest date with Dee the young woman said, "Okay, it's time for some advanced tips and hints."

"I'm ready."

"One." The young woman twirled a blond curl around her pencil. "At your age, it's borderline on whether a guy's been married or not, but if they get close to forty and they've never been married or had a significant relationship, that's a big red flag. Mommy issues? Can't commit? Do some investigation before you commit to anything."

Karen thought about Ron, the CPA who at thirty-seven had never been married. She suspected she'd already met one of those.

"Got it."

"Two. If a guy says he's divorced, when you e-mail him make sure—"

"Oh, I've got this one. First question I should be asking is how long they've been divorced."

Her dating mentor nodded. "And make sure they're living on their own."

"Huh?"

"Catholic divorce. It's where the wife lives on one level of the house and the ex lives on the other. With this bad economy, lots of couples are doing it, but I wouldn't go there."

"Right. That could be complicated."

"Kids is another issue."

"I like kids."

"I know you do. That's my point. If you're going to have kids, no offense, you don't have a lot of time to waste, so if a guy doesn't have any, you want to find out pretty soon if he's open to kids. And if he has some, find out if he sees them a lot. Best way to discover if a guy is going to be a good father is to see if he already is one."

"Wow. This is more like landing a great job than finding eternal love."

"Love won't last if you don't share basic goals and values," Dee informed her.

She was filled with affection for her assistant. "So young and so wise."

By paying more attention to the details in a profile she did manage to avoid a couple more disasters and no one jumped out at her as the potential father of the kids she'd better have quick according to Dee, before she ended up barren as well as alone.

The following Wednesday, against her better judgment, she went to the movies with Ron. Who probably had mommy issues, possibly also commitment phobia. But he was a nice man and she didn't really like her own company right now. Afterward, they stopped at a coffee shop and found, as they had before, that if they talked about their businesses, they got on fine. But on the personal front, they didn't have much in common.

"Is this how most of your dates go?" she finally asked him.

He shook his head. "No. Most are much, much worse."

To her surprise she burst out laughing. "So you're saying this is bad?"

He immediately tried to reassure her that they weren't bad. He liked her a great deal and it was refreshing to be able to spend time with someone who enjoyed discussing business.

She reached out and touched his hand, which was cool and dry. "But there's no spark, is there?"

The gray eyes she liked so much lifted to hers. "No."

She sipped her coffee, thinking she'd miss this quiet, unassuming man who was so easy to talk to and who she'd never imagine getting caught with a half dressed woman on his arm. "I'll miss you."

"I hope we can still see each other. This can be a lonely city when you're not part of a couple. I'd like for us to stay friends." He shifted the sugar until it was exactly in line with the napkins. "At least until one of us starts seeing someone seriously."

She was oddly flattered. "I don't have many male friends. I'd like that."

When they parted he kissed her cheek and she went home alone. Even though she'd changed the sheets after Dex left her, and that had been almost a week ago, she still couldn't seem to get the elusive scent of him out of her bed. She knew it was only her memory playing tricks on her, but oh, it had been a mistake to let him into her bed again.

She'd gone out and bought all new furniture after they split up and the first item she'd purchased had been that bed because she never wanted to sleep alone in the place they'd once shared so much.

Now he'd come and polluted her bed with his presence, and the room was thick with the memories of their night together, the passion, the heat, the searing intimacy.

Oh, she'd slept with a couple of men after her divorce, but not for a while now, mainly because no man had ever come close.

So she went back to planning joyous occasions for brides who didn't know what they were letting themselves in for, giving them the magical day that would seal their doom. Then she came home to a house that had never felt empty until Dexter forever stamped his presence onto it.

Another week and one more dismal date with a guy

who claimed to be a marathon runner, a millionaire investor and a philanthropist. Ten minutes in his company told her he was a compulsive liar since he was overweight, smoked, seemed to think Dow Jones was a baseball pitcher, and sneered at a sad-looking street person.

Would you like to go to dinner tonight? Ron asked her. They had fallen into the habit of e-mailing a few times a week and she enjoyed a certain quiet humor about him, plus the fact that he was pretty much who he said he was.

She was busy with meetings and a bridal show, plus she had a meeting with Sophie Vanderhooven scheduled for the next morning. Sophie had said Dex would probably be at the meeting, which meant he would probably drop by her place since they seemed to have fallen into some kind of ex-with-benefits scenario.

Of course it was a bad idea to sleep with her ex. But ice cream and chocolate bars were bad ideas, too, and she was just as addicted.

I think I'd better— She stopped herself with a start before turning down this nice, uncomplicated single man in order to sit home in case her cheating ex should decide to drop by for sex. What was she doing?

She resumed typing. I think I'd better start inviting you places since you always seem to do all the work. But yes, I'd love to.

Do you like Chinese food?

Heat washed over her. She e-mailed back. No food that involves chopsticks.

Then he mentioned a popular American eatery downtown, which could have no awkward memories attached to it. She agreed.

I'll pick you up at seven.

Perfect. He was the kind of man who treated her like a date even though they were friends which was fine with her. It was nice not to have to drive in heels and figure out parking.

He was prompt as always, but she was ready when he arrived.

Over dinner she finally told him that she might be interested in his services and described a few accounting muddles.

He nodded. "I think I might be able to help you. What I should do is give you a couple of references of other customers so you can get a sense of my work."

Once dinner was over he drove her correctly home. It was only ten o'clock and she got the feeling that he was in no hurry to head to his lonely house. "Would you like to come in for coffee?" She hesitated, then clarified, "And I do mean coffee."

"Do you have decaf?"

"Of course."

"Then I'd like to."

Since he was more worried about caffeine than her hot bod she didn't fret about him getting the wrong idea about her invitation. While she went into the kitchen to make the coffee, he settled himself in her living room with the day's newspaper.

When she returned, he politely folded the paper and accepted his coffee.

"Can I ask you something?" she asked.

"Of course."

"Do you really think there's someone out there for you? A soul mate if you like?"

Ron pondered the question, the way she found he

tended to ponder most inquiries. "I think it would be sad to live the rest of my life alone," he said at last. "I have Beth, of course."

"Beth?"

"My new golden retriever."

"Oh."

"I'll be picking her up Thursday. She's a pup. Would you like to see a picture?"

"Of course I would."

He pulled out his wallet and showed her a truly adorable puppy that she could tell from the snap was all bounce and bubble.

"But I'd like to have a family and someone to come home to. I don't think I'm meant to live alone."

"I can understand that."

He crossed his ankles neatly in front of him and frowned down at them. The light from a table lamp glimmered on his glasses. "I was never the guy all the girls went crazy over. I suppose I keep hoping that someday I'll meet a nice woman who doesn't need to be dazzled, but is willing to settle down with a very average, reliable man. I realized years ago that I was never going to set the world on fire. But I'm a good accountant and I think I'd be a good husband and father."

She found herself warming to his honesty. "I think you'd make a wonderful husband."

"What about you?"

She made a face. "I found my soul mate. Didn't work out quite the way I planned."

"I'm sorry."

"Oh, well. At least I found out while I'm still young enough to try again. But I seem to keep meeting the most horrible men."

"I'm sure the women are worse."

She reviewed her brief dating history. "Couldn't be."

"I had a kleptomaniac who stole all the cutlery off the table when we had dinner, and then lifted the tip off the table. It wasn't until I realized my credit card was missing and went back to the restaurant that I found out what she was like."

"Oh, no," she cried in ready sympathy. "Did you get your card back?"

"Yes. Fortunately I cancelled the card before she could do much damage." He sent her a wry grin. "But I can never show my face in that restaurant again."

While they chatted companionably over coffee, and shared dating disasters, she discovered what she'd begun to suspect, that apart from his years away at college, he'd lived with his widowed mother until she died and still occupied his childhood home.

"Have you thought of moving?"

"Why would I? It's a nice solid home in a good area of town. No, I plan to stay."

"I think we're both stuck in the past a little bit. Maybe we simply need to shake things up a bit. We could move." She placed her empty coffee cup on the table in front of the couch.

"But I don't want to move."

She glanced around her town house. "I don't want to move, either."

He put down his own cup. "I should go." But the way he said it she felt that he didn't relish going home to an empty house just yet.

"I was going to watch the late show, do you want to join me?"

"Yes." He took off his jacket and settled beside her on the couch. It was nice to have the company, she realized. Nice to relax and not have to talk after the stress of the past few days. She'd been knocking herself out putting on back-to-back weddings and then trying to get ready for an upcoming bridal show, plus there was the whole Dexter situation. He either kept her awake all night in passion or in trying to figure out what she was going to do about him.

She yawned, hugely, tried to concentrate on what Jimmy Fallon was saying. After the commercial break he was going to interview a young actress about an upcoming movie.

But she never saw the interview. Before the opening monologue was over, she was sound asleep.

SUN STREAMING IN HER WINDOW woke Karen. She blinked, slowly, wondering where she was and what was different from most mornings.

With a start, she realized she was dressed in last night's clothes and the warm weight resting against her wasn't Dexter.

It was Ron.

Sound asleep and looking rather forlorn, he had an arm thrown around her while her head rested on his shoulder.

"Ow," she said, raising her head and trying to rub the stiffness from her neck.

Either her speaking or moving woke Ron, who blinked owlishly a few times and glanced around.

"Oh," he said, when his puzzled gaze encountered hers. "I guess we fell asleep."

"I guess so."

She didn't know which of them was more embarrassed, as they moved to opposite sides of the couch. She rose, pulling her skirt into place as she did so. "Would you like some coffee?"

"Oh, uh." He cleared his throat, put on the glasses that had fallen onto the floor, glanced at his watch. "No, thank you. I've got to get back to my place and get ready for the day. I'd better be going."

"All right. Well." She had no idea what to say. "Thanks for last night."

He stood up and seeing him so rumpled made her realize what a meticulous dresser he usually was. He looked exactly like a man who'd slept in his clothes. His hair was up on one side and his sweater askew. "I had a nice time, too. I'm sorry that I fell asleep."

This was the most ridiculous situation. In spite of herself she laughed. "I won't tell if you don't."

He smiled perfunctorily, slipping his feet into his loafers. "No. I won't be telling anyone." He rubbed at his stubbled face. "Sometimes, it gets lonely. Living alone."

"I know. Look, I'm putting on coffee anyway. You should at least have coffee."

He shook his head. "Perhaps I could use the bathroom before I leave?"

"Of course."

She started coffee and then he appeared in the kitchen. He'd obviously washed his face since the hair above his forehead was damp. A droplet of water clung to one eyelash. He looked oddly adorable and she felt more like his mother than a date as she led him to the front door once he'd refused once more to stay for coffee.

"Why don't you come to my office tomorrow? I could show you around and then show you my books which are, I admit, a bit of a mess."

"Certainly. I could do that."

"I'll even buy you lunch. You haven't lived until you've tried Chelsea Hammond's lasagna."

"I'll see you tomorrow, then."

She opened the door as he leaned in to kiss her cheek.

"Good morning," a cheerful male voice boomed out from the other side of the open doorway.

Ron's lips hadn't even reached her cheek before darting off again.

Oh, horror of horrors. If there was one person in all the world she wouldn't have wanted to know about her little escapade, it would have to be the man currently striding up her front walk with a box in his arms. She said the first thing she thought of. "What are you doing here?"

"Delivering a bridesmaid gown." He nodded to the man standing awkwardly by her side. "Not for me, you understand."

"Of course."

She and Ron stood rooted foolishly in her front doorway. The day was overcast and cold. A light frost covered the ground. Dexter removed one of his driving gloves and held out his hand to Ron. "Dexter Crane, delivery boy."

Automatically, the men shook hands. "Ron Turgison, CPA," the befuddled man beside her replied.

"Ah, a good man to have around."

Another beat passed. Finally, she reached for the box Dex was holding and at the same time Ron said, "Well, goodbye. I'll call you."

He left and Dexter walked into her house without an invitation. "Now that's nice. A man should always call after he spends the night at a woman's place. Good manners."

"Would you drop the Cary Grant act?" She put her head in the hand that wasn't holding the box. "This is so not what it looks like."

"No?" Dexter said mildly. "It looked pretty clear to me."

The sheer enormity of trying to explain what had just happened was too much for an uncaffeinated woman to handle. "I need coffee. Before I speak, I need coffee."

He followed her.

When she reached the living room she discovered the television was still on. She'd somehow slept through an entire night of late-night, even later-night, after-late, late shows and infomercials and early, early, early shows without ever waking. She put the dress box down and picked up the remote to snap off the TV.

She stomped into the kitchen and then snapped, "Why are you delivering things to my house at seven-thirty in the morning?"

"The slick answer is that Andrew surprised Sophie with a first-class plane ticket to Italy. She sends her apologies, she won't be able to make your meeting. However, she picked up a sample of the bridesmaid dress in New York for you to match flowers and things. Since I had to come back to Philly, she asked me to deliver the dress." He stuck both gloves in the pocket of his overcoat, slipped it off and laid it over the back of one of her kitchen chairs. It was too long and the gray wool bunched on the tile floor. "The honest answer of course is that I wanted to see you."

And she supposed he'd come early enough that they could indulge in a pre-work quickie. Except that he'd found another man leaving her house as he was arriving. What a mess.

She shouldn't be embarrassed. She was a single

woman. Why shouldn't she have men coming and going at all hours? But she did feel foolish. "I never should have slept with you again," she snapped.

"Pour the coffee. You're never at your best before the first cup."

"Stop reminding me that you know me so well."

"But I do," he said softly. He didn't sound irate or angry, but she could tell he was waiting for the explanation she'd promised him.

As she turned to pour coffee, she wished she were at least wearing her heels and didn't look as disheveled as she was certain a mirror would confirm. She poured two mugs of coffee, adding milk only to hers, milk and sugar to Dex's as she knew he liked it.

She pushed the mug at him and drank her own gratefully. Then she caught his gaze. If anything he was looking slightly amused.

"Let's sit down. I can't stand you towering above me."

They sat at her kitchen table since she didn't even want to think about what had happened when they'd sat side by side on the stools at her counter.

She said, "Ron's a guy I met online." She glanced up and then down at her coffee. "He's nice."

Still Dexter didn't say a word.

"We went out for dinner last night and then we came back here to watch the late show. I know it sounds unbelievable, but we both fell asleep watching TV. We'd just woken up when you got here." She traced her finger over the handle of her green pottery coffee mug. "I didn't sleep with him."

"Thank you for telling me," he said and sipped from his matching green mug. "You still make the best coffee of anyone I know. Maybe it's the beans. I should find out from you where you get them."

Coffee beans? He wanted to talk about coffee beans? What kind of emotional game playing was this?

"Dexter, I'm telling you the truth. I know it looks like Ron and I spent the night together—" She stopped, realizing they had in fact spent the night together. "I mean, had sex, but we didn't."

"Yes. You said that. I heard you."

Irritation, completely irrational but red-hot, geysered through her. "Fine. Don't believe me. I don't know why I bothered trying to explain anything. Forget it. Think whatever you want."

A hand, long-fingered and strong, came to rest on hers where it lay fisted on the tabletop. He squeezed her fingers, causing her to look up and meet his gaze. To her astonishment, he smiled at her, with warmth and humor. His hand felt warm and comforting enclosing her own.

"Here's the part where I get to give you a little lecture, for your own good, and you get to listen."

If it was anything about safe sex she was going to hit him over the head with her coffee mug, she decided, tensing.

"Maybe nine out of ten men would see a man with really bad bed-head leaving your house at seven-thirty in the morning and figure you'd spent the night doing more than watch Craig Ferguson—"

"Jimmy Fallon."

"Whoever. The point is, you told me you didn't sleep with him, and I believe you."

She glanced sharply up at him, having a hard time accepting that he was telling the truth. Her eyes narrowed. "Why?"

"Here's the really good part, so listen carefully." He leaned closer, and she saw that he'd shaved extra close this morning, and that his eyes were direct and honest. "I trust you."

"But—"

"That's it. I trust you. If you tell me you were annotating some obscure line in your taxes, or calculating your 401K contributions all night, I'll believe that, too."

She yanked her hand out from under his, no longer feeling comforted but smothered. "Oh, no. I'm not going to let you do this. You're trying to compare Ron leaving my house fully dressed to finding that woman half-naked and wound all over you? The two aren't even remotely similar."

He leaned back in his chair and raised his mug in a mock toast. "They are so similar that poetic justice is written all over this scenario." He slugged back another jolt of coffee. With a well-pleased expression on his too-handsome face, he rose. "Well, I've got a meeting at nine. I'd better get going. I'll see you around."

He walked out and she jumped to her feet to follow him.

"Don't you dare try and suggest that you're a better person than I am because the cases aren't remotely similar. You can say whatever you like but you knew from the first second that I hadn't had sex with Ron."

He'd reached the front door but he turned, laughter sparking in his eyes.

"Karma may be a bitch, but today she's my bitch."

14

WITH A DEFT TWIST of her wrist that she'd perfected over the years, Laurel created the pink icing petal of a rosebud just bursting into bloom. Sure, she could create any kind of cake she was asked for, but it was always reassuring to come back to tradition.

No one would believe her, so she never bothered to voice the thought, but she loved creating the traditional wedding cakes. This one was a perfect delight of white icing over three separate layers of traditional fruit cake, which she made herself from her Irish grandmother's recipe. The only color was provided by the pink roses which exactly matched the color of the bride's bouquet. She'd sourced a few extra roses from the florist and matched the color perfectly, adding darker shadings with a paintbrush.

Laurel loved her job. She'd always enjoyed baking and art growing up and had never realized she could put the two together in the perfect career until she landed a part-time job working in a bakery one summer.

She'd been hired to fry donuts, but when the do-nuts were done she was free to help whoever needed her. Sometimes she greased the bread pans, sometimes she washed gunked cooking pots in a deep stainless steel sink, but her favorite task was helping the cake decorators. An apt and eager pupil, she was soon learning everything she could about the art and science of cake making and decorating and before long she had certainly outstripped her mentor in originality if not technique.

Her cakes might have remained nothing more than a fun summer job if she hadn't been asked to make a wedding cake for a young couple who begged for something different. After asking them about their interests and discovering they were avid skateboarders, she created a skateboard park out of cake and icing, assuming at worst that she'd be fired and at best that she'd give the two getting married what they actually wanted.

She didn't get fired. She started getting orders of her own and, luckily, the senior cake decorator didn't seem to mind. In fact, she helped Laurel turn some of her crazier ideas into reality, teaching her how to perfect her fondant and how to add tensile strength to her icings.

At the end of high school, she'd gone to a baker's college and after working in New York for what was basically a wedding cake factory, she'd come home to Philly and started out on her own.

Meeting Karen the wedding planner and then Chelsea Hammond, the caterer, had been amazing. She didn't like selling herself, she loved to create cakes. By joining up with Karen and Chelsea, they did the selling and she did the baking and icing of fantasy to traditional cakes and everyone was happy.

In the big industrial kitchen where Chelsea's catering business was located, she had her own section. Originally, the idea had been for the two to share the kitchen but the truth was that Chelsea's business had grown so fast that she could well afford the space all to herself.

And Laurel was doing so well with her cakes, frankly shocked at the prices Karen and Chelsea charged for her creations, that she could have moved to a new place.

But she liked working here and Chelsea claimed that she was the kitchen muse so they'd worked out a deal where she paid much less than half the rent and enjoyed working in the busy kitchen. If the noise got too much, she could always slip the Panda earbuds into her ears and turn on her iPod, but she rarely did. She found that she worked best with the bustle of a busy kitchen surrounding her, the good-natured back and forth of the catering staff and the occasional rushes.

Today, however, there were no rush orders, it was midmorning and she was alone in the kitchen but for Anton who was brewing up a batch of leek-and-potato soup for the front takeout crowd.

The kitchen door swung open and she heard Karen's voice. She turned, surprised, for Karen didn't spend a lot of time in the kitchen being, as she'd admitted to Laurel, too much of a food junkie to trust herself.

"You'd be amazed how much food comes out of this kitchen in a busy week," she was saying in a tour guide tone. Laurel noticed the man at her side was nodding, looking around him with interest.

He was the most nondescript person she'd ever seen. Average height, average weight, average build, his hair so indeterminate a color you couldn't call it dark or light. On a woman it would be termed mousy, she supposed.

He wore the dullest gray suit she'd ever seen with a burgundy tie like the kind her dad wore. His face was pleasant without being in any way remarkable. He had no distinguishing marks. His glasses probably came from a big distributor. If someone had asked her to describe him, she couldn't have made him sound any different than half the male population.

"This is Laurel, our genius cake decorator. Laurel, Ron."

"Hello, Laurel." Even his voice was average, neither high or low-pitched, not loud or soft.

"You'd make a perfect spy," she said, not realizing she'd voiced the thought until she heard her own words.

Behind his glasses his gaze sharpened on hers and it was the first thing about him that was noticeable. He had beautiful gray eyes. But still, gray. "Pardon?"

She spent so much time with tiny plastic brides and grooms and animals made of fondant that she'd forgotten how to be around normal people. She felt the foolishness of her remark, saw that Karen was looking at her in a funny way, and blurted, "I read a lot of spy novels. I was thinking you'd be hard to describe. It's one of the things that makes a good spy." *Like keeping your mouth shut.*

Karen gave a social laugh, the kind that says, *let's move on,* but Ron seemed to consider her remark seriously. He said, "I'm a CPA. Being the kind of guy who disappears in a crowd is very useful for that profession, too."

"I'm sure it isn't. I mean, you're not…" Oh, Lord, what did she mean? A blush started to mount her cheeks.

"Laurel's very artistic," Karen said, in a way that suggested she wasn't good with words or people. Which was, of course, basically true.

"I can see that," Ron said, gazing at the cake behind

her. He was so incredibly neat, his not too long and not too short hair parted precisely, his shirt wrinkle-free, his shoes shining.

Today, as she often did, she wore clothes in Indian cotton that were already wrinkled, and she had a bad habit of getting icing in her hair. Her apron was certainly well-splotched with food coloring, bits of icing, and she noticed, glancing down at her plastic clogs, that there was a lump of marzipan on her toe. Next to this extraordinarily tidy man she felt like a disaster.

"This cake is incredible."

"Thanks. It's obviously a traditional cake, but I do all kinds."

"There's a book out front with samples of her work. You'll have to take a look when you get a second."

"I'd like that," he said.

"And this is Anton. He's one of Chelsea's people," Karen said, smoothly leading him to another part of the kitchen. They both admitted that Anton's soup smelled amazing, and then Karen whisked Ron away to meet the caterer who was upstairs.

Chelsea arrived in the kitchen herself not half an hour later and Anton said, "Why do we have a CPA prowling around the kitchen? We're not getting audited, are we?"

"No, of course not. Karen's dating him and I guess they got to talking and she decided to hire him."

"Karen's dating Ron?" Laurel gasped.

"Sure, why not?"

"I don't know, he seems so…" She couldn't find the word she was looking for. All she could come up with was "understated."

Chelsea grinned at her. "Well, they do say that opposites attract."

She thought of herself, One Big Mess—and a colorful mess at that—and the tidiest, most understated man in the world and the strange, instantaneous attraction she'd felt toward him. "Yes, I guess you're right."

"So, WHAT DID YOU THINK of our operation?" Karen asked Ron as they settled themselves back at her office. Lasagna was a treat she didn't allow herself very often, but she felt she needed to do something special for Ron after his embarrassment yesterday morning when Dexter had shown up at her door far too early in the day. Or maybe she felt some urge to punish herself by porking out on hundreds of calories of all her favorite things. So, she'd work extra hard at the gym tonight on her way home.

"You've got a great setup here. I think you're smart to have alliances with other businesses without setting yourself up as their employer. Makes your life a whole lot easier." He paused, took off his glasses and reaching into his pocket removed a cloth and began to polish the lenses. Then he replaced his glasses carefully. "Now, let's take a look at your accounting setup."

Karen was only too happy to have an outside expert look over her books and her systems. Ron was an easy person to have around, he didn't irritate her or ask her a million questions when she was busy, he simply got on with his work quietly.

And, much less quietly, she got on with hers.

"You want a live streamed video feed of your ceremony to go online?" she said into the phone, rolling her eyes as she grabbed a pen. "Right, I'm sure it would be nice for the folks back home to watch you live. Mmm-hmm. Yes, I'm sure they do offer that in Las Vegas."

She sighed. Scribbled notes. It was always something. "It's not a service I get called on to do very often, but let me look into it and get back to you." And she hung up the phone.

"People want to have their wedding televised?" Ron asked, looking startled.

"It's like everybody wants their own reality show these days."

"Can you do it?"

She glanced up from her notes. "Provide a live feed? Oh, sure. I can do pretty much anything if it's legal and somebody's willing to pay for it."

"If I ever get married, I won't want it on TV."

Chelsea strolled in just then with a menu in her hands. "Won't want what on TV?"

"Ron doesn't want his wedding televised."

Chelsea blinked at him and then at Karen. "You're getting married?"

Ron looked understandably harried by this turn in the conversation and Karen had to laugh at his hunted expression. "No, we were talking about some of the outrageous requests I get from brides and grooms."

Chelsea stepped forward and placed the menu on Karen's desk. "This is the menu for the underwater crowd. Let me know what you think. I may have gone overboard on the fish courses." She stepped back and added, "I've always said if you call your business If You Can Dream It, you have to expect strange requests."

"There's a perfect wedding for everyone. I simply help make it happen." She looked up at Chelsea, so busy with her catering company that she wasn't getting her own wedding planned and decided this was the perfect moment to find out a few details subtly, so she asked Ron, "What would your perfect wedding be?"

He removed his glasses and polished them, which she was beginning to recognize as a stalling gesture. "Well, I can't say I've given it too much thought," he said to the lenses. "But now that my parents are both gone I suppose something very simple would suit me. A nice lunch, perhaps, for a very few friends and colleagues. And then my new wife and I would fly to Ireland."

"Ireland?" both women said at once.

He replaced his glasses and blinked at them. "Why not? I've always wanted to go there."

"Well, it's not exactly the top honeymoon destination." Chelsea smiled her lovely smile. "But maybe you'll find an Irish woman to marry."

"I only meant—"

"What about you, Chels?" Karen interrupted, knowing Ron was uncomfortable discussing something so theoretical. "What's your ideal wedding?"

"Honestly? I cater so many weddings and there's still so much post-divorce bitterness between my parents that my dream wedding is to hop on a plane, go to a first-class resort and be waited on." A dreamy expression floated across her face. "No sourcing fresh ingredients or worrying about food allergies. We'd laze around all day and order room service when we got hungry. Or just stay in bed all day. Perfect bliss."

"Why don't you do it, then?"

She fiddled with her engagement ring. "It's sort of complicated. First there was the whole fake engagement thing last year, and now that we're really getting married, David's entire firm is getting involved. Somebody's brother-in-law will play the fiddle, another has a friend who's a photographer, you know how it is."

"You wouldn't want to have your friends witness the event?" Ron asked.

"Not really. Weddings are starting to feel too much like work. We could always take pictures."

"Go to Las Vegas," Ron suggested. "You can have your own live TV wedding there."

"I'll keep that in mind." Then she turned the question to Karen. "Well? What's your perfect wedding?"

An image filled her mind. Her and Dex in a garden in June. The weather was perfect, the scent of roses hung in the air and she'd known in that moment that she was meant to be with the man beside her.

Apart from her mother refusing to sit anywhere near her father, and crying through the entire service, her wedding had been perfect.

"A garden wedding. But I already had my perfect wedding once. I doubt I'll get a second chance."

15

LAUREL WAS FEELING flustered when she arrived at work. With two wedding cakes to bake and decorate and a birthday cake for an obnoxious-sounding twelve-year-old boy who wanted a *Lord of the Rings* theme, she knew she couldn't waste any time. For a perfectionist, that was always difficult.

She changed her black boots for her plastic clogs, tied her hair back and slipped on a clean apron.

She was the first one in and the quiet kitchen, gleaming with stainless steel and hulking appliances still and quiet like sleeping giants, made her happy.

Her own small area wasn't completely uncluttered, however. A paperback novel sat in the middle of her counter. Puzzled, she picked it up. The book was well-thumbed, an old paperback that was clearly loved by its owner. She knew because she had a shelf of books like it at home.

The Thirty-Nine Steps, by John Buchan. The novel had a lurid red cover and when she opened it inside was a yellow Post-it note which said, "From a fellow spy novel enthusiast. This is one of my favorites. Ron."

If the man had sent her two dozen red roses she couldn't have been more thrilled. There was something so personal, intimate almost, about the sharing of one's own copy of an oft-read book. A tiny thrill went through her as she turned to the first page, imagining the times when Ron must have had his hands exactly here, turning the page for himself, perhaps in a coffee shop on a Saturday morning, or maybe sitting up in bed at night before settling to sleep.

Then the fatuous smile on her face snapped off like a light that's been switched off. What was she doing getting all romantic about this man? He was dating Karen. Chelsea had said so herself and Chelsea wasn't a person to make things up.

She closed the book carefully and slipped it into her bag to take home after work. She'd misread the situation. He was simply being nice. He wasn't showing interest in her.

He didn't want to date her, he wanted to be her book buddy.

With a sigh, Laurel hauled out a tub of cake flour and got to work creating yet another artistic fantasy that would be gobbled up in no time by greedy twelve-year-old mouths.

Hours later, she was well into the decorating when a soft male voice said, "That looks amazing."

She turned to find Ron looking over her shoulder. "Thanks. Do you know what it is?"

"The Eye of Sauron. From *Lord of the Rings*. I don't know how you did it, but the colors look like fire."

Like any artist, she was happy to have her work recognized. "Oh, good. I've got some really cool sparklers that will shoot red and orange sparks into the air. I figured a twelve-year-old boy is going to want something spectacular." She glanced up to find him still admiring the cake, and for a second she could imagine what Ron must have looked like as a twelve-year-old. "Thank you for the book."

"You're welcome. Have you read it?"

"No. I saw the movie once. During a Hitchcock phase I was going through."

He seemed pleased that she hadn't already read it. "It's a classic early spy thriller. You'll have to let me know what you think."

"I will." She continued piping red gel onto the rim of the eye.

"Maybe we could have coffee sometime?"

Her hand spasmed and splat: a great squirt of red spat out of her bag so the eye now had a huge red jujube of a tear hanging from it. "Oh, crap," she cried, grabbing a spatula and easing off the mess she'd made.

"I'm sorry. I didn't mean to startle you. Of course we don't have to have coffee. I thought you might like to discuss the book." He seemed as nervous and flustered as she felt.

She had no idea how to respond. She didn't even know what he was asking her. Was it for a date? Which is what she'd first assumed, but now she wondered if perhaps he hadn't meant anything more than a friendly coffee.

But what if she said yes, and it was a date, and then Karen might be upset and she loved her job here and didn't want to cause any trouble to a woman she liked enormously.

On the other hand, maybe it wasn't a date at all and she'd sound all stuck up and full of herself if she refused.

Which was why she pretty much stayed away from

the whole male/female personal interaction thing. It was all simply too confusing, like a game whose rules she'd never grasp.

She'd attempted to play chess a few times and felt absolutely bewildered. When was a playing piece allowed to go sideways and which ones could only go forward, she'd never quite understood. And as for that horse thing that went over and up, it was enough to drive a creative brain crazy.

Silence seemed to echo around the kitchen. It had never seemed so huge, or so empty. "Of course I'd like to discuss the book sometime," she finally managed to say, keeping her attention on the icing, but not daring to continue her task in case he said something that made her completely ruin her cake.

"You don't drink coffee?" he asked seeming a little puzzled.

"I love coffee," she snapped. One of them was being incredibly dense and she had a horrible feeling it was her.

"But you don't want to go out with me?" he finally asked with a kind of humble tone that made her glance up from the cake and meet his gaze.

"No. I would like to go out with you." She sighed. How could a woman spend so much time strengthening her core and believing in the essential oneness of all people and still be such a weenie? She decided to speak her truth. "But you're seeing Karen. At least that's what Chelsea said."

The second the words were out she regretted them. She didn't want Ron to think she'd been asking about him. How embarrassing.

He didn't make the obvious conclusion, but a puzzled frown settled on his face. "Karen's a wonderful person," he began. "But I don't think you could say we're seeing each other. Not romantically. We both realized that we'd rather work together than," he gestured helplessly, "you know."

"Oh."

"So, will you?"

The world made sense again. Speaking her truth was as wonderful as all the yogis in the world told her it was. "Go for coffee with you?"

"Yes."

"I hardly ever date," she admitted in a rush. "I'm not very good at it."

He breathed what seemed to her to be a sigh of relief. "Me neither. I am so happy we both like books. At least we'll have something to talk about."

She turned to him, not even realizing she still held the spatula. The connection she'd felt the first time she saw him was only strengthened by his words and she felt a rush of understanding. "I know exactly what you mean. Isn't that the worst part? Sitting there, racking your brain for something to say? And my mind always goes blank when I start to panic. I'll blurt out something ridiculous." He smiled at her and she suddenly recalled her brilliant conversational repartee of yesterday when she'd told a man she'd never met before that he could be a spy because he looked so innocuous. She supposed she didn't need to tell him another word about her little problem with blurting out the strangest things.

"Have you ever tried online dating?"

"No. I'd never have the courage." Her eyes widened in awe. "Have you?"

"Yes. I decided that mathematically it made sense to widen the scope of potential females as far as possible since I only meet a very narrow selection of women in my daily life."

"Impressive logic. How did it work?"

"Well, let's see, over the last four months I've gone on approximately twenty-five first dates."

"Twenty-five first dates?" Her eyes widened.

"Mmm-hmm. A few of them progressed to second dates, but nothing felt quite right."

"I don't know how you had the guts to keep going."

"I'm tenacious that way. Once I've determined on a course, I try to continue until I've achieved success or accepted that success is not possible. It's important not to give up too soon."

"Wow. Did you meet nice women?"

"Yes. Quite a few. It's how I met Karen."

She gestured wildly. "Get out of here. Karen went through with it? She tried online dating?" With a cry of horror she realized she'd swiped his neat blue and white striped tie with a slash of red icing gel. It looked like the tie had tried to slit its own throat.

They both looked down, but she was the one who gasped.

"Oh my gosh. I'm so sorry."

He continued as though the disaster had never taken place. "And through Karen, I met you."

He swiped his finger over the red gel on his tie and sucked the red goo off his finger. "I'd say it worked quite well."

"I've ruined your tie," she cried, holding her palms to her cheeks.

"Yes, you have. Let me know when you finish that book and we'll go for coffee." And he left looking surprisingly happy for a man wearing a suicidal tie.

16

When Karen waltzed into the kitchen, Laurel experienced a pang of uneasiness. She'd finished *The Thirty-Nine Steps* and was getting together with Ron Saturday morning for their promised coffee to talk about the book. But she only had his word for it that Karen and he were friends. She'd heard of men who used Internet dating to pull together their own personal harems.

Not that she could imagine Ron with a harem, but then how well did she know him?

Karen was in full business mode and checking timing on the various cakes that Laurel was making for her over the next two months. After they'd finished confirming delivery dates, she said, "Um, there's something I need to tell you."

Karen grabbed at her arm. "Oh, God. You look guilty. Please don't tell me you're leaving. I can't take it. Really. Your cakes are so spectacular, you're part of our success."

"No," she said, half laughing. "It's nothing to do with my cakes. I'm really happy here."

"Oh, that is such a relief." Karen slapped a hand

over her heart. Her manicure was perfect. Laurel really should think about getting one of those. She imagined her fingernails with that shiny pink finish, then couldn't. She wasn't the nail polish type. "I've finally got my dream team, I can't bear to lose one of you."

"It's more, um, personal." She looked down and suddenly wished she hadn't opened this conversation. She had no idea how to explain herself and felt foolish even trying.

"You can trust me," Karen said gently. "If you're in any kind of trouble…" The hand on her arm was both warm and soothing.

"Oh, I'm being stupid. It's nothing. Only Ron asked me out and then he said you and he… And I don't want to do anything you wouldn't feel comfortable with, because I am so happy here and…" Her voice petered out and she continued to stare at the floor until she couldn't stand it anymore and raised her gaze.

But Karen didn't look at all angry. More stunned. She said, "You and Ron?" the way a person might say "ice cream and horseradish?" As though the two things couldn't possibly belong together.

"You're surprised?"

"Well, yes, to be honest. You don't seem like you'd have a lot in common."

"We both like spy novels. And he has such nice eyes."

"Yes, he does." She tapped her pretty pink nails against her binder. "Wow."

Laurel couldn't gauge what "wow" meant. "So, are you okay with that?"

The wedding planner seemed miles away. She came back with a start. "Oh, absolutely. Ron and I met through a dating site but we had absolutely no spark. I think he's a very nice man and he's a talented accountant and I think we're becoming friends, but we're definitely not dating. I've hired him to do some work for us."

"Okay then, that's good."

"You and Ron. Who should know better than a wedding planner that opposites attract." She shook her head. "You'll have to tell me how your coffee date goes."

"How did you know we're having coffee?"

"That's how he always starts a relationship." Then as Laurel's eyes widened she hastily added, "At least, that's what he told me. It's not like I know him intimately or anything." She cleared her throat, obviously embarrassed. "Because, in case you're wondering, there was no, you know, between us."

Laurel was insensibly cheered by this news. Not that it was any of her business, obviously, if Ron and Karen, who had met before she'd ever met Ron, had hooked up. Still, she was glad they hadn't. She couldn't imagine how weird it would be to have sex with a man who'd also slept with a colleague who was the closest thing she had to a boss. Not that she was thinking of having sex with Ron. The very idea had her thinking as muddled as one of her crazy icing color experiments that failed.

LAUREL ALMOST MISSED the letter grade.

It wasn't until she'd made sure she hadn't left a bookmark or a smudge or anything that might lessen the book—or her—in Ron's eyes that she noticed the neatly penciled letter *A* marked on the inside back cover of the paperback.

An A and then a line of equally neat handwriting. It said: *Book that began a genre. Masterpiece?*

She loved the question mark at the end of *masterpiece,* as though he didn't want to give out superlatives too easily. Was the *A* a letter grade like a teacher would give a student paper?

She traced the comment with her fingertip. She thought of the way so many people throw out words like *masterpiece, genius, brilliant, groundbreaking* and so on and how rarely the rave was deserved. She'd often heard ridiculously over-the-top praise for her own efforts. But then, Laurel, who was modest about most things, knew that some of her cakes were, in fact, masterpieces. Which suggested that not only mastery of one's medium of work was necessary, but also something more. Some whiff of the creative, the unusual, that took a creation to a new level.

She'd never thought of herself in the same realm as artists—she made bakery goods to be consumed, her works of art were no more permanent than a sand castle or an ice sculpture.

And yet, she liked to think that she lifted the mere cake to a new level, infusing it with meaning and giving joy to those first viewing it and then consuming it.

A shy woman, she spoke through food.

Usually.

Sometimes other forms of communication were necessary and she never found it easy to converse. She was shy, loath from a child to put herself forward. She'd always admired bold women, like Karen, who could go out and meet new people, sell products and services, fight when she had to. Laurel was much happier alone in her corner of the kitchen putting her thoughts into icing rather than words.

Somehow, she recognized in Ron a kindred spirit. The fact that he'd made this short and measured judgment of a book appealed to her. She couldn't imagine him in a book club arguing the merits of chaining oneself to a stranger of the opposite sex as a way to solve crime, or discussing the sexual undertones of the book and how they related to the mores of the time. The very notion of Ron arguing in public about sexuality made her want to giggle.

And if he did want to discuss the book with her over coffee she knew she'd find herself tongue-tied and stupid.

But she had to say something. In the end, she took a Post-it note, so impermanent it wouldn't even leave a mark in the book, and below his A and comment she put her own. She said, after much thought and the wanton waste of half a dozen yellow sticky notes:

He's an ordinary man who, when forced to save his country, can do extraordinary things. As in so many thriller novels, things aren't what they seem to be on the surface. I think that's true of people, too.

She realized that her note was hardly significant literary criticism, but she didn't care. Her last line was more of a personal observation that had nothing to do with the novel but she was trying to tell Ron, in her own way, that she wasn't exactly what she appeared either. She hoped there was more to her than she could articulate.

As the date approached, she realized, she wanted to be different from all the other women he'd had a first date coffee with. Well, it stood to reason she would be because she was different from pretty much everyone she knew. But ever since Karen had told her that Ron started all his relationships with a coffee date, she'd decided that she wasn't going to tell her grandchildren that she and Grandpappy had got together over coffee in cardboard containers.

Nothing as permanent as love should start over anything involved in takeout.

Laurel wasn't a bold woman, but she was intuitive and if she'd learned anything in the years she'd studied and practiced yoga and meditation it was to honor her instincts. Of course, she could be wrong. Ron might be entirely wrong for her in the long term but she wasn't willing to ignore the strong feeling she had that the way they began would be important to their future.

Wanting to respect his idea of a first date, and yet still make it special, she called him.

When she picked up his business card to call him on Friday she accidentally left a purple icing thumbprint on the pristine card stock. When she identified herself he sounded instantly distressed. "You're not cancelling, are you?"

"No. I'm not. I have an idea. Instead of meeting at a coffee shop, I thought we might have a picnic."

There was a tiny pause. "A picnic coffee?"

"Yes. I will meet you at JFK Plaza." She didn't call it by its more familiar name, Love Park, named for the famous red-and-blue sculpture that spelled *LOVE* with the *O* tilted sideways.

"But it's almost winter."

"Wear something warm. I'll bring the coffee."

She was inordinately pleased with herself when he agreed. A first date at Love Park was the kind of outing to tell her grandchildren about. Even if the fountain wasn't operating, there was a great view of the city by looking northwest down the Benjamin Franklin Parkway, which was supposedly modeled after the Champs Elysées in Paris.

Laurel had no idea whether that was true or not. She'd never been to Paris, but she liked the idea that she could pretend. Besides, the art museum was at the other end of the plaza and she never tired of going there.

As she imagined their first date, thought about Ron, she began to create a perfect first cake to go with a perfect first date.

17

DEX HAD TAKEN TO texting her. She had no idea why, but the short, sexy, sometimes funny texts were getting to be a bad habit. Of course, it would be rude not to respond, so they began exchanging increasingly steamy messages.

Every time I see a takeout container I get hard, he texted.

She shut her phone and tried to ignore the surge of lust his words invoked. After her next appointment, she texted back: I can still feel your lips on my nipple.

The texts continued in this manner until she got one that puzzled her. Have dinner with me Friday night.

That's not sexy, she texted back.

Trust me, it will be.

She laughed aloud from the parking lot where she'd picked up the message. Replied, I don't trust you.

Hardly a minute had gone by when she had her reply. I know.

Even though a text message couldn't have a tone, she felt sadness coming from the words. As she looked at her phone, wondering how to reply, it rang.

"Hey," he said.

"Hey."

"So, dinner on Friday night is with the building owners and their wives. What do you say?"

"I'm not your wife anymore."

"I know. But you're a beautiful, interesting woman and I'd enjoy your company. Then, after dinner, we'll head to my hotel room and I'll demonstrate how much I've missed you."

I've missed you, too, she wanted to say. Instead she managed, "I think I can make it."

"Thanks. See you Friday."

SHE'D NEVER LOOKED MORE GORGEOUS, Dex thought as he escorted Karen into the restaurant. In her simple black dress, she somehow managed to appear both elegant and sexy at the same time.

He'd loved her sexiness when he'd first met her but he liked looking at her even more now she was a little older. He liked her confidence and the tiny lines at the edges of her eyes. They lured him in.

She was still a great corporate wife, too, he thought, watching her charm the building owners and make friends with their wives. What could have been a boring business dinner ended up being so much fun that everyone exchanged hugs at the end.

As they walked away making the short stroll to his hotel in overcoats and gloves, he said, "Thanks, that was more fun than I expected."

She squeezed his hand through their two gloves. "Thank you. Louise has a niece getting married next year. I schmoozed."

He laughed down at her. Her face was alive, her

cheeks pink with cold, her eyes sparkling. He couldn't help himself, he leaned over and kissed her full lips.

Her hand slipped up to his shoulder. "What was that for?"

"Schmoozing, smooching, I get confused."

"Come on, walk faster."

"You cold?"

"No. I want to get naked with you, and fast."

"That's my girl," he said, pulling her along the pavement at top speed. If he hadn't been staying on the seventeenth floor he'd have run for the stairs. As it was, the time spent waiting for the elevator was agony. Once the car came and they were inside and alone, he pulled her to him, kissing her hungrily, pulling off his gloves and slipping his hands inside her coat to feel her up.

She giggled, but slipped off her gloves to do some exploring of her own.

By the time they reached his room they were both panting. His hands were unsteady as they pulled off her coat, her dress.

When he saw her underwear he nearly expired. Under that classy dress she had the sexiest, barely-there black wisps of nothing that he'd ever seen.

He had them off in no time. She pulled back the covers and slid into bed, watching with frank enjoyment as he ripped his own clothes off and then rolled into bed. And paradise.

"GOOD THING we slept over at the hotel," Dex said next morning as they got ready to go down to the restaurant just off the lobby for a late breakfast.

"Why?" Karen asked.

"I don't have to worry about a certain CPA showing up this morning and forcing a showdown."

"Very amusing. To be honest with you, I think he dumped me for my cake decorator."

"Wow. She must be hot."

She swatted him and then gave him a shove that sent him sprawling. Luckily he'd had the forethought to grab her on the way down so they bounced onto the mattress together, still damp from the shower, still hungry for each other.

At some point, he knew they'd have to face up to what they were doing, but right now he was so happy to have her back in his life that he didn't want to go there. Having that sweet, willing body back in his bed was enough.

For now.

"Dex," she said, in a sexy, breathless tone, as she unbelted her robe.

He suspected breakfast would be late. And it would be room service.

_18_

WHEN RON ARRIVED for their coffee date, bundled in an overcoat, gloves and warm boots, his nose red from the cold, Laurel was already waiting on a bench. She got up and hugged him. He seemed a little taken aback but hugged her in return. She thought they fit nicely together, being of a similar height. When you were both average, average could be perfect.

She was wearing a man's winter coat that she'd picked up at a thrift store, a woolen hand-crocheted hat with a pink crocheted flower on the side that an aunt had sent her for Christmas, and purple mittens.

"This is a very nice spot," he said, seeming to see the LOVE sculpture for the first time in his life though he must have viewed it hundreds of times.

She was so happy he approved. He sat down on the bench and she reached into her bag and pulled out the thermos of coffee she'd made earlier. She only drank fair trade coffee, of course, and the brew was excellent.

She poured the coffee into china mugs she'd brought from home. They were pottery, made by hand at a women's collective in Guatemala and she loved their heft and the connection she felt with these women who were using their own artistic talents to make a better life.

She handed him his coffee, then realized she hadn't brought milk or sugar. "Um, I hope you like it black."

"I do."

Finally, feeling both bold and foolish, she unearthed a reusable cake box and handed it to him.

"What's this?"

"A little something to go with your coffee."

He opened it slowly and the grin that split his face made him look anything but unremarkable. He put down the coffee on the bench and removed his gloves so he could ease the cupcake out of the box.

She'd spent more time on that one cupcake than she'd spent on some four-tier wedding cakes. And his response was everything she could have hoped for.

The cake was spherical, with a flat spot on the bottom so it would stand. On it, she'd iced a simple variation of the continents, using blue gel with touches of green as the sea. On top of the world was a man made of fondant, a man with glasses and average-colored hair, in a gray suit—including a tiny blue-and-red striped tie—holding a briefcase in one hand and a gun in the other. She'd considered writing Top Secret on the briefcase but decided that was too obvious.

At first he simply looked at it, turning it every way so he could see the cake from all angles, not saying a word, but she could tell from his expression that he was pleased.

"This," he finally said, "is the nicest cake I've ever had. Thank you."

"You're welcome." She felt absurdly pleased. It was so rare for her to be present when her creations were consumed. Sometimes she never even met the final customers, she'd get commissions from Karen or Chelsea. To have the opportunity to watch someone she liked enjoy the fruit of her artistic vision and stove labor made her bubbly with excitement.

She anticipated his first bite. Would he be delighted at the cake she'd chosen for him? A plain white with lacings of hidden lemon flavor? She wanted to see him with icing smeared around his clean and proper mouth, to watch him gobble the tiny figure of himself she'd crafted so painstakingly.

After admiring the cake again, chuckling over the details and peering closer until his nose almost touched Africa, he said, "I can't believe how accurately you've delineated the continents in such a small space. It's quite remarkable."

Then, as carefully as he'd eased it out of the box, he began to replace the cake.

She couldn't stop herself from crying out in protest.

"What is it?" he asked, the thriller cupcake half in and half out of the box.

"You're not diabetic, are you?"

"I don't think so."

"Then why don't you eat it?"

He appeared as shocked at the idea of eating the cupcake as she was at the notion of him not eating it. "I can't do that, it's a work of art. I want to enjoy it. Make it last."

"You can't," she said, understanding the joy of her profession in that moment as she never had before. "Any more than you can make a perfect sunset last, or an amazing live concert, or a belly laugh. If you put that cake in the fridge until it rots, you'll have missed the joy of eating it. Please." She leaned over and touched his leg with her purple-mittened hand. "I made it for you."

He blinked at her slowly, then with a nod that contained a hint of sadness, he withdrew that perfect cupcake. And, after staring at it again from all angles, as though to commit the image to memory, he bit into Australia.

He didn't seem to mind that he got blue gel all around his mouth, didn't stop for a second to wipe up. Instead, he gave himself over to the pleasure of that first bite. "Mmm, mmm, that is so good," he finally said, licking his lips. "Usually commercial cakes are so disappointing, as though all the work went into the decorating for show, and then inside it's a boring cake. But this." He seemed unable to find words. Closed his eyes briefly. Then smiled at her. "I think I get it. You made an ordinary cake and filled it with a surprise flavor."

She nodded, pleased with his perception, and so he went on.

"It's like a thriller novel. Everything seems normal on the surface, but there are secrets to be uncovered. And the protagonist may seem like one thing on the outside but be full of surprises."

"Exactly. It's what I love about thrillers."

"And new relationships?"

He was gazing at her with those warm gray eyes that were anything but ordinary. Her stomach jumped and then settled. "Exactly."

He offered her the cake and she bit into the other side. Even she had to admit it was one of her tastiest, most inspired creations.

"This is a very different first date for me," he said, sipping from coffee that steamed in the cold air.

"I'm glad. How do they usually go?"

"I have a list of questions I can ask to keep the conversation flowing."

"Such as?"

"Tell me about yourself," he said.

"That's a good one to start with."

"I think so. Well? How about it? Tell me about yourself."

She sipped her coffee, thinking. What was there to tell, really, that a down-to-earth man like Ron would find interesting? When she reviewed her history, even with careful editing, she knew she'd sound like a flake. So she cut to the chase. "I'm a flake."

A quiet rumble that could have been a chuckle shook him. "Really? Have a bit of Antarctica."

He passed her the cake and she bit into it.

"I am, you know," she said around the flavor. "I don't like schedules or do normal things. I practice a lot of yoga—and I started a long time before it became popular, by the way. I've spent much of my life drifting."

She tipped back her head and contemplated the gray sky above. "All of it, really."

"Perhaps I could have some specifics?"

Suddenly, she laughed. "You see what I mean? I can't even have a normal conversation with details. I'm even a flake in conversation."

"I like that about you."

"You do?" If he'd told her he liked that her hair was four colors because she could never decide on one she couldn't have been more shocked.

"For the same reason I like your hair," he said, knocking her mouth wide open. As though he could hear her thoughts. "It's free and unfettered by rules and order. Oh, don't misunderstand me. I like order, I live by rules. Accountants have to, you know. Numbers don't have a great deal of room for whimsy. I saw you and something lightened in me. I think I have a tendency to be too serious."

She thought of the way he'd described his dating strategy to her, playing some kind of mathematical numbers game, and she had to agree.

"If you want whimsy, you've come to the right girl." She blew out a breath. Usually she was uncomfortable talking about herself, but she figured if she liked the guy enough to spend half a day making him a cupcake, she liked him enough to tell him about her life. So she tried.

"The only truly constant thing in my life has been cakes. I knew that's what I wanted to do when I was a teenager. But apart from that, I've moved around a lot, spent some time in India, never really been able to settle. My parents were hippies and somehow I never got out of the habit, I guess. I'm thirty-two years old and my longest ever relationship was two years. Everything I own fits into the world's tiniest apartment. Which I rent."

There was nothing left of the cupcake now but the little fondant man in the gray suit. Ron glanced at her as though he were about to ask if he could keep the little icing guy, but he surprised her, he leaned forward, holding the replica of himself between his thumb and forefinger. His eyes held hers. "I want you to take the first bite," he said softly.

Maybe it wasn't the sexiest remark a man had ever made to a woman, but it was the most erotic statement anyone had ever said to her. Perhaps because of the way he was looking at her. This buttoned-up accountant had sexual intent blazing in his eyes and she knew he was inviting her to do more than chomp a chunk of icing.

She leaned forward slowly. Opened her mouth. Like a perfect sunset, a great concert or a belly laugh, she knew this moment would be gone all too soon, and all she'd have would be the memory, so she tried to imprint every sensation. The feel of the cold breeze on her nose, the sound of traffic in the city, the cry of some hardy seabird in the distance, and the warmth of the man beside her. The expression of tender lust on his face, the way his lips curved slightly, a tiny smudge of blue lodged adorably on his chin.

He slipped her version of himself between her lips and she bit down, taking half of him into her, enjoying the burst of sweetness and the punch of almond. Because, as with the cake, she hadn't wanted the icing to taste predictable.

She licked her lips. He continued to gaze at her as he pushed the other half of his fondant self into his mouth and chewed. His eyes widened slightly as the unexpected flavor hit him, and they went squinty at the sides with humor.

Then he leaned over and, taking her chin in his hand, scanning her face for a long moment, he kissed her.

She was flighty and dreamy and whimsical and—deep to her core—romantic. She'd dreamed of Princes Valiant and Charming and every variation in between. The kind of men who rode steeds and crashed down doors and swept innocent, heart-pure maidens off their feet.

Ron wasn't anything like that. She couldn't imagine him on a steed. He seemed like the kind of guy who might be afraid of horses. She couldn't imagine him sweeping her off her feet, but he'd hold a door open for her, he'd be able to figure out even her income tax, which was a lot more practical in the real world.

It was only his kiss that made her feel like a fairy tale princess.

This was sweeping her off her feet, the way he took possession of her mouth, teased her with his tongue, so she tasted again the sweetness of sugar and almond, the hints of lemon from the cake.

She got the feeling he was as stunned as she was by the powerful attraction between them when their mouths met. She made a sound in the back of her throat, embarrassingly like the purr of a well-stroked kitten, and he pulled her in closer, until their bodies rubbed together. She felt all the frustration of winter. Coats and sweaters, possibly thermal underwear on one of them, which oddly enough didn't put her off but kind of excited her since it was so new and strange compared to what she'd been used to.

Guys who could unerringly find their Chi but didn't always have as much luck finding the clitoris.

Not that she knew a great deal about Ron, but somehow she felt he was the kind of man who, once shown, didn't forget important details like that.

His hands were rubbing up and down her back. She could tell he wanted to do more and was holding himself in check.

For her benefit or some odd notion of his own?

She rubbed her breasts provocatively against his chest, as provocatively as she could with all the layers between them and she was pretty sure he groaned in a quiet, self-contained way.

Hmm. She let her hand stray to his knee, slowly track north. He sucked in his breath when she brushed against a flatteringly hard erection. But he didn't pick up on her obvious invitation to do some more exploring of his own.

She thought about everything she knew about him and nuzzled a little closer. "How many dates do you usually have before you get intimate with a woman?" she asked softly.

For a second he didn't answer her. Then, with a trace of humor in his tone, he admitted, "Ten."

They kissed again. His glasses were fogging up as was her entire body.

"Would you ever make an exception to that rule?"

There wasn't a breath of hesitation. He panted, "Yes."

19

LAUREL AND RON STAYED on the bench necking for a while longer, until she couldn't stand it anymore, then she said, "I live in a tiny walk-up apartment."

"Does it have a bed?"

She giggled. "Yes."

"Let's go."

She thought he might have wanted to go to his place, but it seemed he didn't. So they went to her apartment in a Bohemian walk-up in the South Street area. They passed secondhand bookstores, places that sold nothing but incense, funky boutiques.

They entered the narrow hallway and walked up the three flights of stairs to her small apartment.

Ron walked in and hung his coat neatly on the brass hooks hanging on the wall. Then he helped her out of her coat and hung that, too. He neatly placed his gloves in the pocket of his coat while she dropped her mittens in the basket she kept for the purpose. When she pulled off her hat she felt her hair rise with static. She probably looked like a science experiment gone wrong.

"I like this place," he said, looking around. "It suits you."

"There's not much here," she said, trying to see it through someone else's eyes. Indian prints on the wall, her yoga mat stretched out on the floor. The modest shelf of books, mostly spiritual and thrillers. Only now, seeing it through his eyes did she see that it was an odd collection.

The ceilings sloped on both sides, so there really wasn't a lot of room to stand up unless you stayed in the center of the suite. Her bed took up most of one side of the apartment, covered in a tie-dyed spread she'd bought on impulse at a street market.

He glanced at the bed and away again. He wandered toward her books, studied the thrillers but didn't say anything. He stood there, staring at the books without uttering a word or even reaching for one, so that she wondered if he thought she had lousy taste in fiction.

"Would you like some tea?" she asked, seeing as now that they were away from that cold bench they didn't seem quite so hot for each other. Correction: *he* didn't seem so hot for her all of a sudden.

She didn't think it was because he didn't approve of her modest living conditions, so she had to consider other possibilities.

"Yes, I would like some tea," he said, as though they hadn't just filled up on coffee and cake.

She took the few steps to the tiny alcove where her kitchen consisted of a two-burner hotplate, a toaster oven and a microwave that she never used because she didn't believe that any appliance that cooked food that fast could possibly be healthy.

She plugged in the kettle and checked her stash of teas. "Happiness? Calm? Or peppermint?"

He looked at her. "You don't have one for Confidence?" he asked only half joking.

She turned to him. "Is that what this is about? Confidence?"

He shoved his hands in his pockets and turned his face up to the ceiling. "This is the reason I decided on a ten-date timeline."

"But—"

"You're so open, so giving. You live in the moment and I'm always planning for the future."

"I'm not sure I—"

"Laurel, I've only slept with two women." He shot the words out like bullets.

She forgot about the tea and moved toward him. "What difference does that make?"

The ceiling seemed to fascinate him, requiring all his focus. "And the last one was…a while ago."

He was so brave and honest, she felt warm all over and somehow protective of this sweet man who worked with numbers all day and read thrillers for excitement. She suspected he spent far too much time in his head. "Are you worried about—"

"I think I might be terrible in bed."

She resisted smiling. It would be counterproductive, she knew. If there was anything she'd learned to trust it was her intuition, and hers was telling her that a man who could kiss the way Ron did was not going to be a disaster in bed. But he was obviously feeling concerned. She'd messed with his careful plan, hadn't waited for ten dates to sleep with him, and she could see that he was feeling rocked out of his comfort zone.

So she contained her smile. She might be flaky and whimsical and a mess in a lot of real world ways, but there were a few things she knew to the core of her being. She rose on her tiptoes, linking her hands around his neck until he was forced to look at her, and kissed him softly. Instinctively, his arms came round her. "I'm very flexible, you know."

"Are you?" His voice was pitched higher than usual.

"Mmm-hmm. It's all the yoga."

His eyes lit with interest.

"When you're with me? It's impossible to be bad in bed."

And then she pulled his sweater over his head. And then his long-sleeved T-shirt, and finally his thermal underwear. She'd never been with a man who wore thermal underwear and for some reason she found it incredibly sexy.

His body was about what she'd expected. Pale skin. A nice compact body with the average amount of body hair, the average musculature. She'd always been a step outside of normal and it was nice to be with someone who was a step too far inside the rigid boundaries of the acceptable, the expected. The average.

He seemed completely happy to let her lead, so she dipped down to help him remove his jeans, his blue long johns, his thick socks.

She sighed with pleasure as she pushed him back onto her bed, leaving him in only his boxer shorts— boxers so dull they didn't even have funny sayings on them or hearts or something. They were plain navy cotton. The poor man needed her.

At least there was a nice tent in the middle of his boxers, so his supposed problems weren't anything that needed drugs most often advertised on the Internet.

He gazed at her with a kind of neediness and she realized he wanted to see her but was too shy to ask.

She probably should invest in something that would pass for lingerie, but she could no more see herself in silk nothings than she could imagine herself with a manicure. Her underwear was organic cotton, an oatmeal-colored camisole and simple matching panties.

But she did her best, stripping off her sweater slowly, putting some wiggle in it when she slipped out of her jeans, pulling off her socks and then climbing onto the bed beside him.

She was slim and slight, but she felt good in her body. It was toned and strong. Ron didn't say anything, but she thought he liked her body fine, too.

Leaning over, she kissed him until the guy who'd kissed her senseless on the bench was back.

He took his glasses off and reached to place them on her bedside table where they hit with a clatter in the quiet room.

Then she reached for the waistband of his shorts and peeled them slowly off him. And gasped.

He might be unremarkable everywhere else, but her Mr. Average CPA was definitely above average in some departments. What an incredible surprise.

She felt looser in her muscles than she ever had, more flexible, more…sexy. She peeled the cotton camisole over her head slowly, letting him watch his fill, which he did with his slightly myopic gaze fastened on her. She'd never felt so right with a man. His gaze on her was like a caress, heating her skin everywhere it alighted.

She slipped her panties down over her legs and snuggled into the bed beside Ron.

He turned his body toward her, touched her shoulder. "I never knew, under all those flowing things, you were hiding…that body."

Silent laughter shook her. The simple man or woman with much more to them than meets the eye; it seemed to her she and Ron were both like that.

"I could say the same."

She wrapped her arms around him, rubbing her naked body against his, enjoying the pleasure of her skin against his without any hurry. She loved foreplay, loved every second of it, so that when orgasm snuck up on her it was all part of a holistic experience.

Ron seemed a little shy, receiving her caresses but not initiating any of his own. "My hands and feet are cold," he warned her.

"Bad circulation, probably. I bet I can warm them up." And once she got him into yoga, which she fully intended to do, his circulation would definitely improve.

She took his hands in hers and found that they were a little cool, and placed them on her breasts. He tried to pull them back, telling her he didn't want her chilled but the minute her nipples hit his palms, he closed his hands over her breasts and began to knead the warm flesh.

His excitement was buzzing through his body, she could feel it. "I think I might…" he panted, but couldn't finish his sentence.

She thought he might, too, if he was worried about going off too soon, and since it was obviously a big deal for him she decided that the best course of action was to let him get rid of that first head of steam. She reached for her bedside table and the condoms she kept there, sheathed him efficiently without giving him a chance to protest.

Then she rolled on top of him and took him slowly into her body. His sheer size was an absolute joy to her, stretching and filling her. He made helpless noises indicating distress and she said, "I want you to come inside me, right away."

He lay below her staring up, all his half-uttered apologies stilled. "What did you say?"

"I really need to feel you come inside of me." She leaned down to kiss him full on the mouth. "Please. Now."

He groaned as though Santa Claus had just brought him the best gift ever, and grabbing her hips, thrust in and up, staying with her rhythm as she rode him.

It wasn't a long ride, she'd known it wouldn't be, and as he grew more frenzied in his movements she encouraged him. "Yes, I want you, now." When he exploded, she stayed with him through the roar of release and the tremors that shook him.

After they'd cleaned up, they lay side by side and he gazed at her ruefully. "I'm so sorry, I wanted to last longer but—"

She kissed him.

"Feel better now?"

"Immeasurably."

He rolled over and kissed her, and, as she'd hoped and half expected, his cock was already rising for more action.

"Do you have to be somewhere?"

"Not for hours," he said.

"Then quit apologizing."

He chuckled, running his hands through her crazy hair. "Why don't I make love to you instead?"

She loved his intelligence. "That would be a much better use of your time."

As she'd already suspected, he knew exactly where the clitoris was and it seemed to fascinate him. She found that he was particularly good at focusing on her needs and pleasures.

Maybe he was a little rusty at first, but he soon grew comfortable and there was definitely chemistry between them. She'd probably been with technically superior lovers in her time, but she'd never had more fun in bed.

Never.

He was indeed a thriller.

RON DIDN'T LEAVE until the next morning. "Well?" she asked as she watched him get dressed. "How do you think our first date went?" She felt sleepy and satisfied, her entire body replete. She supposed a man who worked with accounts and spreadsheets all day had to be good at focusing and staying on task and she'd found that once he got over that first eager climax he'd been as focused and generous as she could have wished.

"I think," he said, as though giving the matter profound thought, "that was the best first date of my life." He regarded her for a moment, his eyes twinkling behind his glasses. "If I were a man given to hyperbole, which I am not, I might characterize that as the greatest first date in all of history."

She hadn't thought he could make her feel giddy, but she was wrong. A foolish grin split her face. "Really?"

"Really."

"Me, too."

"Oh, I almost forgot," he said and went to his jacket. From the right pocket he withdrew an early John le Carré novel. "Have you read this?"

"No," she lied because she wanted to get her hands on his copy. When he handed her the book, the first thing she did was flip to the inside back cover and find

the letter grade and accompanying comment. A again.
How they made her smile, his comments. So measured,
so restrained.

"Do you grade all your books?"

"Yes. It's a habit of mine."

"Do you give every book an A?"

"Of course not. I only keep the books I consider a B
or above."

"So you're sharing with me your favorites?"

"Yes." Maybe some men wooed a woman with roses
and candlelight dinners, but for her, this was so much
better. He was sharing the books he loved, letting her
put her hands where he'd put his. Even sharing his comments about the book, which she instinctively knew he
wouldn't do easily.

"Do you ever give a book an A+?"

"Not so far. My feeling is that if you give an A+ and
then a better book comes along, the A+ loses its meaning. I'm not of the opinion that one can keep adding
pluses. So the A+ is the greatest spy novel I've ever
read."

"And it's still out there?" For some reason she found
the idea charming. And optimistic.

"I suppose, if it exists, that it's still out there, yes."

"Or hasn't been written yet."

"Another possibility."

"How do you decide to give a book an A?"

He was on safer ground here, she could tell.

"I have a grading scale. A book has to answer all the
questions it sets out, if it's a mystery, the reader must
have had the clues to solve the puzzle. The writing must
be of high quality, obviously, and the general story must
interest me. That's a subjective way to rate a book, but
it's the one I use."

She got out of bed, naked, but she didn't care and walked over to him.

She put her arms around him and thought she could never have enough of this man. She barely knew him and yet she knew him so well.

"I had such a great time," she said.

He pulled back slightly so he could see her face. "You are the A+ I never thought I'd find."

20

"No, NO, NO!" Karen yelled at her computer screen.

"What is it?" Dee cried, running in at top speed to where Karen was yelling obscenities at an electronic device, no doubt looking as demented as she felt. "Has your system crashed?"

"Yes!"

"I'll call the tech guy. Don't worry, I'm sure they can restore your hard drive. And remember, we got that automatic backup after the last time."

"Not that system." Karen waved her away. "It's personal, not business."

Dee blinked at her for a moment, then seemed to appreciate she was having a really bad day and backed away. "Ah. Well, if you need me, I'm out front."

"Thanks. Sorry for the panic." She had to get a grip. She really, really had to get a grip.

System crash. Dee had the terminology right, but it was her internal system that was crashing. The one that kept her functioning and sensible. All it took was one text message.

From Dexter. He'd called earlier to say he was back

and staying the weekend. Since she hadn't seen him for over a week, she was more pleased than she should be to know she'd be seeing him tonight. She was just beginning to think that this sex with Dex the sexy ex was actually working out when he had to go and ruin everything.

Again.

The text was still on her phone. She called it up and stared at it again. Do you want to spend Christmas together?

Why did he do this to her? No, why did he still have the power to do this, to make her feel young and foolish and in love again? Did he have any idea how very badly she wanted him? How desperately she'd tried not to notice when he wasn't in town and she wasn't seeing him.

But Christmas? That was what married people did. She knew exactly what it would be. A big dinner with family who would all ask impertinent questions, and then he'd suggest a quick trip. Skiing for a few days, or the Caribbean. They'd spend New Year's Eve shushing atop a mountain, or sailing under a heavy, golden sun. It sounded heavenly.

She couldn't do it. She could not go down this path again.

As much as she'd tried to deny it, she had to admit to herself that she wasn't simply enjoying casual booty calls with her ex. She was making love with the man she loved with all her heart.

And that heart couldn't take another break.

She decided that Dexter Crane had been put on this earth to drive her insane.

And that it was her job to cut him off at the pass.

She didn't text back.

But as the hours crawled along she could think of nothing else but getting naked with the man who'd given her so much physical pleasure and so much emotional pain.

When she booked a wedding night suite for a soon-to-be married couple, she ended up drifting into a reverie where she recalled her own wedding night. In fact, she didn't think they'd stopped making love for three days, practically pausing only to eat and shower.

Well, she wasn't going to go running over to his hotel tonight. She'd moved on. She was a woman in her prime who wasn't getting regular sex. That was the only reason Dex's call had her squirming on her office chair all day imagining all the things he could do to her at night. All she had to do was go to him.

Which she had no intention of doing.

What she needed was a distraction.

She'd be so busy tonight that she wouldn't have time to think about Dex waiting for her in his hotel room. All hot and naked and... No. She wasn't going there.

Around four, Karen stomped into Chelsea's office feeling twitchy and irritable.

Since Dexter had stormed back into her life and, even worse, into her bed, she'd been feeling this way a lot. "What's up?" Chelsea asked in surprise when Karen let out a frustrated howl as she entered her friend's private space.

"We're going partying tonight."

"We are?"

It was a Friday, and a perfectly reasonable request, except that she and Chelsea had never partied together before. "Remember when you promised me a girls' night out?"

Chelsea slapped a hand over her mouth. "Oh, my gosh, I did. I forgot."

"Well, we're going to have it tonight."

"We are?" she repeated.

"Yes. We are."

Chelsea had appeared mildly surprised, but now a frown of concern pulled her perfectly maintained eyebrows together. "Honey, what is it?"

"He wants to spend Christmas with me. I could kill him."

"That jerk." But she seemed a little amused and her words didn't hold much heat.

"It's not funny. I thought we were having a fling, no strings, no commitment, simply sex when we're both around and feel like it. Now he wants me to spend the holidays with him. But it's impossible."

"Why?"

The truth burst from her. "Because I still love him."

"I know," Chelsea said, her brown eyes warm with sympathy. "I know." She put a hand on Karen's and said, "Do you think maybe he loves you, too? Why else would he ask you to spend the holidays with him? Honey, he wants you back."

"But he cheated on me."

There was a pause. "I don't know what's right for you. But don't you think that sometimes, people can change?"

Shock held her speechless. "Are you suggesting I should take the cheating liar back?"

"I think, maybe, he's trying to get your forgiveness, maybe a second chance. Of course, it's up to you to give him one."

"Men don't change," she said, thinking of her father and the destructive pattern of his relationships.

"Sure they do. People change all the time. Sometimes, for the better."

"I'm so mixed up. I can't see him right now."

"And you don't have to."

"Maybe if we go out tonight, I'll have the strength to stay away from him."

"Well, I did promise you a girls' night out."

"Good. Besides, it's time we took control of our lives. You, with a guy who won't commit, me, even poor Laurel, what are we? Some kind of wimps? We sit around and wait for men to decide our futures?"

"Did I hear my name?" Laurel floated in all wispy and fragile, with a streak of purple icing in her hair that looked as though a psychotic hairdresser might have put it there.

"Yes. You're coming too," she decided on the spot. "I was telling Chelsea that we need a girls' night out. The three of us. All we ever do is work and where's it getting us? I'm sleeping with my ex-husband—"

Laurel's eyes widened in shock. "You are?"

"Yes. But you can't tell anyone that because it's insane."

"Who is—"

"Never mind." She waved an imperious hand. "The point is, it's got to stop. And look at you two." She waved a slightly shaky hand between the two of them. "Chelsea's the most beautiful woman I've ever seen and she's engaged to a guy with commitment problems—"

"Actually," Chelsea began, but Karen cut her off.

"And you?" She turned to Laurel. "You're like Cinderella, Sleeping Beauty, Rapunzel, all those fairy tale princesses you put on cakes. All your passion is going into butter cream!"

She hauled in a breath. "This has to stop."

Laurel took a step backward. "I'm sort of see-ing—"

Karen interrupted as though she hadn't spoken. "That is why, we three are going out tonight and we will have so much fun that men will be a distant memory."

Laurel and Chelsea glanced at each other and if she wasn't so mad she couldn't see straight she'd probably have been able to interpret their expressions. As it was, she didn't really care what they were thinking. Her plan was a good one. "This is exactly the thing we need to get us all unstuck."

Chelsea frowned. "You know, I have an idea. How about the three of us head back to my town house for a bottle of wine." She glanced at Karen. "Or two."

"Sitting around drinking wine in the town house you share with the man who won't commit to marrying you isn't my idea of a fun time." She shook her head. "I'm going downtown. Who's with me?"

For a long moment no one said anything. Finally, Chelsea closed her computer file with a click. The light caught the big honking engagement ring on her finger that had sat for too long waiting for its mate, rather like its owner.

"I'm with you. You're right, it will be fun."

"I don't really…I'm not sure I can…" Laurel began then, taking a deep breath, she said, "I'm in."

Chelsea said, "Thanks, Laurel," which seemed like a stupid remark, but Karen was too happy to know they'd seen the light to cause an argument.

"Good, that's settled then."

21

THE TECHNO MUSIC in the club beat into Karen's body
with the thrusting insistence of her mood. Her blood
picked it up, her hips joined in, already swaying.

"Oh, boy," Chelsea said behind her.

After enjoying a couple of cocktails in an after-work
hangout, she'd suddenly remembered she wanted to
check out this club as a possible wedding venue and
dragged the women along.

The place was dimly lit, and crowded with a restless,
moving throng of people, mostly in their twenties and
thirties with a smattering of older people and teens with
fake IDs.

The dance floor was a pumping, swaying crowd.
It was a good size, the wedding planner in her noted.
A waft of air-conditioning brushed the exposed skin
above her low-cut top, reminding her how hot her skin
felt everywhere.

She would not think of Dex touching her there, of
Dex, even now, waiting for her in a hotel only blocks
away from here. She would not.

"I think there's an empty table in that corner over

there," Laurel said, gesturing into the quiet area at the back.

"We'll sit at the bar," Karen decreed and without waiting for argument she led the way into the most crowded part of the club apart from the dance floor.

When they got to the bar, she ordered a Kamikaze. She wasn't entirely sure what was in the cocktail, but the name sounded full of alcohol, and deadly, which was good.

Chelsea ordered a Pernod, and Laurel, after dithering through the menu, and Karen thinking that if she ordered herbal tea or something she'd have to smack her, settled on a glass of white wine.

"This is fun," she shouted over the music. "Isn't it?"

"Really great," Chelsea said, sounding absentminded. Karen saw that her hands were beneath the level of the bar and immediately made a grab for them, yanking away Chelsea's cell phone before the other woman could stop her.

"No texting," she ordered.

"I was telling David that I won't be home until later. That's all."

"Huh. I've got a few things to say to David myself."

Laurel seemed as though she'd gone to bed in a normal universe and woken up on a different planet where she didn't know the rules. "You're acting a little strange," she finally said in her soft, tentative way.

When Chelsea turned to talk to her in a low voice, no doubt about how Karen was having some kind of breakdown, which she had to consider was a possibility, Karen took the opportunity to finish Chelsea's text and push Send. Overhearing the last of her companions' conversation, which contained the words *complicated* and *confused* she said, "It's not complicated. And I'm not confused."

"Do you want to dance?" a thirty-something guy asked her.

"Yes," she told him. "I would." Then she turned to her companions. "Isn't this better than the Internet?"

Karen loved dancing, she'd forgotten how much.

She was soon joined by her friends. Chelsea danced in a more restrained manner, but you could see that she was comfortable with her body and enjoyed moving in it. Laurel seemed to hear a different song than they did, something softer and more melodic. She floated through the rhythm rather than conforming to it.

Her partner moved over to dance with Chelsea and then a blond boy, for boy was all he was, stared at Karen, dancing his way closer until he said, "You know who you look like?"

"Your mother?"

But he hadn't heard her. "Amy Adams." He considered her for another moment. "With bigger breasts." And he moved closer, dancing as near her as he dared.

"Whose idea was this?" she shouted to Chelsea who drilled her pointer fingers her way in time to the beat.

He was adorable, though, with big blue eyes and a flop of hair. Skin so smooth she doubted he had to shave every day. Still, he was dancing with her and he was cute.

"How old are you?" she asked him.

"Twenty-five." He said it so fast she knew it was a lie.

"I'm too old for you."

"I've been with an older woman before," he said with immense pride.

"Yeah? How old was she? Twenty-six?"

He grinned at her. "You're so sexy. I am really into you right now."

"You are balm to my ego. But I think that girl over there is trying to get your attention."

He glanced behind him at a pretty brunette who was gesturing to him.

"Oh, yeah. Don't move. I'll be back." And he was gone.

He was replaced by a second, older version of himself. This guy was probably thirty. And shaved every day.

"I was watching the way you move," he said as he came up to her as though he had every right to invade her personal space. "You're a very sexy woman."

"So I hear."

"I'm serious. You radiate sex. It's really powerful. I want to take you home and do you, right now." He grabbed her hand and twirled her. She kind of liked the macho way he assumed control of her.

"I'm John."

"Hi, John."

"I'm only in town for a couple of days. What do you say?" There wasn't a lot of finesse in the way he eyed her the way the big bad wolf eyed Little Red Riding Hood but it was nice to know she had options if she wanted nothing but sex.

The gleam in his eye was purely carnivorous and on some deep level she responded. It was nice to be reminded that she was still a desirable woman. She spent so much time obsessing about what was wrong with her and wishing she was taller and thinner that she forgot she'd always drawn male attention.

Keeping a man's attention for a lifetime seemed to be the problem.

She glanced around. Chelsea was making nice to an older man who had "freshly divorced" written all over him, and Laurel was now dancing with the fresh-faced blond kid.

She was suddenly filled with affection for both these women who were here for her, since it was clear neither of them would have chosen to come out dancing if she hadn't made them.

Her partner nuzzled her neck, which she found mildly annoying. Where was the teasing, the finesse, the... Oh, she had to stop thinking about Dex.

"What's your name again?" she asked.

"John." He laughed down at her. "And you have a great ass. You know that, right?"

"Right now, I don't know anything."

He seemed to take that as a come-on rather than what it was: a true expression of how she was feeling, a wail of despair from some deep unexplored part of herself.

"I've got a bottle of scotch in my room. It's open so I can't take it on the plane. Might as well drink it. Come on up."

"Wow," she said. "It's a tempting offer, but I don't think so."

"Why not?"

"I can't leave my friends. But thanks." She pulled away. "Have a nice evening."

"No. Wait. You're so hot. I could make you feel real good. Let me tell you what I'm going to do to you." He tried to kiss her, but she resisted.

"Some other time."

Laurel and Chelsea were as ready to leave as she

was, so they jumped in a cab and headed out into the night.

"You know, that was fun," Chelsea said. "We should hang out more."

"It was fun. Thanks for coming out with me. I needed the company."

"Why don't you stay at our place tonight? There's a very nice guest room. You'd be welcome."

"No, thanks. I'm not good company right now. I think I'll just go home to bed or something."

The cab drew up outside the town house Chelsea shared with her fiancé, David. She opened the door and as she exited leaned in to give Karen a hug. "Be careful about that 'or something.'"

She dropped Laurel off next, and then the cab driver asked, "Where to?"

She opened her mouth to give him her home address. She was certain that's what she intended, but what came out of her mouth was the name of the downtown hotel where Dex was staying.

22

DEX DREAMED he was on a construction site and the crew was really going at it with the hammers. It took him a minute to realize he'd been wakened by pounding. He glanced at the bedside clock and wondered who had visitors at two in the morning?

Another minute went by before he realized it was his door taking the pounding.

No doubt some partiers had the wrong room. He yawned and rolled out of bed, somehow knowing from the intensity of the banging that ignoring whoever was on the other side of his door wasn't an option.

He dragged on the hotel robe and padded barefoot to the door. An eye to the peephole showed him, not partiers, but Karen, dressed to kill.

Even through the distorted lens of the peephole he felt her sensuality. A woman only came banging on a man's door at 2:00 a.m. for one reason. He was hard before he had the door opened.

She didn't tumble in his arms as he'd half expected, or open a coat to show she was naked underneath, a persistent fantasy that she'd never yet fulfilled. She pushed

past him like a dynamo, he could feel her body heat as
she brushed past him and a scent that smelled like sex
and danger.

"I didn't think you were coming," he said on a yawn.
He didn't bother to tell her that he'd waited like a fool
for her to show up until all the ice in the bucket cooling
the champagne had melted. He'd finally called down
to room service for a burger and a beer and watched a
Flyers game on TV.

"I wasn't," she said. "I went out with the girls, but
this guy came on to me on the dance floor. And his
body was the wrong shape and his smell was all wrong.
And all I could think about was that I wanted you."
There was something about the way she wailed that
last line that told him everything he needed to know.
The woman he loved, loved him right back.

Then she did tumble into his arms. Or maybe he
pulled her in, it was impossible to tell.

All he knew was that she was a bundle of heat and
needs and passion and when his mouth closed over hers
it felt right. She tasted right. She smelled right. The
thought of her being with anyone else made him crazy,
but he was also honest enough to admit to himself that
the idea of her being out there, attracting the attention
of other men, and then rejecting them to come here to
him was darkly exciting.

He pushed his hands down the front of her top and
released her breasts, taking them into his mouth, sucking and licking her the way she liked, easing her closer
to the bed. But she didn't want to be eased anywhere.

She reached into his robe and took him into her hand.
Her skin was so hot when she closed over him. Then,
her eyes sparkling with excitement, she pushed the robe

off his shoulders so it fell to the floor and then knelt before him and took him into her mouth.

Oh, if he'd thought her skin was hot it had nothing on her mouth. He wondered if any two people had ever known each other as intimately, had fit together so perfectly, knew so instinctively what the other craved.

She loved him with her mouth, teased him with her tongue, and he let her control him until he was mindless. But being taken by this woman in her crazy mood wasn't good enough.

In some primal part of himself he recognized the need to give as good as he got. Hauling her to her feet, he pushed her backward, angling her so her butt sat on the arm of the maroon-and-blue striped armchair. He stripped off her panties in one practiced motion. He started to lean in, to use his mouth on her as she'd used hers on him, but what he saw in her eyes stopped him.

Slowly, he leaned forward and kissed her. He didn't say the words, not yet. Instead he took her by the hand and led her to the king-size bed. He made love to her as he never had before. Letting his emotions out, through his skin, his mouth, his hands. They were both trembling when they came together.

A slow grin spread over her face. "Whatever you did, do it again."

He smiled at her tenderly. "You never replied to my text. Spend the holidays with me."

"Why would I do that?"

"So we could spend some time together. We could take off and go skiing or spend a few days in the Caribbean. I'd rub suntan lotion on your body and—"

"We're not a couple anymore, Dex."

"Are you sure? I still love you."

She turned her face away from him. "No."

"I never stopped. And when you accused me of cheating I was so angry and so hurt I never fought hard enough for you. For us. Karen, I want another chance."

"I can't deal with this right now," she said, jumping out of bed and grabbing her clothes, pushing them on at random.

"Here's the thing," he said as she pushed her feet into her heels and simultaneously stuffed one arm into her coat sleeve while opening the door with the other hand. "I think you love me, too."

"I—I wish you'd never come back, Dex."

"If you leave me again, I won't come chasing you. Kiki, don't do this."

His answer was the door shutting behind her.

CHELSEA LET HERSELF INTO the town house. The muted buzz of a TV told her where to find David. After watching her friend lose the program today she really needed the calm good sense of the man she loved.

One thing about David, he never went on any psychological roller-coaster rides.

She walked in to find him with a beer in his hand watching the replayed highlights of a Flyers game. She went over and put her arms around his neck. "How you doing?"

"Just sitting here being an emotional cripple. Yourself?"

She eased to sitting beside him on the tasteful couch his designer had picked out before she met him and that she'd made more personal with pillows and a colorful throw.

"Did you have a bad day?"

"No." He glanced at her, looking sort of huffy. "It was fine until around ten tonight."

"What happened at ten?"

"You sent me a text. Remember?"

"Yeah, I sent you a text saying I'd be home late." A horrible feeling gripped her. "Karen wanted to go out with the girls and she's my friend. I went. We didn't have plans or something, did we?" She wasn't one to forget social engagements and besides, they usually checked in with each other during the day. He hadn't mentioned anything when they'd spoken earlier.

"I figured I'd wait until you got home to see if you were drunk or something."

"I had two Pernods. I am not drunk. What is going on?"

"You seriously don't remember?"

"Remember what?"

He pulled out his cell phone and showed her. There was her text. Which she remembered writing. It said, I'll be home late. Eat whatever's in the fridge. That part she remembered perfectly well. Then the message continued. And why don't you man up? Get married like you promised instead of avoiding the issue like a typical male emotional cripple.

She put the phone down on the table. "Ah," she said.

"I don't understand. You know I want to get married. I've tried to set a date about twelve times but you always have an excuse. Everybody at work is starting to piss me off with their offers to help and somebody's cousin who's a photographer and have we decided on the color of ribbon for the freaking pew bows and I don't even know what pew bows are."

"I know, but you see—"

"I wasn't ready last year, and I know how stupid it was of me to pretend to get engaged to you so that I could get a promotion at work. How many times do I have to apologize?"

"You don't have to—"

But there was no point trying to interrupt him. He was on a roll and she got the feeling this was a rant he needed to get out of his system.

"I was blind and so incredibly focused on my career that I forgot what life was about. Then I met you and I was so busy trying not to get married to you that I didn't notice I was falling in love with you and that all I wanted in the world was to be with you forever."

"Oh, David." She felt love and tenderness for this man well inside her.

"But ever since we got engaged for real you've been avoiding the issue of getting married. And now, now that I've practically given up asking you when it would be convenient to marry me, you send me a text like that?" He shook his head, "Just tell me. What do I have to do to make you my wife?"

She stared up at him and thought that the great thing about loving someone was that they could always surprise you, no matter how well you figured you knew them.

"I hurt your feelings."

"You're damn right you hurt my feelings. Who wants to be called an emotional cripple?"

"No. I didn't." She picked up the remote and muted the TV. "I didn't write that part of the text. Karen took my phone away from me. I didn't send you that message. If you'd read it over a second time you'd probably have realized that."

He blinked at her. "Karen wrote it?"

"Yes."

"Karen? The wedding planner?"

"That Karen."

"But— I thought she liked me."

"She does like you. She's going through something with her ex-husband and she was in a crazy mood, not helped by mainlining a couple of drinks called Kamikazes."

He sat down. Still not as close to her as she'd like, but at least they were on the same couch. "So, you didn't write that text."

"No. I don't think you're an emotional cripple." She couldn't resist teasing him a little. "Because I fixed you. You totally used to be an emotional cripple. Now you're not." She leaned over and put her hand over his. "I didn't realize getting married was a big deal to you. I'm sorry."

"Well, it's…a man has certain expectations. If he asks a woman to marry him and she accepts…" He drilled her with his eyes. "I mean for real and not in some bogus fake fiancé way—"

"Right."

"Then he expects that she'll find a weekend in her busy schedule to marry him." He leaned forward, so earnest and eager that her heart went squirmy. "You know, you have to book these places six months in advance and then there's the photographer to book and well, the pew bows."

"I know. I've been putting everything off. I have."

His hands tightened painfully on hers. "Tell me the truth. Are you having second thoughts?"

Her heart began to hammer. "No." She couldn't bear it if he did so she asked very quickly. "Are you?"

"No. I love you. I don't want to wait another half a year to be married to you."

"Are you really stuck on a big wedding?"

"For all I care we could go down to the courthouse and get married on our lunch hour."

"Really?"

"Yeah. Of course. Weddings are for brides." He seemed to consider that statement. "And families."

"And friends." She flopped back on the couch still holding his hands. "I keep thinking I'm too busy to get married but the truth is I am avoiding it. Weddings are starting to become associated with hard work in my mind."

"But I need to seal the deal."

"Seal the deal? What am I? An insurance policy?" As the top salesman for an insurance firm, he had a bad habit of thinking in sales speak.

"Okay, okay. I want to marry you."

She glanced up at David under her lashes thinking that marriage to him was never going to be dull. He had that look in his eye, the one that suggested they'd be naked and she'd be seeing stars before too long. He only had to look at her like that to get her hot. "I might have to try you out first."

David made a sound deep in his throat, part moan, part growl. "You are the sexiest woman on seven continents." He took a fingertip and traced the line of her V-neck silky top that revealed just a hint of cleavage. He trailed the line of her shirt down to where it ended and then nudged the fabric a little farther.

"Yeah?" She felt liquid and sexy and his eyes were getting that heavy-lidded expression that made her melt. She traced her hand up his thigh. "I remember when you tried to pick me up on the street."

"Greatest night of my life," he said.

He picked up the remote, and pushed another button. Music flooded the room. He pulled her gently to her feet and pulled her against him. She closed her eyes and settled her head against his chest, moving with him. He simply led her around the floor, her body pressed to his. He took a lock of hair that had fallen across her cheek and wound it around his index finger. He traced her lips. "You're the sexiest, most beautiful woman I've ever seen." It sounded like he was telling her the truth in his heart.

"Oh, David," she said, and lifted her face for his kiss.

And as he wrapped his arms around her, she realized she was tired of playing games. So she'd have a complicated wedding with parents who hadn't been able to put their bitter divorce behind them, interfering but well-meaning work colleagues and David's parents whom she loved, but who didn't have enough to do now they'd retired. They wanted this marriage so badly they'd offered to pay for it, organize it and host it. She'd found her future mother-in-law knitting yellow baby booties and when she'd claimed they were for a friend, she hadn't quite believed her.

But really, in the big scheme of things, was she going to let all those things stop her from marrying the man she loved?

"Are you sure you can put up with me forever?" she asked him, her head still against his chest where she could hear his heart beating its steady, reliable rhythm.

"Yes. I want to be with you forever. Longer if I can

figure out how that part works." He pulled away long enough to look down into her face. "I love you."

"Let's get married," she said.

23

KAREN CREPT into the kitchen as though she were about to commit a felony. Laurel watched in surprise as she crossed to her side, checking over her shoulder before speaking.

"Where's Chelsea?"

"She said something about driving out to Kennett Square. She went to source mushrooms."

"She drives miles out of town for mushrooms." Karen shook her head. "And I think I'm obsessed with food."

"Did you need her for something? She's got her cell phone with her."

"No. I'm having lunch with her fiancé and I don't want her to know anything about it."

Laurel blinked, pausing from airbrushing clouds onto a sky-blue background to concentrate her full attention. Since Friday when they'd had their girls' night out, Karen had been acting strange. Now she was becoming seriously worried. "You're dating Chelsea's fiancé?"

Karen's laugh was sudden and loud. "No, not that

kind of a date. As if he'd ever look twice at me when he's got Chelsea."

"It's weird they don't get married."

"It's men. They can't commit. They're all like 'too many first dates, Ron.'" She suddenly stopped, looking at Laurel fully for the first time. "Oh, that was rude. I forgot you were one of them. Um, how did your coffee date go?"

Laurel wondered if it was even possible to put into words how that first coffee date had gone, decided it couldn't be done, not without a thesaurus and a lot of time. Besides, their relationship was all so new and special she didn't want to spoil it by talking too soon. She settled on "Fine."

"Really? I wouldn't have thought you two would have much in common. But that's great. Are you seeing him again?"

Laurel was an honest person, but she didn't feel any need to share with Karen that apart from when they were working, she and Ron spent most of their time together. When they'd exhausted themselves making love, sometimes they read together in bed. He'd even taken her to the house he'd inherited from his parents, introduced her to his dog, Beth, and she was helping him make the family home over into his.

After her telling him his ideas were too conservative and him telling her that hers were too wild, they were meeting there tonight with a designer. She was flattered that he wanted her input, but she thought they both knew she'd end up living there one of these days.

Not that he'd said anything, or she had, but sometimes you just knew.

Karen was looking at her, obviously waiting for an answer, but Laurel had discovered the best thing about everyone thinking you were flaky was you had the luxury of taking time before answering. At last, she simply said, "Yes. I'm seeing him again." And taking him a first edition copy of an old Raymond Chandler novel that she'd found in one of the used bookstores near her place.

No doubt Karen hadn't noticed that Ron had removed his profile from the dating site and she suspected he wouldn't be going on many more first dates. Coffee or otherwise.

"Huh. Well, there's no accounting for tastes, no pun intended." And Laurel was left wondering which of them Karen had just insulted.

"Anyhow," Karen continued, "I think it's time I stepped in and had a little talk with the reluctant groom."

"You called him?" Laurel liked Karen, she really did. It was impossible not to, but she was getting the feeling that the wedding planner was going through a phase of some sort that wasn't entirely conducive to helping Chelsea and David find perfect happiness.

"No. He called me."

"Really? What did he want?"

"I don't know, but he's going to get some advice. If he lets that amazing woman get away because he is too scared of commitment, then he's the biggest fool alive. And that's what I plan to tell him."

Laurel never thought of herself as a brave person. She more liked to stay in the background of life and observe, but she cared about Chelsea and she didn't think she could live with herself if she didn't try to protect her from Marriage's Avenging Angel.

"Are you sure this is about David and Chelsea?"

Karen was such a strong woman, always in control.

But as she met Laurel's gaze, the tough attitude collapsed and her eyes filled with emotion. "You mean, am I interfering in other people's business out of some twisted need of my own? I don't think so. Dex has gone back to New York. I doubt I'll be seeing him again."

"Why? What did he do?"

"He told me he loved me." She seemed for a second as though she might cry, but she pulled herself together. "And I walked away. Now he doesn't send me sexy texts anymore and he's back in New York and I… I just want David to understand that he could lose Chelsea if he doesn't stop being so scared of love and marriage."

"Maybe you should call him."

"But I'm seeing him in half an—"

"Not David. Dexter. Maybe you should call him. I don't know, go for counseling or something. You seemed so happy when he was around."

"I think it's too late. Anyhow, today is about Chelsea and David."

"Are you sure Chelsea would want you to—"

"No! Of course she wouldn't. And I don't want Chelsea to know I interfered. That's why I need you to keep her focused on mushrooms or whatever until I get back. Can I trust you to keep it a secret that I'm seeing her man?"

Laurel called on the universe to shore up her courage. "Only if you promise not to make things worse."

"Of course I won't. David loves her. He probably just needs a gentle nudge." She looked at Laurel and her blue eyes started to dance. "With a cattle prod."

DAVID WAS WAITING for her at the restaurant he'd chosen. It was an Italian restaurant halfway between both their offices and the kind of place where neither of them were likely to bump into anyone they knew.

She felt momentarily guilty at meeting Chelsea's fiancé without her knowledge, but she knew she was doing this for the best so she sucked up her courage and went forward. She'd planned to hug him since she'd met David a few times and he'd always been friendly. But he stuck out his hand in a formal way, so she shook his hand instead. Weird.

When the hostess seated them, he asked for a quiet table in the back of the room and her feeling of subterfuge was heightened.

They made small talk over menus but she wasn't really reading what was listed. It was too tempting. When the waitress came for her order she asked for salad. No dressing.

David, of course, went for a rich pasta dish. No doubt there'd be garlic bread. Garlic bread was one of her weaknesses. Maybe this place wasn't the ritziest Italian restaurant on the planet, but it had all the right scents. Garlic and tomato sauce, rich cream and who knew what else? All she knew was that if she breathed in too deep she'd gain a pound.

She needed to think about something else before she called the young woman with the dyed black hair and the nose stud back and changed her order. "I was surprised to get your call," she said.

"I bet." His brows pulled together. "I wasn't sure I was going to call after the other night."

She reached for a bread stick. Snapped it in half, told herself she'd only nibble. "The other night?"

He had really great eyes, and usually they were full of charm, but right now they seemed pretty chilly. "Do you really think I'm an emotional cripple?"

"No. Of course not. I—"

He was looking at her with skepticism all over his face and suddenly that awful night when she'd forced Chelsea and Laurel out dancing came back to her. "Oh. I texted you, didn't I?"

"Yep."

"Did I really call you an emotion—"

"Yep. I thought the text came from Chels. It was pretty intense."

She put her head in her hands. "Oh, David. I'm so sorry. I can't believe I did that. I was a little…" What was the word she was going for here? Oh, yeah, she knew. Where Dex was concerned, it always came back to the same thing. "Crazy."

"I figured drunk, but okay. It probably turned out to be a good thing, Chelsea and I had a long talk that night."

Her guilt lifted slightly. "Oh, thank heaven. I really wasn't myself that night. I hope you'll forgive me."

His eyes were warming already. He seemed like the kind of man who didn't stay mad for long. There was a twinkle in his baby blues when he said, "For a price."

Putting the bread stick down, she reached for her water. "What kind of price?"

"I think I'm beginning to understand why she doesn't want to get married."

"Well, it's good that you—" She glanced up at him, but he didn't look like he was toying with her. "Did you say *she's* the one who doesn't want to get married?"

"Yep."

"But, I thought—"

"I know you did." He paused here as their food arrived. She was so busy thinking she barely noticed the scent of freshly baked garlic bread wafting over her naked greens like a very bad boy trying to corrupt a determined girl.

When their waitress left, he continued. "Last year I was an ass. I know that now, but when I figured out that I love Chelsea and she's the woman I want to spend my life with, I thought we'd just do it, you know?"

"Get married, you mean?"

"Right. Instead, she's got one excuse after another."

"Chelsea is the one dragging her feet on the wedding?" She felt she needed to clarify this fact once more.

"Yes."

When had she ever been so wrong about anything? Karen always prided herself on being so smart about people. "Wow. I had no idea."

"You want a piece?" He offered her the plate of garlic bread which she'd been eyeing hungrily. She should resist but right now she needed comfort food.

"Sure, thanks."

While she bit into the garlic bread, enjoying it so much she almost moaned, he said, "I'm giving her all the time and space I can because, obviously, I wasn't exactly the most stand-up guy when we were engaged the first time. But that wasn't real. This is real."

He looked so sincere she could see his love for Chelsea shining out of his eyes. *This,* she thought, *this is why I do what I do.* Bringing people together and helping them start their lives together with the most perfect wedding ever.

She leaned forward. "Okay, I was wrong about you. Instead of apologizing again, I'd like you to tell me, what can I do to help?"

"I was hoping you'd say that. Here's the problem.

Chelsea feels like weddings are part of her work life, plus her folks aren't exactly the poster parents for divorced couples with families. Then there are my parents who are so eager for this wedding, it's sort of scary, and everybody at my work wants to be involved. Honestly, I think she's freaked out."

"I can imagine how that could feel."

"The other night, after we talked and I told her how much I wanted to marry her, she suddenly said, 'Okay, let's get married.' But I could tell she was doing it for me."

"David, she loves you, I'm sure of it—"

"Oh, yeah, it's not that. I'm sure she loves me, too. It's the wedding that's making her crazy."

"So, what are you going to do?"

"We're going to elope. And I need your help."

She frowned. "I don't think I've ever planned an elopement."

"I know it probably sounds insane, but I want to surprise her. If I suggest we elope she'll argue with me, she won't want to let down her parents and mine and all our friends and coworkers."

Karen thought about how much she'd been looking forward to planning Chelsea and David's wedding and knew exactly what he was referring to.

"You're right. She will. So what do you need me to do?"

He looked boyishly excited as he pulled out brochures. "Here are three resorts that do weddings. What do you think?"

He shoved them across the table at her. All featured crystal water oceans, beaches, weddings with tropical sunsets pictured in the background. She pushed them all back across the table. "These are all really beautiful, but

I don't know, David. I think she'd want to get married in Paris."

"Paris?"

"Yes."

"But the weather's so crummy there this time of year."

"It's Paris. Who cares?" She glanced up at him. "Anyhow, it's your honeymoon. When are you going to be outside?"

"True. And they do have some incredible hotels there."

"Yep, you could stay at George V or Crillon. Oh, and think of the restaurants. She could eat in all the best places, restaurants she couldn't afford when she was living in Paris and studying." Her enthusiasm built as she thought of all the positive aspects of Paris as an elopement destination. "She could have her good friend give her away, what's his name? The one she met in cooking school."

"Phillipe?"

"That's the one. Then after a few days in Paris maybe you could go somewhere in the Mediterranean. That's what I think she'd like. But, you know, it might be better if you asked her. A wedding is an important part of a woman's life. If you surprise her and get it wrong, her memories will always be a little bit tainted."

He shoved the brochures back into his pocket. "I wish you weren't so right. I'll talk to her. Paris—why didn't I think of that?"

She crunched some salad, still in planning mode. "Maybe we could have a simple reception when you get back? So the parents and friends can still be part of your celebration. I know I'd like that."

"Thanks, Karen. That's a great idea."

He pulled out his BlackBerry and made a notation. Then he glanced up.

"How do you say *I do* in French?"

She and Dexter had talked about going to Paris. Well, doing all of Europe. She'd never been and Dex had promised to show her all the sights. She doubted she'd ever go now.

"Oui," she told David. "Whatever anyone asks you, just say, *Oui."*

24

"MAYBE ANOTHER I-beam," Dex suggested to the construction foreman as they stood contemplating the fact that the Philadelphia hotel's structure had a few weaknesses they were uncovering as the renovation began.

In his experience there were always unforeseen issues in a building this old, but with the wonders of modern technology and building materials, most could be fixed while still maintaining the architectural integrity.

"Yeah. I was thinking the same thing."

"Then we could use some of the reclaimed brick—"

"So you are still in town," a cool female voice hailed him.

He turned. "Sophie? How did you get in here?"

She smiled at him. Nodded to the foreman. "Never doubt the abilities of a tenacious woman."

Since she had a look in her eye that suggested he didn't care to have a bunch of construction guys hear their conversation, he said, "How 'bout I buy you a coffee?"

"Why don't you?"

He gave the foreman a few instructions and then left with Sophie on his arm and a wary feeling in his gut.

She waited until they were out of earshot before saying, "I haven't seen you since Christmas. You don't return calls."

"I'm busy."

"I had my last wedding planning meeting today, and it was weird without you."

He'd known it, of course, since Sophie had e-mailed him the date and texted him and left a phone message. He grabbed his thick coat and held the door for her to exit. "How's Karen?"

"She looks pale. And like she's not getting enough sleep. Sort of like you look. When I walked in for our meeting, she definitely was hoping you'd be there. I could tell she was disappointed you weren't."

"Like I said, I'm busy with work. Besides, the wedding's all planned. You don't need me. Karen's fantastic at what she does."

"I know. I like you both being there, that's all. I'm used to it. And you have good ideas."

He led her into the closest coffee shop and when they were both settled with lattes, he said, "You didn't come here to tell me I missed a meeting. What's up?"

"Honestly, I want to make sure you'll be at the wedding. Andrew's counting on you as his best man. If you're going all high school on me and can't be in the same room with your ex then I need to know about it."

"Of course I'll be there for the wedding. I'm looking forward to it."

"Good."

"Aren't you?"

Sophie shrugged her slender shoulders. "I guess. Mostly I just miss Andrew. I wish he were here."

"I'm sure he feels the same way."

"He does. In fact, he went ahead and booked me a flight to Italy for the week before the wedding."

"Really?"

"Yep. I'll be able to relax and spend some time with the man I love. Then we'll fly home for the wedding. It'll be so much better than hanging around waiting. And this way, I don't spend Valentine's Day on my own. You know?"

"Sure."

She sipped her drink. "She asked after you, by the way."

A flicker of hope stabbed at his chest. "Really."

"Yep. She asked how you were. And she'd really dressed up for the meeting."

"She always dresses well."

"It was a dress designed to get her man back. A woman can tell these things."

He thought this woman was too filled with romantic notions to be a reliable witness, but he appreciated the effort. "All she has to do is call me," he said. He'd been waiting for that call for so many weeks that he knew now it wouldn't come.

He'd been wrong about Karen. She didn't love him enough to battle back her demons. And the loss of her for the second time was more painful than he'd imagined possible.

As bittersweet as it would be to see his ex-wife again, he was all but counting the days.

They finished their coffees and Sophie gave him a big hug as she was leaving. "I'm telling you, she misses you."

He hugged her back. "Have fun in Italy. Tell Andrew hi."

"See you at the wedding."

"SOME DAYS I FEEL like I was put on earth to help people celebrate true love," Karen said to Laurel, in a particularly good mood since the Vanderhooven wedding was today and everything, including the weather, seemed to be smiling on the event.

"Which is weird considering you don't believe in love."

"Yes, I do."

Laurel had changed subtly over the past weeks. Karen couldn't put her finger on what it was, but the woman seemed more outspoken than she used to be. And she had a certain glow about her as though she knew all the secrets of the universe. It was both attractive and, to someone who felt that all the secrets were forever hidden from her, kind of annoying.

The cake creator was working on the finishing touches to Sophie Vanderhooven's cake and it was, perhaps, her greatest achievement yet.

"That is so beautiful," Karen said, pleasure gushing through her. The cake was tiered in traditional style but Laurel had taken the garden theme and made a whimsical, tiered garden, with a twist. It was a Tuscan garden complete with olive trees, lemon trees and cascades of purple bougainvillea, all done in icing.

Just looking at the cake made her happy.

She'd even dressed to match the garden theme in a dark green suit, the color of rose leaves, with a white silk camisole underneath and brand-new shoes to match.

Everything was on track for a wedding that would be as close to perfect as any wedding can be. Of course, she'd have to see Dexter again, but she planned to stay as far in the background as possible and out of his way.

Then, after today, she'd never have to see him again. If the thought brought more pain than she'd imagined, she knew she'd get used to it. Experience had taught her that heartbreak dulled over time.

While she was admiring the cake, and trying to ignore the racket of Chelsea's crew preparing the food that would be served at the reception later, Chelsea came up behind them. There was a sparkle in her eyes and a glow that had nothing to do with cosmetics.

Laurel glanced up, gazed at Chelsea for a few moments and then went back to her task of piping tiny green leaves. "When are you leaving?" she asked.

Chelsea put her hands on her hips and tried to pout. "I thought I was going to surprise you. How did you know David and I are eloping to Paris?"

"Your fiance's not very good at keeping secrets. He's getting us to organize a reception for when you get back."

"Yeah, I wanted to talk to you about that." She tied her white apron tighter around her slim waist. "Who's catering the reception?"

"You are," Karen informed her.

"What?" She looked both horrified and relieved.

"Come on, you know you wouldn't be happy if we got one of your competitors to cater your reception, so we have a plan. Don't we, Laurel?"

"That's right. You pick out what you want and Anton and I will manage your staff. You know Anton can make your recipes almost as good as you can yourself."

"Well, his puff pastry is excellent, but he has a tendency to put too much salt in his sauces. I should—"

"Relax, that's what you should do." Karen took her friend by the shoulders and gave her a little shake. "We all love you. We want to do this for you. After you're back and married and there's no stress."

The women exchanged a quick hug. "Thanks," Chelsea said. Then, as though she couldn't help herself, added, "I'm so happy."

"You should be. You deserve it." Since such sentiments threatened to make both women damp-eyed, Chelsea turned to Laurel and asked, "What kind of cake are you making me?"

"The Eiffel tower."

"Isn't that a little—I don't know. Unlike you? It's so obvious."

Laurel chuckled and adjusted a tiny lemon on a tiny lemon tree. "Sometimes I surprise even myself. But I thought about it and the Eiffel Tower is the perfect metaphor for the relationship between you and David. It's strong and yet elegant, iconic and unforgettable."

"Wow. Thanks."

"I think most people associate the Eiffel tower with romance and Paris, obviously, where you trained and where you're getting married." She bent close to her cake to nudge a purple petal. "I can change it if you want."

"No," Chelsea said. "You are right as always. It is perfect."

"When are you leaving?" Karen asked.

"Whenever you can do without me for a couple of weeks."

"How does Sunday sound?"

She and David had already planned the dates, but she didn't feel any need to share that with Chelsea.

"Really?" she squealed. "You can do without me so fast?"

"It's all arranged."

Chelsea put a hand on her belly and breathed deeply. "I can't believe I'm finally getting married after being engaged twice. To the same man."

"I know," Karen said. "It's so great."

Anton's voice interrupted them. "Chels, can you check this pomegranate infusion? I'm not sure it's thick enough."

The wedding was taking place at the bride's aunt's estate, one of the grand old homes still remaining in the Main Line suburbs.

After checking that everything was running smoothly on the food end, Karen grabbed her binder, her pack of supplies and headed for her car.

She arrived to the usual scene of organized chaos. Flowers were arriving right on schedule, her delivery guys were carrying in stacks of chairs for the ballroom where the actual wedding would take place.

In order to convey the garden theme for a winter wedding, the floral designer, Bertrand, had brought in fresh flowers by the truckload. The effect made her smile. To see pots of daffodils, irises, tulips and hyacinths sending out their evocative fragrance, and tubs of roses arranged in formation to give the idea that the indoor space was a garden of different beds representing different seasons.

The designer was directing the placing of pots of chrysanthemums himself. Even though she'd seen a sketch of the design she was still enthralled by the real thing.

"You have outdone yourself, Bertrand," she cried.

"I think so," he said. Bertrand was not a man who underrated his own talents. He came forward to greet her, an urbane man with a goatee and wearing a black silk blazer, to kiss her on both cheeks. "By holding the ceremony in an ever-blooming garden we suggest that love is always in season."

Trite, perhaps and, given the national divorce rate with a slightly higher than fifty percent chance of being true, she still loved the notion.

"It's gorgeous, better even than I'd imagined."

He nodded, not at all surprised that he'd impressed her yet again. But then with the prices he charged, he should be impressive.

She slipped back into the ballroom after the floral crew had finished, as she always did, checking that everything was perfect.

As she walked among the rows of chairs, adjusting this one, moving a potted plant a half an inch that way, her gaze fell on a pot of yellow roses, very like the ones she'd carried at her own wedding. As she walked forward to touch a soft, creamy yellow petal, she felt an odd peace steal over her.

Love did matter.

Couples every day were brave enough to make a commitment before friends and family, cynics and romantics, and do their best to make a go of it. She took a moment to silently wish Sophie and Andrew success in their married life.

She'd been alone, with two hundred empty chairs and hundreds of blooming plants representing the four seasons, from snowdrops to chrysanthemums and even a tub or two of holly. Suddenly, she knew she wasn't alone anymore. She felt a presence.

Turned.

Dexter was standing before her in his tux, and in that moment she was transported back to her wedding day. They were both older now, but her heart still jumped painfully to see him in that outfit, so reminiscent of the day she'd promised to love him forever, for better or worse.

Trouble was, nobody had explained that the worse might include infidelity. She'd put up with a great deal, but after living with a father who couldn't keep his pants zipped, and a mother who made excuses, she knew she couldn't repeat that pattern.

She forced her racing pulse to slow—and when that didn't work, she hoped he wouldn't notice his effect on her and walked calmly forward.

"Place looks great," he said. His eyes warmed as they looked her over. "And so do you, Kiki. I always liked that color on you."

"Thanks. This is my favorite part," she admitted. "These last few hours when everything's all excitement and coming together into the most perfect wedding."

"Do you ever get tired of it?"

"Never. Every wedding is unique. Every story is theirs to be written."

"Seen the bride yet?"

"No." A tiny frown tried to settle but she wouldn't let it. There was time yet. "She should be here any minute to start getting changed. How 'bout you? Seen the groom?"

"No. I think he's coming straight from the airport."

She shook her head. "I really hate it when people cut the time that fine. What if the plane's late?"

"Relax," he said soothingly, which was easy for him to say when he wasn't the one planning the wedding. "Everything's going to be fine."

"I'm sure you're right."

"I've—" The door opened and he stepped back. She wondered what he'd been going to say. *I've missed you?* It's what she would have said if she had the guts. She'd missed him. Seeing him again only reminded her of how badly.

Sophie's aunt entered the space. "Sorry to interrupt, Karen, but the wedding party seems to be arriving."

"Sophie and Andrew?"

"Not yet. Only the minor royalty so far."

Bridesmaids and groomsmen streamed in the big front doors and Karen sent them to their assigned rooms and still there was no bride or groom. "Where's Sophie?" she asked the maid of honor.

"She's coming in with Andrew, I think."

"You mean she's picking him up at the airport? I specifically told her to—"

"No. She's there. With him. In Italy. They're coming in on the same plane."

"But—" There was no point telling the poor maid of honor that the bride wasn't following agreed-on protocol. "Never mind," she said with her reassuring smile. "They've got plenty of time."

She was slightly less reassured when the guests began arriving. Sophie's aunt sent her increasingly questioning glances and she could only reply with an uplifting of the shoulders. She had no idea where the bride was. Sophie wasn't answering her cell phone nor the groom his.

To get away from the melee, Karen walked into the kitchen where Chelsea was overseeing food and drink and David was serving as a bartender as he sometimes did in order to be with his fiancée on a big night.

He was exuberant and surprised Karen by picking her up and swinging her in a circle. "I got her to commit. Did you see that?"

She laughed. "I did."

He was so happy it was impossible not to laugh. "Oh, David," Chelsea said, her apron covering one of her designer Paris dresses. "Stop goofing around and slice lemons or something useful."

"Henpecked already," he complained, before heading off to do as he was bid.

"Coming through," Laurel's voice could be heard, louder and more commanding than usual.

Laurel was bringing in her cake. This was always a tense time for her as one slip and fall meant that days of hard work were lost and the wedding would be minus one cake. To Karen's surprise, Ron was with her, helping. "Ron, hi," she said, surprised.

"Hello, Karen," he said, as though he was to be found in the back kitchen of all her weddings. Whatever, she had no time to visit.

"Okay, I've got the table all set up ready for the cake. Follow me." She cleared the way and between them they got the cake safely stowed in the large formal dining room. Laurel fussed with it a bit until the confectionary garden was once again perfect.

Ron stepped back to watch Laurel, and she bet he didn't even realize he was smiling like a lovestruck fool.

He was dressed as neatly as always but somehow he appeared more casual. She guessed it was because his entire attitude was so much more relaxed.

And then it hit her like a bolt of lightning. There were only the three of them in the large room. She said, "Ron, would you mind going into the kitchen and bringing me a pair of scissors?"

"I'd be happy to," he said, and left.

"What do you need scissors for?" Laurel asked.

She waited until he was out of the room. "I don't. I wanted to get you alone." It all made sense now, the way Laurel had been so different lately, the glow about her. "You're sleeping with him, aren't you?"

Laurel opened her mouth to reply but it was Chelsea who answered. She'd arrived in time to hear Karen's last words. "Have you just figured that out?" She sounded pretty amused.

"I—I've had other things on my mind. Usually I notice."

"Actually," Laurel said in her soft, diffident way, "he asked me to marry him."

"What?" both women shrieked in unison.

And Laurel—quiet, flaky Laurel—laughed aloud, pulling them both in for a hug. "I never would have met him if it wasn't for you two. I am so happy."

"But it's so fast."

"I know. Honestly, I think I knew the second I saw him."

"Love at first sight. Huh. So it really can happen."

Chelsea nodded. "Happened to me, the first time I saw David. Of course, I was only fourteen at the time and he didn't know I was alive. But I didn't care. I loved him anyway."

At that moment Dexter walked in. Karen looked across the room at him, recalled the first day they'd met, and how she'd taken one look at him and felt as though time had stopped and the world stilled.

"It happened to me, too," she admitted.

25

"WHAT HAPPENED TO YOU, too?" Dex asked.

She ignored his question. "Tell me you have news?"

"I was hoping you'd have some."

She shook her head. "If only the happy couple would show up, this would be a fantastic wedding."

"Don't panic until you have to," Chelsea advised. Her brown eyes were full of sympathy. It was great having a friend like Chelsea. She knew Karen wouldn't worry if there wasn't anything to worry about. "Some things we can't control."

For some reason, they both glanced at Dexter.

Could Chelsea be as aware as she was that where her ex was concerned, she had no control. Not over her feelings, her actions or her heart.

She loved him now, had loved him when she first set eyes on him, would always love him.

"The guests are arriving," Dexter informed her.

But she already knew that. They, at least, were on time.

"I know." There had been no plan for a before

ceremony mingle. This was like a church wedding. Arrive, sit down, ceremony and then reception. The harpist had already started. She could hear the soft strains of music coming from the ballroom.

This had never happened to her before.

Never.

As they stared at each other, twin cell phones began to ring. She reached immediately for hers, saw Dexter do the same.

"It's an incoming text," she said as Laurel and Chelsea watched. As though drawn by some invisible force, David and Ron came into the dining room just as Karen faced her worse nightmare.

"Stuck in Italy," she read aloud. "No way to get back in time. We're going to get married here. We've paid for the wedding so tell everyone to enjoy a great party on us. Sophie."

"My message is shorter but pretty much says the same," Dex added.

KAREN MADE A SOUND she didn't think had ever come out of her mouth before. Could you yell, moan and hyperventilate all at one time? With a little scream thrown in for good measure?

"There's not going to be a wedding," Chelsea said.

Dexter was the only person in the room who didn't seem at all shocked, instead he chuckled. "Good for them," he said.

Finding an outlet for the torrent of emotions swamping her nervous system, Karen swung on him. "Good for them? What are you talking about? I planned a wedding around a bride and groom."

But Dexter simply looked at her for a long moment, a slow smile spreading across his face. How he could

be happy in this time of her worst professional humili-
ation, she couldn't even imagine.

"And all those people out there have traveled a long
way to enjoy a wedding," Dexter said. He glanced
around, spotted a bouquet of cut flowers on a side table,
broke off a yellow rosebud and began stuffing it into
his top buttonhole. "They gave up their Saturdays, got
dressed up."

Chelsea regarded him with interest. "Yes, they
have, it would be a real shame to disappoint them,"
she agreed.

"I'll have to tell them," Karen said, feeling stunned
and stupid. And why, oh why was Dex sticking flowers
in his lapel at a time like this?

Laurel, who'd quietly watched Dex, seemed to have
caught the bug and she'd abandoned her cake to choose a
selection of blooms from the bouquet. "I need a kitchen
towel," she said urgently to Chelsea. "And some ribbon.
Do we have anything in green?"

"What are you lunatics doing?" Karen demanded.

Dex walked forward, laughter deep in his eyes, and
an emotion so strong it made her pulse pound in spite
of the fact that she had really important things to do
here. He reached for her hands.

"I love you, Karen. In front of all these witnesses,
I swear to you that I have always loved you. I never
was unfaithful to you, never could be. You're my muse,
my insanity, the thorn in my side and the woman I
dream about at night and want to wake up to every
morning."

He laughed as her mouth opened and closed a few
times but nothing came out.

"Come on, Kiki. Accept the truth. You let your in-
securities get in the way of the best thing that ever

happened to either of us. What say you give us another chance?"

"But, I can't just—"

"Seems to me," Chelsea said, helping Laurel tie her makeshift bouquet, "that a good wedding planner should be prepared for every eventuality, including supplying a bride and groom if the original pair go missing."

"But I—"

"What, Kiki? You what?" Dexter was still holding her hands, still looking at her with his heart in his eyes and she knew.

Crazy, with no way to prove anything, she knew.

"Oh, Dex, are you sure?"

"I'm game if you are."

Strains of harp music penetrated the dining room as the door opened and Sophie's aunt came in looking as distracted as a seventy-year-old society matron can look. "The guests appear to be getting restless," she said.

Chelsea moved to the woman to speak to her quietly since Karen only had eyes for Dexter. "But I'm impossible. I'm jealous and neurotic and a perfectionist."

"I know."

"And I'll never get any taller. And probably not a lot thinner. I'll probably gobble up that entire cake and get fat."

"I love you exactly the way you are."

Tears filled her eyes. "Do you, Dex? Do you really?"

Instead of answering her with words, he leaned in and kissed her with passion and warmth. Felt like all the answer she needed.

She nodded, decision made.

Then, as everyone in the room was looking at her, she did what she did best. Planned a wedding.

"Chelsea? I'll need you to be my maid of honor."

"I'm touched and I accept." Chelsea removed her apron and looked as chic as any bridesmaid could in her Paris gown.

"Best man?" Dex asked David.

"Happy to help. I'm David by the way." The men shook hands.

"But who's going to walk me down the aisle?"

Ron stepped forward. "I would be honored, as a friend who thinks the world of you, to walk you down the aisle."

"But Laurel? You'll have to be a bridesmaid. I can't leave Laurel out."

"I'm not really dressed for it." They all looked at her in one of her usual flowing numbers and Karen thought she'd never looked better.

"You're perfect."

"What would you like me to do?" the aunt asked, seeming much less hysterical about this change of plans than Karen would have imagined.

"Perhaps you could make an announcement," Dex said. "If you're up to it."

"I suppose it's no more complicated than speaking to the Ladies' Auxiliary," she informed him tartly.

"Then let's go."

He held her hand tightly and they walked to the double doors that led to the conservatory.

Sophie's aunt opened the door and two hundred faces turned to look. Some were bored, some irritated and some simply enjoying the music and the day.

Dexter spoke to her in a low voice and she repeated

the words, putting her own spin on them, naturally, to the rather stunned looking congregation.

"Dear friends," she said, every inch the grand lady. "I've got some rather surprising news for you. My niece and her fiancé were unable to fly back from Italy in time for today's ceremony."

There were a few startled cries and an immediate rustle of comment and shuffling. But a congregation of two hundred restless and confused wedding-goers were no match for a woman who'd been a top society matron for decades. She simply raised her voice.

"I know it's unfortunate, but I promised you a wedding in this house today, and a wedding you shall have."

She waited another moment for the latest batch of murmurs to die down. "Many of you know Dexter Crane, if not personally, then by reputation. He's a dear friend of the family and I'm delighted to help him celebrate his wedding to Philadelphia's favorite wedding planner, Karen Petersham, whom many of you know personally or certainly by reputation.

"Karen and Dexter would like your support and congratulations as they celebrate their marriage here, today."

"Rings," Chelsea whispered urgently. "You don't have rings."

Karen had never been more glad that she always had emergency supplies. She slipped off the gold band she always wore on these occasions, kissed it quickly for good luck, then passed it to David, Dexter slipped off the signet ring he always wore and followed her lead, kissing it quickly before passing that to David.

The aunt took one look at the homemade bouquet and shook her head. She walked over to where a gaggle of confused young women in blue bridesmaid dresses stood and took the bridal bouquet from the maid of honor and handed it to Karen. "Something borrowed."

She then took the heirloom pearls from her own neck and looped them around Karen's. Who was so surprised she blinked. The older woman's eyes crinkled when she smiled. "I wore these on my wedding day. They've been worn by all the brides in my family, and we've all enjoyed very long, successful marriages."

Karen glanced at Dex in panic, then back at the woman. "But Dex and I were married before and it didn't work out."

"Well, whatever foolish mistakes you made before, don't make them again," she told Karen quite forcibly. Then she surveyed her once more. "Right, that's something old, something borrowed, your clothing's obviously new. That just leaves something blue."

"I'm actually wearing blue underwear," Karen said, feeling a little foolish.

"Excellent foresight." The woman nodded briskly. "Now who is going to walk you down the aisle?"

"I've offered, ma'am," Ron informed her.

"Good. Now," she motioned to Dex and David, "you two skedaddle up to the front, then I'll take my seat and motion to the harp to begin. Oh, and you'd better give the minister your full names so he doesn't muff it up." Then she beamed at them both. "Good luck, my dears."

It was perhaps the oddest wedding party Karen had ever been a part of. Six confused young women in designer blue bridesmaid gowns trooped up the makeshift aisle, followed by Laurel and Chelsea both stylish in their own ways, but very different from the other attendants. Then Karen followed on Ron's arm, in her green suit and the most glorious bouquet of flowers. The pearls were warm around her neck, warm with tradition and generations of successful brides.

She wouldn't have worn them if she'd thought she'd break the tradition, but she knew she wouldn't. She and Dex had broken faith with each other once. They wouldn't do it again.

Of that she was certain.

When she walked down the aisle, before a congregation of people who seemed as delighted to celebrate her wedding as they would have been to celebrate Sophie's, she felt a connection with all the women who'd dared to believe in love, dared to make a commitment.

Her gaze rose and she met Dex's, his eyes so warm and full of promise.

And love.

"Dearly beloved," the minister began and she looked at Dexter and thought how dearly beloved he was to her.

The service, so unexpected, so perfect, could have been designed with them in mind. Then she realized that Sophie had pretty much left it to Dex and Karen to plan her wedding.

No wonder they'd planned the perfect wedding for themselves.

When the minister said, "You may kiss the bride," Dexter took her in his arms and kissed her, managing to be both decorous and passionate. As he pulled away, he held her for a moment.

"We'll do better, this time, Kiki."

"We'll do better, Dex," she promised. "We will."

* * * * *

WHAT HAPPENS
IN VEGAS...
KIMBERLY LANG

To Shelley Visconte, MA, LPC, LMFT and soon-to-be PhD—I'm so proud of you and terribly impressed by that alphabet soup behind your name, but the letters that make me the proudest are the ones you've had all along: BFF.

Kimberly Lang hid romance novels behind her textbooks in school and even a Master's programme in English couldn't break her obsession with dashing heroes and happily ever after. A ballet dancer turned English teacher, Kimberly married an electrical engineer and turned her life into an ongoing episode of *When Dilbert Met Frasier*. She and her Darling Geek live in beautiful North Alabama with their one Amazing Child—who, unfortunately, shows an aptitude for sports.

Visit Kimberly at www.booksbykimberly.com for the latest news—and don't forget to say hi while you're there!

CHAPTER ONE

THAT WAS AN ACTUAL mirrored disco ball spinning over a lighted dance floor. Hundreds of sweaty bodies crowded the dance floor, moving to a techno dance mix, and the bass line thumped like a heartbeat. This club—The Zoo—had strobe lights, LED-lit jungle vines hanging from the ceiling and zebra-striped furniture. This place took tacky to a whole new level.

And Evie Harrison loved it. In fact, she loved everything about Las Vegas: the neon lights, the over-the-top, let-it-all-hang-out attitude, the sheer unapologetic gaudiness of the entire city.

Las Vegas wasn't Dallas, that was for sure, and *that* made Evie love Vegas all the more.

"Wanna dance, gorgeous?"

Evie's eyes watered at the alcohol exhaled in her face as the offer was made. "No, but thanks. I'm waiting on some-one."

Thankfully, her would-be dance partner was still in the "happy drunk" stage, and he only shrugged as he moved one table over, presumably with the same question.

The truth was, she *would* like to dance. But hitting the dance floor alone wasn't an option. Not that she cared who saw her or what they thought—the joy of anonymity was part of what brought her to Vegas in the first place—but a woman dancing alone would bring every drunk guy in the bar immediately into her personal space, and she couldn't guarantee they'd all be as easily rebuffed as the last one.

A cocktail waitress with tiger ears on her head and whiskers painted across her cheeks picked up the empty glass off the table. "Can I get you something?" she shouted over the music.

"A vodka tonic," Evie replied, as her tiny silver purse began to dance across the table from the vibration of the cell phone inside. She pulled out the phone and looked at the number displayed on the screen.

Will.

There was no way in hell she was answering that. The phone quit vibrating as the call went to voice mail, and Evie noted it wasn't the first time her brother had called tonight. A quick scroll through the missed-call log showed this was the fourth time in the last two hours Will had called. She was busted.

She'd left Will a message at his office telling him she was leaving town. He wasn't supposed to get it until Monday morning. The workaholic butthead must've checked his messages already.

She would not feel guilty. She was twenty-five years old—even if Will still thought she was a wayward teenager—and she didn't need her brother's permission to leave town for the weekend.

Her drink arrived at the same time as a text from Sabine. *Going to casino @ Bellagio with Toby. Don't wait up.* The last sentence was unnecessary; she'd recognized the look in Bennie's eyes when she'd left thirty minutes ago and known their girls' night out was officially over.

She was a little disappointed, but at least Bennie had dropped everything to come to Vegas with her last night when she asked.

And honestly, being alone in Vegas sure beat being in Dallas at the moment. Being *anywhere* beat being at home right now.

So she lost her patience and said a few things at that brunch she shouldn't have. Evie frowned into her drink. If that witch from the *Dallas Lifestyles* gossip column hadn't been standing right there minding everyone *else's* business, no one would have ever known. But *no,* the whole embarrassing thing got prime treatment on page three yesterday morning.

She'd apologized to the Dallas Beautification Committee's president *and* doubled the amount of the company's donation to make up for implying that new benches in the city's parks weren't equally as important as curing cancer or feeding the hungry.

No one reported *that* in the paper. No, they were too busy getting as much ink as possible out of her big mouth. Again. Then Will had jumped on her case about it, and she'd gotten a nice long talking-to from Uncle Marcus—*again*—about not embarrassing the family—*again*—but neither of *them* was sitting through endless brunches and endless speeches just to be the smiling face that presented a check on behalf of HarCorp International.

Why had she even bothered going to college? A trained monkey could do her job. Hell, a *well*-trained monkey might manage not to make the paper while doing so.

So what if Will was all bent out of shape that she was AWOL? It wouldn't be the first time he'd wanted to strangle her, and it probably wouldn't be the last time, either.

Her phone vibrated again. This time it was Gwen's number. Did Will honestly think she'd answer a call from his wife's phone when she wasn't taking calls from him? How dumb did he think she was?

She made a face at the phone before she tucked it back into her purse. With Bennie off with her new friend, Evie reassessed her options for the rest of the evening. She could be good and go back to the hotel, but that defeated the entire purpose of running away from home in the first place. She just needed a time-out from her life, the chance to have some fun without worrying everything she did would end up in the papers.

That ad campaign for Las Vegas claimed What Happens in Vegas, Stays in Vegas. That sounded fantastic.

It was time to go find something to do.

Whoever designed this club should be shot. It *was* possible to take a theme too far. And if they were aiming for a zoo theme, why on earth were jungle vines hanging from the ceiling?

Nick Rocco mentally tallied up how much it would cost to completely gut and refurbish the interior of The Zoo and added it to the total cost.

If he bought The Zoo—and that was still an if—he'd have to close it completely during renovations. But it was in a prime location, and a big, splashy, grand reopening might give the club a boost and added publicity. Any loss from the closure *could* be recouped if he handled the reopening properly.

Even with the added cost and delay, adding The Zoo to his collection of properties made good business sense. He'd also readily admit it gave him no small sense of satisfaction to purchase a place where he'd once mopped floors and tended bar. Even if it hadn't been called The Zoo back then.

Nick made a practice of visiting any potential purchases during business hours before making firm offers to get a true feel for their potential. And any potential problems. That's why he was here on a Friday night, trying to blend in with the clientele.

The dance floor heaved with bodies, most of the low sofas and chairs were occupied, and the waitresses and bartenders were moving at a fast clip. It wasn't packed, but it wasn't dead, either. If The Zoo could pull in this much business as is, a makeover and a fresh launch could turn it into a gold mine.

Kevin O'Brian, who handled much of the day-to-day business and promotions at all of Nick's clubs, returned from his reconnaissance mission and joined him at the bar.

"Well?" Nick shouted over the thumping bass line.

"Other than the occasional drunk-and-disorderly, the cops aren't required to come by very often. I asked around, and no one seems to be picking up tricks or selling anything this place isn't licensed for." Kevin had the kind of friendly, good-ol'-boy personality that made gathering that kind of behind-the-scenes information easy. People opened up to Kevin without any effort on his part, but Nick himself didn't have the patience—or Kevin's unassuming frat-boy looks—at his disposal. The ability to play good cop/bad cop was one of the secret weapons in their business arsenal. Kevin was a valuable asset to Nick's business—as well as his oldest friend. "You'll need to fire that DJ, though."

That got his attention; Kevin rarely weighed in on staffing issues. "Why? You think he's—"

"No. His taste in music sucks." Kevin grinned and motioned for the bartender to bring him another beer. The blonde delivered it with a smile and winked at Kevin as she pocketed the tip. "Keep her, though. I like her."

"You're assuming I'm going to make the deal."

"You know you are. I'd bet this beer you've already figured how much it's going to cost you to expand the dance floor and pull down those god-awful vines."

Nick shrugged, acknowledging nothing, but Kevin knew him too well. They'd grown up together in one of the toughest parts of Las Vegas, yet unlike so many other of their childhood friends, they'd managed to get out of the circular grind of poverty and drugs. Luck *had* been involved—he'd helped fund his first major club purchase with poker winnings—but it was their common desire to escape that past that bonded them together in the hard work of the climb out of the Vegas projects to UNLV and finally to the top of the food chain.

"So, we're done now?" In the old days, Kevin would just be gearing up, but Lottie had put a stop to his partying ways.

"Go home to your wife. I'm going to stay a little longer and see how the crowd changes after the shows let out."

"You could *try* to have some fun, you know. It wouldn't kill you. You know what they say about 'All work and no play…'"

"Keeps us in the black?" Nick challenged.

"I know the books as well as you do. You don't need another club to stay in the black. You're just buying this one because you *can*."

"And that, my friend, *is* fun."

"You're twisted. Look around—there's a lot of pretty girls here tonight…." Kevin raised his eyebrows suggestively. "I'm sure any of them would love to help you rediscover the meaning of fun."

Nick hadn't picked up a woman in a bar in years. Hooking up with a party girl out for a good time was just asking for trouble he didn't need. "Go home."

"Gone." And he was.

Nightclubs weren't Nick's idea of a place to have a good time—possibly because he'd spent too many years working in them, ensuring everyone else did. He scanned the crowd, making plans and evaluating.

Two men seemed to be having words over a small red-headed woman's attentions. From the posturing, Nick knew exactly what was coming, and he left his spot at the bar rail.

He didn't quite make it in time. The blond-haired one pushed the other one back, causing him to stumble backward into the crowd and crash into a woman behind him. Nick reached for the woman as she fell, catching her before she hit the table.

She slammed into him, her weight landing in his arms as

her feet nearly went out from under her. Something cold sloshed down his chest as he tightened his grip and turned her away from the combatants. A second later, a burly bouncer pushed past and put himself between the men, effectively stopping the fight by virtue of size and scowl.

The scuffle ended before it really began, and the two men were escorted to the door by security with the redhead trailing behind a moment later. The speed and ease with which the bouncers handled the problem impressed Nick, and he made a mental note to be sure to keep them on staff.

Looking down at the woman sprawled in his arms, he asked, "Are you okay?" as he helped her regain her balance.

The woman pushed dark auburn hair out of her face and tugged her dress back into place, calling his attention to the length of leg exposed by a tiny silver skirt and the gentle swell of her cleavage over a black top. His body seemed to remember the feel of those breasts pressed against his chest and his skin warmed a fraction.

"I think so," she replied, before she lifted green eyes to his and smiled. "Thank you for the save."

The smile lit up her face like the Vegas strip, drawing attention to her slightly exotic bone structure and causing something in him to stir.

"Oh, my God, you're wearing my drink. I'm so sorry." Her hands were on him, brushing at his chest and sending jolts through him as they did. *Damn. What was wrong with him?*

"It's fine."

"It shouldn't stain, but I'll pay your dry…" She trailed off as he grabbed her hands and held them away from his chest. "Um…your dry-cleaning bill." She slid her hands out of his grasp and extended one to him. "I'm Evie."

"Nick." Her hand disappeared inside his larger one, but she squeezed gently.

Evie looked as if she should be gracing a stage: she was

tall and willowy, with that dark hair cascading over her shoulders, and she carried herself with grace and self-assurance. Kevin would say Evie looked "expensive"—and she did—but without that fake plastic look or the sense of entitlement that normally accompanied it. He knew all too well how to spot women like that and avoid them.

"It's very nice to meet you, Nick. And you have excellent reflexes. I never even saw that guy coming."

"It happens. Testosterone, alcohol and a pretty girl is a bad mix. A common one, but a bad one."

"So *that's* what it was about." Evie seemed to think for a minute, then she turned that electric smile back on him. "I feel like I should at least offer to buy you a drink or something."

"That's not necessary."

"But—" Evie stopped and shook her head. "Oh, I'm *so* sorry. You're probably here with somebody. I don't want to start another fight, so I'll just—" She stepped away and indicated she would leave.

Oddly enough, for someone who'd come strictly to case the joint, he was now uninterested in the club itself. Evie, on the other hand. "I'm not," he heard himself say.

Evie caught her bottom lip in her teeth, and the sparkle came back to her eyes. "Then I can buy you that drink after all."

"Isn't that my line?" A couple abandoned a zebra-striped couch in favor of the dance floor, and Nick steered Evie in that direction.

"I believe the rescu*ee* should buy the rescu*er* the drink." She sat gracefully and sighed. "At least it's a bit quieter over here. I can barely hear myself think out there."

"That's kind of the point. Most people don't come here in search of stimulating conversation."

Evie cut her eyes at him. "I guess not."

A waitress appeared almost immediately to get their order. Evie ordered a vodka tonic, and though he didn't normally drink anything stronger than water when he was working, he asked for the same.

It was slightly quieter in the corner, but Evie still had to move close to him in order to hear him. As she did, the faint spicy scent of her perfume tickled his nose. It suited her perfectly—just slightly exotic and very natural.

"So where are you from, Nick?"

It took him a second to get his mind back in the conversation. "North Las Vegas."

"Really?" Her eyes widened.

He was used to looks of pity or scorn when he revealed his less-than-blue-chip background, but Evie's reaction was unexpected. "Why do you seem so surprised?"

"Because I am. I mean, I just never thought of people actually being *from* Vegas, you know? It seems like one of those places where everyone is really from somewhere else." As Evie spoke, her hands moved animatedly—until she seemed to realize she was doing it and clasped them in her lap.

"Everyone has to grow up somewhere. What about you?"

"Dallas." There was a touch of exasperation behind the word, and her mouth twisted the tiniest bit. If he hadn't been so focused on her lips, he'd have missed it. "I'm only here for the weekend."

"Not on business, then."

"God, no. Just fun."

That phrase—practically the code word for *trouble*—should've sent him to the nearest exit, but something about Evie kept him in his seat. "On your own?"

"Oh, no, I came with a friend."

He looked around pointedly, and Evie laughed. The sound caused a physical reaction—almost as if she'd run her hands over him again.

"But my friend made a new friend, so…"

Evie was on her own tonight. The same part of his brain

that was overriding his common sense took that knowledge and ran with it. He shifted on the sofa, looking for a comfortable position as his body's physical responses took over.

Thankfully, the server returned with their drinks, shifting his attention as he reached for his wallet. Evie stayed him with a hand as she handed over a bill to the server and told her to keep the change. "Smart women don't let strange men buy their drinks in bars." She winked. "It can lead to misunderstandings later."

Evie wasn't naive. He liked that. "Then I'll get the second round."

Her eyebrows went up in challenge. "That assumes there will be a second round."

"I'm not assuming anything. Just thinking positively."

"Hmm, I've heard folks talk about the power of positive thinking. Does it work for you?" Holding her drink carefully, Evie smiled as she leaned against the sofa back and crossed those unbelievably long legs. Although the action didn't look rehearsed or intentional, it was still outrageously seductive. His imagination sprang to life, and all the reasons why he didn't pick up women in bars anymore were blotted out by the images.

"I'm positive I'm glad your friend made a new friend...."

"Leaving me to make a new friend of my own?" Evie finished.

"Exactly."

That word sent a shiver down Evie's spine and kicked her heartbeat up another notch. The power of positive thinking? Hell, she was positive she wasn't thinking straight, but she was also *very* positive there was no place on earth she'd rather be than here, with Nick's dark eyes causing her stomach to turn funny flips.

When she'd landed on him and his arms tightened around her, it felt like time stopped. The imprint of his chest against hers, the heat of his skin under the silky cotton shirt, the thump of his heartbeat seeming louder than the music. And when she'd looked up to see her rescuer…

The strobe light kept sending parts of his face into shadow, emphasizing the sharp cheekbones and the strong, square line of his jaw. Dark hair fell across his forehead, nearly covering a scar above his left eyebrow that gave him a dangerous look. She'd had to break eye contact before those eyes of his sucked her in completely and turned her to mush.

Then she'd noticed how the dampness of his shirt caused it to mold across his chest, and her hands had been on him before she realized it. The electric tingle he caused in her fingertips only intensified when he grabbed her hands, and Evie had sent up a fervent prayer of thanks that God made men that looked—and felt—like him.

Only the years Gwen had spent trying to teach her to be a lady had saved her at that moment, letting her fall back into simple conversation instead of throwing herself into his arms. Her sister-in-law would be horrified at the very *un*ladylike way Evie was flirting with Nick *now,* but someone else seemed to be inhabiting her body at the moment.

Exactly. Was that a challenge? A promise? Nothing at all? Evie knew she was flirting way out of her comfort zone—and probably flirting with disaster at the same time—but she couldn't seem to dredge up a care. This was a whole new world, and she felt as if she'd slipped out of a confining costume and was finally herself.

It was scary and thrilling, and if she had an ounce of sense, she'd go back to her suite at the Bellagio and forget she'd ever laid eyes—or hands—on this man.

How many times had Will accused her of not having that ounce of sense? Obviously, he was right.

"Are you saying you'd like to be my new friend?" Dear

Lord, had she really just said that? And where had that husky tone come from?

The corner of Nick's mouth twitched. "Yeah."

Oh, yeah, she was way, *way* out of her league. *Switch to small talk.* Small talk would give her a graceful retreat while she regrouped. *You can do small talk.* Maybe not, she corrected herself as no words came to mind. Flustered by, well, *everything,* she reached for her glass to help calm her nerves. The vodka burned as she swallowed, and she coughed painfully. Nick signaled the waitress and she quickly brought a glass of water over.

Embarrassed, she could only smile gratefully and hope the darkness of the club would hide the blush on her cheeks.

"Since that drink doesn't seem to be to your liking, would you like to go somewhere else? Someplace a bit quieter with better-quality vodka?"

That offer nearly caused her to choke, and the water burned worse than the vodka. She cleared her throat. "Like where?"

"There's a club not far from here—the Starlight—that I like, but the options are wide open. This is Las Vegas, Evie, anything you could ever want is available twenty-four hours a day."

Her mind went to a dozen inappropriate places—complete with visuals—before she managed to rein it back in. "That sounds good to me."

Nick stood and offered her his hand. "Then let's go."

She hesitated for a millisecond and covered by reaching for her water glass one more time. Out of habit, she immediately wondered what the gossip columns would make of her and Nick, but then she remembered where she was. *What happens in Vegas, stays in Vegas.* No one here knew or even gave a damn who she was, what she did, or whom she did it with.

She placed her hand in his and her insides turned warm and melty when his fingers closed around hers and he pulled her to her feet. Feet that weren't very steady at the moment, dancing as they were around excitement, desire and the knowledge of her freedom.

Then Nick smiled at her, and her knees wobbled.

Viva Las Vegas.

CHAPTER TWO

EVIE KNEW SHE WASN'T DRUNK—she'd only had a couple of drinks—but she certainly felt like it. The freedom, the not-caring who was watching, the feeling of lightness—the intoxication was coming from Nick, not a bottle.

Who needed alcohol when every time she inhaled, his scent coiled through her, making her blood sing in her veins? And if there was anything more perfectly thrilling than the feel of his body pressed close to hers on the dance floor... Sweet mercy. She was about to spontaneously combust. This wasn't dancing: it was rhythmic public foreplay, and the bass line vibrating through her body was an unnecessary additional stimulant.

Oh, no, Nick was more than enough.

But something more than just her libido was awake. At this moment, she wasn't "Evangeline Harrison, heiress to half of HarCorp International." She wasn't under the lens of Dallas society's microscope. No one was judging her or expecting an appropriate level of behavior from the sister-in-law of Texas's leading etiquette expert.

She was just "Evie"—random girl-on-the-street—and *that* Evie was enjoying her time out of the Dallas fishbowl. Nick didn't know any differently, and he certainly didn't seem to care who she was when she wasn't here in Las Vegas. Not only did he have no expectations of her behavior, but he also seemed blissfully ignorant of the kinds of rules she was used to.

Drinking beer straight from the bottle? He didn't bat an eyelash. Joining the band on the stage and singing backup on her favorite song? He lifted her up there and then watched her with a fire in his eyes that had her stammering into the microphone.

Nick seemed sure of himself; he wore his rough edges with pride and did what he wanted without apology. She'd spent her entire life with the "right" boys who came from families much like hers and were members of the right country clubs. Even with a veneer of civilization, Nick was what the other girls in her debutante class had called a Bad Boy.

And she'd never wanted someone so bad so *badly*.

The music ended with a crash of cymbals, and the band announced they were taking a break. Her fingers dug into Nick's muscular shoulders in protest. *No.* She didn't want this dance to end.

Nick's hand tightened around her waist, keeping her close, and her heartbeat jumped up another notch. From the way he was staring at her, she got the feeling he felt the same way. Her mouth went dry, and she swallowed hard.

The arms holding her pulled her another fraction of an inch closer until she could feel the beat of his heart against her chest. The blood roared in her ears and everything that wasn't Nick ceased to exist.

Then his mouth landed on hers.

Oh, *yes*.

His lips were warm and firm and hungry, and they fired the hunger in her. Her hand slid over the solid muscle of his shoulder, to the nape of his neck, where she was finally able to run her fingers through the inky-black silk of his hair.

She felt, more than heard, him growl low in his throat as Nick's tongue swept into her mouth to find hers.

Then she began to burn.

The fire started low in her belly, moving down through her core until her thighs began to quiver. It spread up, causing her breasts to feel heavy and her nipples to harden against the silk of her bra.

Nick's hands cupped her head, his thumbs brushing over her cheekbones to her temples as he held her steady against the onslaught.

If she'd had any worry that the tension—the want—had been only one-sided, Nick dispelled that erroneous notion with one press of his hips against hers.

"Get a room!" someone shouted, and she broke away quickly, putting distance between them.

Oh, *no.*

The lovely heat of Nick's kiss receded as the hot flush of embarrassment rushed to her cheeks. Nick didn't seem to notice—or care—as he placed one last kiss on her temple and tilted her face back up to his.

The wry smile she saw answered her question. Nick didn't care that a crowd was watching. But he did release his hold on her waist, taking her hand and twining his fingers through hers as he led her off the dance floor.

But he didn't lead her back to the table they'd occupied earlier, winding his way instead through the crowd to the bar, where he ordered another round of drinks for them. He pressed a twenty into her hand and leaned close to her ear. "Wait for the drinks, and I'll be right back."

She didn't have a chance to question him before he disappeared into the crowd. A couple of minutes later, she saw him in the back corner, next to a staircase, talking to a burly bouncer with arms the size of Texas. The bouncer nodded, and Nick headed back in her direction as the bartender set their drinks in front of her.

"What was that about?" she asked, as Nick handed her a drink, took her other hand and picked up his own glass.

"You'll see."

They approached the stairs and the bouncer standing there looked rather ferocious from up close. Without saying anything, he reached behind him, unhooked a velvet rope and waved them past.

The noise of the bar receded as they climbed the stairs to the second floor and walked down a dimly lit corridor past several closed doors. Nick finally stopped in front of one marked simply Six.

The door swung open easily, and curious, Evie stepped inside. A large window covered one wall, giving an unobstructed view of the stage and dance floor from above, and two leather-covered sofas were arranged in front of it. It was a small, intimate room with low lighting.

And privacy.

Her heart skipped a beat and she moved to the window. "This is one of those VIP rooms, isn't it?"

Nick nodded as he closed the door behind him. Evie heard it snick into place, and the muscles in her thighs tightened.

"It is—a small one, though. Usually they're a bit bigger. This one is designed for small business meetings as opposed to parties." The thick carpeting muffled his footsteps as he moved across the room toward her.

"And we managed to get it how?" Forming words was very difficult, and she was pleased she wasn't stuttering.

"I know the bouncer minding the rope. Dave owes me a favor, and since this room wasn't being used at the moment…"

Wow. They'd been told to get a room and now they had one. Evangeline Harrison—the one who went to nice dinners at the Club and smiled her way through cocktail-party fundraisers—reeled in shock. The Evie she'd rediscovered tonight shivered at the possibilities.

"That panel to your left controls the speakers—you'll be able to hear the band once they start up again."

Who cared about the stupid band?

"And that—" he pointed to what looked like a key fob to a luxury car on the table "—signals for a server. They won't enter unless you call for them."

Nick was only an arm's length away, and his intent was obvious. But he didn't take the last step that would close the gap. She guessed he was leaving that up to her. Suddenly, she felt gauche and naive and unsure of herself. "Wow, they think of everything."

Her hands were starting to tremble from the proximity and the need to touch him, and her drink sloshed over the rim. Nick held out his hand, and she handed him the glass. He set it on the table and held his hand out again.

There was a clear path to the door. She could push a button and have someone in here in just another minute.

It was her choice.

This time she placed her hand in his and welcomed the electricity that arced through her. One small step, and those strong arms closed around her, and the fire in her belly pulled the oxygen from her lungs. She required no encouragement at all to pull his head down to hers.

That hunger she'd felt earlier roared back to life full force, causing her to sway dangerously on her feet, and Nick's arms tightened, steadying her.

One hot kiss melded into another as her greedy hands traced over the contours of his back, learning the musculature. Nick's hands massaged the small of her back, sliding under the hem of her shirt to scorch her skin as his lips slid down her neck and his tongue dipped into the hollow behind her collarbone.

How they covered the short distance to the couch, she didn't know, but then Nick was easing her down and moving over her.

Evie wanted to cry at the exquisite sensation of Nick's

body on hers, the heavy weight of him settling between her legs. The cool leather of the couch was such a contrast to the scorching heat of his skin. This was heaven; this was bliss and she wanted more. She wanted all of him.

Now.

A push and a tug and Nick was upright on the couch, and he helped settle her onto his lap with a lazy, appreciative smile. With her legs on either side of his strong thighs and her knees snugged up next to his hips, she pressed against the bulge in his pants and gasped as a bolt of heat shot though her.

It was easy to push his shirt up and over his head, baring sculpted bronze skin to her eager hands. The dusting of crisp black hair tickled her fingers as she explored the lines and planes of his chest, and she felt the muscles jump when she brushed her thumbs over his nipples.

She was shocking herself with her actions, but not Nick. His hungry look told her that much. Again she sent up a word of thanks for Las Vegas and men like Nick. Nick was unlike any of the men at home—they were too polished, too urbane, too domesticated. Nick's rough edges excited her, made her feel as if she was dealing with something powerful and raw and untamed. It reached inside her, past the years of behaving herself, and released her.

More importantly, Nick seemed to like that part of her. Encourage it, even. It was a heady combination—the power and the freedom—and it frightened her a bit with its intensity.

Nick's hands locked around her arms, pulling her down for another soul-stealing kiss. A moment later, she felt the straps at her shoulders give way. Then the zipper of her skirt. The fabric bunched under his hands as they made their way up her body with excruciating slowness. She lifted her arms and Nick pulled both items over her head, and she fought back a blush as his eyes moved appreciatively over her body.

His fingers brushed over the top of her lacy strapless bra, teasing her nipples and causing her thighs to clench. A quick twist of the clasp and it joined the rest of her clothes on the ground.

She hissed as Nick's tongue snaked out to tease, then bit back a cry when he pulled her aching nipple into the moist heat of his mouth. His hands went to her waist, pressing down as he lifted his hips and pressed against her very needy core.

Oh, *yesss.*

A tug on his hair and Nick was kissing her again, his tongue sliding across hers in a way that made her insides melt and her breathing ragged. His hands cupped her face gently as she worked on his belt and slid his zipper down.

She caught his groan in her mouth as she palmed him, running her hand over the hard length of an impressive erection that made her shiver with anticipation. Nick's eyes closed and he leaned back, his fingers digging into her thighs as she stroked him. Evie felt powerful, sexy, pleased she could make Nick feel even a part of that burning ache he stoked in her.

Nick suddenly surged forward, capturing her mouth in a savage kiss as he lifted her to the side easily with only one arm, using the other to slide her panties down her legs and off. That same dexterity had the rest of his clothes off in a blink, and he settled her back into her original position.

With a bravado she didn't know she had, she managed to meet his eyes and hold the stare as he tickled his fingers along her inner thigh, teasing her before his thumb slipped between her damp folds and wrung a moan from her with barely a touch.

Nick cursed, and holding her in place, leaned forward and reached for the table. Confused, she turned her head in time to see him slide open a drawer. Condoms filled the small space.

They weren't the first people to use this room for... She tried to swallow her shock. "Oh. Goodness."

"These rooms are for private parties, too."

Of course they are. Nick must think she was some kind of naive country girl. She tried to sound airy and sophisticated. "They really do think of everything here, don't they?"

Nick's smile caught her off guard. "Thank God they do."

She couldn't argue with that, and she was thankful Nick was coherent enough to remember the basics. Her brain had definitely checked out. Nick placed the condom on the cushion next to him and settled back into place.

In no rush, his hands began exploring her body again, teasing her nipples, sliding a strong finger inside her until her nails were digging into his biceps and she was gasping for breath.

An eternity later, she heard the beautiful sound of a condom packet being ripped open, and Nick was guiding her hips into position.

Evie couldn't stifle her groan of pleasure as she sank slowly onto him, savoring each centimeter until they were completely locked together. Her thighs shook as she started to move, Nick's hands helping her set the pace.

Sweet *mercy,* she was going to die, right here, from the sheer bliss of the feel of him in her. She let her forehead fall against his as the movement became more frantic, the pleasure sharper and more intense. She felt light-headed as the pressure built, radiating out until her entire body began to shake, and she threw her head back and screamed his name as she shattered into a thousand glittering pieces.

He'd never used one of his VIP lounges for sex before. He'd hosted a small gathering in this room only once: last year when they'd celebrated the purchase of the Starlight. He had good memories of that night, but tonight guaranteed he'd never look at this room the same way again. Every piece of furniture, the floor, even the long wall of windows, would now hold the image of Evie, naked and panting and crying out his name.

Evie lay back against the couch, her hair a tangle of curls cascading over the edge to nearly touch the carpet. The picture she created was more than enough to get his blood pumping again, although it shouldn't be possible after he'd taken her so many times he'd lost count. But the band had long ago called it quits for the night, and the slowdown on the dance floor told him how late it was. He checked his watch to be sure.

He ran a hand over the leg Evie had draped across his lap, and she sighed contentedly. "Starlight closes at four. We should probably get dressed."

Evie switched from sensual to shy in a heartbeat; the woman who'd clawed his back and screamed his name—repeatedly—couldn't seem to meet his eyes now. A blush stained her cheeks as modesty returned about three hours too late, and she fumbled for her clothes.

"Um, okay...sure. Just give me a minute."

Her face was redder than the desert sunset, and she practically ran for the attached bathroom, giving him a lovely view of her backside as she retreated.

He untangled his own clothes and pulled his shirt on over his head, surprised to find that the scent of Evie's perfume clung faintly to it. The smell wasn't a familiar one—he couldn't place it. It was heady, yet subtle, exotic and unique.

Much like Evie.

She was tempting and seductive, yet there was a wholesome genuineness underneath. She seemed cautious to approach new things—even hesitant at times—but she had an adventurous streak that couldn't be denied. Her honeyed Texas drawl wasn't affected, but it gave way sometimes to something else, leading him to believe she wasn't a true Dallas native.

Part of him thought she had to be from that Southern aristocracy he'd heard about; she had class, elegance and she could be unbelievably polite and well-mannered. At the same time, she lacked that air of superiority Old-Money people had: that belief they were somehow better than everyone else just because great-grandpa once owned half the town.

He had personal experience with Old Money and New Money. Vegas was full of New-Money people—hell, he was one of them—and he far preferred the New Money over the Old, even if he was, technically, *biologically* at least, both.

Evie returned—dressed, hair somewhat tamed—but still looking as if she'd been…well, having sex for the last four hours. Her lips were slightly swollen, and her jaw was a little red from where his stubble had rubbed.

Still not quite able to make eye contact, Evie retrieved her shoes from under the table and grabbed her purse. "I'm ready," she claimed, as she hurried to slide her feet into the strappy silver sandals.

"Don't rush. No one's going to be banging down the door."

"Well, I don't want Dave to get in trouble for letting us up here."

He bit back a smile at that.

"Here. Take these." She pushed glassware into his hands and started straightening the cushions on the couch.

"You don't have to do that, Evie."

"If this room wasn't supposed to be used tonight, they'll know someone was up here when they see the mess."

"Don't worry about it."

Evie frowned. "Nick…"

With no way to explain that wouldn't tell her more about his finances than he wanted her to know, he bit his tongue and took the empty glasses.

Evie *had* to notice the number of strange looks sent their way as they came down the stairs. Earlier, when the place had been hopping, only a few people had noticed he was here. Now, with so few customers still hanging on, he could see the questions on every face of the Starlight staff.

Evie's cheeks grew redder and redder and her feet moved faster, until she was out the door in almost a full trot. Outside, she leaned against a wall and covered her face with her hands. "Oh, my *God,* that was so embarrassing."

"What?"

"Did you not see everyone staring at us? I felt like I was carrying a giant neon sign that said We Just Had Sex."

He laughed, but smothered it with a cough when Evie turned stormy eyes on him. "It's not funny."

"You don't know these people, and you'll never see them again, so why do you care?"

Evie leaned her head back against the concrete wall. "I guess you're right. That only makes it *slightly* less embarrassing."

He'd never seen anyone die of embarrassment before, but Evie had to be close, so he took pity on her, even though he was loath to end their evening. "It's late, and I have to work in the morning. I'll take you back to your hotel. Where are you staying?"

"The Bellagio." Her voice sounded small and he wondered why.

A taxi coasted to a stop, and he opened the door for Evie to climb in. In the backseat, Evie seemed even more withdrawn, a huge change from her brightness earlier. Unable to ask why when the cabbie was listening, he settled for lame small talk. "That's a nice hotel. Have you had a chance to explore it?"

"Not really. Bennie—Sabine," she corrected, "and I did a little shopping earlier today."

"Bennie's the friend who came with you?"

Evie nodded. "But I haven't been to the casino yet. I'm not much of a gambler."

"Don't like it?"

"Don't know how to play any of the games. I've played penny-ante poker with my brother and blackjack on my laptop, but that's about it."

"I could teach you." Why had he offered that? He hadn't been in a casino in years.

"You'd do that?" Evie brightened considerably. Maybe she really did want to learn to gamble.

"If you'd like."

Her mood improved exponentially at that point, and by the time they pulled in at the Bellagio, Evie was almost back to her earlier self.

Including using her best manners. "I had a great time tonight, Nick. Thank you."

"My pleasure." *Understatement of the year.*

A Bellagio doorman opened the taxi door, and Nick slid out and extended a hand to Evie. Once she was on her feet, he slid a hand under her chin and turned her face up for a kiss.

Evie's response was as voracious as before, and he let the kiss continue until the cabbie started complaining about the wait. Evie stepped back, another adorable blush rising over her cleavage.

"Do you know the bar that overlooks the fountain?"

She nodded.

"Meet me there at seven tonight."

Evie's smile could be breathtaking, especially when she rose up on her tiptoes to kiss him one last time before finally turning to the doorman patiently holding the lobby door open.

At the door, she turned and waved.

He directed the cabbie to take him back to The Zoo, where he had left his car in a not-great alley off a side street. At the time, he only planned to be in the club for a couple of hours, tops. If he'd known it would be more like six, he'd have found a safer spot. Hopefully, it would still have a stereo and all four tires when he returned.

Hell, who was he kidding? He didn't care, even as he noticed the broken window. A night with Evie was well worth the consequences.

CHAPTER THREE

EVIE FELT LIKE SKIPPING through the Bellagio lobby, but ladies didn't skip through hotel lobbies. She stamped down the urge.

She'd just had what was possibly the best night of her entire life, and even better, Nick wanted to do it *again* tonight. Ladylike or not, *that* thought put a bounce in her step anyway.

Even at this time of the night—or technically, morning—the lobby was active, the employees greeting her politely as if she didn't look as if she'd just come in after a night of debauchery. She should feel exposed and embarrassed, since it was obvious what she'd been up to, but she realized that probably wasn't an uncommon occurrence in Las Vegas.

And, as Nick had reminded her, it's not as if she'd ever see these people again.

In the elevator, she slipped out of her shoes and stretched tiredly. The adrenaline and endorphin rush she'd been on all night dissipated quickly now that Nick wasn't around to fuel it, and exhaustion settled heavily on her shoulders. An enormous yawn cracked her jaw, and she really, really needed to sleep.

She closed the door to the suite behind her quietly. Sabine's shoes and evening bag were on the couch, and the door to her room was shut. Evie had no way of knowing if Bennie was alone in there or not.

And to be honest, she was too tired to care.

Evie collapsed on her bed and stared at the ceiling. She was keyed up mentally, sated physically and totally exhausted. She should shower, maybe eat something, but her legs felt too heavy to move. Getting out of her clothes almost sounded like far too much work, but she managed to shimmy out of them and wrap a robe around herself before she pushed the button to close the drapes and crawled under the covers.

When she closed her eyes, Nick's face was there. She could feel the imprint of his hands on her hips, taste him on her lips, hear that low growl. She wanted to relive every moment and savor the anticipation of tonight, but sleep was dragging her under quickly....

"Jeez, Evie, wake up. How hungover are you?"

Evie felt Sabine land on her bed next to her. "I'm not hungover. Just tired," she mumbled. "Go 'way."

"The day is half-over, and I still haven't heard about your night. What time did you get in, anyway?"

"Dunno. Four-ish. Maybe?" She pulled the pillow over her head as Bennie pushed the button controlling the drapes and light flooded the room. "Late."

"Way to go, Evie! I want details. Graphic ones." Sabine shook her shoulder. "Spare nothing."

Evie pried open her eyes and looked at the clock. After ten. "You lie. The day is not half-over. Wake me in another couple of hours." She could go back to the dream where she and Nick were swimming in that cove not far from where she grew up on St. Kitts....

"Evie Harrison, I am *dying* for details." Another shake. "Get up or I'll call Will and tell him you stayed out all night."

She didn't believe Bennie would do such a horrible thing, but... "Fine. I'm up." She untangled herself from the covers and sat up slowly.

Sabine giggled as Evie pushed her hair out of her faced and yawned. "You look awful."

Bennie, as always, looked like one of Botticelli's angels: adorable round face, curly blond hair, big blue eyes. Petite, thin and perky, Bennie was the perfect debutante. On the outside, at least. On the inside, she was more trouble than a biker gang at a Sunday School picnic. Sabine—unbeknownst to her family—was what Uncle Marcus would call a Bad Influence. It was why they were such good friends. "Thanks, Bennie. Just what I needed to hear. I feel awful, too."

Sabine handed her a bottle of water and eyed her critically. "Good thing I made reservations at the spa. It'll take them all afternoon just to take care of those bags under your eyes."

"Oh, that sounds excellent." Evie unscrewed the lid and drank deeply. Some of the cobwebs left her mind, and she felt better almost immediately. Nick had warned her that the desert air would dehydrate her. "How was your night? You and Toby have a good time? His name *was* Toby, right?"

Bennie smiled angelically. "What Toby lacks in finesse, he more than makes up for in enthusiasm and stamina. He's not the sharpest tool in the shed, but who needs conversation, anyway?" Bennie nudged her. "If I want to talk, I'll call you."

Evie scrubbed a hand over her face as she laughed. "I'm glad you had a good time."

"I *am* a little achy this morning." Rolling onto her back, Bennie stretched, then grinned. "But enough about me. I want to know who *you* hooked up with. I nearly died when I saw your text, and then when I beat you back to the room, I couldn't believe it. Spill."

"His name's Nick." A little smile tugged at her mouth.

Bennie nearly crowed. "I know that smile. Was he that good-looking or just that good?"

"Both. Tall, dark, drop-dead-oh-my-God *gorgeous*. Broad

shoulders. Great arms, too." Evie sighed, feeling like a school-girl with a crush.

Bennie echoed her sigh. "Oh, I love good arms."

"I had a fabulous time, though." Evie scooted to the head of the bed and leaned against the headboard.

"I can tell."

"Not just *that*." She tried for a disapproving frown, but Bennie laughed it off. "Well, the sex *was* fabulous, too, but we danced and talked—"

"Why on *earth* would you waste time talking if he was that hot?"

"Because I like to get to know people a little bit before I get naked with them."

Bennie shrugged.

"So much fun and absolutely no pressure at all to do anything except enjoy myself. Have I mentioned how much I love this town?"

"I would, too, if I'd hooked up with a hottie like your Nick. Are you going to see him again?"

She could feel the goofy smile tugging at her cheeks. "He wants to do something again tonight. If you have other plans, that is. Are you seeing Toby again?"

"Lord, honey, even if I wasn't, I'd expect you to go with Nick. That's why you came here, after all."

Evie felt her jaw drop. "You think I came to Vegas just to hook up?"

Sabine was wide-eyed. "Didn't you?"

"It wasn't my primary agenda, no. I wanted to let off a little steam, drink a little, let my hair down and dance." She raised an eyebrow at Bennie. "*I* came to Vegas to have a girls' weekend."

"Then I misunderstood. My bad." Bennie was wonderfully unrepentant. "But now you've found someone yummy, so you should make the most of it. And take a few pictures tonight. I wanna see this god who's got your libido doing the lambada."

"I'll try," she promised and her stomach growled. She pounced on the distraction eagerly, not really sure she wanted to go into too much more detail with Bennie at this point. She wanted to hug it all to herself for a little while longer. "I'm starved. Is there anything in the minibar besides pretzels?"

"I took the liberty of ordering brunch. If you can hang on a little longer without falling away to a shadow, it should be here about another twenty minutes or so." Bennie gave her a once-over. "I'd recommend you use that time to grab a shower and sort out your hair. You really do look a mess."

"I do not!"

Sabine merely raised an eyebrow. "Our first appointment is at twelve-fifteen. I've booked the works—massage, manicure, pedicure, facial and a detoxifying hydrotherapy bath. What time are you meeting him?"

"Seven." Her pulse kicked up at the thought.

"What are you wearing?"

Damn, she had no idea what Nick had planned. "Not a clue."

"Then we'd better get moving. We may have to shop."

"You are an angel, Bennie." Evie leaned over and kissed her cheek. "What would I do without you?"

"Based solely on today? Sleep all day, starve and be celibate and inappropriately dressed." Sabine threw her legs over the side of the bed and started to leave. In the doorway, she paused and turned around. "Hmm, I think I'll call the spa back and add a wax for you." She winked.

In the shower, Evie debated whether she should go tonight. Last night had just *happened*. The stars or whatever aligned to give her one wonderful night, and she should just leave it at that—a perfect memory. What if tonight didn't turn out, as well...? Who was she kidding? Tonight would be just as good as last night.

Although she would like to have a bed this time. She had a bit of a crick in her neck from last night.

She didn't even sound like herself. Standing here planning to… This wasn't like her at all. There was her usual life, and then there was…

Then there was Nick.

Bennie was right. She'd needed this. Needed someone like Nick to shake her up a little. Las Vegas had to be the next best thing to heaven.

Evie turned the tap off. Sabine must've been listening for the water to stop, because a second later, her voice drifted through the open door. "Food's here. And your phone was ringing."

Evie wrapped her hair in a towel and pulled a robe around her. Sabine was already at the table, munching on a bagel, and Evie's stomach growled. Grabbing a muffin, she took a hungry bite as she picked up her phone. Three missed calls and three messages: the first one time-stamped at eight this morning.

And every one of them was from her brother.

Damn.

The mystery and memory of Evie—and her unbelievably long legs—had haunted Nick in the four hours of sleep he'd managed to get last night before Kevin and business forced him out of bed.

By the time lunch rolled around, he'd almost convinced himself that Evie hadn't been real. Or at least not as he remembered. Beautiful women were a dime a dozen in Las Vegas; tourists out for a good time were even more plentiful. Evie was just one in a crowd—maybe he'd built more into it simply because he'd been so immersed in business he had, as Kevin insisted, gotten jaded and forgotten how to have plain ol' fun.

But that rational knowledge didn't stop him from spending way too much time deciding on a plan for tonight. He could call in a favor, get seats to the best shows or a table at the most exclusive restaurant, but he didn't want to try to impress Evie like that. He liked not having a woman know how much his bank account was worth—it tended to skew the genuineness of their reactions. And after last night, he knew that wasn't really what Evie liked anyway. She had simple tastes and didn't need ostentatious displays to have a good time.

Since he didn't want to waste all that time at shows and restaurants anyway... That gave him the perfect idea.

Kevin was in the offices at Blue—the first club Nick had purchased outright and, for sentimental reasons, still the main hub—when Nick called. And while Kevin had a mouthful of things to say about it, Nick knew it would be done.

And when Evie turned out to be less than he remembered? He shrugged. They'd still have a good time, and he'd go easily back to normalcy tomorrow.

At just a minute after seven, Nick was on the Bellagio patio watching the door while everyone else watched the fountains do their thing. When Evie walked in, nervously chewing on her bottom lip, he felt as if all the oxygen had been sucked out of his lungs.

A shimmery green dress hugged those luscious curves he'd memorized last night, the neckline plunged to reveal generous cleavage, and the hem stopped high enough to showcase her long legs. She'd piled her hair up on her head, exposing the line of her neck and emphasizing her bone structure.

If anything, his memory of last night couldn't compete with the reality.

She scanned the crowd, and when her eyes met his, she smiled shyly—at complete odds with the sensual picture she created. He wanted to meet her halfway, but his feet seemed rooted to the floor.

Then he noticed the attention she was garnering from several other places in the bar—one man was even on his feet and headed in her direction—and that kicked him into motion, a need to claim her taking hold.

"God, you're beautiful," he muttered as Evie turned her face up to his.

"I didn't know if you'd actually come tonight or not."

"How could you possibly doubt that?" He inhaled deeply and her scent shot through his veins, sending all of his blood south. They were in a hotel, for God's sake; he could have a room and have her in it in less than five minutes.

And that seemed like far too long to wait.

Evie smoothed a hand along his arm, scorching him with her touch. "You look nice." Her hand moved to his jaw. "You shaved. I kind of miss the sexy stubble."

She was killing him.

"Should we get a table?" she asked, looking around.

That brought him back to the conversation. "No. I've got a surprise for you."

Evie's eyes lit up. "A surprise? What kind of surprise?"

"If I told you, then it wouldn't be a surprise, would it?"

Evie brushed at her dress. "Is what I'm wearing okay for this surprise? I wasn't sure about the dress code…."

That scrap of fabric barely counted as a complete dress, and he was already imagining peeling it off of her. "Like I said, you look beautiful. Let's go."

Evie's heels clicked against the floor of the lobby, reminding him to slow down. He wasn't an animal dragging Evie off to mate—regardless of what his instincts were urging him to do. He could at least attempt civilized conversation. "What did you do today?"

"Slept late, hung out with Bennie. You?"

"Got up early, went to work."

"Ouch. Sorry."

Even the valet gawked at Evie as he returned with the car, but a frown from Nick put a stop to it. Evie didn't seem to notice that attention any more than she'd noticed the men in the bar. She was a danger to herself and others if she really didn't know the effect she had on men. But how could she not? Beautiful women knew they were beautiful, knew what it could do for them.

It only took a few minutes to get to Blue, and Evie looked around eagerly as he pulled into the parking lot. "Blue. Is it a nightclub? Are we going dancing again?"

He flashed back on the memory of Evie moving against him on the dance floor and groaned. That would kill him for sure. "Patience."

"Sorry. I know it's rude to ask so many questions. I'll be good."

That promise brought a visual he really didn't need at the moment, and he quickly opened the door before he mauled her in the parking lot. The hand Evie tucked under his arm caressed his bicep as if they were truly lovers, and he wondered if she was intentionally trying to drive him insane.

Blue was almost deserted at this early hour, which was fine by him. The bouncers merely nodded as he and Evie passed and the bartenders waved.

"Everyone seems to know you," Evie said.

"I know the owner, so I'm here a lot." He led her past a velvet rope and down the back hallway.

"I don't think we're supposed to be back here," Evie whispered as she tugged against his hand.

At the elevator, he pulled her close. "I told you, I know the owner. Don't worry."

She looked around, clearly unconvinced. "Is there anyone in Vegas you don't know or who doesn't owe you a favor?"

"I've lived here a long time, Evie."

"I do *not* want to get arrested in Las Vegas." Her eyes narrowed as the elevator doors opened, and she stared pointedly at the sign marked Private.

"You're not going to get arrested. I promise." Evie still looked suspicious. "I thought you'd like to do something a bit different, so I made a couple of calls this afternoon. Look," he added as the doors opened onto the roof.

Evie gasped. Facing west, they had a great view of the sun starting to set.

"Later in the summer it gets too hot to be up here at this time, but it's about perfect now." And he wasn't just referring to the weather.

"It's gorgeous," Evie said as she crossed to the chest-high wall that enclosed the patio. "Is this another VIP-type room?"

"Sort of." Blue's rooftop was very exclusive, but Evie had no way of knowing that. He'd hired one of the best designers in Las Vegas to create an oasis here: plenty of green plants, indirect lighting, low couches canopied with gauzy fabrics, small fountains. A giant shade stretched overhead to keep the worst of the sun off, but also gave the roof an intimate feel. Kevin called it the Sheik's Tent.

"This is…wow."

He agreed. Evie looked fabulous backlit by the sunset— she seemed to glow. She moved away from the edge to run a hand along the back of a chaise, then moved to examine the table set for two.

She raised an eyebrow as he lifted the champagne out of its bucket. "A private party?"

"Only a very select guest list."

A smile tugged at the corners of Evie's mouth. "Be sure and thank the owner for me. This is absolutely perfect." Before he could respond, Evie was pressed against him, her hands sliding to his shoulders as she rose up on her toes. "The elevator is locked? All the guests are here?"

He slid his fingers into her hair and found the combs holding it up. One small tug and it tumbled around her shoulders. "Uh-huh."

"Good." Then Evie's mouth met his.

The want that had slowly simmered in his veins all day boiled over in that instant, and his hands tightened in her hair to hold her. Evie's fingers gripped his shoulders, and her nails stabbed against his skin when his mouth moved to the column of her neck and her head dropped back to allow him better access.

She sighed, then shivered, as he tasted her, and the shiver moved through him, as well. Nimble fingers made quick work of the buttons on his shirt, and she slid her hands across his bare chest before she wrapped her arms around him and pressed herself against him again.

Evie's height had their bodies aligned perfectly—her breasts rubbed against his chest and he felt the hard points of her nipples through the thin material of her dress.

He walked backward, pulling Evie with him, until he felt the edge of the couch butt against his calves. Evie groaned in protest as he broke the kiss to lower her down, her hands fisting in his shirt to pull him down to join her.

Déjà vu. Only better.

Maybe Kevin was on to something calling the roof the Sheik's Tent. Nick certainly felt like the Sultan of Something, lying on a couch with a mostly naked Evie draped across him as they nibbled on fruit and cheese and watched the city lights cause the sky to glow.

Evie's bag started to ring, and she wrinkled her nose. But she didn't move beyond examining another strawberry.

"Aren't you going to get that?"

"Not just no, *hell* no." She picked up her champagne flute and drank deeply.

He'd never met a woman who could resist a phone. "Why not?"

"That's my brother's ringtone. And I am *not* in the mood to deal with my butthead of a brother."

It was the first time she'd mentioned anyone in her family specifically. "Family problems?"

"Yeah. No. Sort of." She sighed and pushed her hair back from her face. "I left town without telling him, and he's a bit peeved about it. He's left me several voice mails this weekend telling me exactly how much."

"Your *brother* is upset you left town?"

"My parents died when I was young. Will and Gwen—she's his wife—took me in and raised me. So Will treats me rather like a child."

"And you're dodging his calls? No offense, but isn't that a little childish?"

Evie smacked him playfully. "You don't know my brother."

"As you said, you are an adult. What could he possibly do to you?"

"Nothing but yell at me, but that's never stopped him before. Will's just… He's a…" She sat up and pulled his shirt closed around her. "Something happened earlier this week—nothing major—but it got blown a bit out of proportion. He got mad, and I got mad and now I'm AWOL because I wanted a *break* from the drama. I certainly don't want to hear it while I'm here." She sighed and grimaced. "Will thinks he's the master of the whole freakin' universe and, therefore, in charge of everything."

"Including you."

Evie rolled her eyes. "Definitely including me. I know he means well, but, dear God, it gets old. It got old about the time I turned twenty-one. Do you have any siblings?"

"No." *Thank God.* It was tough enough getting himself out, if he'd had to worry about siblings, too… "It was just me and my father after my mother left."

Evie's eyes clouded. "Your mom left?"

He stiffened at the question. He very rarely spoke of his

mother, and those that knew the story had learned long ago not to broach the subject. He couldn't fault Evie for asking since he'd brought it up, but he was surprised at himself that he'd let it slip out.

Evie blanched. "I'm sorry. That was terribly rude of me to ask such a personal question. Please don't feel like you owe me any response at all. Forget I said anything."

She seemed so sincere, he almost wished he could explain. "No apology necessary, Evie. I just don't like to talk about it."

"Why don't we just *not* talk about our families? Everyone has some nuts on the family tree—some are just more annoying than others."

"And some think they're the master of the universe."

"Indeed. He'll have plenty of opportunity to yell at me tomorrow when I get home. Why settle for the telephone version when the live action is *so* much more interesting."

It seemed Evie had an interesting family dynamic. But they'd called a halt to all uncomfortable family discussions, so he didn't press the topic.

"It's a shame you have to go back so quickly."

Evie shrugged as she settled her head against his chest and traced circles on his skin. "But if I ever make it back to Vegas..."

"Give me a call," he finished.

She pressed a kiss on his chest and he responded by rolling her to her back and settling his body between her legs. Evie looked adorably mussed—hair tangled from his hands, mouth slightly swollen—and sexy as hell. He rested his chin on her chest, enjoying the silky feel of her skin as she toyed with his hair.

Evie ran her thumb over his eyebrow, and he knew what was coming next. "How'd you get this scar?"

"Bar fight."

She laughed, causing her body to move under his in a way guaranteed to get his attention. "No, seriously."

"I am serious. A guy swung a bottle, and I got this."

"Oh, my gosh, I've never met anyone who's even witnessed a bar fight, much less been in one." She looked at him oddly. "Who started it? Was it over a girl? Like last night at The Zoo?"

"I wasn't *in* the fight, Evie, I was trying to break it up." Understanding crossed her face, and she nodded. "It was part of my job—breaking up fights, that is. I was working at this sleazy joint when I was in high school—"

Evie's eyes went wide. "High school? Isn't that a little bit illegal?"

"Maybe. But I needed a job and Henry—the owner—needed a bar back and someone to help break up fights."

"The fights were a regular occurrence?"

"I told you, testosterone and alcohol are a dangerous mix." She grinned. "What about the pretty girl?"

"Not always necessary—especially in sleazy joints."

"Were you this big in high school?" She ran her hands over his shoulders as she asked, and the openly appreciative look on her face caused his body to harden again.

"About."

Evie's hands were now on his arms, tracing his biceps. "Linebacker for the football team?"

He could have been, had he not had to work. "Nope."

"Let me guess, between your size and your scowl, you're good at breaking up bar fights."

To the best of his knowledge, he hadn't scowled since Evie landed in his arms last night. That had to be a world record—but Evie didn't know that. "What makes you think I scowl?"

She ran a finger across his forehead. "This crease here. Definitely caused by scowling." Evie trailed her finger down over his cheek and to his lips. "Who do you scowl at now?"

"Drunks in bars. Such is the hospitality industry in Las Vegas." He captured her finger between his lips and sucked gently. Under his chin, he felt her heartbeat accelerate.

"So that's how you know the owner of this place—and everyone else." She smirked. "Well, you certainly are hospitable."

He nipped at her finger, causing her to jump. He pushed himself up, wedging his hips firmly between hers, and caught her gasp in his mouth.

Evie's hands slid up his back as her tongue slipped inside his mouth to torment him. She echoed his groan as his hands tangled in her hair, and her legs wrapped around his waist.

Faintly, he heard her phone ring again.

CHAPTER FOUR

EVIE PACED WHILE THE TIMER counted down the last few seconds. The cool blues and greens of her apartment decor were supposed to create a soothing and relaxing environment. They were failing miserably.

When the timer dinged, she jumped. "Please, please, please," she mumbled as she walked through to her bathroom—also done in soothing colors and also falling down on the job.

She looked carefully at the array of tests lined up on the vanity. Six different brands, purchased at four different stores in the next county this morning after she'd called in sick to the office.

Every last one of the damn things said "positive."

Oh, she really felt sick now. She sat on the edge of the tub while the horrid reality settled on her shoulders.

Last night, she'd turned the calendar over to June and realized she hadn't had a period in May. That thought lead her to her day planner, where she realized she last had her period the week before she went to Las Vegas.

Sleep was impossible after that.

But she'd kept calm—sort of—telling herself there was no need to panic until she had a reason to. She looked at the line of tests. Oh, she had reason to panic now. Good reason.

She was pregnant.

She was going to be a mother, and, dear God, she wasn't
ready to be someone's mother. She wanted children—several,
in fact—but motherhood had always seemed like a distant
prospect. Motherhood would come after she'd built some
kind of career for herself, when she could have a house in the
suburbs and do the whole nuclear-family thing with a white
picket fence and a dog. And, most importantly, a husband.

Instead, she would be raising a baby alone. Well, not alone,
exactly—she *did* have family—but it wouldn't have a father.
How would she tell her child one day, "Your dad? Well,
honey, I met him in a bar in Las Vegas…."

The child wasn't even born yet and she needed to start
looking for a good therapist to help it through the issues of
growing up without a father because its mother was stupid
enough to get pregnant during a two-night stand in Vegas.

She ran her hands through her hair and pulled at it. "I'm
so screwed. *This* is so screwed."

And it would only get worse from here. This news would
kill Uncle Marcus. His heart wasn't very strong these days,
and the shock and horror would kill him for sure. Pain
throbbed behind her left eye. Of course, the upside was that
Will was going to kill her anyway, so she wouldn't have to
live with *that* guilt on her conscience for very long.

Oh, and the papers were going to have a field day. It wasn't
enough that she was unwed and pregnant—and that would be
plenty for the gossips to chew on its own—but they were also
going to brand her a giant slut because her last breakup had
been quite public and fodder for the gossip mill four months
ago. All of Dallas knew she was single.

"Nice" girls didn't sleep around and get knocked up. She
was supposed to be some sort of role model for the youth of
Dallas—a "real lady," as Gwen put it. She was, as Uncle
Marcus continuously preached, a Harrison—not some trashy

Hollywood starlet. Promiscuity might fly for the rich and famous somewhere else, but not here. Not in her world. That's why she'd gone to Vegas in the first place.

Society had rules: they weren't fair, and they weren't right, but they were still rules. And she'd just broken a major one.

Oh, God. She'd pulled a lot of stunts, garnered a lot of publicity—both good *and* bad—but nothing like this.

This was a nightmare.

Would anyone believe she'd gone the single-mother route intentionally? Used a sperm bank or something? She snorted. Not likely.

The tests with all their positive results seemed to mock her, and she swept them into the trash with one hand. Then she went to the bed to lie down.

In her freshman year of college, she'd invented a boyfriend because she'd seemed like the only girl in her sorority who didn't have one. Leonardo had been Italian, gorgeous and conveniently studying architecture in Rome. Leonardo had served her well that first uncomfortable semester, and she wondered if an imaginary boyfriend would work now. Maybe he'd been tragically killed in a freak scuba-diving accident off the coast of Australia before he even knew she was pregnant....

Right. Even if she could resurrect Leo—and promptly kill him off—there was no way she could claim a long-distance romance. She'd been too visible lately, too often in the society pages to have anyone believe she'd had time to go overseas. In fact, she'd barely left Dallas—aside from one little trip to Las Vegas.

One little trip, that until just a few minutes ago, had held the top spot on her Greatest Memories list. One trip so far outside her reality she hadn't even talked about it to Sabine— beyond the basic details—so she could keep it special and untouched and perfect just as it was in her memory. She didn't bother analyzing or deconstructing it, but she found herself revisiting it a lot, reliving that feeling of freedom...

And Nick.

She thought about Nick much more than could possibly be healthy, remembering his dangerous good looks, the sensation of his body against hers, that devil-take-it attitude that he also brought out in her. Her dreams had become complex and erotic, and she often awoke frustrated and needy, but, even worse, they'd sowed discontent in her waking hours. None of the men in her circle were as good-looking or disarming as Nick, and none of them seemed to understand the real her the way he had—much less bring the real her out from its hiding place behind her family name and social responsibilities.

In short, none of the men here were Nick. And while Nick was totally wrong for her in so many ways, that fact hadn't checked her overactive imagination or made a bit of difference beneath the surface.

Of course, she'd have to tell him at some point. He had a right to know she was carrying his baby. But while she'd fantasized about going back to Vegas in the future and looking him up, *this* hadn't been part of that fantasy. She couldn't even fathom how he might react to the news. Would he be upset? Did he even want children? Or would she be saddling him with a responsibility he didn't want?

Much like Will and Gwen had been saddled with her.

No, this was different. It may have been an accident, but babies were a possible side effect of sex, and if Nick didn't want that responsibility, he shouldn't be...

Jeez, when had she started channeling Uncle Marcus? Evie snorted. Next, she'd be demanding Nick marry her like this was the Dark Ages or something....

The proverbial lightbulb went off. The answer to all her problems was unbelievably simple: she needed a husband.

Everything would be fine if she got married: there'd be no embarrassment to the family, no heart attacks for Uncle Marcus, no explosions from Will, no gossip in the society pages.

Well, there'd be a little of that, considering she was getting married so quickly to someone whom she hadn't been connected with in the past, but she could survive that fallout. The romantic idea of eloping—and that gossip—could be ridden out, and in another month or so she could announce she was pregnant.

This was perfect. Relief spread through her body, and feeling much better, she rolled out of the bed and to her feet. She had the bones of a plan now; she just needed to flesh them out. Energy flowed through her as the plan started to solidify. She'd go to Vegas tomorrow and marry Nick.

What if Nick doesn't want to get married? the little voice in her head asked.

That was the hitch in her plan. She didn't know how Nick would respond to the news he was going to be a father, and she really didn't know how he felt about marriage. What would she do if he said no?

Nick wasn't going to say no. He couldn't. He'd want to do the right thing.

And if he didn't? Well, she was a Harrison, and she'd just have to make him an offer he couldn't refuse.

Nick crossed the lobby, his body and mind at odds. Something wasn't right—possibly even very wrong—but he couldn't have stayed away if he'd wanted to. His skin had felt tight and hot since he'd found Evie's message on his phone after his meeting with the soon-to-be-former owners of The Zoo.

Her message was the stuff of teenage male fantasy: "I'm at the Bellagio. I'll be here all day, so call or just come on by when you can." She'd left a phone and room number, and his body had reacted like she'd run a hand over him.

But when Evie left almost four weeks ago, she'd seemed unsure when—or even if—she'd be back in Vegas. To hear from her so quickly...well, it was a stroke to his ego, but also disconcerting. He knew something wasn't right—he could hear it in her voice—but he was headed for her hotel right now because he wasn't thinking with his big head at the moment.

Maybe he was just being paranoid. Looking for problems where none existed. He couldn't shake the feeling, though, even as he knocked on her door.

Evie was a bit slow answering, and while she looked happy to see him, her smile was hesitant—not that dazzling, mega-watt one he remembered so well. "It's good to see you again. Come on in." She held the door open for him, turning her cheek up for a chaste kiss as he passed.

Not exactly the greeting his body had hoped for, and the alarm bells rang louder. The bells were temporarily muted, though, by the realization he wasn't in an ordinary hotel room. Evie was staying in a suite—and a damn nice one at that.

"How've you been?" Evie led him to the sofa and indicated he should sit. Her spine ramrod straight, she perched on the edge of the sofa and clasped her hands in her lap.

"Good. And you?"

Evie's smile faltered, but she recovered quickly. "I'm well, thank you. I'm glad you came." Her voice was strained, tee-tering on the edge of something.

"And I'm glad you called. I didn't think you'd be able to return to Vegas so soon."

This was awkward. Evie was acting strangely—too polite, too formal and totally unlike the woman he remembered. She was casually dressed in jeans and a green top that brought out the color of her eyes, and her auburn hair was tied back in a long ponytail that draped over her shoulder. But she could have easily been wearing white gloves and a ball dress for all the cool formality of her attitude. If it weren't for the suffocating tension and the pinched look she wore, he almost expected her to offer him tea and a crumpet at any moment.

"Would you like something to drink? A snack, maybe?"

He bit back the absurd laugh and hid it by clearing his throat. "Evie, what's wrong? You're acting…" He searched for the right word. For lack of anything better, he added, "Weird."

Her shoulders sagged a little and she ran a hand across her face. "I know. I've been trying to figure out how to say this, but there's just no good way."

There were those alarm bells again, clanging with intensity as Evie took a deep breath. "Then spit it out."

She blew out the air noisily and met his eyes. Hers were bleak, slightly haunted. "I'm pregnant."

The surprise at her announcement was minimal, but it didn't keep him from feeling as if he'd been punched in the stomach with the confirmation. Where to start…? "You're sure?"

Evie cocked her head. "Very. And, yes, I'm also sure you're the father."

"I wasn't going to ask that." The sick feeling in his stomach and the million other things his brain was trying to process put more bite in those words than he intended.

"Sorry. There was no offense intended, but it is—*would be*—a reasonable question for you to ask, especially since we used protection."

"Fat lot of good that did, huh?" He'd known Evie was going to be trouble; he just hadn't known how much at the time. Now, he was in deep.

Evie shrugged. "Nothing's one hundred percent. However, you should know that I also plan to keep the baby."

He'd come to that conclusion already. She wouldn't spend the money coming here to tell him if she planned to terminate the pregnancy. The first of the knots in his stomach untwisted with that knowledge. Which meant she... "So you need money?"

Her eyebrows went up in surprise. "No. I don't need any money. I'm fully able to support this baby by myself."

A moment too late he realized that was a stupid question to ask. Evie was staying in a suite at the Bellagio; that in itself was proof she didn't need financial support. He'd thought before how Evie looked "expensive," and obviously she was. But just *how* expensive was a question mark. He shouldn't judge her based on his mother's actions, but beautiful rich women...

Evie continued, unaware of his thoughts. "And I'm also happy to work out a visitation agreement that will be agreeable to us both—totally dependent on how much involvement you'd like have to have with the baby, of course."

Involvement? Visitation? Damn it, he'd forgotten for a moment that Evie lived in Dallas. His child was going to be a thousand miles away, and his mind began to race with questions and possibilities and...

"But there *is* something I need from you."

That stopped his thoughts. Evie was about to drop the other shoe. Her eyes were serious, and she looked as if she was steeling herself for what she wanted to say. If she didn't need money, then what? Cautiously, he asked, "And that would be...?"

She took another deep breath. "I need you to marry me."

The words hung in the air as he waited for the punch line. There didn't seem to be one. "Excuse me?"

Evie shot to her feet and began to pace. "I know, it sounds old-fashioned in this day and age, but I need you to marry me."

"You said you didn't need financial support."

"And I don't. *Seriously*. I have more money than I know what to do with." Evie rolled her eyes, making that sound like a bad thing. "What I don't have is a hus-husband," she tripped over the word, "and for me, that's a *huge* problem." Her hands were moving frantically as she spoke, and she finally clasped them together. Maybe he'd read this situation wrong. Evie was certainly agitated; maybe she was worried, scared... "I know this sounds really strange, but I have to get married. I can*not* be an unwed mother."

So much for *that* thought. Or any quaint thoughts about a child needing two parents or even a token compliment thrown his way. This was about her. "Embarrassed, are you, for getting knocked up?"

"It's not embarrassment—at least not for me. I'm going to end up in the papers, yes, but it's my family I'm concerned about."

Her pregnancy was newsworthy? That sick feeling started to settle in his stomach again. There was more to this story, and he wasn't going to like it. "You're not making any sense at all."

"My family is... They're...well...hell." She met his eyes steadily. "We're what you might call 'prominent' in Dallas, if you get my meaning. My brother runs the family's company and my sister-in-law is Gwen Sawyer-Harrison—the one they call 'Miss Behavior'—and she wrote all these etiquette books. We are society- and gossip-column fodder no matter *what* we do, and I'm their current favorite topic at the moment. Don't believe me? Look me up on Google. Evangeline Harrison. If I so much as *sneeze* in public it makes the news. Turning up pregnant... I can't even imagine what they'll say." She shook her head and shuddered. "Actually, I can. And it's going to be ugly."

The implications of her words finally sunk in. Evie was a socialite. An attention-seeking, famous-for-being-rich-and-beautiful socialite. His stomach turned over. Of all the women who came to Las Vegas looking for a good time, *he* managed to find the one who represented everything he most despised.

And she was carrying his baby.

Good Lord. It had to be a Rocco family trait: knock up a

rich-girl-gone-slumming. He had turned into his father. And his kid was going to be severely messed up when Evie decided being a mom didn't mesh well with her high-glam lifestyle. No, he could protect his child from that. He had what his father didn't: money. His child wouldn't grow up in the projects once its mother got over the urge to play Mommy and wanted her old life back—the life that didn't have a child in it.

Evie was staring at him wide-eyed and expectant, but there was worry in that stare. Three weeks ago, he wouldn't have pegged her as a socialite, but then she hadn't been acting like one. And he didn't have reason to look beyond the surface.

Not that women like that had much depth, anyway. The fact she was here, more concerned for herself and her reputation, proved that. "So the Dallas debutante can't face the music at home for her little Vegas-escape weekend."

Her eyes narrowed. "Don't 'poor-little-rich-girl' me. You don't know squat about me or my life at home. If it were just about me, I wouldn't give a flip about what the papers said or what anyone thought. But Will and Gwen will be hurt, disappointed and embarrassed. The consequences of my actions are going to affect more people than just me. My family..." Her voice cracked and she cleared her throat. "I'm just trying to mitigate the damage. To contain the fallout so it doesn't land all over the people I love. The easiest way to do that is to get married. Preferably to you, since you're the father of the child I'm carrying."

Interesting how the baby hadn't figured anywhere into that speech. Had Evie given *any* thought to the child? Or him for that matter? He was supposed to jump to attention, relish the opportunity to marry her exalted self? "And if I'm not amenable to getting married?"

The air seemed to rush out of Evie, and she sagged into a chair. "Then I'll figure something else out. I'm not sure *what* that will be exactly….” She propped her elbows on her knees and rested her chin on her hands. “Are you saying marriage is totally out of the question? Or are you willing to hear my proposal?”

He crossed his arms and leaned back in his seat. Oh, he couldn't *wait* to hear this. “I thought ‘I need you to marry me’ was your proposal.”

Evie rolled her eyes. “Want me to get down on one knee?” She shrugged. “So it wasn't flowers and romance. Think of it as a business arrangement if it helps. We get married—as soon as possible if that works for you—and you only need to stay married to me for a year or so. Sometime after the baby is born, we can file for a simple, amicable, no-fault divorce.”

That word slammed into him, driving home his earlier concerns. “I do need you to come to Dallas and make nice with my family and smile for the papers, but otherwise, I won't interfere with your day-to-day life. I'll be moving here—”

That nicely addressed one problem, but… “Why?”

“It makes sense. Why wouldn't I move to be with my husband? And this is far enough away to keep me out of the spotlight at home.” The corner of her mouth curved down briefly.

“And that's a good thing?” Women like Evie usually thrived on attention—the more the better.

“I've spent enough time in the fishbowl. Some anonymity will do me good.” She cleared her throat again. “But, this is the digital age, so for the sake of appearances, it might be better if we lived together—as roommates only, of course— but if that's out of the question for you, we can figure something else out.”

But which part? The living as roommates or living together at all? She'd put some thought into this. But who on earth got married and then lived as roommates only? *Probably the same kind of person who planned their divorce before they proposed.* "That's it?" he asked sarcastically. "You're not asking much, are you?"

"I *know* it's a lot to ask—and it will cramp your dating style a bit—" her mouth twisted, and he disliked the implication he picked up women in bars as a regular habit "—but all I really ask is that you don't do anything that could get back to my family, or Dallas for that matter, and cause embarrassment for me, my family or the baby." She paused and bit her lip. Something else was coming.... "And you'll need to sign a prenup."

Evie had thrown a lot at him in the last few minutes, and he was still trying to process all of the information. She seemed to take his silence as disagreement, though, and reached for a manila file on the coffee table. "I'll give you a few minutes to read it over, and then...and then we'll talk more." She stood without making eye contact and went to the minibar, where she poured a soda with intentional slowness.

Curious, he flipped open the file. It was a pretty standard agreement: anything Evie had before their marriage—and damn, it *was* substantial—stayed hers. Upon her death, her assets went into a trust managed by her attorney for their child—or children, he noted with surprise. Likewise, everything of his remained his, but without a codicil for the children if something happened to him. She obviously hadn't told whoever drew up this contract she was pregnant already, because there were clauses regarding her inheritance and her heirs if there were no children from the marriage. Darkly, he realized that she'd left him a nice settlement in case of her death.

If he'd been looking to get married, it would be a sweet deal. But he hadn't been looking to get married. The baby— *his* baby—changed everything.

But in case of divorce... "What the hell is this, Evie?"

Nick could tell by the tensing of her shoulders she'd been waiting for him to reach that section.

She faced him with bravado. "That's your settlement. It's rather standard, actually, to set a fixed sum for each year of marriage. In our case...well, I wanted to compensate you for the inconvenience of marrying me."

Inconvenience was an interesting word choice. So was *compensate*. "Sounds like a bribe to me."

Her jaw dropped. "It's not a bribe—"

"Then why is the next clause a nondisclosure agreement that forfeits that money if I talk?"

"I'd like some privacy, *some* part of my life I don't have to worry about making the news. That clause isn't anything out of the ordinary, and the money—"

"I don't want your money, Evie."

"But—"

"I believed you when you said you didn't need my money. Trust me when I say I don't *want* yours. I don't need a stud fee. That deed was done for free."

Evie turned a shade of red that clashed with her hair. Then she squared her shoulders and looked at him coolly. "There's no need to be crude. I was only trying to be fair to you."

Politeness dripped off every word. Watching Evie retreat behind a wall of good manners would be amusing in any other situation, but bordered on absurd now. "I don't see anything about custody arrangements."

"Because most people aren't pregnant when they sign pre-nups, and you can't make custody arrangements for children that don't exist yet." Evie was still unfailingly polite, but he could hear the undercurrent of frustration in her voice. "Those arrangements come with divorce papers."

Custody arrangements were foremost in his mind at the moment. Damn it. He had a master plan and marriage—to anyone—hadn't been in it. He was ahead of his schedule, but marrying a spoiled socialite wasn't on that schedule *anywhere*. And a baby...

Risk of fallout or not, he didn't doubt Evie would go home to have this child if he refused to marry her. He didn't give a damn about her reputation or the "problems" that would cause her family, but it did create problems for him. One, he wouldn't be able to keep an eye on Evie while she was pregnant. She could do God-knows-what for the next nine months and cause the baby to have all kinds of problems.

He was a hands-on project manager: marrying Evie would give him oversight of this pregnancy.

Secondly, refusing to marry Evie now could put him in legal difficulties later when he *did* sue for custody. She could use this moment against him later, claiming she'd offered him the chance to claim paternity and he'd refused.

The fact she had money—and a powerful family—added a degree of difficulty to the situation. If on the off-chance she did decide to fight him in the future, she'd have the where-withal; he didn't need to give her any additional ammunition.

That was a slim chance anyway. Her family probably wouldn't want a reminder of Evie's mistake. They wouldn't want his less-than-blue-blood or his blue-collar DNA sullying the Harrison bloodline.

But marrying Evie would give him all kinds of rights and give him some control over the situation. If Evie proved to be a good mother, he didn't *have* to divorce her, and his child could grow up with two parents. People married for less noble causes and managed to live somewhat harmoniously. She'd called it a business arrangement. Crude wording, but true.

Decision made, he took a pen out of his pocket and drew a line through the divorce settlement clause and initialed the change. "You'll need to initial that before you sign. We can get it witnessed and notarized when we get our marriage license."

He didn't realize how tense Evie was until he saw her close her eyes as the relief washed over her. When she opened them, the relief there was tempered by an uncertain discomfort and cautious disbelief.

Nick knew exactly how she felt.

Dear Lord, was she actually going to *do* this? Evie felt a weight lift off her shoulders only to be replaced by a strange sick feeling in her stomach. She'd spent all her time working on the plan to get Nick to agree, but she hadn't thought beyond that. Marrying Nick sounded so good in theory—the baby would know its father, she wouldn't have to face the press—but now that it was about to become *reality,* she was afraid she was about to make a huge mistake.

For both her and the baby. This baby wouldn't lack for anything, and she worried now that bringing Nick into the situation instead of just facing the music alone might not be the best idea in the long run.

Because this Nick wasn't the one she remembered. The fun-loving, laid-back Nick of a few weeks ago had been replaced by a man with a hard jaw who very early on in this "meeting" had began to look at her with what she could only describe as distaste. And she didn't understand why.

After all, she'd worked very hard to make her proposal as palatable for him as possible. She'd rehearsed this; she wasn't coming to him all needy or trying to play on his conscience. She was offering him a very fair arrangement, and he was acting like…like…

His sarcasm, the cold bite in his words, the way he was scowling at her… *Ugh.* Topped with the cool efficiency as he flipped through the prenup and discussed details… She almost backed out of the whole plan because she'd be better off dealing with Will than Nick. At least she knew how to handle Will when he got like this.

For someone whose plan was coming together, who was getting exactly what she wanted, she felt as if she was strapped in a guillotine, unsure whether she dreaded or welcomed the fall of the blade. She gave Nick one more chance to back down. "Are we really going to do this? Like right *now?*"

One dark brow arched at her. "Why wait? This was your idea, not mine. Cold feet already?"

Yes. "No, not at all." *Now what?* Lighten the mood, that's what. "So...what do we do? Go to the courthouse? Elvis at a drive-through?"

Nick thought for a moment, and Evie would have given her trust fund to know exactly what was going through his mind. "I actually have a few things to do first. Give me a couple of hours and then we'll go."

A couple of hours. She felt the guillotine blade slide a little bit. That short of a reprieve wouldn't give her much time to get her head sorted back out. "Okay." What was she going to do with herself for a couple of hours? *Besides* hyperventilate.

"Do you have a dress?"

That snapped her back to the conversation. "Pardon me?"

"A dress? To get married in? I'm assuming you'll want pictures to show your family, and you won't want to be in jeans."

She hadn't thought of that. She mentally sorted through her suitcase and came up empty. That showed how out of it she was; she came to Vegas to get married and didn't even pack a nice dress. Maybe deep down, she'd been expecting—hoping?—this plan would fall through and not happen at all. "You know, I don't. I guess I can shop for something while you...you do...whatever it is you need to go do."

Nick nodded, but his scowl didn't diminish at all. "I'll pick you up at eight, then."

She walked Nick to the door, the uncomfortable tension between them so different than what she remembered from before. When the door closed behind him, Evie leaned against it and banged her head gently. This was absurd; she was marrying a man she barely knew simply because she was carrying his child. How had she ended up here?

She'd allowed herself one tiny romanticized daydream where this conversation worked out completely differently…. But no. This was a business agreement. She knew that. She swallowed her disappointment Nick was treating it as such.

Evie looked at her watch and sighed. She needed a dress, but the last thing she felt like doing was shopping. Thankfully, there were plenty of great shops right here in the Bellagio. They'd have something for her to wear.

By fifteen to eight, she'd showered and redone her hair and makeup and was sliding the zipper up on the simple ivory sheath she'd found. It was perfect for a simple wedding, and were the circumstances different, she'd be thrilled to wear it. This was a far cry from the princess-style wedding she and Gwen had talked about when she was a teenager. Not that that kind of wedding had been her dream—she always imagined something more intimate and private—but this wedding was falling far short of *any* kind of romantic fantasy.

Instead, she was getting ready for her wedding alone in a hotel suite. She should have let Bennie come with her; it just seemed wrong to get married without any of her family and friends around.

Her fiancé was gorgeous and sexy and made her heart pound to think about him; Nick was practically the groom of adolescent fantasy weddings in the flesh. But…

This wasn't going to be a romantic story she'd share with her child in the years to come, that was for sure. The disappointment in her stomach was real—a physical pain. She'd always assumed that when she did get married, it would be forever; a marriage like Will and Gwen's, like her parents'.

The sharp knock at her door startled her. A glance at the clock told her Nick was punctual, if nothing else.

She said goodbye to her girlish fantasy and faced reality.

Evie slid her feet into her shoes and grabbed her purse. With one last deep breath to steady her nerves and fortify her resolve, she went to get married.

CHAPTER FIVE

WHEN EVIE OPENED THE DOOR, she was steeled for the worst. She wasn't prepared, though, for the physical reaction that slammed into her, stealing her breath and causing heat to coil through her veins. She'd seen Nick in jeans; she'd seen him in a work-appropriate shirt and tie earlier, but in black slacks and a black button-down silk shirt…*damn*. He looked wicked and delicious, and only showing up naked at her door could have affected her pulse more.

He had showered and shaved, and his dark hair fell casually over his forehead in a tousle most men would have to spend hours to achieve. If things were just a little different…

But the arching of Nick's eyebrow was a harsh reminder of the reality of the situation. Things weren't different. Things were what they were. He tempered that reminder, though, with a simple, "You look nice, Evie," that caused her heart to stutter regardless.

"Thank you. You look pretty good yourself." She pulled the door closed behind her and gripped her handbag tightly to keep her fingers from sliding over that silk shirt to feel the man beneath. As they walked toward the elevator, Nick's hand landed on the small of her back.

It was a simple gesture—commonplace, even—but Evie

felt as if she'd been touched by a live wire. Had she really offered Nick a marriage in name only? That they'd live simply as roommates? She had to be insane. How had she forgotten the magnetism of this man?

In the close confines of the elevator, each breath she took was filled with his scent, and her thighs were trembling as they descended.

"That's a nice dress. Didn't they have anything in white?"

She cut her eyes at him. Was that an insult or a tease? His dry tone didn't help; he could have been discussing the interior decor of the elevator. "White's not a good color for me. Too harsh against my skin tone."

Nick merely nodded, which didn't tell her anything,

She swallowed. "So, what's the plan?"

"Kevin and Lottie are meeting us in the lobby. We'll go to the license bureau first—"

Whoa. "I'm sorry, who are Kevin and Lottie?"

"Kevin is my friend and business partner. Lottie is his wife. I couldn't get married without telling them."

That caused her conscience to twinge in guilt, and she thought sadly of her family again. "I see."

The elevator doors opened, and Nick took her hand as she stepped out, stopping her just beyond the threshold. "My friends don't know the true circumstances surrounding this wedding, and I'd like to keep it that way—although for different reasons than you."

She hadn't thought about what Nick might tell his friends and family. Realizing all the things she'd forgotten in her plan was quickly becoming a full-time job. "Of course. One happy couple, coming up."

Nick smiled for the first time and butterflies battered her insides. He didn't let go of her hand, either, and a nice warmth moved through her as they crossed the lobby in the direction of a couple wearing bright smiles.

"Kevin, Lottie, this is Evie."

Kevin had average Irish good looks—tall and ruddy—an open, honest face and a contagious grin that put her at ease almost immediately. Lottie, in contrast, was petite, with beautiful olive skin and long black hair that hung to her waist. Lottie immediately wrapped Evie in a hug that made her feel welcome and slightly guilty for deceiving this nice woman.

"You're even more beautiful than Nick said," Lottie gushed, "but I'm sure we're going to be great friends, regardless."

Evie was still reeling over the news Nick had told these people she was beautiful as Lottie rushed on. "Later, you'll have to tell me how you managed to snare Nick. I'd all but given up on him finding someone."

"Let her breathe, Lottie," Kevin admonished his wife. Turning his grin at Evie, he extended a hand and continued, "You're a brave girl, tying yourself to this guy."

Evie felt a bit overwhelmed and unsure of what to say. "I'm very happy to meet you both. Nick has told me so much about you."

From the identical shocked expressions on Kevin and Lottie's faces, she worried she'd stepped in something, but she wasn't sure what. She knew she wasn't the *best* actress, but had she blown it already?

Then Kevin laughed. "Nick talking. That's a first."

Confused, she looked at Nick, who merely shrugged. *Great. That's helpful.*

Lottie took her husband's hand. "I told you she'd have to be something special."

She didn't feel very special at the moment. "He is the strong, silent type, isn't he? That's okay, because I can talk enough for both of us."

Lottie beamed, and Evie wanted to like her—felt as if she *could* really like her and maybe have a friend in Las Vegas already—but the guilt was killing her. If the guilt of deception was this bad just with Nick's friends, how on earth would she survive her family?

Nick continued to hold her hand as they followed Kevin and Lottie out and into a waiting SUV. Kevin held the door open for her with a mock bow. "I'll be your driver for the evening. Sit back and relax. First stop, marriage license bureau."

She'd been surprised to learn that any government agency in the world was open until midnight seven days a week, but as she filled out the paperwork for her marriage license along with several other couples, she understood the necessity of it in Las Vegas.

Her license was still hot off the printer when Kevin herded them back into the car and screeched out of the parking lot. Just a few minutes later, she was entering a chapel, and Lottie was pushing a small bouquet of roses and daisies into her hands.

Her chest constricted, and it became difficult to breathe. *Back out. Run. Forget this whole plan.* Then Nick tucked her arm under his. She jumped in surprise.

He leaned close to her ear and whispered, "You're not planning on ditching me at the altar, are you?"

The humor in his voice banked the onset of her panic attack, and she looked up to see an amused glint in his eyes. "Actually, I am."

"Too late," he countered, as a balding man waved them forward and Kevin and Lottie took their places on either side of them.

She'd never realized how quick a wedding ceremony actually was, and the minister was looking to her for a response before she'd had a chance to catch her breath. Nick's "I do" seemed to boom in her head, even though she knew he'd said it at normal volume.

At least she wasn't in a tacky chapel being married by an Elvis with fake sideburns. This chapel was actually rather nice: understated and charming, lit by soft candlelight and peaceful. While she'd been floundering in confusion and trying to find a decent dress to wear, Nick had been busy planning something nice for their wedding. Her stomach gave a funny flip at the idea.

She panicked when the minister asked for the rings, but Lottie touched her arm gently and passed her a heavy gold band with a faint outline of Celtic knots across the surface. Evie fought back tears as Nick took her hand and slid a matching band over her knuckle. This wedding was perfect and beautiful and totally false. It was killing her.

When she turned her head, she saw Nick's strong profile as he listened to the minister pronounce them husband and wife. Nick turned to her and smiled wryly as he lowered his head to brush a gentle kiss across her lips. Time seemed to stop, and her heart beat faster as that kiss arced through her, stirring her blood with desire. But the gentleness of it caused her stomach to flip over again, making the moment feel poignant and important and one she wanted to remember for the rest of her life. She leaned in, pressing her mouth more fully against his, and she felt his lips soften as if he were going to deepen the kiss, make it…

Then Kevin clapped and Lottie was snapping pictures and horrid reality crashed in. Rice landed on her shoulders and slid inside her dress, and they were back outside with a certificate proving they were married before she could wrap her head around it. Another couple was already taking their place at the chapel doors; a very young couple with ear-to-ear grins and an inability to keep their hands off each other. She was suddenly irrationally jealous.

Needing a moment to regain her equilibrium, Evie pretended great interest in the envelope containing her marriage certificate. The date and "Mr. and Mrs. Nicolas Rocco" were written in fancy script across the front.

Mr. and Mrs. She was now Evie Rocco—a name she hadn't known until a couple of hours ago. Or maybe she should do like Gwen and hyphenate: Evangeline Harrison-Rocco. No. Too many letters. She guessed it didn't matter too much; she wasn't going to be keeping the name for very long.

That bothered her more than she liked.

Nick was being very quiet; something she found a little odd, but Kevin and Lottie didn't seem at all bothered. Evie got the feeling Nick's silence really was normal as far as they were concerned. In the backseat of Kevin's SUV, she leaned as close to Nick as her seat belt would allow.

"Thank you for arranging something so nice. I really didn't want to get married at a drive-through," she whispered, hoping Kevin and Lottie would think they were simply nuzzling newlyweds.

He shrugged. "Thank Lottie. It was mostly her doing."

Oh. So much for warm fuzzies. "I see," she whispered, trying to keep the deflation out of her voice by thinking of the way that kiss at the chapel had almost…

"None of that," Kevin shouted from the driver's seat, and Evie jumped back to her side of the backseat. "I know you're eager to get to your bridal suite and—" Lottie's hand smacking his arm cut Kevin off.

Evie choked back a laugh. Lottie and Kevin reminded her a little of Will and Gwen, the way she kept pulling him back into line. The amusement faded, though, at the thought of how disappointed Will and Gwen were going to be when she showed up at home with her new husband.

"Ahem," Kevin started again. "Lottie has a surprise for you two first."

She felt she'd had enough surprises recently, but it would be ungracious to say so. But déjà vu set in along with surprise when Kevin parked in the lot at Blue and indicated they should get out.

"Obviously your last date here worked out pretty well," he grinned lasciviously and winked, "so Lottie thought it might be a nice place to start off your new life together."

Nick's eyebrows drew together. "The roof is booked tonight."

"It *was*," Kevin corrected. He looked at Evie. "I had to tick off a few B-list celebs by cancelling their party, but they were happy enough to be rebooked in the VIP room at Starlight."

"Kevin," Nick growled.

Kevin waved him off and leaned into Evie as they walked. "Nick's partial to Blue since it's his pride and joy, but really, Starlight will work for them just fine. It's not like he's really losing any money off of it."

All kinds of details were pressing their way through the fog that had entered her brain the moment she met Nick, and now she needed some answers. Answers she *should* have gotten before she waded into this, but Nick and clearheaded thinking didn't come as a package deal. Evie plastered a smile on her face. "Could you excuse us for just a second? I haven't had a chance to be alone with Nick since…"

Kevin lifted his hands as he backed away. "No problem. Lottie and I will go check on your surprise. Just don't get too carried away." He winked and disappeared through Blue's door.

Evie grabbed Nick's hand and pulled him out of the direct line of sight of the door. "Explain to me how you 'know the owner' of this nightclub?"

Nick cleared his throat. "Well…"

"You and Kevin own this place, don't you? This is how you're business partners, isn't it?" Why hadn't he told her?

"Not exactly."

"Oh." She felt foolish and wished it was a little darker in this parking lot so he couldn't see the flush she felt on her cheeks.

"I own Blue. Kevin runs a different part of the business."

She felt her jaw drop. "You own Blue outright?"

He smirked. "And four other clubs."

How'd she miss *that* piece of information? All those details she'd overlooked—first in lust, and then in her marriage panic—jumped to the forefront to scream at her. Nick's expensive car, the obviously custom cut of his clothes, the deference of the employees here at Blue and Starlight…

"Including Starlight?" She waved the question away before Nick could reply; she didn't really need an answer that obvious. "No wonder you didn't need a divorce settlement spelled out in the prenup."

Nick stiffened. "So you did think you could buy me off with money. Go slumming and use your trust fund to get out of the mess?"

She lifted her chin at the insult. "I'm not even going to dignify that with a response."

"Don't bother to try." His jaw hardened. "You're not the only one who can afford to support this child."

That seemed a gross understatement. "I see that now. Why didn't you just tell me this that first night?"

The corner of his mouth curled again, but this time it was in sarcasm. "Probably for the same reason you didn't mention your trust fund."

She would *not* feel guilty, damn it, for not advertising who she was on their first date. "I wanted you to think I was just an average girl." Her voice dropped. "I guess we both surprised each other."

Nick crossed his arms over his chest. "And this disappoints you somehow?"

His attitude rankled her. The last warm fuzzy feeling from earlier evaporated. "Not at all. In fact, it will make things much easier at home. Less speculation about *why* we got married."

He looked at her stomach pointedly. "I think the *why* will become obvious soon enough."

She wanted to hit him just hard enough to knock that sarcastic look off his face. "Yes, but at least no one should be able to accuse *you* of knocking me up just to get a piece of my inheritance."

"Or think you're a fool for letting it happen," he finished for her, the words dripping with bitter disdain.

The urge to smack him was growing stronger by the second. "Exactly. It's all about me, you know."

"Isn't it?" he challenged.

Anger battled insult and came out as outrage. "*Excuse* me? What do you mean by *that?*"

"Couldn't you have just as easily claimed to have fallen hard for your personal trainer and avoided all this? I'm sure he would love the 'settlement' you outlined *and* served your purpose nicely enough."

She opened her mouth to inform him she didn't *have* a personal trainer before she realized the stupidity of that argument. "If you have some kind of problem with me—" Nick snorted and she dug her nails into her palms. "Which obviously you *do,* why on earth did you agree to marry me?"

"As you said, it's *my* baby." Nick's possessive tone grated across her already raw nerves.

"You seem to be taking that at face value. No doubts about paternity? No real fears about my trainer?"

He stiffened. "Like you'd come all the way to Vegas to get me to marry you if the baby wasn't mine. It's too easily disproved."

"Are you two coming or not?" Lottie's head appeared around the door as she shouted for them.

"In a second," Nick called, and Lottie disappeared back inside. "Come on," he muttered at her.

She took a step back. She'd been insulted enough for one day. "No way. I'm going back to my hotel now."

A muscle twitched in his jaw. "This was your idea, Evie."

"It was *your* idea to involve your friends. Not mine."

Nick's eyes narrowed. "If you can't pull this off in front of Kevin and Lottie—who, by the way, are genuinely happy for us—then you don't have a prayer of convincing *your* family."

Dear God, he was right. She needed to screw her head on straight, suck it up and ride out this rodeo. She took a deep breath, trying to calm herself. She was doing what was best for the baby, for her family—for everyone. She needed to stay focused on that. The deed was done—she was pregnant and safely married—now she had to follow through.

If she managed to survive this with her sanity and dignity intact, she would never, *ever,* step outside the lines again. *I swear, God, really.* She'd live the most boring, circumspect, politically correct life Dallas had ever seen.

If she managed to survive.

She nodded her agreement at Nick and plastered a smile on her face as he took her elbow and led her to the door. To her surprise and chagrin, her skin tingled where it touched his, and getting back in close proximity caused an uptick in her pulse.

That *if* was getting more questionable by the moment.

Kevin might have initially been skeptical about this sudden wedding, but Lottie—who just happened to be right there when Nick called—had let her inner romantic out to run free at his first mention of the word *married.* Even Kevin had warmed to the idea rather quickly—thanks to Lottie—trapping Nick in their romanticized reading of the situation before he could tell Kevin the truth. He hadn't planned on misleading Kevin about this wedding, but he got in too deep too fast to extricate himself gracefully.

As the elevator doors opened to the roof, he realized he should have stopped them both long before now. The Sheik's Tent was romantically lit with candles, and Lottie had sent someone up here with flowers and a miniature wedding cake. Kevin popped the cork on a bottle of champagne as the elevator doors closed behind them.

Lottie was beaming, but apologetic. "It's not much, but on such short notice…"

He looked at Evie, whose shoulders seemed to square as Lottie spoke, and noticed the kind smile on her face. "It's beautiful, Lottie. So much more than I could've hoped for. Thank you."

Evie could pull out the grace and graciousness in a milli-second. In fact, he was beginning to notice how the more un-comfortable she got in a situation, the more polite and amiable she became. Except with him. Evie was shooting daggers in his direction every time she caught his eye, but she played her part well, holding his hand, trailing her fingers down his arm playfully and generally driving him insane with her touch. But with Lottie and Kevin, she turned on the charm, accepting their toast with the tiniest of sips of the excellent champagne, admiring the cake and expressing what looked like genuine interest in them both.

All the hallmarks of the society belle she was. He needed to remember that, and not get blinded by her beauty or her charm. Nick could easily picture Evie at her debutante ball, a charity gala, even a polo match, working the crowd with charm and ease. But Kevin and Lottie left as soon as they cut the cake—Kevin making ribald comments about need-ing privacy while Lottie hushed him and dug elbows into his ribs.

Their exit left him alone with his wife, who shut off that charm the moment the elevator doors closed behind their wedding guests.

Evie lapsed into silence, setting aside her champagne glass and foraging behind the bar for a bottle of water. She sank onto the low sofa, only to jump to her feet again as if it burned her. The flush rising over the V of her neckline made clear the memories of that sofa were fresh in her mind, as well.

Although his earlier compliment had been rather offhand, something that seemed appropriate to say in the silence, Evie looked more than just nice. She looked beautiful, as stunning as the first time he laid eyes on her, but tonight her elegance and good breeding were on display, as well as her charms. Her skin glowed in the candlelight, and the simple dress hugged the delicious curves he remembered with stark, haunting clarity.

And while he was touched by Lottie's thoughtfulness, he rather wished they'd not brought him and Evie here, of all places. Returning to the scene of one of his most erotic memories with the woman who played the starring role had his body hard and aching, but tonight was a far cry from last time. Instead of the sensual, exciting Evie of his memory, this Evie was distant, wary and bordering on hostile.

She was also his pregnant wife, and the stunning absurdity of *that* knowledge was enough to send him behind the bar to search for something stronger than champagne.

"So we seem to be stuck here. What do we do now?" Evie asked, as the silence stretched out between them.

He raised an eyebrow at her, and she blushed deeper.

"I mean, the official part is taken care of, so where do we go from here?" She twisted the gold band on her ring finger as she spoke.

His body had a grand idea, and it circled around Evie wearing nothing but that gold band. Somehow, he knew Evie wouldn't be amenable to *that*. "Are you hungry?" he asked lamely for lack of something better. Lottie's minions had left a simple cold dinner behind the bar.

"No. My stomach's all tied up in knots at the moment. Food is the last thing I need. But I guess we *do* need to stay here for a little while, at least. You go ahead, if you're hungry."

Evie pulled out a chair and sat at the small table, the politeness back in her voice and her hands folded neatly on the table. "We can make a few plans, get our story straight."

"What's there to get straight?"

Her tone all business, she jumped into the conversation. "I'd really like to avoid dropping two bombs on my family at once. Our elopement will be enough of a shock for them without mentioning the baby. I can call home with *that* news in a couple of weeks—after they've had a chance to recover."

"Unless your family is stupid, surely they'll make the leap from elopement to pregnant."

Evie shrugged. "Maybe not. This isn't the first time I've done something crazy and unexpected." A bitter laugh escaped.

So she did have a wild streak. "This is merely par for the course?"

"I wouldn't say that. Eloping is definitely an extreme even *I* hadn't considered. There will be speculation, of course, about me being pregnant, but I'll be safely up here before any of that gets spinning." She drummed her nails on the glass tabletop, but when he came to take the chair opposite hers, she slid back and moved her hands in her lap. "Since we're mar-married," she stumbled over the word, "I'd like to break the news to my family as soon as possible, and I think it would be more believable if you were with me. Is your schedule flexible enough for you to come to Dallas for a couple of days?"

It wasn't. Especially not with a sale pending on The Zoo. But something in Evie's wide green eyes stopped him from saying so. "I'll need to make a few calls in the morning to arrange things, but we could go to Dallas tomorrow afternoon."

Evie's shoulders dropped in relief, and she nodded. "You could be back here by the weekend, but it may take me a couple more days to get my things together, tie up a few loose ends at work—"

"You have a job?" He couldn't keep the shock out of his voice. Between the state of her finances and the fact she was in Vegas on a Tuesday, he'd assumed being beautiful *was* her primary job.

Her eyes narrowed at him again. "Of course I have a job. It's not much of one, but it's a job."

Most people would describe a job flipping burgers like that, but there was no way Evie worked for minimum wage. But what did someone like Evie do? Honestly curious, he asked her.

"I work in HarCorp's marketing department."

He'd used Google to look up Evie shortly after leaving her hotel this afternoon. In addition to seeing her smiling face at every society event in Dallas worthy of making the paper, he'd found Evie's description of her "family's company" to be misleading. HarCorp was a huge international company with fingers in many different pies. And she worked in their marketing department? The surprise must have shown on his face, and Evie's mouth twisted.

"I've been regulated to PR mostly—doing all the 'public stuff' like charity work and fundraisers—and it's only part-time, but it was the best I could do considering my brother's extreme surprise I'd even want to work for the company." That hollow, bitter laugh escaped again. "I see you're surprised, as well. I realize you can only judge me based on our current fiasco, but I'm not a complete ditz. I graduated at the top of my class and everything."

Oh, he had no doubt of her intelligence, even if everything *else* about her—including how she used that intelligence— was in question. "From finishing school? Let me guess... France?"

Evie bit her lip and he saw her knuckles whiten. Then she lifted her chin and smiled broadly. "Switzerland, actually. But I was really referring to Trinity University's Business

School. I should be able to get a job up here doing something, don't you agree?"

"Why would you want to?" She didn't need to work—even temporarily while she was pregnant. Did she not want to stay home with the baby?

Genuine confusion twisted her face. "What else would I do for the next nine months? Sit around and knit booties? You don't expect me to become president of the Junior League or join the UDC, do you?"

What was she talking about? "I have no idea what either of those are."

This time Evie's laugh was real, and it echoed off the stone walls of the roof. Even though he didn't understand the humor, her laugh reminded him of the Evie he'd met before. "Really? Oh, that's fabulous. I think I'm going to love living in Vegas."

"It's nothing like Dallas," he reminded her.

"And that's one of the many, *many* reasons I love Las Vegas." She eyed him carefully. "You're not press fodder, are you?"

"I don't know what you mean."

"Do you make the papers a lot? Gossip columns, fashion pages, society blogs, anything like that?"

Evie had a skewed view of the world. "Do you honestly think nightclub owners are interesting to the press? In *this* town?"

"I just wanted to be sure." She looked out at the skyline and sighed. When she didn't elaborate, he let the silence spin out until Evie started to shift uncomfortably in her seat and she cleared her throat. "Have we killed enough time up here? Can we go back to the hotel now?"

The absurd reality of the situation—which he'd managed to forget momentarily—settled around him. This was his wedding night, and he was sitting on the roof of Blue with his bride, debating what to do next.

That spark, that sizzling need that marked their first meeting, had been slightly damped by Evie's revelations and the circus of their wedding, but it was still there. The tightening of his body at the thought of what he *should* be doing with Evie on their wedding night was real enough, as had the light in Evie's eyes she hadn't been able to fully hide behind the variety of emotions she'd spiraled through this evening.

She'd blushed when she said she wanted to go back to the hotel, but she'd wanted a marriage in name only, like some sort of a bad movie plot, so he assumed Evie wouldn't be open to his idea of how to kill some time—here *or* at her hotel.

Her next words confirmed that.

"I've had a long day, and I want to go to bed. To sleep," she corrected. "I'm, um, tired. Really tired."

Well, he had his answer. Although every part of him protested, he wasn't going to push as if he was some sort of desperate teenager trying to get into her pants.

This marriage thing had to have some perks attached to it—beyond custody of his child. He'd let Evie think whatever she liked until they got back from Dallas, and then he'd explain the situation to her.

CHAPTER SIX

COWARD. EVIE PUNCHED her pillow into shape and curled around it as her stomach churned at the thought. She may have become more cautious, better behaved, over the years—with varying degrees of success, granted—but never had she been such an outright, chicken-livered, all-hat-and-no-cattle *coward.*

So now she was alone in her hotel suite on her wedding night, unable to sleep because she couldn't quit berating herself for her cowardice and unable to shake the feeling that, regardless of the circumstances surrounding their wedding, she should be having mind-blowing sex with her new husband right now.

Her blood heated with the memory, the fantasy of what could've been on the agenda for tonight, if she hadn't been such a weenie when Nick turned her question around on her. Despite everything else going on, she'd felt the tension in him, seen the barely banked desire in his eyes. He might not like her very much, but he *did* want her.

And while her body had been all in favor of taking what she could get, her pride was still smarting from his revelations and his treatment of her, and she'd backed down.

If she wasn't such a coward, she'd have asked him straight out *what* his new problem was, but how could you ask someone "Why don't you like me?" without it sounding like a pathetic whine? Was he angry she was pregnant? Did he blame her? Think she did it on purpose? Or had he only been out for a good time and now resented the result? Had she been suckered in by a player and fallen for his lines? That was an unpleasant thought.

The deed was done now. She was married to Nick—at least for the near future.

They'd killed a little more time on the roof—Nick booking plane tickets back to Dallas while she sent Gwen a text inviting herself and a friend over for drinks the next night—before they snuck out the back door of Blue like thieves. Nick had delivered her back here without much conversation, then left. She assumed he went home—wherever that was.

God, she didn't even know where he *lived*.

She couldn't help but wonder if she'd made a grave mistake in her rush to try to fix this situation before it exploded in her face. Nick, at least, seemed game to hold up his end of the bargain—even though he had no real reason to do so—so she should be thankful for that.

Still, it seemed wrong to be married and not have any of the benefits that went with it. *Why* had she opened her big mouth? Hadn't she learned anything about negotiating a contract from listening to Will over the years? Obviously not, or else she wouldn't be burning with frustration right now.

With a groan, she rolled to her other side and looked at the clock. Maybe she'd feel better once she got the showdown at home over with. After she dealt with her family, she could concentrate on sorting out the mess she'd already made of her marriage.

Nick had never been taken home to meet the family before. He wasn't the type of guy women took home to their parents—not since he picked up his prom date had he been expected to make nice with the family. This would be awkward no matter what the circumstances were, but the tension radiating off of Evie had his own nerves on alert in response.

Their conversation—if that's what it could be called—on the flight to Dallas had been stilted at best and circled around their "story." Evie seemed lost in thought most of the time, staring out the window and often dropping off to monosyllabic replies to his questions.

The flight had been delayed, and they'd barely dropped their bags at Evie's place before she was ushering him out the door and muttering about not being late as if tardiness was a capital crime.

He let Evie drive without comment since she knew the way, but her knuckles were white from her grip on the steering wheel. She seemed to be carrying on an interesting conversation with herself, and he couldn't get a word in edgewise. But that graciousness he'd seen her pull out before came into play when they pulled to a stop in front of a high-rise building, and she turned that dazzling smile on the doorman as she handed over her car keys.

In the elevator, she finally looked at him directly, and he saw a spark of energy there he recognized. Evie was steeling herself for a fight, and she was ready for it, even. "Just let me take the lead on this, okay? This won't take long. Just stick to our story like the gospel, and the ugliness will be over quickly."

Ugliness?

He saw her set her jaw and take a deep breath as she slid her key into the door, and he wondered *what* the hell kind of family Evie came from. He rather felt as if the guard escorting the princess into the dragon's lair for the sacrifice.

"I'm here!" Evie singsonged as she pushed open the door, and the turnaround in her attitude floored him. She was all smiles and sounded completely carefree. "Anyone home?"

"Evie!" Two boys, maybe six or seven years old, came

thundering down the hallway and launched themselves into Evie's outstretched arms.

"Hey, monsters! Whoa, someone's feeding you too much. You keep growing." She dropped her voice to a whisper. "I thought we had a deal about that."

She gave each of them a big kiss, showing a facet of her personality he hadn't seen yet. Evie liked children—or at least *these* children—and they loved her. That knowledge alleviated a tiny bit of his primary concern.

The boys giggled as they wiped the kisses off, then turned curious green eyes exactly like Evie's on him.

"Nick, these two monsters are Justin and Patrick, my nephews," Evie offered. "This is my friend Nick."

Both boys nodded and extended small, slightly sticky hands for him to shake. "Nice to meet you," they chorused carefully before taking back off down the hallway with shouts of "Mom! Dad! Evie's here!"

"Well, that still needs a little work." Evie laughed. "Don't run," she called after them, and Nick could hear a woman saying the exact same thing as she dodged the children on her way through a doorway to their right.

He'd been expecting a veritable dragon, not a petite woman half a head shorter than Evie with soft, gentle features. She wrapped Evie in a tight hug. "Evie, honey, it's good to see you." She then turned to Nick expectantly.

Evie reached for his arm, her fingers tightening around his bicep. "Nick, this is my sister-in-law, Gwen. Gwen, this is Nick. Nick Rocco."

The possessive touch and the deliberate lack of even a brief explanation of who he was weren't lost on Gwen. She raised an eyebrow at Evie briefly, a smile tugging at her mouth, before she extended a hand to him. "It's lovely to meet you, Nick. Welcome."

"Thank you. And it's nice to meet you, too."

Evie's hand loosened a bit, and her shoulders slipped just a little. What had she expected from him? Did she think he was so low-class he couldn't handle meeting her family without causing embarrassment? His manners might not be as polished as Evie's, but he did have them.

Gwen waved them out of the hall and toward a large room with a great view of Dallas. "Will is on the phone in his office, but he should be out any second now. We can have a drink while we wait."

Hard on her words, a man he assumed had to be Will joined them. Evie's brother didn't seem to be a fire-breathing dragon, either, as he kissed Evie on the cheek and she repeated the introductions. Nick knew he was being assessed as Will shook his hand and cut his eyes at Evie. The man was not subtle at all.

But Evie's family seemed remarkably normal—not at all worth the stress he'd seen from her or the tension she was holding in check behind her smile. The older couple—he really couldn't call them "old" since they only looked to be in their forties—knew something was up. It was clear that they were waiting for Evie to make some kind of announcement, but they were still friendly enough.

He settled back onto a leather sofa and accepted the wine Gwen offered. Evie sat her glass on the table as Will took a chair opposite them and Gwen perched easily—if oddly, considering there wasn't a lack of seating available—on the arm with her husband's hand on her waist.

Gwen leaned forward, her face kind but curious. "Nick Rocco. I don't think I've heard the name before. Would we know your family?"

Evie jumped in before he could answer, her voice bright as she took his hand and twined her fingers through his. "No, Gwen, you wouldn't. Nick's from Las Vegas."

And the air in the room changed at that moment. Evie's statement had been simple and delivered with friendliness, but a gauntlet had been thrown down. Will's eyebrows drew together in a frown, and Gwen's eyes darted toward Evie's hands. Gwen was quick on the uptake. Surprise registered on her face before she lifted her glass and drank deeply.

Will, however, was busy glowering at his sister and hadn't made the same leap his wife had. "Surely I didn't hear that correctly. You met him in Las Vegas, Evie?"

Evie's spine straightened an inch. "Yes, I did."

"When, exactly?" Even Nick could hear the dangerous growl under those words. Evie hadn't been kidding when she said her brother was unhappy about her taking off for a weekend in Sin City.

"Four weeks ago." She took a deep breath. "And I wasn't at work yesterday or today because I went back to Vegas. To get married." She held her hand up to show the gold band on her finger.

"What the—" Will started to roar, only to have Gwen's elbow fly sharply into his ribs. Now Nick understood Gwen's choice of seating. And a little of Evie's stress.

"That's quite a surprise, Evie." Gwen came to hug Evie again, and this time, she hugged him, as well. "Congratulations to you both. I wish you'd given us a little warning, honey. We would've liked to have been there."

While Gwen was all smiles and hugs, Will was shooting dark daggers at him and no doubt planning how to dispose of his dead body. "Did you know she was an heiress?" he snapped.

"Will!" Gwen scolded as Evie tensed. He tightened his fingers around hers in support. He opened his mouth in their defense, but Evie shook her head slightly. She'd asked him to let her take the lead on this, and he'd honor that.

For the moment, anyway.

Will's face was red as he pushed to his feet, every inch the outraged parental figure. "If he married her thinking…"

"He didn't," Evie interrupted, an edge to her voice. "He

didn't know how much I was worth when we met, and when he did find out, he signed my prenup without hesitation. Nick has his own money, Will. He doesn't need mine."

"Everyone needs that kind of money." Evie's brother looked directly at him as he spoke, and Nick bristled at the insult. "At least you thought far enough ahead to have a prenup."

"I'm not stupid, Will."

"*That* seems debatable at the moment."

Okay, that crossed a line. "Now just wait—"

Evie interrupted him, holding up a hand. "Stay out of this, Nick."

This was the fight he'd seen her steeling herself for in the elevator. He had to admire her chutzpah; she'd known her brother would react like this—not that he didn't understand where Will was coming from—and yet she hadn't chickened out and simply called with the news. In a strange, train-wreck kind of way, the showdown was fascinating to watch.

Will crossed his arms over his chest. "Who wrote your prenup?"

Evie mirrored the movement. "Sabine's brother."

"*Jackson* drew up a prenup for you and didn't tell me?"

"Well, it's not really your business, now is it, Will?"

"The hell it's not."

Both Harrison siblings were on their feet now and the volume was rising. He was getting hard-pressed not to get involved, regardless of Evie's wishes. Based on Gwen's reaction, though, he didn't jump in the middle. She seemed strangely calm, as if these kinds of fireworks were commonplace.

"Are you pregnant?"

Evie paled at her brother's question. *"What?"*

"I can't think of a single good reason otherwise for you to elope like this. To someone you barely know."

"Maybe I'm just a romantic at heart, swept off my feet by love," she responded.

Nick had never seen someone's head actually explode, but Will had to be close as his voice dropped dangerously. "Evangeline…"

"William…" Evie gritted out.

Gwen cleared her throat. "Voices, please."

Without a word, but still glaring daggers at each other, Will and Evie went out onto the balcony and shut the door. He could no longer hear their battle, but it was certainly still raging. So much for thinking her family was *normal*. Gwen seemed unperturbed by what was going on outside.

She patted him on the shoulder. "Don't worry. Neither of them will end up over the balcony rail. They're volatile, but not homicidal."

"They do this a lot?" He couldn't keep the shock out of his voice.

"Will's a bit overprotective of Evie, and she's always chafed against that. When you throw in that Harrison temper they both have…well, it can get explosive."

Still… He could see Evie's wild gesticulations and Will's increasingly deepening frown. Will didn't seem like the kind of man who would take a swing at a woman, but at this point he wasn't sure about anything as far as Evie's family was concerned.

Gwen's eyes followed his to the balcony. "It was hard for me to watch at first, too. It still is, but I understand them both better now. I don't like the boys to hear it, though, so they take it outside. Can I refresh your drink?"

This family was truly nuts. Gwen was playing gracious hostess while Evie and Will fought it out on the balcony. He'd witnessed plenty of violence growing up, and it usually started with people shouting at each other much like Evie and Will were. Rich people—those so-called "good families"—weren't supposed to have that problem. Maybe that was a myth. But he'd be damned if he was going to stand here…

He moved for the glass door, but Gwen stayed him with her hand on his arm.

"They need to get it out, Nick. I promise you, she's fine." Gwen's eyes darkened in understanding, and her voice turned serious. "Really, she's perfectly safe out there. Will has never raised a hand to Evie—*would* never." She led him away from the door, explaining the whole time. "Evie is probably the only person in the world who will go nose-to-nose like that with Will. And, oddly, I think they both enjoy it. I do know that they won't be able to discuss anything like adults until they get *this* out of their systems. They fight fair, though. Don't worry about that." She cocked her head. "I can't believe Evie didn't warn you."

"She did. Sort of." He wondered what else Evie hadn't fully prepared him for. But Gwen didn't have that scared-rabbit look most women wore when they knew someone was about to get hit and were powerless to stop it. If anything, she looked exasperated. That relieved his mind a little.

"Why don't you tell me a little about yourself while we wait? I'll admit I'm terribly curious. Evie's very picky and wouldn't marry just anyone, so you must be something very special. What do you do in Las Vegas?"

This was surreal, but he tried to keep up his end of the conversation while keeping one eye on the balcony. "I run nightclubs."

Gwen beamed. "Oh, Evie should enjoy that."

Here was a chance to learn a few things about his new wife. Like how *much* she loved the nightlife. "Why?"

"Well, she does love to dance, but she had to give up clubbing a couple of years ago just because the press gave her so much grief over it."

He bit back the remark he wanted to make. "She has mentioned that."

"Evie does her best to avoid the limelight whenever

possible, but that's just not possible for someone like her. Not here, at least. I'm glad you two met in Vegas—you've been allowed a little privacy at least." Gwen leveled a steady look at him. "How *did* you two meet?"

The question was simple enough and her tone was simply curious, but that steady look carried weight. Will might have exploded loudly, but Gwen's inner Mama Bear looked eager to eat him alive if necessary. He tried to put himself in their place and not take offense. It was getting harder by the moment, though.

Evie had wanted to handle this part of the conversation, as well—something else she'd asked for while they were getting their story straight—but since she was occupied at the moment… "Evie came into one of my clubs."

"And it was love at first sight?" Gwen sighed, but he wasn't about to believe he'd tamed the bear that easily. "How romantic. Evie never mentioned a word about what happened on her little Vegas getaway."

He nodded toward the balcony. "I'm not surprised."

Evie chose that moment to pull the door open. She was flushed and her eyes were snapping, and she blew her hair out of her face with a deep sigh. "Will's being a—" She stopped abruptly as her nephews came into the room. "He's, um…I think he needs a little time to calm down, so we'll just go now."

Gwen shook her head. "Leaving me to listen to it? Gee, thanks, Evie."

"Hey, you *chose* to live with the big—*ahem,* with him. I'll call you tomorrow, okay?" Evie hugged Gwen and her nephews, and her face twisted when she looked out on the balcony where her brother stood looking out over the city, the tension in the man's shoulders evident even from where they were. "Tell *him* he can call me when he's ready to admit I'm not fifteen anymore."

With that, Evie grabbed his hand and led him out.

Dear Lord, he hoped insanity wasn't hereditary.

Why did Nick keep looking at her as if she'd grown an extra head? She *had* warned him her brother wouldn't take the news well.

Just this once, she'd hoped Will would be able to keep a lid on his temper—especially in front of company. Oh, *no,* that would be too easy. She'd prepared for the worst, but hoped it wouldn't be necessary. It wasn't the first time she'd been wrong. As she pushed the button for the elevator, she turned to Nick. "Sorry about that. I love my brother, but I'd also love to strangle him at the moment."

One of Nick's eyebrows quirked up. "The feeling seemed to be mutual."

She leaned against the elevator wall, trying to look unconcerned as they made their descent, but the energy of the fight with Will was still thrumming through her veins, making her antsy and itchy.

"He pegged the pregnancy, though."

"That was a lucky guess. And I didn't confirm it." Nick still looked at her as if she was an alien, and it was starting to grate across her nerves. Not that she needed much help there; between his attitude of the last twenty-four hours—God, had it really only been twenty-four hours since Nick had shown up at her hotel?—and the still-unresolved fight with Will, her nerves were raw and ready for a fight.

"I'll drive," Nick told the valet when he tried to hand Evie her keys, and Mike looked at her for confirmation. Nick's jaw tensed as he repeated the statement. "You're in no shape to operate heavy machinery at the moment."

Although *she'd* known Mike for three years and Mike didn't know Nick from Adam's house cat, her keys were now in Nick's hand, and Mike was holding the passenger door open for her.

Who the hell did Nick think he was? This was *her* car, her *town,* and he...

Nick revved the engine of her Mercedes. "Are you getting in?"

Mike and the other doormen were watching the exchange with undisguised interest. Evie bit her tongue until she tasted blood to keep from ripping into the lot of them—starting with Nick. *Private matters stay private:* she could hear Gwen's voice in her head, and she let that calm voice be her guide.

Once they got home, though...

"Do you even know where you're going?" she snapped as Nick pulled into traffic.

"I paid attention on the way over. I can handle it. Why are you so testy?"

Because everyone is trying to run my life for me. "Switching to decaf is tougher than it sounds."

Nick looked at her oddly before he switched lanes and accelerated around a truck. She turned her head and stared out the window. The familiar sights of Dallas seemed alien, as if everything had been swapped out overnight with something different. But the "something different" in the equation was her.

She was married to a stranger, pregnant with his baby, fighting with her brother—*again*—and her attempts to bring her life under control were only causing it to spiral faster out of hand.

Maybe Will had been right: maybe she did need a keeper. *No,* she didn't. She lifted her chin as the self-pity that was starting to creep in was pushed back by anger and determination. Her life in Dallas was the least of her problems, as it was about to take a backseat anyway to far more pressing issues.

Like moving to Las Vegas. Becoming a mother.

Figuring out the silent man beside her.

Was the Nick she'd met and flipped for—flipped enough to have a fling with, at least—the real Nick? Even with his dangerously rough edges, he'd been fun and exciting and easy to get along with. *That* was the Nick she'd thought she was marrying; in fact, *that* was the reason she'd thought this was a good idea in the first place.

Or was this darkly brooding Nick the real thing? Even allowing for some initial shock time, she wasn't seeing any *real* signs of adjustment that would lead her to believe his attitude would level off into something more acceptable. Or easier to live with.

For a few moments, though, when they'd been at Will and Gwen's, she'd almost felt as if they were a united front. Nick had held her hand and even bowed up those massive shoulders in response to Will's blustering. It had given her a tiny spurt of hope. But Nick's caveman attitude and continuing silence now that they were alone had killed that hope, and she knew the disappointment of *that* was partially fueling her ire at the moment.

The whole thing was giving her a pounding headache, and she couldn't even have a glass of wine to take the edge off.

Nick wasn't lying when he'd said he'd paid attention on the way to Will's, and he never once asked her for directions as he drove. He navigated the tricky entrance to the parking deck under her building with ease and pulled into her assigned parking space without hesitation. He even remembered to insert her key so the elevator would take them up, and the fact he still had her keys instead of giving them back to her irked her even more.

She'd been so deep in thought, due in no small part to his continuing silence, that when he did finally speak to her again, she jumped. "What?"

"I asked you how much of your stuff you were planning to move to Vegas."

"I guess that depends on where I end up living." She reached past him as the elevator doors opened on her floor and pointedly removed *her* key.

"Yesterday, you wanted to move in with me," he said quietly as they walked down the hallway and she opened her condo door.

"Yeah, well, things are a little different now."

"Not worried about your reputation anymore?"

As the door closed behind him, providing them privacy, she let loose some of the frustration that was about to cause her head to explode. "The only people I really care about are Will, Gwen, the boys and Uncle Marcus. Will or Gwen will let Marcus know the news tonight or in the morning, and I'll go see him tomorrow afternoon. The papers will report that I'm married, but once I'm in Las Vegas, no one will really care anymore. Separate living arrangements won't matter since no one in Dallas will know."

Nick leaned against her couch, his face stormy. "And *my* friends?"

"That's your problem, not mine." Tossing her purse and keys onto the table, she went to the kitchen for something cold to drink.

"That's a bit selfish," he challenged.

Her feet froze to the rug, and she bit her lip, trying very hard not to take the bait. She failed. "And you're a bit of a bastard, so this will work out great."

Nick caught up with her in two steps, grabbing her arm and forcing her to look at him. "What the hell is your problem, Evie?"

She was so close to him, she could feel the heat of his skin and see the rapid pulse in his throat. His eyes were dark, though, and she wasn't able to read anything from them. Her body reacted, but she kept her focus. "I could ask you the same question."

Nick's jaw tightened, but the dam was cracked now, and Evie pushed through with a bravado she didn't fully feel. "You obviously have a problem with me. I don't know what it is, and at this point, I'm not sure I really care, but I would like to know one thing—why did you marry me in the first place?"

CHAPTER SEVEN

EVIE THREW THE QUESTION DOWN like a gauntlet. Frustration and anger charged the air around her, and her eyes were lit up and snapping. But Nick knew this wasn't all just residual anger from her showdown with her brother looking for an outlet; something else simmered beneath the surface.

Although they'd been in close proximity all day, Evie had been distracted, distant even, and he'd had his own thoughts to occupy him. But now her full attention was focused on him, and his body reacted immediately, his skin tightening and muscles tensing. Evie's spacious living room suddenly felt smaller.

He knew Evie felt it, too, even through the heat of her anger, as the tension in the air shifted and heated in a completely different way.

Color rode high on her cheekbones, and her hair tumbled wildly around her face and shoulders. She took a step back, her feet faltering under her the tiniest bit.

She cleared her throat and tossed her hair out of her face, resolutely lifting her chin. "Well? Why?"

The obvious answer was the easiest. "Because you're carrying my baby."

"That was *my* option to solve *my* problem making it all about me, as you've so helpfully reminded me, but it doesn't explain why you'd marry me when…" She stopped as she bit her lip.

That flush now colored the cleavage swelling gently over the neckline of her shirt, and her breath stuttered when she followed his gaze down. "When what, Evie?"

She shook her head slightly and took another step backward. Her back was almost against the wall now—literally—but she squared her shoulders and met his eyes. "When—based on your attitude—you don't even seem to like me very much," she finished baldly.

Oh, he had a multitude of reasons to support his "attitude," as she called it, but only time would tell how accurate his assessment of her would turn out to be and how they'd work out the details. He knew the importance of timing his battles, and it wasn't time for *that* battle with Evie just yet.

This situation, though, demanded his immediate attention. The rush of hot blood under Evie's skin had warmed her perfume, and the heady scent filled his lungs and fired through him every time he inhaled. He took another step toward her, and her eyes widened, the pupils dilating as the sexual tension grew stronger than the anger fueling her. He could tell when her body finally switched gears fully; Evie's breath turned shallow, and a tiny shiver moved over her skin.

"I never said I didn't *like* you." Another small step and only inches separated them. He braced one hand on the wall beside her head, and her breath stopped completely as he ran a finger over her shoulder and down her arm. Her stance loosened as he leaned forward, pressing his hips against her, letting her feel exactly how much he "liked" her at the moment.

"Nick…" Her voice was a husky whisper, the honeyed drawl of his name on her lips fanning the slow burn in his groin into a bright, painful flame.

God, he wanted her. From the first moment he'd touched her, he'd wanted her, and although that want had landed him in one hell of an awkward situation, it didn't affect the way Evie heated his blood. And regardless of how they ended up here, the primal part of his brain wouldn't let go of the fact they were married, that Evie was *his* and he should be taking full advantage of that fact.

"Nick...I...I mean, we...shouldn't...um..." Her body contradicted her words as it moved ever-so-slightly against his, her breasts rubbing against his chest, her hips returning the pressure against his straining zipper. Her breath hitched slightly, and a second later her mouth met his.

The force of Evie's raw hunger stole the air from his lungs as her arms locked around his neck and she pulled him fully, possessively, against her. His other hand went to the wall for support, caging Evie between his body and the wall as he ground his hips and felt her shudder in response.

Her taste intoxicated him, leaving him light-headed and craving more. He moved his lips to the column of her neck, causing her to moan low in her throat, and the vibration rippled over his skin. Evie's foot rubbed against his calf, bringing her knee up to nudge at his hip. He slid a hand under her thigh, around to the curve of her bottom, and lifted. Evie's legs twined around his waist like a sinful promise, her head falling back against the wall, giving him access to the cleft between her breasts.

She hissed as his tongue moved over the smooth skin. A quick tug on the thin straps of her shirt at her shoulders, and her breasts were bare, allowing him to pull a nipple into his mouth. Evie arched as his tongue moved over the hard point, and her fingernails dug into his shoulders.

Sweet mercy. Evie didn't know whether to shout or cry at the sensations Nick caused. He felt heavenly; the hard heat of his body locked firmly—blissfully—between her thighs while his mouth...oh, *God,* his mouth...

Her brain was a mess of conflicting thoughts—she still wanted to hit Nick with something hard, but at the same time she wanted to finish their fight and get some truths out into the open. But neither hurt pride nor anger—as strong as they were—could hold up against the overwhelming, aching *need* that had hold of her.

This was what got her into this predicament in the first place, and letting it sweep her away again was just asking for more trouble she didn't need right now. But her brain wasn't in control right now; her body was, and it was quite sure what it wanted.

Nick.

There was too much fabric, too many layers, separating them. She craved skin-to-skin contact, and the constriction of their clothes was maddening.

Nick seemed to share her frustration. His hands worked busily at clasps and buttons, but it wasn't enough. It wasn't fast enough, and she'd go insane if she didn't touch him soon.

With a groan, Nick pushed away from the wall and carried her easily, never once breaking the connection of his lips on hers. She expected the cool softness of her bed to be the next stop, but Nick only took her as far as the table, setting her on the lacquered wood surface and pressing her back with the weight of his body.

A second later, he broke the kiss long enough to sweep her shirt up and over her head, sending it sailing. A tug and her bra was gone. His shirt joined hers on the floor, and she finally had the contact she craved.

Crisp hairs tickled her nipples, teasing the sensitive skin and shrinking her awareness of the world to just the two of them and the tidal wave of pleasure that threatened to engulf her. The slide of denim down her legs barely registered, but the hot sweep of Nick's hands over her calves and thighs had her hands shaking as she tried to work the snap of his jeans. She only had a second to run her hands over the smooth skin of his hips appreciatively before Nick's tongue dipped into her navel to tease and traced a slow, teasing path down to her core.

She arched as he tasted her, and her hands searched futilely for purchase on the slick tabletop. Nick's hands held her hips, and she closed her fingers around his wrists, anchoring them both as he pushed her toward her climax.

When she got there, the explosion shook her to the marrow of her bones, forcing his name out in a cry as she rode the shockwave.

Then Nick was over her, *in* her with a powerful thrust that kept the wave from abating. His fingers twined through hers, pinning her to the table, as Nick set the rhythm and she matched it.

Those deep dark eyes met hers and held her captive, the intimacy of eye contact startling her. Even more surprising was, that for the first time since she'd proposed to him, that guarded, slightly snide expression was gone. Instead, she saw only desire—desire for *her*. Her brain tried to tell her it was simply a physical thing—just sex and hormones overcoming anything else—but that rational thought couldn't deflate the feeling that expanded in her chest.

Just before Nick took her over the edge again, she identified that feeling.

It was hope.

The sound of Sabine's ringtone woke her up, and out of habit she reached to the nightstand to retrieve the phone. It wasn't in its normal spot, and that confused her sleep-muddled brain. So did the heavy weight pinning her legs to the bed...

Nick. The weight was Nick's leg, and the memory of last night rushed in in stunning Technicolor detail. The light peeking in around her drapes told her it was late in the morning—later than she normally slept—but considering how Nick had kept her occupied until the wee hours of the morning...

The ringtone blared again, and Evie slid carefully out from under Nick and the duvet. He muttered and rolled over, but didn't wake. She grabbed her robe off the vanity stool and tiptoed quickly to the living room, closing the bedroom door behind her.

She opened the phone to silence the noise and told Bennie to hold on. Setting the phone down, she slipped her arms into the sleeves and knotted the sash. Then she took the phone to the couch and sat, groaning slightly as her hamstrings lodged a late protest against the gymnastics of the night before.

"'Morning, Bennie."

"You got *married?*" Sabine's voice was an octave higher than normal and twice as loud. Evie winced as she held the phone away from her ear.

"I guess good news travels fast. How'd you hear?"

"Will called Jackson this morning raising all kinds of hell over him writing a prenup for you without telling anyone what you were planning. Jackson called me assuming I knew you'd run off to Vegas to get married, and I didn't even know you'd gone back to Vegas at *all.*" Sabine finally paused to breathe, and Evie could hear the hurt creep into her voice. "Why didn't you *tell* me? Why wasn't I there? And exactly *who* did you marry, anyway? Did you and Tucker get back together?"

Oops. "Um, no. I married Nick."

"Nick? Who's Nick? Wait—" Sabine sounded incredulous. "Nick, the-guy-you-hooked-up-with-in-Vegas Nick? *That* Nick?"

"That Nick."

"Oh, Evie… *Why?*"

Evie pulled a cushion into her lap and picked at the seam. What to tell Sabine? Bennie wouldn't believe the "love at first sight" line she was feeding her family, simply because Bennie had been there. She'd talked to her almost every single day since then, and Nick hadn't entered their conversation at all.

That left the truth. The truth only she and Nick knew. She could trust Bennie to keep the truth to herself and not go blabbing to the gossip columnists—Evie knew that in her soul; they had too many years of friendship—but at the same time, she didn't want *anyone* to know.

"Evie, talk to me. Something's not right here. I can tell. What is going on?"

"Bennie…"

Sabine's voice dropped to a near whisper. "Are you *pregnant?*"

Will had asked her the same thing, but Bennie asked with concern in her voice, not outrage, and Evie's resolve cracked. "Yeah," she said quietly. "I am."

"And that's why you married Nick?"

"Pretty much." At Sabine's sharp inhale, Evie hurried ahead. "But you can't tell anyone. Promise me you won't. No one knows about the baby yet."

"I figured as much. Will would have mentioned it to Jackson, and Jackson would have said something to me. I can't believe…I mean… Honey, you didn't have to *marry* him just because you accidentally got pregnant. This isn't the Middle Ages. You have—or at least you *had*—other options."

"Nick has the right to know he's a father. The right to know his child. And the baby…" Evie pulled the cushion against her chest and wrapped her arms around it. "The baby deserves to have a father in its life." That much she was sure of; ethically, she'd done the right thing by Nick and the baby both. It gave her *something,* a piece of moral high ground to stand on.

"All of which could have been achieved *without* getting married." Sabine had a wide practical streak and wasn't one to romanticize anything. "Evie, you barely know him. How could you tie yourself permanently to someone you knew for two measly days?"

No, she couldn't tell Sabine *that* part of the truth. Not right now. The fact this was temporary, just a business arrangement, left a bad taste in her mouth as it was. Thinking about it after the night she'd spent in Nick's arms...that just turned her stomach.

"It's not like there's anyone here I had hopes of marrying one day." *That much was true.* "I like Nick, and we get along great—" she nearly choked on that lie "—and I'm sure things are going to work out great for us. Once I get settled in, we'll—"

"Excuse me? 'Settled in?'" Sabine's voice took on an edge. "Exactly where are you planning on settling in?"

"Well..." Evie hedged. Will and Gwen seemed to accept her moving as a given—and it had fueled a bit of Will's fit last night—but Bennie had a key piece of knowledge they didn't have...

"You're *not* moving to Las Vegas." She paused. "*Are* you?"

"Well, yeah. It's where Nick lives."

"Nick can move his butt down to Dallas. You can't just pack up and move to Vegas. Your whole life is here."

An excellent reason right there to run away. "And Nick's life is in Las Vegas. Plus he has a business to run there. It makes much more sense for me to move there."

Sabine huffed. "You've lost your freakin' mind."

How right she was. But not about this. "No, Bennie. I'm doing the right thing. For everyone." Evie forced herself to sound upbeat. "I'm really excited. Nick's wonderful, and I know I've made the right decision here. We may be off to a weird start, but there's a happily-ever-after for me out there."

She just didn't know with whom.

"Evie, are you positive? I'm sure Jackson can untie whatever legal knots need to be untied to get you out of this."

"I'm not in anything I need out of. Thanks, though." She needed to end this conversation before it killed her. "Look, I have a really busy day ahead of me—lots to pack, and I need to go to the office..."

"I'll come help," Sabine offered.

"No!" The last thing she needed was a witness today. Especially a witness who knew her so well, she'd be able to see right through the lie. "I mean, we just got married two days ago. We'd like a little privacy, know what I mean?"

Sabine snorted. "Yeah. I think I do."

Evie had the sinking feeling Sabine understood a little *too* much.

Then Sabine sighed. "Look. Just pack up what you need for the immediate future. Make a list of everything else you want done or sent to you, and I'll take care of it. You have enough on your plate."

Tears burned Evie's eyes. "You're the best, Bennie."

"And don't you forget it. You know I expect to be this baby's godmother, right?"

Evie laughed as she swiped at her eyes. "You bet. 'Bye."

She closed the phone and tossed it aside. Leaning forward, she buried her face in the cushion she held. Dear Lord, there was no end to the lies. But she was hip-deep in it now.

Coffee. Coffee would help her face this day, even if it was decaf. She certainly needed a cup before she had to face Nick. Maybe two. She stood, grabbed her phone so she could call Gwen to take the temperature of things there, and turned.

Nick stood in the doorway, bare-chested and barefoot, his jeans riding low on his hips, looking yummy enough to eat with a spoon and nearly causing her nervous system to overload. But his arms were crossed over his chest, an inscrutable look on his face.

Damn.

Evie shouldn't look so tempting first thing in the morning. Her hair was mussed from both sleep and where his hands had tangled in it repeatedly the night before. Without makeup, she looked fresh-faced and exotically innocent, but her eyes were red-rimmed with unshed tears. He'd heard enough of her conversation to catch the general gist, but something her friend said had gotten to her.

She shifted, tightening the belt of her robe and pulling the collar closed. The tiny silky robe barely covered anything; it clung to her curves, stopping midthigh on those long legs.

He'd spent the better part of the night with those legs wrapped around him, trapped between her thighs, and the sensation seemed burned into his memory. The temptation to drag her back to the bedroom was strong, but in the harsh, bright light of day, the intimacy they'd shared last night seemed far away.

Evie pushed her hair back, tucking the mass behind her ears. "'Morning. I'm after coffee. Want some?" A perfectly normal and expected set of sentences, but the slight shake of her hands and the too-careful tone of her voice gave her away.

Evie was a complicated creature. It was hard to believe the same woman who railed at him and called him a bastard last night was now treading so carefully. Evie had helped expand his definitions of great sex, but now she mumbled and blushed like a virgin with regrets the morning after.

As she passed him, he could smell her—the scent of sex, him on her—combined with sleep and sweat and her perfume. The smell rekindled that primal need to take her....

But Evie was smiling at him shyly, guardedly. "Breakfast might be more difficult to produce."

"Just coffee. I'm not much of a breakfast eater."

"Me neither." She cocked her head at him. "Wow. We're so compatible, we're practically soul mates."

His body chose to interpret "compatible" in a different way, and his blood immediately rushed south. But Evie's voice lacked sarcasm or snark; she sounded almost teasing with the statement.

"So what are we going to do with all this privacy you asked Sabine for?"

An eyebrow went up, but the blush that stained her cheeks ruined the effect. "You were eavesdropping?"

"Just enough to hear how wonderful I am," he teased, enjoying the way the blush deepened.

Evie handed him a cup of coffee. "I had to tell Bennie *some*thing."

"Like we got married because you're pregnant."

"Bennie knows me too well to believe it was love at first sight or anything like that." Evie drank and then wrinkled her nose, staring at her cup in distaste. "Ugh. This part of being pregnant is not fun at all."

It was the first time she'd mentioned the physicality of being pregnant, and he realized he'd never asked, either. "Morning sickness?"

She sighed sadly. "Not that. Not yet, at least. It's the lack of caffeine. I don't care what people say—decaf just doesn't taste the same as regular. And facing the day without caffeine just sucks."

"So you've given it up entirely?"

"Caffeine, sushi, Brie, alcohol, pâté…there's a whole list of wonderful stuff I'm not allowed to have anymore. Plus there's a whole list of things I *should* be eating that just doesn't balance out what I'm giving up. It's almost depressing. Oh, and the prenatal vitamins—*yuck*. They're the size of horse pills *and* they stink."

How did Evie know all of this? The question must have shown on his face.

"I did some reading on the plane," she said by way of explanation and dismissed it with a shrug. "By the way, you don't happen to know who's the best obstetrician in Las Vegas, do you? I'll need to get an appointment soon."

"I didn't realize you were so organized." He'd assumed

Evie's actions to this point had all been reactionary, but now it seemed she had put *some* thought into this beyond saving her own reputation.

"I have layers." Her mouth twisted and she lifted her chin. "I just might surprise you."

"You already do." He could tell she didn't know how to respond to that candid statement.

"Ditto."

To be fair, he'd been a little reactionary himself the past couple of days, and that wasn't something he was used to at all. He still had a lot to figure out about Evie and how he wanted this to shake out in the end, but for now… "So what is the plan for today?"

Go back to bed and stay there was too much to hope for.

She leaned a hip against the counter, and he mirrored the movement, as if this was just a normal morning chitchat between husband and wife. "Well, I need to go see Uncle Marcus, and I need to check in with Gwen and see if Will is still acting like a butthead about this. I have to call my assistant, and I need to start packing."

Back to the topic that set her off last night. Not that he minded how *that* worked out. But living arrangements did need to be settled. "I assure you my home is fully furnished with all the modern conveniences. But feel free to bring any personal items you'd like to have around. We'll find someplace for them."

"I don't know…"

"Your original plan involved you moving in. And it does make sense. I have plenty of room, and it will be much easier in the long run." *Right.* And he'd be able to keep an eye on her and the baby.

Evie frowned as her hands went to the collar of her robe again, pulling the edges even farther over each other. In light of last night, she had to be thinking about her earlier plan to just be roommates. But last night had changed the game.

Even if she hadn't figured it out by now, *that* idea was out of the question. If Evie was moving to Vegas, she was moving in with him.

And if she was moving in, she was moving into his bedroom.

CHAPTER EIGHT

EVIE DIDN'T RECALL SIGNING a treaty or even participating in peace talks, but she and Nick seemed to have called a cease-fire. A truce of sorts.

Which should have made her happy, especially since Uncle Marcus had called with an invitation to lunch—and there was no way to get out of an "invitation" from Uncle Marcus—in order to meet "her young man," and it was just too nerve-racking to play happy couple when Nick looked at her as if... Well, as if there was something *wrong* with her.

But it was an uneasy, superficial truce—at least for her, because the only thing that was different from yesterday was the completely mind-scrambling sex they'd had last night.

It was hardly what relationship experts would suggest as a way to broker peace, but somehow, it had worked. Some-what. Nick wasn't being overly friendly, but he was less monosyllabic today. He wasn't quite the same man who'd shifted her out of her usual orbit in Vegas, but he wasn't that same cold-eyed man she'd left the wedding chapel with, either. Somewhere in the middle was the man who'd done things she didn't think were humanly possible to her body last night and made her love every minute of it.

And yet this morning...well, it was weird, to say the least. Neither of them mentioned last night. Or the future. Or anything really. Their conversation had been well, not *easy,* but not difficult, either. It had been a surprisingly simple morning full of surprisingly normal conversation like "Would you like the shower first?" and "What channel is ESPN?"

It was nerve-racking at the same time it was oddly comforting, but in the grand scheme of things *that* was still a major improvement.

More importantly, it had made lunch a little easier. Uncle Marcus was buying their story, and Nick seemed to be passing this interview with flying colors. She tried to feign interest in their spirited discussion of...what? Mutual funds? *Seriously?* At least it was something.

It still bothered her a lot, though, that the *one* thing Nick did seem to like about her was how good she was in bed.

For one, it would mean she had completely misjudged Nick—both when she'd made the decision to sleep with him in the first place and again when she'd decided to marry him. She didn't want to think she was that naive. Or so easily blinded by her hormones.

"You're not eating, Evangeline. Is there something wrong with your salad, my dear?"

Uncle Marcus's question snapped Evie back to the conversation. Damn, her brooding over Nick had caused her to forget where she was. Uncle Marcus might be closing in on eighty and his heart problems had left his body frail, but he still had the ability to make her feel like an uncouth tomboy with little more than a pointed stare.

"No, Uncle Marcus, it's delicious. I'm just rather tired today. I didn't get much sleep last night."

Nick coughed slightly, and she cursed herself silently as she added, "Between all the traveling and then dealing with Will yesterday... Well, you know."

Marcus nodded. "Oh, I got an earful from William this

morning, but I'll be sure to let him know that your Nicolas seems to be on the up-and-up and not at all a gold digger."

Evie bit her lip as Nick stiffened at the label. Nick had borne Uncle Marcus's pointed and unrelenting interrogation—however cloaked in politeness it was—with a restraint and patience she admired and envied.

Now, in typical Uncle Marcus fashion, he seemed to believe that his stamp of approval—or disapproval—marked the end of all discussions on the topic. She could wish, but she and Will still had a conversation on the horizon. Patting Nick on the arm, where she could feel the tightened muscle, she smiled at Uncle Marcus. "Thank you. Will trusts your judgment so much, I'm sure that will go a long way in easing his mind about our marriage. I know this caught him off guard."

"You must realize, Evangeline, this has caught all of us off guard." His mouth curled just the slightest bit down in disapproval. "I still don't see why you had to run off to Las Vegas for some quickie wedding, when we've looked forward to your wedding day for so long."

Oh, let's not go there. "I know, Uncle Marcus." She tried to sound appropriately contrite. "But you know sometimes I just get caught up in things." Her cheeks were hurting from the smile she'd worn for the last hour, but she forced herself to keep it up and just prayed it looked like sincere excitement. "Nick kind of swept me off my feet."

"I had hoped you had outgrown your occasional penchant for the dramatic by now. It embarrasses the family and the company when those dramatics hit the papers."

Ouch. Uncle Marcus sure knew how to score a direct hit on her conscience. As if he somehow felt her inner wince, Nick took her hand. Everyone else might see it as newlywed-itis, but she took it as a much-needed pillar of support. If only Uncle Marcus knew how she was trying so desperately *not* to embarrass everyone with even more drama….

"I'm afraid I'm to blame for this," Nick interjected and she nearly choked. "Evie's spontaneity is part of her charm, and I encouraged her more than I should have."

She couldn't believe her ears. Nick was defending her?

"I'm not accustomed to the level of attention Evie attracts," he continued as she tried to hide her shock behind her water glass. "I hoped an elopement would make a quick splash and be forgotten, whereas planning a big white wedding would draw endless amounts of attention. I don't like the idea of being fodder for the society columns."

She was still reeling from that statement, but when Uncle Marcus nodded in agreement, it took everything she had to keep her jaw from hitting the table in shock. Her world spun off its axis, and she could only hope her eyes weren't bugging out of her head as Nick and Uncle Marcus bonded over the tiresome burden of being grist in the gossip mill.

"That's probably a wise attitude to have, young man. Beat the busybodies at their own game. I've always felt there was far too much speculation about everyone else's personal business going on. Never cared for it, myself."

Evie looked around the room carefully. It was the same dining room where she'd eaten hundreds of lunches the last decade, filled with the same people she'd known for years, yet she felt she'd landed on another planet. She'd love to know exactly when the pod-people had taken over Marcus's body and implanted this new aversion to "what everyone else thinks." She'd spent the last ten years worrying about what everyone else thought and might say—primarily because *Marcus* worried about it so much. In fact, Uncle Marcus was usually the first in line to raise an eyebrow.

Her world was now completely, officially askew.

Did pregnancy cause insanity? Maybe she was caught in some wishful daydream? The hand holding hers felt real enough: warm and strong and just calloused enough to remind her he wasn't a pretty boy with a desk job at his daddy's firm. And the way his other hand was sliding over her forearm…gooseflesh rose behind the feather-light touch.

No, this was real. Weird, but real. That cautious bubble of optimism inflated in her chest again. She had three people on her side—Bennie, Gwen and now Uncle Marcus. Between the three of them, they'd have the gossip columns under control, and eventually, they'd get past Will's pigheadedness, too.

Which meant she only had Nick to deal with. And, for now at least, they had a truce. She might not like how that truce came about, but she was rapidly learning to take what she could get. She'd build on what she had and go from there.

It wasn't *that* bad of a start. At least half her plan was working out. A little voice in her head, though, wouldn't stop wishing the half that was working out already was the half that involved Nick.

Evie lived in a very strange world, Nick decided. Lunch with her Uncle Marcus—who must have been from a different branch of the family tree—had driven that point home.

In all honesty, her family's reaction wasn't unexpected considering Evie's inheritance and the fact she was the youngest and obviously doted on. But it was the last two hours that had him shaking his head at the world Evie inhabited.

It started when they arrived at the country club and a person stepped in front of them to snap off a photo before the doorman shooed the cameraman away.

"What was that?" he asked.

Evie shrugged. "That's Malcolm Wilson. Amateur paparazzo. You just made the 'Texas High-Life' blog. Congrats."

"Because I'm here?"

"Because you're here with *me*." A tentative smile crossed her face. "I did warn you. People are interested in my family."

Belatedly, he realized that now included him. Great. "Why?"

"Because we have money? Because we're considered influential? Maybe Dallas doesn't have enough real celebrities? I don't know for sure why, but it comes with the territory. If I got all bent out of shape every time someone took my picture and posted it somewhere..." She shrugged again. "Let's just say I don't leave the house without makeup."

Still reeling from that, he'd borne Evie's uncle's interrogation with all the patience he could muster, drawing on his last reserves when Evie sent him a grateful look and squeezed his hand.

But what really had him shaking his head had nothing to do with paparazzi or elderly relatives. In two hours at the country club—and the majority of that spent at a table with her uncle—no fewer than fourteen people had waylaid them. He'd expected some of it, simply because this was Evie's family's club and she was bound to know a lot of people, but these hadn't been fourteen simple "Hi-how-ya-doin" quick conversations.

Some knew of their marriage already, causing Evie to mumble something about Gwen being quick to the punch this morning with all the appropriate spin, but even he could tell people were fishing for details. Evie deftly deflected the questions without once losing her smile or seeming ungracious in any way.

He was more impressed, though, at how easily Evie handled the requests for her time or her money for everyone's various pet projects. He dealt with his fair share of that at home—and it was getting worse every day as his bank balance grew—but he could tell Evie had lots of practice in this area, as well.

In many ways, Evie was a different person in Dallas. Her smile was brighter but less genuine, and she seemed more reserved than he remembered—and it couldn't be him causing it. It took him a little while—about five or six sets of introductions and conversations—to figure it out.

These were superficial relationships; they were far more

interested in what she could do for them than how she was. No wonder she didn't want these people to know she'd gotten pregnant accidentally; they'd eat her alive and relish every bite.

And the reason why she often spoke of "Evangeline Harrison" as if she was a different person became clear. Evie had a role to play, and she played it well. No matter how much it chafed against her true personality.

But what was her true personality? He needed to remember who she was, not be blinded to the truth and how women like Evie could be. He needed to keep that reminder front and center.

So another piece of the Evie puzzle fell into place, but it still was far from a complete picture. No wonder she'd run off to Vegas to blow off steam. And no wonder she was so willing to move there now that she had an excuse. But was Vegas where she'd want to stay? Did she need all of this—as superficial as it was?

Her polite smile didn't falter until they were safely inside the car and he eased the car out of the club's driveway. She blew out her breath noisily as she leaned back against the seat. "Well, that wasn't so bad."

"You expected worse?"

"I always expect the worst. It helps keep my mouth in check, and curbs that penchant for the dramatic that bothers Uncle Marcus so much." Her mouth twisted. "The family's image, by the way, used to be Marcus's number-one thing. I don't know *who* that man was, telling you your private life was none of anyone's business."

Evie sounded so grumpy about it, he couldn't help but laugh, and she shot him a dirty look for it.

Casually, as if he wasn't fishing for information, he asked, "Is he as tough on his own kids, or are you the only dramatic Harrison in the clan?"

"There aren't many Harrisons in the clan. Will and I are the only ones—plus Gwen and the boys, of course. But Will doesn't make the papers much since he married Gwen, and the boys are too young, so I'm the only one they're interested in right now. Uncle Marcus is a committed bachelor, and if he has any family at all, I've never met them."

Wait. He'd been through a military-grade interrogation and the man wasn't even a true relative? "You mean Marcus isn't really your uncle?"

"No. He and my father were great friends, and he's been with the company since the earth's crust cooled. He kind of adopted our family, but I didn't really know him until I moved back here."

It was slightly shocking how little he knew about Evie personally, especially since he knew so much about her *physically.* At the same time, they hadn't had much time to really talk, and this was the most open and approachable Evie had been since she left Vegas the first time. He needed to take advantage of it. "I assumed you grew up in Dallas."

"No. I was born here, but we moved away when I was five. I told you how Will had to take me in after my mom died, right? I came back to Dallas when I was fifteen." She laughed, but it was a slightly bitter sound. "It was a huge adjustment because I just walked into the fishbowl and was totally unprepared for any of it. That's a whole different story, but that's what Uncle Marcus is talking about when he mentions my 'penchant for dramatics.'"

He could almost feel sorry for her, growing up under a spotlight like that. But then he thought of Evie up on the stage at Starlight...if she was that free and adventurous in a strange place around strangers, what kind of trouble did she stir up in her hometown?

Maybe the reserve he'd seen recently was unusual for her, a by-product of the situation. Evie obviously knew what was expected of her—today was proof of that—but if her family was on her case a lot, it had to be deserved. When he'd researched her family briefly just to get a feel for what he would be walking into, maybe he should have read past the who-wore-what-where.

He should've been looking closely for clues, information to tell him how much Evie and his mother had in common....

"It's funny, you know," Evie continued, unaware of his brief lapse of attention. "Gwen is the etiquette expert, so you'd think she'd be the one to really worry about, but Uncle Marcus is the real stickler. I love him, but..."

"And your brother?"

"What about him?"

"Does he agree with Marcus about your 'dramatics'?"

"Will doesn't care so much that it ends up being news, if you understand my meaning. He doesn't like the gossip, but it's not the gossip that bothers him. Uncle Marcus focuses on the gossip, while Will is more focused on *me*."

"That sounds like a pain. Especially after what I saw last night."

She shook her head. "Don't worry about last night. Will's a lot of bark, and he tends to forget I'm an adult now, but he'll come around. He always does." She sounded sure of that.

"*Always?* You've eloped before?"

"No, like I said, this is definitely the *biggest* stunt I've pulled, but it's not the first. And it won't be the last."

"Planning to rob a bank or something?" Even with all his doubts and questions about Evie, he was still enjoying himself. She was certainly entertaining.

"Nope, just giving birth barely nine months after the wedding and then getting a divorce. It's gonna be fun," she added sarcastically. "That will make everyone's head explode."

"So why bother with getting married?"

"Because divorce is too common to be hugely newswor-thy. It will get reported, dissected and speculated about, but ultimately, that's a family matter very few people can throw stones about."

Evie might end up in the press a lot, but she also had a savvy understanding of it. "Great. I'll have your big brother coming after my hide."

"I'm pretty sure you can hold your own against Will."

Oddly, he took that as a compliment.

Lowering her voice, she added conspiratorially, "And if it comes down to a fistfight, I got a fifty on you."

Was she teasing him? This was definitely a different Evie, reminiscent of Las Vegas. He feigned affront. "Only a fifty? Your brother's got... What? Twenty years on me?"

"Hmm... From what I saw on our marriage license—and happy belated birthday, by the way—it's closer to fifteen. But you *do* have all that experience in bar fights.... Still, I think a fifty is a safe bet." She grinned broadly at him, turning the charm on high.

"If you're going to live in Las Vegas, we need to work on your betting skills. You'll never make any money that way."

Evie laughed. "Not everyone gambles because they need the money. They gamble for the thrill."

Very true. And that knowledge would help her immensely in acclimating. "You checked out my birthday on the marriage license?"

"I was curious." She thought for a minute, then added, "I figured since we were getting married, I should at least know your birthday and middle name."

He pretended he needed to concentrate to navigate the entrance to the parking deck as a stall for time. Evie must really think he was a first-class bastard if she wasn't willing to ask even the simplest of questions. "Those aren't state secrets."

"Well..." Evie looked at him over the rims of her sunglasses. "You're not exactly Mister-hey-ask-me-anything."

How many times had Kevin said much the same thing?

That's why he and Kevin made a good team—Kevin could do all the talking so he didn't have to. Unfortunately, Kevin wasn't here to answer Evie's questions for him. "Try me."

She fell silent and he could almost see the gears turning in her head. She must be coming up with something really...

"What's your favorite color?"

All that thought for *that?* "Black."

"I'm not surprised. It's a good color for you. Do you listen to country music?"

This was Evie's idea of getting to know each other? His earlier hopes of Evie's depths were being quickly battered down. "No."

"Umm...favorite movie?"

"Shaun of the Dead."

"Really?" Her mouth dropped in disbelief.

"Really. It's a great movie. Next question."

He pulled into her parking space and killed the engine. Evie didn't wait for him to open her door or hold out her hand for her keys. He couldn't decide if that was a good thing or not.

She fired her next question as they waited for the elevator. "Cats or dogs?"

"Neither. I'm never home. But you can get one if you like after you settle in."

A wistful smile flashed briefly. "How about hobbies?"

He fought to keep a straight face. "I collect stamps."

Evie's eyes grew wide and her mouth fell open. "You're kidding me."

"Of course I am." He rubbed his arm where Evie smacked him. "Seriously, Evie, *these* are the burning questions you have for me?"

She fiddled with her purse. "I'm trying to get to know you. Since we're going to be living together..."

"At least that's settled."

"Did I have much of a choice?" she challenged, an edge creeping into her voice.

He tried to dull the edge from his own voice even though she was trying his nerves again. Evie barely clutched before she shifted gears. "It's a free country. I can't force you to do anything."

She snorted as he opened the door to her apartment, and she passed him to go inside. She hung her bag on the back of a chair and leaned her hips against the table. Evie frowned as she ran a hand over a large smudge on the shiny finish.

Her handprint. The image of Evie on her back, her hair spilling over the table and off the edge, slammed into him, and he no longer cared about silly get-to-know-you questions. The most important knowledge was that the bedroom was only steps away.

He knew the moment Evie realized what caused that smudge. She jumped up as if she'd been burned. "Wh-what were we talking about? Um… Oh, yeah, um, getting to know each other."

Evie moved busily around the room, avoiding eye contact as she straightened magazines and fluffed cushions.

"Then it's my turn now to ask you some questions."

She cleared her throat. "Of course. My favorite color is blue, and I like dogs and *The Sound of Music*…"

Evie might be willing to waste her Q&A time on shallow topics, but he didn't have that kind of patience. He needed some answers—some truths—and now was as good a time as he was likely to get. "Those were your questions. Not mine."

"Oh. Right."

And there was that unexpectedly quick shift in gears. From teasing, to turned on, to nervous in less than a minute. Now she squared her shoulders, took a deep breath and switched gears again. Hands behind her back and chin up, she faced him as if he was a firing squad. As if she read his thoughts, she smiled weakly. "Fire away."

Why did Nick make her so nervous? She felt like a babbling fool half the time—make that *most* of the time—she tried to have a conversation with him. He'd handed her the golden opportunity to ask him all the questions she'd been storing up, and she'd chickened out. She wanted to know, *really* know, this enigmatic man she'd married, but she'd defaulted to stupid questions instead because she was a coward.

Even worse, she had the feeling he knew it.

Oh, and the look on his face when she'd noticed the smudgy handprint on her table. That only made it worse, because it reminded her how she'd ended up here. How much she wanted him to like her for something more than...*ugh.* For something *more* than how they ended up here.

God, she was pathetic. For a minute there, she'd let herself believe their act; that what they were presenting to Will and Gwen and Uncle Marcus and the rest of Dallas had even a grain of truth in it.

It was just too easy to lose sight of the reality of their situation when faced with a memory like last night. How Nick made her feel as if... As if this could be real. Even if it wasn't.

His voice was hard. "What made you decide to marry me? And what would you have done if I'd said no?"

Nick obviously didn't have the same yellow streak running through him that she'd recently discovered in herself. He went straight for the tough questions. The kind she didn't have the guts to ask when they weren't shouting at each other, and she had an actual chance of getting an answer.

"I decided to marry you for the same reason you decided to marry me. I'm carrying your baby. It's pretty straightforward." She took a deep breath and squeezed her fingers together. "And, honestly, I didn't have a backup plan."

"Because you always get what you want?" There was that mocking tone again.

If he only knew. "Hardly. It just didn't occur to me that you'd say no. You seemed like a decent, upstanding guy who'd want to do the right thing for his child—however unplanned it was."

That earned her a skeptical look. "Exactly how did you come to this great understanding of my psyche? We didn't do a whole lot of talking."

"Just a feeling I had. But look," she said, trying to sound upbeat, "I was right. And here we are."

A black eyebrow arched up. "And you don't think this is an enormous mistake?"

All the time. Definitely every time you look at me like that. That eyebrow, though... It infuriated her at an elemental level she didn't quite understand. And his tone. He was just like—

Will. A clarity she wished she'd had much earlier settled on her shoulders.

Oh, *damn it.* After ten years of butting heads with her brother, somehow she'd managed to find a man just like Will. And she *married* him, for goodness' sake. No wonder...

Dear God, she needed some *serious* therapy.

But if she could handle her brother... Something inside her solidified, and she found her backbone again. It felt good. "Is it?" she challenged. "You tell me."

Nick's other eyebrow joined the first at his hairline, and the shock on his face made her feel much better. Like herself again. She might be Evie Rocco now, but she was still Evangeline Harrison, damn it, and it was high time she remembered that. "Well? Are you going to make me regret this?"

"Me? It was your idea."

"Yes, you keep reminding me of that, thank you. But no one forced you to the altar at gunpoint. Why is that, Nick? You've made it very clear that this wasn't your idea, *and* that you don't think it was a very good choice, yet you agreed pretty quickly." Oh, she was really getting warmed up now. "Why, Nick? Was it the money? My family's connections? Planning on expanding to Dallas and figured you could get your foot in the door?"

She was goading him, trying to force him to react, hoping he'd drop a bit of that shield and answer her with some honesty. Nick's face reddened in anger and his jaw locked, but he didn't take the bait quite the way she hoped. His voice was dangerously quiet and mocking as he said, "It had nothing to do with your money, Evie. It was all about you."

Her heart jumped in her chest, an involuntary reaction to his words before the tone fully registered and squashed the feeling.

"I know your type, Evie. Vegas is full of women just like you—rich, beautiful..." He sneered the word, killing the compliment as he stalked toward her. "But spoiled and out only for a good time. Their children make great accessories—until they don't anymore, and then they're an inconvenience. I won't let that happen to my child."

She held her ground as he got closer and his voice grew even more mocking. "It's very simple, Evie. Marrying you gave me legal rights to my child—rights I couldn't be guaranteed as easily otherwise. You aren't the only one able to make plans, Evie. Marrying you won't be a mistake—at least not for me. You might come to regret it, but I assure you I won't, because I'm getting *exactly* what I wanted out of this."

His words punched her stomach like hard fists, and she wanted to curl into a ball to protect herself—and the baby, too—from such ugliness. She didn't doubt the truth of the words; she pushed and goaded to get the truth out of him and now she had it.

In her anger, she'd made a tactical error: she couldn't handle Nick the way she handled Will, and she shouldn't have tried. Will loved her and acted only in her best interest—however misguided he was about that interest. Nick didn't like her, had his own interests to protect, and she'd just backed herself into a very bad corner.

Oh, yes, she'd made a huge mistake. And now she couldn't find her tongue to say anything at all.

Nick looked her up and down with hot eyes before shaking his head and walking out the door. The sound of the slamming door echoed through her apartment like a gunshot.

Her knees began to wobble and she found a chair before they gave out entirely. At least she now had a reason for why Nick didn't like her—even if she didn't quite understand why or how or when he'd made such dramatic judgments about her character.

When would she learn to watch her mouth? Just a few minutes ago they were talking about *movies,* and she'd been so hopeful. But now…

What was she going to do now?

CHAPTER NINE

A TWENTY-MINUTE WALK AROUND Evie's neighborhood helped cool his temper, but now he felt exactly like the bastard Evie accused him of being. For someone Evie had called the strong, silent type, he sure had a big mouth.

He knew he lacked patience, but he'd always managed to keep a lid on his temper—even when his patience was pushed to its limits. It was a point of pride with him as well as a business philosophy. Anger led people to say and do stupid things, and hotheads rarely prevailed.

So where was his trademark silence and self-control when it came to Evie? One toss of her hair and he wanted to bend her over the nearest table. Then she'd grin at him and make him laugh. But that determined and stubborn lift of her chin made him want to strangle her.

Tease to tempt to temper with unbelievable speed and zero warning. He'd learned quickly *she* was capable of those extremes, but finding those extremes in himself? Good Lord. Dealing with Evie was like driving a fast car with no breaks around sharp curves while wearing a blindfold.

No wonder he was losing his mind. There just wasn't another explanation for any of this. Something had to give before they either killed each other or…

Or what?

He and Evie could draw up legal agreements all day long, but those weren't going to be much use in the day-to-day trenches. How was he supposed to create a decent home for his child when he and Evie kept snapping each other's heads off?

And Evie was getting more complicated with each passing minute. Accidentally pregnant or not, Evie had looked rather shocked—and offended—when he matter-of-factly informed her he didn't expect her to be much of a mother. *That* reaction had been real; Evie wasn't that good of an actress. It was such an honest look, he'd almost felt bad for saying it in the first place.

He shouldn't. There was too much riding on this bet.

But he did. It was absolutely infuriating.

To make matters worse, *none* of this did a damn thing to damp the fire that burned in his veins for her. It was insult to injury, salt in the wound, to want a woman *that* much even as she tore through his life like a flash flood.

Even now—not half an hour after he'd stormed out of her apartment—he wanted nothing more than to drag her into her bedroom and bury himself in her for the foreseeable future.

What he needed was to get Evie out of his system. Eventually, he'd get enough of her and the drugging, addictive effect she had on him.

Maybe then, he'd be able to think straight again.

Otherwise, this was never going to work. For any of them.

She simply couldn't go on like this. The stress was tearing her apart—and it couldn't be good for the baby, either. She and Nick had to come to some kind of real understanding, or else she simply wouldn't make it a month—much less a year—without killing him or driving herself insane.

She took several deep breaths, trying to calm herself.

Work the problem, Evie. One step at a time. Right now, the problem looked insurmountable and complex, but that was because Nick was at the middle. *Work the bits you can, then. Start at the edges.*

Where had he gone? Her keys were still on the table, so he didn't have access to a vehicle….

That's not your problem. He's an adult. He'd come back when he was ready, and hopefully, he would be calmer then. She needed to use this time to get her head together, to formulate a plan. She'd be able to function better if she had some solid ground under her feet. She'd been running on instinct for days now simply trying to mitigate the damages—no wonder she was half-crazy.

Right. Time to make a plan, then.

She dug a legal pad and a pen out of the drawer and pulled a chair up to the table. She tapped the pen against the paper as she tried to focus, but those smudged handprints kept drawing her eyes like a magnet. Muttering a curse, she went to the kitchen, grabbed a dust rag from under the sink and went to work removing the evidence.

It was torture, and it stirred up images she needed *not* to think about if she was going to be able to think straight at all. Her body wasn't getting the message, though. Her pelvic muscles contracted, sending a ripple up through her body until it reached her jaw and made her swallow hard.

Work the problem, damn it. Sex wasn't the problem. Well, not one she could really address at the moment. *Focus.*

She drew columns, labeled them and started orderly numbered lists of what she needed to do, what she needed to pack. The lists grew, the numbers moving into double digits, but she pressed on, not letting the length of the list panic her. She even added a couple of things to the list that she could cross off already—like telling Uncle Marcus—just to make herself feel as if she'd accomplished something.

Evie ran her finger over the last item in the list. *Nick.* In reality, he was number one, but she'd refused to think about it until she had everything else down on paper, simply because he was the most complicated and the most likely to overwhelm her if she thought about it too much.

Oddly, though, it didn't overwhelm her. She traced over his name, and a strange serenity settled on her shoulders. She did it again, and the feeling intensified.

This was ridiculous. *He* was the source of all her problems. *He* had just shouted at her and stormed out of her apartment. He didn't even like her, so why on earth was his entry on the list making her feel...

Better?

No, not really better. He brain stuttered and scrambled and butterflies battered her insides when she thought of him. Her heart beat faster and arousal heated her skin. That didn't fall under the category of "better." But there was no mistaking that odd feeling of serenity.

That had to be a good sign for the future. Either that, or she was a glutton for punishment and cracked in the head. She drummed the pen on the table. *Maybe?*

It made no sense at all. Nick was the center of the storm: everything unsettling and destructive in her life swirled around him.

The eye of the hurricane is the calmest.

She scrubbed her finger over the shiny surface of the table, leaving a smudge. With just a touch, Nick certainly let loose a hurricane inside *her.* The first time, the intensity had both excited and scared her.

Now she craved that feeling—and that explained a lot.

What it didn't explain was why when Nick touched her, she felt as if she was in the eye of the storm at the same time. The only time these days she felt as if her life *wasn't* spinning completely out of control, threatening to destroy everything and everyone she loved, was when Nick held her.

Evie jumped to her feet at that disturbing thought and began to pace. She *had* lost her mind this time. If not for Nick, her life wouldn't be spinning out of control in the first damn place.

It's the hormones. Something biological was causing that feeling. Residual caveman instinct to connect her to the father of the child she carried. Genetic programming from her evolutionary ancestors.

Because if it wasn't… Oh, dear Lord, she was in *big* trouble.

Two hours later, Evie's doorman waved him past the desk and straight to the elevator. Nick had to respect a building that ran with that much efficiency and attention to its residents that they already knew who he was.

He tried the handle of Evie's door before he knocked, and he was surprised to have it open easily under his hand. Either living in a limited-access building had Evie's guard down or else she'd left it unlocked in anticipation of his return. If it was the former, she'd have to break that habit once she moved to Vegas; his neighborhood might be gated, but it was isolated and a tempting target for burglars. If it was the latter…

That was a good sign, right?

Evie was on the couch, her laptop open and a phone pressed to her ear. From the sound of it, she was speaking to someone at her office, tying up loose ends and making arrangements for business to go on without her. She looked up as he closed the door, and ended the call quickly.

Three large suitcases sat next to the door.

With a careful—if slightly forced—pleasantness, Evie said, "You're back."

Good. Evie had cooled down as well and wasn't going to immediately reopen hostilities with an opening shot. He carefully kept his voice level, as well. "Yeah. I spent some time at that Internet café two blocks from here taking care of some business back home."

"Oh. You're welcome to do that here, too. Use the computer…whatever."

He indicated the phone and laptop. "Is that what you were doing? Taking care of business?"

She closed the computer and set it on the coffee table. "Yep. It's all taken care of."

"That was easy."

"Well, Will's been slow to hand over much responsibility to me. It's not that he doesn't trust me, he just still sees me as his little sister and…" She stopped and shrugged. "Most of my job could be done by a well-trained monkey. My assistant is pretty sharp and could easily handle everything, so she just landed a nice promotion. I'll keep a few fingers in a couple of projects while I'm gone and finish up a few things long-distance, but otherwise, I'm now free to do whatever."

An odd smile crossed her face as she spoke. Evie didn't seem upset to be leaving her job at all. Then she nodded at the suitcases. "And I'm pretty much packed, so we can leave whenever you're ready."

This was much quicker than expected. Either Evie was very well-organized or else she was leaving a lot undone. Why the big hurry to leave? "That's all you're taking?"

"I know. It's weird to me, too. I think I took more than that on my last vacation. I'm not normally what you'd call a light packer."

Guilt nagged at him—a new, unusual feeling—that he had implied she shouldn't, or couldn't, bring much with her. "You can bring anything you want with you, Evie. I have plenty of room."

"I know," she quickly interrupted, "and I started to pack all kinds of stuff. Then I realized I didn't know what I would need. I don't even need a lot of clothes, because I'll be outgrowing these soon anyway." She rubbed a hand over her still-flat abdomen. "Sabine or Gwen can mail me anything I decide

I do need, and, in reality, I'm not going to be gone all that long. No sense dragging everything I own to Las Vegas only to move it all back in another year."

Evie sounded upbeat about the move—and the move back. That bothered him more than he liked. He had no doubt her attitude would change, but for the moment, she sounded downright chipper, not something he'd expected to return to after the way he'd left earlier.

"Hey, Evie…"

"Look, Nick," she said at the same time. She stopped and clasped her hands in her lap. "I'm sorry. Go ahead."

"Ladies first."

"Okay." She stood and circled the couch, ending up standing right in front of him. Then Evie set her shoulders and lifted her chin, and he braced himself for another volley. "I'm sorry."

The apology caught him off guard, but Evie didn't seem to notice as she hurried ahead.

"For a lot of things, but primarily for earlier. Well, my attitude has pretty much sucked recently, and I've taken it all out on you. And I am sorry for that." He opened his mouth, but Evie held up a hand. "I really need to say all of this before you respond. You're holding up your end of the bargain admirably, and I can't thank you enough for how you've acted around my family. I'll sleep a lot better and worry a lot less now that I know they're satisfied. Now, I'd really like for us to come to another agreement. One where we don't snipe and yell at each other."

That was quite a speech. She'd been thinking while he was gone. "I think that sounds like an excellent plan."

He didn't realize how forced her pleasantness had been until her shoulders sagged and she laughed. A genuine laugh this time; the one he didn't hear very often. "Thank goodness. I know you might not believe this, but most people say I'm pretty easy to get along with."

Her voice was both earnest and lighthearted at the same time—a combination only Evie could ever manage. "Is that so?"

"Yes, it is," she responded primly. "My only explanation is that this situation has put me under a lot of stress, and I'm learning that I don't handle stress all that well."

Regardless of her light tone, she'd swallowed a lot of her pride to make that speech; it was only fair that he do the same. "It's been stressful for me, too, and I'm learning a similar lesson."

"Oh, good, we're *both* growing as people then. Gwen talks about building and showing character through adversity. I think I've been building a whole cast of characters." Her mouth twisted. "Not all of them are shining stars of the show, though."

Evie's charm; he'd forgotten how captivating she could be when she turned on the charm like that. "So now what?"

She took a deep breath, and he waited. "Well—and I know this sounds really strange, considering—I'd like us to be friends."

"Friends?" He nearly choked on the word. They may not have been very friendly lately, but they'd passed "friends" eight orgasms ago.

"I think it will be much easier as we go forward. We're going to be together for a very long time—um, I mean, the baby will always connect us, and it will be much easier for everyone if we're on good terms."

"I agree."

"Good." She blew out her breath and leaned her hips against the couch. "Wow. That was both harder and easier than I thought it would be. But I feel a whole lot better. Now, what were you going to say?"

"Something similar, actually." He was rewarded for his honesty by the look of surprise that sent Evie's eyebrows arching upward. "We certainly couldn't go on as we were."

"I'm *so* glad we got that sorted out." She rubbed her hands on her thighs and pushed to her feet. "And now, I'm suddenly very hungry. What about you? There's a wonderful Lebanese place not far—"

"There's one more thing we need to discuss, Evie."

"Oh. Okay." She resumed her earlier position, and braced her hands on the top of the couch. "What?"

"This." It was all the warning she got before he closed the distance between them and captured her mouth. Her gasp of surprise pulled air from his lungs. Then Evie melted into his embrace, her lips molding against his as her tongue slid greedily over his. Her hands roamed restlessly over his back before coming to rest at his waist, her thumbs hooking under the waistband of his jeans.

He'd meant the kiss as a simple demonstration—a reference for the point he was about to make—but desire soon took over, and he deepened the kiss as his hands slid up around her neck and into the mass of her hair.

He broke the kiss before he lost all control and hauled her into the bedroom, pressing his forehead against hers as he listened to her short, panting breaths.

"*This* is still an issue, Evie."

Her head was spinning now. "I think...." She had to pause to compose herself. "I think *this* crosses the line of 'friends.'"

"We can't ignore it."

Damn. He was devastating to her higher brain functions when he looked at her like that. *Think, Evie.* "But that doesn't mean we should explore it, either. Not immediately, at least."

"We're married, Evie. For the first time in your life, the people you're so worried about gossiping about you are actually expecting you to have sex. You should take advantage of that." Nick's hand slid around her waist, and the hurricane began to swirl.

"Marriage of convenience" was taking on a whole new meaning for her.

The dangers, though, of a marriage of convenience to Nick were quickly becoming clear. Nick's magnetism was almost irresistible, his eyes and voice hypnotic, but that feeling of serenity was sucking her in. Turning her on.

This was a perk, and as wrong as it seemed to build on it, it was a foundation of sorts. At least she and Nick had *something*.

But what happened in seven or eight months when she became too big and bulky and awkward to interest him? Was she signing up for even more misery later by not drawing a bold line in the sand now?

The hand around her waist tightened, and the pressure from his fingers increased, pulling her incrementally closer to him.

Her body was on board, practically screaming at her mind to quit thinking and just *do*. It was a foundation, and she reminded herself that she wasn't trying to build a foundation for forever. It wasn't the key to happily-ever-after, but it could be the key to happy-enough-for-now.

It would buy her some time so they could get to know each other better, find some common ground, and maybe, just maybe, change his opinion of her.

Even just a little. She'd settle for that.

Threading her fingers through Nick's belt loops, she tugged his hips to hers. Those dark eyes seemed to light from behind, and she was rewarded for her decision with a kiss that held wicked promises.

As far as "settling" went, she could settle for worse.

CHAPTER TEN

SETTLE WAS RAPIDLY becoming her least favorite word in the English language. Two weeks after moving to Las Vegas, Evie had to bite her tongue every time someone said the word *settle* in her presence or else she might scream.

Gwen kept asking how she was *settling in.* Bennie wanted to know if she regretted *settling* for a quickie marriage. Will wanted to know if she'd *settled* all of her outstanding jobs and accounts before she left and how she was *settling* the ones she still had some activity in from Las Vegas. Her obstetrician promised her stomach would *settle* soon and recommended crackers and ginger ale for breakfast.

Settle, schmettle. It was a stupid-sounding word in the first place, Evie thought as she moved from a down dog into a plank position. *Settling* sounded passive, as if something would magically happen on its own, and she had no patience at this point for just waiting around for something to happen.

Fortune favors the brave, she thought, breathing in through her nose and lowering into a crocodile. Her arms trembled a little as she held the pose and counted under her breath. Dr. Banks had given yoga his stamp of approval at her first prenatal appointment yesterday, but she was now paying for the three weeks she'd taken off.

She couldn't claim to be brave, but she was certainly not

passive, either. Since she and Nick called their truce seventeen days ago, she'd plastered a smile on her face and jumped into her new life with great amounts of—however forced at times—enthusiasm.

Evie rocked her chest and hips forward to push through into an up dog and felt the stretch in her back. She held the pose and opened her eyes to enjoy the view. Nick's pool deck looked out over the desert's colors to the mountains in the distance. It was a far cry from the urban landscape she'd had from her windows the last ten years, and it had been a surprise to find that Nick didn't live among the lights of Las Vegas proper. She'd fallen in love with the view and spent as much time as possible out here in the shade of the awning, enjoying it. She almost hated to move back into down dog and lose the sight. Her calves protested, but she pulled her chest toward her thighs for a better stretch.

Yoga, like everything else, had to be done full-out whether she wanted to or not and regardless of how uncomfortable it was. But at least she was reaping results from that approach to her life.

She'd never be a perfect wife, but she was trying. Nick had a huge kitchen, and Evie discovered she really liked to cook. After some initial suspicion of her culinary talents and surprise that she not only planned to cook, but also claimed to enjoy it, Nick seemed pleased with her efforts and results.

The goal she'd set for herself sounded rather simple on the surface: try to get along. It wasn't as if she didn't have practice in that area. Years of Gwen's training provided her with a full set of skills designed for that, and Evie had had plenty of practice perfecting them.

After the first couple of days, it got easier, as she and Nick both kept to the unspoken terms of their cease-fire. Even though she could tell Nick still didn't quite like her, at least he didn't seem to actively *dis*like her, either. He was pleasant—friendly, even, at times—and it was getting incrementally better every day.

Slim results were better than none, she kept reminding herself. Hell, it was practically a mantra for her these days, and she repeated it as she moved into warrior two.

Her nights, though…

Her thigh trembled in a way that had nothing to do with the deep lunge. There were definitely perks in this arrangement, and sometimes, in the nonsense talk of afterglow, she felt as if she and Nick were coming to some kind of understanding—she hesitated to use the word *relationship*—that just might be genuine and beyond the ground rules of peaceful coexistence.

Work the bits you can….

"Evie?"

She jumped and turned to find Lottie at the door. "Lottie! Is it eleven already?"

"I knocked, but there was no answer so I let myself in…." Lottie looked worried. "I didn't mean to interrupt."

"Please don't apologize. I'm glad you let yourself in. I just lost track of time. Can I get you something to drink?"

Lottie's unreserved acceptance of her had made Evie's transition much easier, and she was glad for the friendship. In many ways, Lottie reminded Evie of Bennie: practical and funny and straight to the point, only without Bennie's wild streak. Plus, Lottie was her husband's best friend's wife, and therefore a fount of information about Nick.

And Lottie's open personality meant Evie didn't have to pry for any details, either. Bonus.

But Lottie was Evie's savior today for an entirely different reason, and she sent Lottie to the sitting room while she got the snacks and drinks from the kitchen. When she returned with the tray, Lottie frowned at her slightly. "Are you sure about this? You don't have to."

"Believe me when I say I really *want* to. I did this all the time at home. Not to brag, but fundraising is something I'm pretty good at. That and PR. And y'all do so many great things, I'm just blown away."

Four days ago, when Lottie casually mentioned what the nonprofit center she worked for actually did and how they were trying to raise funds to rehab a community center in one of Las Vegas' poorest neighborhoods, Evie had pounced gratefully on the project.

"And you've saved me from going stir-crazy." While she *loved* the fact no one in Las Vegas knew her, and therefore had no expectations of her, not having anything at all to do had lost its luster after about four days. "I'm not used to not being busy and doing things, and the walls were already starting to close in."

Lottie looked around the spacious room and laughed. "You really do need something to do, don't you?" Picking up the pile of papers Evie had left on the table, she flipped through and whistled in appreciation. "When you do something, you go all out, that's for sure."

This wasn't park benches or the garden club; this was real effect on people's lives. Social-services counseling, after-school programs, drug and gang and teenage-pregnancy prevention—the Gleason Street Center provided it all. And, yes, Evie was fired up about it. Both HarCorp and the Harrison Family Charitable Trust had funding requests on the appropriate desk—Will's—already. The computer center and the basketball court were as good as done deals, but Lottie didn't know that yet.

"You have a very worthwhile project, and I'm just pleased you'll let me help." *Where was that spreadsheet?*

"I bet Nick's happy. What did he say when you told him?"

That got her attention. "I haven't mentioned it. Should I? Is Nick a donor already?" She frowned at that thought;

she'd planned to bring Nick on board later. Maybe with the library project…

Lottie choked on her drink. "You could say that."

When Lottie didn't elaborate, Evie knew she was missing an important piece to the puzzle. She leaned back into the corner of the couch and folded her legs under her. "Okay, spill. Give me all the details."

"Gleason Street is Nick's—and Kevin's—old turf. They both grew up not far from there. Did you not know that?"

Evie shook her head. "Nick told me he grew up in North Las Vegas, but since I didn't know the city, it didn't mean anything to me at the time."

And she'd forgotten until now. *Damn.* As part of preparing herself for this project, she'd spent some time researching the area, but she hadn't made the connection. The whole neighborhood was far below the poverty line; there were drugs and gangs… Evie chose her next words carefully. "Has the neighborhood changed much since then?"

"It's gotten a little better."

Oh. She knew Nick had earned his money and built his business with his own hands, but she hadn't realized his climb had been *that* steep. "They've come a long way, haven't they?"

Lottie nodded. "And they're proud of it. Nick actually uses it as a test on people sometimes."

"A test?" Alarm bells went off in her head. "How?"

"Oh, like when he meets people, he'll drop it into conversation to see how they react."

"Really?" Evie thought back to that first night. Nick *had* dropped that nugget of information before he knew she was from Dallas. She'd passed a test without knowing she was even taking it. No wonder Nick wasn't happy when he found out…

"If you think about it, it's a good way to cut to the chase with people. Especially the Old-Money types. Just because your daddy had money that doesn't make you any better than anyone else."

Evie's head snapped up, and she looked carefully to see if Lottie had directed that comment at her, specifically. But Lottie was still scanning printouts and budgets. That "you" must have been a general, nonspecific pronoun. "True. Money doesn't mean anything about a person's character."

"I know that, and you know that, but tell that to some folks." Lottie laughed, and Evie felt sick. Lottie obviously didn't know much about her background.

"Don't you think that's a bit of a broad generalization? Not all wealthy people are like that." Granted, Evie knew a lot who were, but not everyone with family money had a superiority complex.

"Precious few, Evie." Lottie's eyes grew wide as she read more of Evie's proposal. "Do you really think we could get some NBA players to come?"

Evie smiled weakly. "We can ask. The worst they can do is say no." Her stomach tied itself into a painful knot. "Still, you don't think testing people like that... I mean, it's a bit childish."

Lottie smirked. "Tell Nick that."

"I think I will, as a matter of fact." *One day.*

Lottie shrugged. "You can't really blame him, though, considering..."

"Considering what?" She wasn't sure she wanted to know at this point, but she *had* to ask.

Lottie looked at her wide-eyed. "Nick hasn't told you?"

Would I be asking otherwise? "Guess not, because I'm clueless."

"Well, it's probably not my place to go telling you..."

Evie tried hard to keep her voice light. "You have to now. I'm curious."

"Well, Nick's mother is—*was*—Farrahlee Grayson."

Evie wracked her brain but came up empty. Lottie must have been able to tell.

"I keep forgetting you're not from here. The Grayson family goes way back in Vegas. Not quite a 'founding family,' but definitely part of the boom years. There were even rumors that some of the family's money came from the mob, but that's neither here nor there. Either way, the Grayson family had bucket loads of money and they made sure everyone knew it."

The knots in her stomach were getting worse with each word. Evie knew she wasn't going to like this story at all, but glutton that she was, she had to hear it. And she probably couldn't stop Lottie now if she tried.

"So, Farrahlee's a bit of a rebel, and to tick her family off, she finds a guy her parents are guaranteed to hate and swears he's the one."

The alarm bells clanged with greater urgency. "Nick's father."

"Right. Gus. Farrahlee was just out for kicks, but she ended up pregnant. So, Gus and Farrahlee had to get married. I mean, you couldn't knock up Big Buddy Grayson's daughter and *not* marry her."

Oh, dear Lord.

"Farrahlee's father buys them a little house, gets Gus a good job and then cuts Farrahlee off without a dime. They last maybe a year or so after Nick was born before Farrahlee didn't want to play house anymore. She wanted her life, her money, her place as Big Buddy Grayson's daughter, back."

This was not good....

"Before Gus knew it, Farrahlee had divorced him, signed away parental rights to Nick and left the state. Gus went to Farrahlee's family, but they denied that they had any responsibility for Nick at all. Gus slowly began to drink himself to death at that point. He lost his job and the house and they ended up on Gleason Street. Nick had it rough. Really rough."

Evie sighed as the full meaning of the story landed in her chest like a rock. "Hence the chip on his shoulder."

"Exactly. His selfish, self-centered, stuck-up rich mother destroyed Gus's life and damn near destroyed Nick's. Evie, are you okay? You look pale."

She felt pale. "Just a little light-headed all of a sudden. I guess I didn't hydrate enough while I was out there in the heat."

Lottie, unaware that the world had just shifted, jumped topics. "I've always wanted to learn yoga. It seems like a good workout."

Evie dug deep into her bag of polite tricks. "And I'd love for you to come over sometime and exercise with me. It's a wonderful way to stretch." She tried to keep her voice at the same calm level, hiding her desperate curiosity. "So, where are Farrahlee and the rest of the Graysons now?"

Lottie shook her head as if it was a shame, but her voice belied the sentiment. "The family fell on hard times about ten or fifteen years ago. Big Buddy died about then, and they lost pretty much everything. Some folks had to leave town, some folks went to jail.... Farrahlee never came back to Vegas, and she died about five years ago. Nick was able to pick Starlight up for a song when they were selling off the last of the Grayson properties."

"A little comeuppance for the family?"

Lottie laughed. "Nick's whole existence—much less his success—is a big ol' poke in the eye for what few Graysons are still around."

Her nausea grew worse. "Success is the best revenge, they say. Nick's come a long way. And Kevin, too, obviously."

"They make a good team. I love him, but I don't know if Kevin would have had much drive to change his circumstances if Nick hadn't pushed him. He's not lazy or anything—he's just too laid-back to push too much."

"Kevin and Nick have known each other for a while?"

Which meant Kevin would share Nick's feelings toward Old Money, and therefore, *her.*

"Oh, they've been friends since they were like five or something. But Kevin's story is pretty much the same as half the kids' at Gleason Street—absent father, mother on drugs…"

"Would you excuse me for just a moment?" Without waiting for a reply, Evie stood and managed to walk calmly from the room. She closed the bathroom door and gripped the edge of the sink. He head was spinning, and she didn't quite know where to start processing the information Lottie so causally tossed her way.

She was horrified and indignant on Nick's behalf. His mother—hell, that whole family—was an insult to the decency of the human race. But, wow, it certainly explained a lot about why Nick didn't trust her, why he thought she would be a terrible mother…. Her shoulders dropped. Why Nick didn't like her much.

Because he thought she was just another Farrahlee. There were plenty of parallels, but still…

Talk about irony. Her life had plenty of examples of people who wanted to be her friend—or boyfriend—simply because she had money and came from the right family. Until now, she'd never faced anyone who didn't like her *because* of her family's wealth.

It wasn't as if she asked to be a Harrison. It was unfair of Nick to paint her as something simply because of her trust fund. It made her nauseous—like the morning sickness gone ten times worse.

It also made her want to kick Nick in a sensitive area. Who was he to accuse her of being shallow when he was the one passing judgment based solely on bank balances? That was a hell of a double standard.

Of course, the big question was now that she had new pieces to the puzzle, what was she going to *do* with them?

* * *

The volume of his stereo made him feel as if he had a teenager living in his house. Evie's musical tastes ran the spectrum from jazz to Top Forty, but the volume control only had one position: max. Granted, he tended to push the volume up a bit himself, but he'd spent too many years in bars and nightclubs where loud music and the subsequent slight hearing loss were expected. What was Evie's excuse?

He was getting used to coming home to the sound of music blaring, and, more recently, the smells of dinner coming from the kitchen. For the first couple of days after Evie moved in, she seemed uncomfortable with his house, but that had passed and she'd put her stamp on the place. Arrangements of fresh flowers graced tables. Art that had sat on the floor since the day he moved in now hung on the walls. She'd moved his furniture around and hired a different maid after finding the dust accumulated underneath.

After almost a year of living here, his house finally felt—for lack of a better word—homey. He had started looking forward to coming home, and a part of that, he wasn't ashamed to admit, was Evie.

He found her in the kitchen, her back to him as she stirred something on the stove, her head bobbing slightly with the beat of the music. She wore a simple cotton sundress with a low-cut back, and with her hair pulled up in a ponytail, he was treated to a lovely view of the elegant line of her neck and spine. She shifted her weight, leaning a hip against the counter and balancing one foot on top of the other.

Evie was barefoot. Pregnant. In the kitchen. He laughed out loud, and Evie dropped the spoon as she turned around.

"Nick! I didn't hear you come in."

"I'm not surprised."

Evie frowned as she slipped past him through the door, and a second later, the music volume dropped dramatically. When she came back in, she arched an eyebrow at him. "Are you sure you're only thirty-two?"

He arched an eyebrow back at her. "Are you sure you're really twenty-five?"

"If it's too loud, you're too old," she challenged as she opened the fridge, took out a beer and offered it to him. "How was your day?"

"Good. The sale on The Zoo went through."

"That's great. Congratulations."

"I'll keep it open for a little while, give the staff some notice, but I'd like to get started on the refurbishing soon."

Evie returned to stirring. "How sad. I'll miss those lighted vines. Hey, bring them home, and we'll hang them by the pool."

"Very funny." But he did like the way Evie referred to this as "home." "So what did you do today?"

"Picked up some paint samples for you to look at for the baby's room. Sent a resume to Circus Circus…"

"I told you I'd hire you if you wanted a job."

Evie shook her head. "Thanks, but after looking at the pitiful state of my resumé, I think I need to get some experience at places *not* owned by people I'm related to by blood or marriage." She paused and took a deep breath. "And I had lunch with Lottie."

Such a simple domestic scene: Evie puttering around in the kitchen while they discussed their respective days. It was almost as if they'd been doing it for years. And it hadn't been at all what he expected when Evie moved in. "Good. I'm glad you and Lottie are becoming friends."

Evie leaned against the counter and crossed her arms over her chest. "I'm going to be helping her with the Gleason Street Community Center project." She tossed it out like a challenge, but he wasn't sure why.

"I think that's great, Evie. You've certainly done a lot of fundraising and PR in the past." He chose his words carefully, wondering why she seemed so on guard about this. "I'm sure Lottie will appreciate your expertise."

"So I can count on you for a hefty check and ongoing support?"

Was that sarcasm? "Of course." When Evie didn't respond, he decided not to beat around the bush. "*What?* What's the problem?"

"Why didn't you tell me you grew up in that neighborhood?"

"I distinctly remember telling you that very thing."

She rolled her eyes. "And if I'd told you I grew up in Turtle Creek, would that have meant anything to you? Didn't think so. I'm from Dallas, how was I supposed to know what you meant by that?"

"Considering you were just on vacation, it didn't seem that important to elaborate."

"And now?"

"What do you want to know, Evie? I grew up in the projects. My dad was a drunk who couldn't keep a steady job. I didn't want to end up like him, so I worked my way through school, won a lot of seed money at the poker tables and bought Blue."

She smirked. "A true American success story. Making good through hard work, determination and luck."

Somehow, Evie made that sound like a slam. "I guess. And your point is?"

She sighed. "Nothing."

So much for that nice, homey feeling. "Go ahead. Spit it out."

Pushing out of her lean and wiping her hands on a towel, she shook her head. "You know, it's not worth it. I'm not going to pick a fight."

It was a little late for that, in his opinion.

Waving in the direction of the stove, she added, "Dinner will be ready in a few more minutes...."

"You brought this up, not me. If it's bothering you…"

Evie spun to face him. "Fine." With her hands on her hips, she met his eyes evenly. "What about those people who only needed luck? The luck to be born into the right family."

"Like you?"

She nodded. "That's one example, sure. It seems like the height of arrogance to assume those born into money aren't as appreciative of it or that they're somehow not as…as *good* as those who started with less."

"Evie, here's a news flash for you. Money doesn't always bring out the best in people."

"And poverty does?" Sarcasm dripped off the words. "No offense to your personal Bolshevik uprising, but money is nothing more than a tool. If that's the only tool in your tool-box, you'll never be happy. It'll warp your brain. Surely you've seen that."

"Spoken by someone who has a trust fund greater than the GDP of some small European countries. You lack credibility on this particular topic."

"And that huge chip on your shoulder makes you an expert on what, exactly? You know, a good therapist could help you work through some of these issues."

What the…? "My issues? Jesus, Evie, you're one to talk. You're not exactly the poster child of self-help and empower-erment."

Her chin went up. "But I'm not your mother, either."

He froze. "You don't know anything about Farrahlee Grayson," he said slowly, narrowing his eyes in warning and hoping she'd realize he didn't want to continue on that course of conversation.

No such luck. "Oh, I know enough. And while it doesn't make anything she did right or fair, I can see where having money and being Farrahlee Grayson was the identity she had and how losing that identity could have pushed her over the edge."

"You're defending her?" Three weeks ago he wouldn't have been surprised, but after everything recently...

"God, no. Not at all. The woman is an evil bitch and her whole family should be shot. Understanding *why* someone did something doesn't mean I sympathize or approve."

"You're assuming *I* don't understand why she left."

"Actually I think you *do*. And it's made you mad enough to live your entire life for the sole purpose of spiting her and her family. You're basically a good man with lots of potential, and you should be proud of your accomplishments. But you've got to let this go at some point."

Evie let her hands drop to her sides. "You've passed judgment on me, assuming I'm self-centered and selfish because of my bank balance." Her words were clipped, precise. "I'm actually relieved to find out that's where it's coming from, because my trust fund isn't me. I don't even know how much money you have, so I have to base my judgment of you on your actions. I think my judgment has a lot more creditability than yours."

"You're the one who showed up with a marriage proposal, a prenup and a divorce plan because you found yourself pregnant. Those actions just scream credibility."

She opened her mouth, paused and closed it with a snap before scrubbing her hands over her face and huffing. "Dinner's ready. Help yourself. I'm not hungry anymore."

She walked out of the room with her shoulders held back, but there was resignation in her step. A moment later, he heard a door close; not with a loud slam—just solid noise that spoke volumes.

He drained his beer, hoping the liquid would help cool his temper. Evie had made several valid points during her rant, telling him he that needed to reevaluate a few things. But *he* wasn't totally wrong, either, he reminded himself.

But if that were really the case, his conscience argued, why did *he* feel like the complete tool now?

CHAPTER ELEVEN

EVIE DROPPED INTO THE ROCKING chair she'd purchased for this room with a groan of disgust at herself. Shooting off her mouth—and thereby shooting herself in the foot—had moved from being an occasional lapse to a full-time occupation.

And things had been going so well. Well, better, at least. The rocking chair she was currently sitting in was proof of her belief in that. And her hope. Why else would she be decorating a nursery unless she harbored the hope it would see good use?

Oh, she'd rationalized it, telling herself that Nick would want the baby to have a nice room of its own for when he or she came to visit. But now, as she berated herself for her astonishing inability to keep her trap shut, she had to admit that wasn't really the complete truth.

She'd been designing this room for the long term. It was a long-shot, secret hope—one she didn't really want to admit: the hope she and the baby might be here for much longer than originally planned. And that was totally stupid, considering the situation.

Because that meant... Well, damn. She shouldn't even go there. Crossing that bridge wasn't a good idea. Madness lay on the other side. As did heartbreak.

Evie leaned back and set the chair rocking, allowing the movement to calm her. Or trying to, at least. She heard the quiet knock a few minutes later and opened her eyes as Nick stuck his head around the door.

She searched his face carefully, examined his body language for clues to his mood and temper level. He seemed oddly…friendly? No, *friendly* wasn't the right description, but he wasn't openly hostile, either—amazing considering how she'd just blown her top and flounced out of the room in such a mature way.

"You like to get the last word, don't you? Make the dramatic exit?" Nick's mouth twitched in amusement, and Evie felt her muscles relax. He wasn't here to reopen hostilities.

Cautiously teasing, testing the waters, she tried for a small smile. "It's one way out of uncomfortable situations."

"Is it approved by your sister-in-law?"

"Oh, no. Flouncing—of any sort—is definitely not Miss Behavior-approved. It's a hard habit to break, though."

Nick crossed his arms and leaned against the wall. The silence stretched out, but it wasn't stretching her nerves. The energy in the room wasn't tense or angry. Nick wasn't mad, wasn't here to fight more, but the truce had been upended—thanks to her—and she got the feeling Nick was here to reestablish the treaty. And since she'd fired the first shot, she needed to extend the olive branch, as well.

She took a deep breath and swallowed her pride. "I'm sorry I blew up like that. I shouldn't have said—"

"Maybe those things needed to be said."

That was hope rising out of the ashes of her pride. "I lack finesse when I get angry, though."

"So do I."

Fortune favors the brave. She met Nick's eyes and made a cautious step out onto that bridge. "I'm not like her, you know."

Nick nodded. "I realize that. You're not the only one with bad habits, though."

It wasn't exactly a gushing declaration, but Evie grabbed

the hope it offered with both hands. Mentally steadying herself, she edged another foot out on the bridge. "And I don't want to be like her, either." *There, she'd said it. She'd gone there. Sort of.*

Surprise registered on Nick's face, replaced a moment later by a slow, easy smile that made her insides melt. "History doesn't have to repeat itself."

Evie figured that was about as good as she could hope for at the moment and it was a good start. She put her feet down and stopped the rocker. "You know, I'm hungry after all."

Nick extended a hand to her and she took it. "Let's eat."

She took it, and with that, she was across that bridge and on the other side.

And it scared the hell out of her.

"Lord, you're such a butthead." Evie rolled her eyes at him as she made that pronouncement and flopped dramatically back onto the pillow. Then she ruined it with a giggle.

Nick pushed up on his elbow to face her. She was a vision: her hair all tangled and flowing across her pillow onto his and her cheeks flushed. "Did you really just call me a butthead? I haven't been called a butthead since third grade."

"Hey, I call 'em as I see 'em."

He picked up a lock of her hair and brushed it across her nose. "But you're not in third grade anymore. You can't come up with something better?"

"Other appropriate descriptions would not be very ladylike," she responded primly. Completely unselfconscious of her nudity, Evie looked like an exotic goddess—not a buttoned-up "lady" worried about appropriateness.

He used her hair to paint a line down the valley between her breasts before lazily circling a nipple and watching the shiver slide over her skin. "Is 'butthead' part of the Official Debutante Vocabulary?"

"It's not in the handbook, no, but—" Her forehead creased slightly, and she arched her back. "Ouch."

"You okay?"

She nodded as she sat up and rubbed at her lower back. "Muscle cramp."

"Roll over."

She grinned. "Again?"

Desire sliced through him. "Don't get cheeky. I'm offering to rub your back. However—" he let his eyes roam over her until she started to blush "—I'm certainly willing to rethink that offer."

"Back rub first." Evie flipped to her stomach and wrapped her arms around a pillow.

He knelt over her, straddling her hips, and savored the smooth warmth of her skin against his thighs. Gathering her silky hair in one hand, he lifted it out of the way and tucked it over her shoulder, leaving her back completely bare. He slid a finger down the indentation of her spine and watched goose-flesh rise. "Are you cold?"

"Not at all," she mumbled huskily, then cleared her throat. "Lower back, please."

Massaging slow circles at the base of her spine earned him an appreciative moan. His erection stirred to life, hardening against her backside.

"This is what I get for not exercising for three weeks. I knew I felt tight in my up dog this morning. It started bothering me a couple of hours ago." She shrugged, and he looked up to see her cheek move as she smiled. "I guess tonight's activities just aggravated—*damn*."

His hands hadn't moved much; he couldn't be responsible for that pained curse. He quickly moved off her. "Evie?"

Evie rolled to her side and curled her legs up into her body, her arms wrapping around her waist. Her face had lost all its color, and her eyes squeezed closed in pain. A muscle in her jaw worked as she gritted her teeth and breathed in slowly through her nose. "Are you all—"

Fear—real fear like he hadn't felt since he was a child—slammed into him as Evie groaned again and pressed her hands against her stomach. His blood turned icy.

The baby.

Heart pounding, he scrambled for the phone.

Everyone was so kind. The doctors and nurses in the emergency room. The hospital volunteer who'd found her a set of scrubs to wear instead of her bloody clothes. The counselor who stopped by her little curtained-off bed in the E.R. to check on her and give her a card for a "recovery group." And especially Nick, who had worry lines etched into his stone face, but had sat by her bed while folks came and went and did all kinds of things to her—none of which stopped her from losing her baby.

They were all so damn *kind,* she'd wanted to hit something. And now, ten nightmarish hours later, she was still careening between that need and the need to lock herself in a dark room and bawl. But instead she had to sit here and listen to Dr. Banks talk about recovery time and coming back for a follow-up scan, when just two days ago, he'd been writing prescriptions for prenatal vitamins and pressing nutritional information pamphlets at her.

She'd taken so much for granted. It never occurred to her she wouldn't have this baby. And now she didn't. This had to be some kind of karmic payback for not wanting to be pregnant in the first place. The depth of the ache surprised her and killed her at the same time.

It was hard to focus on what Dr. Banks was telling her. "It's not uncommon to miscarry this early. It's nothing you did or didn't do." She should take comfort in that, but the wound was too fresh. "I can't find anything wrong with you physically, so there's no reason to assume you'll have any problems in the future conceiving or carrying a baby to term."

She opened her mouth, but Dr. Banks put a hand on her arm and squeezed gently. "It's not your fault." He turned to Nick. "Or yours, either. I'm so sorry about the baby, but you're perfectly healthy and these things really do just happen sometimes." She nodded because he seemed to expect it. "Now, do you have any questions for me?"

She did, but they all started with *why* and she already knew Dr. Banks didn't have any of those answers for her. No one did. She shook her head, which felt as hollow as the rest of her right now.

Dr. Banks had a kind face and a bedside manner that made her feel she could trust him at the same time it made her feel as if he really cared, but all that kindness and caring just rattled around in her hollow chest like marbles in a can. "I wrote you a prescription for some pain medicine if you need it over the next few days. Just rest and take it easy. And no sex for at least two weeks."

Out of the corner of her eye, she saw Nick's shoulders stiffen at the "no sex" edict. Did that mean he was upset it was off the cards, or insulted it even came up? And while she couldn't fault Nick's behavior or support through all this, he'd fallen into a silence that made his usual lack of communication seem positively chatty in comparison. He'd said all the right things at the right time, but none of them had *meant* anything. Nothing to let her know what he was feeling.

And then there was shaking of hands and patting of shoulders, and she and Nick were back in the car, headed home in silence.

Home. Where was that now? Nick's house? Not really; she was merely a guest there, just a step above an incubator for the baby. But home wasn't Dallas, either. She wasn't the same person she was even a couple of months ago, so she couldn't just go back and pick up her life where she'd left off. Her focus, her center, had shifted so dramatically recently, but that focus was gone now, and she was more than a little lost.

"How are you feeling?" Nick asked, breaking the quiet and causing her to jump.

What wasn't she feeling? Everything was all tied together, though, confusing her. "Tired."

He nodded. "Then you rest, and I'll go get your meds and something to eat."

He looked just as tired as she felt; there were shadows under his eyes, and she wondered if he'd slept at all in that plastic hospital chair. She'd had drugs—drugs that allowed her to sleep and escape the knowledge of what was happening for a little while.

There was something she should say—a lot she could say—but the words were trapped in her throat behind that backlog of conflicting emotions. "Thanks."

Nick followed her into the house "to help her get settled"— the word still grated across her nerves, but in a whole new way now—and she searched for words.

He stopped at the bedroom door, not following her in as she sat on the bed and toed off her shoes. She noticed the sheets were still tangled from last night's activities and askew from their hurried exit. She wanted to crawl under them and cry herself to sleep at the same time she didn't want to be there at all. As Nick turned around, she finally decided what she wanted to say. "I'm sorry."

His response was quick, but his voice was tired. "You heard the doctor—it wasn't anything you did or didn't do. It wasn't your fault."

"I can still be sorry." *For a lot of things.*

"Me, too." He was quiet for a moment, but he didn't meet her eyes. "But the doctor did say you would be able to have other children."

You. Not *we.* What had she expected? She lay down, the weight of everything just too much to bear any longer. "Yeah. He did say that. Maybe one day."

Nick looked in her direction—but not *at* her—a moment longer, the muscle in his jaw working, before he nodded. "Yeah. One day. I'll, um…I'll go get your meds."

He closed the door behind him as he left, and Evie burst into tears. Burying her head in the pillow that smelled like Nick only made her cry harder. She heard the crash, but couldn't bring herself to care enough to investigate.

She hadn't meant to get pregnant, but she did. And now she wasn't. She should feel relieved, but she didn't. Smelling his pillow made her think how happy she and Nick had been just hours ago, but she knew now that had been false. Just like their marriage license, it had been window dressing for the sake of the baby.

A baby she didn't have now.

She wrapped her arms around her stomach, berating herself for grieving so hard for something she'd barely had to begin with. But she couldn't help it. The baby hadn't been far from her thoughts simply because of the situation, but she hadn't realized that emotionally, at an elemental level, she'd connected to the baby and the idea of being a mother. Her rational brain hadn't really been focusing on *that,* but obviously something in her had. And now it hurt. Badly.

Following hard on that hurt—as if it wasn't enough or something—was the pain of knowing she'd lost everything. Her whole life—the new one she'd been working so hard to build—was crashing down around her. And she had no one to turn to.

She wanted Nick, but *that* wasn't what their relationship was about. How many times had he spelled that out to her? She'd just lost what their relationship was about, and Nick had just beaten a hasty path to the door. But that didn't seem to stop her from wanting him to be here with her now. She needed that. She needed him to talk to her, to tease her, to make her mad. Something. *Anything*.

Because otherwise, she had nothing.

In the car, Nick examined the blood on his knuckle. He didn't feel any better, and now he'd have to explain the hole in the drywall to Evie.

Provided she ever spoke to him again.

He'd never been so scared in his entire life. He'd known the baby was gone long before the doctors in the E.R. made their official pronouncements, but that pain had been held at bay as his real fear had centered on Evie.

She'd been whiter than the sheet on her hospital bed, but the blood… He hadn't expected that much blood. For a few minutes there at the beginning, he'd been sure she was going to die, but then her pain meds finally kicked in. It had been the longest time of his life.

But the worst had been—still was, actually—the hollow look in Evie's eyes that seemed as if she'd checked out mentally from the whole situation. He hadn't known what to say, and for the first time ever, Evie hadn't been very talkative. She hadn't needed him, and he hadn't been able to tell her… Well, anything.

So they'd sat there in silence. That silence had finally driven him to punching holes in the drywall in frustration and grief. The grief—he hadn't been prepared for that feeling.

This was his fault. No pregnant woman should have to deal with the level of stress he'd been putting on Evie. And he should have been more careful in general—Evie had said her research had said sex was perfectly safe, but hours of it? In multiple positions even the *Kama Sutra* didn't know? Had he once checked to make sure she was eating right? Resting enough?

At times, he'd almost forgotten the only reason she was

even there was because of the baby. He'd gotten used to having her around, started looking forward to coming home to her, and he'd forgotten this was a business arrangement.

And now their business was concluded. Once she recuperated from this, she'd want to go back to Dallas. Back to her life. What had she said last night—dear God, had it only been last night?—about Farrahlee wanting her identity back? Evie probably wanted hers back.

And while he could continue to hate his mother for her selfishness, he didn't blame Evie one bit. This situation was different, and it was only right for him to encourage Evie to do what she wanted. He owed her that much.

To prove it to her, he'd start by giving back some of the things she'd given up. Mikato's Sushi Bar was just a few more blocks. He'd get her sushi for lunch. And some regular coffee.

It was the least he could do. He didn't want to, but he owed her that much.

CHAPTER TWELVE

THREE WEEKS. TWENTY-FOUR DAYS, if she wanted to be exact, since she'd given up hope, swept up the pieces of her heart and come home.

Evie lay on her couch and watched the ceiling fan turn, bored by the blur of the blades, but unwilling to find anything else to do. That would require energy, and it took all the energy she had just to get through each day, so she didn't have any to spare.

Physically, she was fine. Fully healed. Back to normal. No sign she'd ever been pregnant at all. And since she was fully caffeinated again these days, she had no reason to be so lethargic.

Mentally, she was a mess. Emotionally, she was a disaster area worthy of federal funding. She got up every day and put on a happy face, but she was simply going through the motions. "Evie Harrison" felt like a costume—an ill-fitting costume, at that—but the show had to go on. She didn't even feel as if it was her life anymore; instead, she felt as if she was the understudy, stepping in to fill a role that really didn't belong to her.

And she wasn't sure if she wanted to star in that show again, anyway.

She was safely back in the bosom of her family and friends and she didn't want to be here. She wanted to be in Vegas.

She wanted to be with Nick.

It had taken her a long time to admit that, because it was more pathetic than she could stand. In the days right after her miscarriage, Nick had been supportive and helpful, yet distant. He'd moved into the guest room without a word, and they became nothing more than polite roommates overnight. Then he'd started talking about Dallas as if it was the best place on earth, and she'd expected him to slap a plane ticket on the table at any moment.

As if it wasn't enough she lost the baby. She had to lose Nick, as well.

The double whammy on her heart had been more than she could take. She was trying to process and heal from two different, yet related, events. She could separate them in her mind to cope, and while she was starting to come to terms with the loss of the baby, the loss of Nick weighed her down like a sack of rocks.

After only a week, she couldn't take it any longer and she'd called HarCorp's pilot to come get her. Gwen arrived with the plane, and Evie had cried on her shoulder all the way home to Dallas. Though she never mentioned her pregnancy or her miscarriage, something in Gwen's eyes told her Gwen knew a lot more than she was letting on.

That was twenty-four days ago, and while she wasn't getting worse, she wasn't getting better, either. It seemed as if everything inside her had just shut down. She couldn't—*wouldn't*—cry anymore, but she wasn't bouncing back, either. Other than the constant pain in her soul, she felt…nothing. Bennie was threatening to send her to a therapist if she didn't "perk up" soon, but Evie didn't want to perk up. She wanted Nick, and since she couldn't have Nick, she wanted to wallow in the pain for a while longer.

That would teach her to fall in love with someone who didn't even like her, much less love her. The more painful the lesson was, the less likely she was to forget it.

And this hurt so bad….

The phone rang, and she wanted to ignore it, but she couldn't. *The show must go on.*

It was the doorman downstairs. "Mrs. Rocco…"

That was another knife in the chest. She wouldn't be Mrs. Rocco for much longer. And when *that* happened…she just prayed the numbness would continue so she wouldn't care what *Lifestyles* had to say about it.

"Yes, Howard?"

"Your brother is on his way up."

Great. Just what she did *not* need. "Thanks for the warning."

She swung her feet to the floor. The door was unlocked, but she couldn't be wallowing on the couch when Will arrived. She might as well make coffee.

A minute later, she heard the door open and Will was calling her name as he entered.

Evie forced herself to smile as she kissed his cheek. "Hey, Will, what brings you by?"

"I figured we should talk."

Ugh. That's never good. Play ignorant. "Okay. About what? Want some coffee?"

He shook his head at the offer and pinned her with a stare instead. "You haven't come back to work."

The truth would serve her well here, but it still needed to sound nonchalant. She shrugged. "Well, I think it's time I got a job on my own. Get out from under my brother's shadow for a while."

Will continued to stare at her. It made her a little nervous.

"And Kelley is doing such a great job—much better than I ever did—and it didn't seem right to give her a promotion and then take it away so quickly…." Still nothing from Will. *"What?"*

"Jackson tells me he's helping you file for a divorce."

"Remind me to talk to Jackson about what client confidentiality means," she muttered. "Yes, he is. I assumed you'd figured that out anyway when I moved back here. You were right. It was a stupid, impulsive thing to do." *And she was paying for it. Dearly.*

"But understandable under the circumstances," he said quietly.

Did Will... She searched his face carefully. *Damn it, he did.* "How'd you find out?"

A crease, so reminiscent of Nick's it cracked her heart, formed on his brow as he scowled. "I'm not stupid, Evie."

"Gwen told you, huh?"

Will didn't answer that. "*You* should have told me, Squirt."

The nickname brought tears to her eyes. "I thought y'all would be disappointed in me. Upset that I was about to embarrass the family again and give the gossips more to talk about."

"You worry too much about what other people think. I'm your brother, remember?" His voice softened a little. "And how are you feeling? Better?"

"I'm fine." She settled for a half-truth. "Early miscarriages don't have a lot of lingering effects."

He frowned again. "So why are you hiding in your apartment? You're practically a recluse."

Argh. "If you want me to present the checks and cut the ribbons for HarCorp again, I will. Just not yet, okay?"

Will lifted an eyebrow at her. "Evangeline..."

She held up a hand in weak protest. "Not now, Will. I don't want to fight with you."

The exasperation left his voice, and concern took its place. "Now I *know* something's very wrong with you. You've never backed down from anything in your life. Much less me."

"What?"

"Something's got you whipped."

How dare he... "I just had a miscarriage. I think I'm allowed to be whipped for a little while."

"No, I don't think that's it."

Anger prickled along her neck, causing her jaw to tighten. "How would you know anything? I didn't want to get pregnant, but I did. And I didn't know how much I wanted the baby until I lost it." Her voice cracked a little at the end. *I will not cry.*

Will crossed his arms over his chest and tried to stare her down. It was so irritating when he did that. "Then why aren't you in Las Vegas trying to have another one?"

A red haze clouded her vision, and blood pumped to her extremities. "You want to fight? Fine. Bite me, *William.*"

He didn't bite back. Instead he mocked her. "Or did you find out that Nick was a loser after all and now you're ashamed of the whole—"

Son of a— Her hand curled into a fist, her nails digging painfully into her palm, and she had to consciously release her fingers. "That's it," she snapped, her voice rising to a near shout. "How dare you come into *my* home and pass judgment on *anything,* much less my husband? You don't know squat about Nick or where he came from, or anything about *us* or our marriage, so just shut your mouth, you…" She trailed off as Will started to laugh. "What is so damn funny?"

Will's voice was warm as he reached out to touch her face. "There you are. I was afraid this guy really had damaged you in some way."

"So you picked a fight on purpose?" Will merely shrugged. "You like to live dangerously, don't you? No wonder Nick thinks my family is crazy." She flopped on the couch and rubbed her eyes. Will's plan had been dangerous, but it did shake her out of her funk and make her feel something beyond the pain and self-pity. That wasn't necessarily a good thing; too many emotions kept at bay for too long were now crowding in on her.

"We've been worried about you."

"We?"

"Gwen. Me." He sat next to her. "Gwen's been after me for a week now to go to Vegas and beat some sense into Nick—"

Add flabbergasted to that list of emotions. "Gwen? *Gwen* is on the warpath? Promoting violence?"

Very serious now, Will nodded. "And *I* was going to be next on her list if I didn't go rip Nick a new one."

Didn't she have a fifty on Nick in that fight? A hysterical giggle bubbled in her throat and she choked on it. "Will, *no.* Don't."

"I tried to remind her you were a Harrison and no one needed to fight your battles for you. Not even your big brother. I figured if you really wanted him, you'd go get him yourself. You didn't, though, and now that Jackson is serving papers on your behalf, I figured you didn't want him. But then you kept moping…"

"I'm not moping." Will snorted, and she rushed ahead. "I'm wallowing. There's a difference. Moping would involve ice cream."

"So you're 'wallowing.' Why?"

She couldn't seem to find her voice, and when she did, it came out small. Whipped. Pathetic. "Because I don't want a divorce."

She heard the sigh and waited for Will's patented exasperated-with-Evie tone. He didn't use it. "Then why are you here and not there?"

"Because Nick wants one." Saying that out loud hurt. "We only got married because I was pregnant, and now that I'm not…" She sighed. "My feelings changed. His didn't."

Will shifted uncomfortably. "If we're going to talk about boys and feelings now, maybe I should call Gwen. She's much better at that whole thing."

That made her laugh. "Just *a* boy. I thought for a little while he might be *the* boy. But he doesn't love me."

"Then he's stupid. And I thought we covered the whole you-dating-stupid-boys thing years ago."

This time, the laugh did make her feel better. "Thanks." She patted his leg. "Now you can get Gwen off your back without a trip to Las Vegas."

"I don't know. Sounds like Nick could use a good kick in the—"

"Very funny."

"You think I'm kidding?"

"I think it's best to let this go, no matter what I want. Nick and I have probably done enough damage to each other." She stood and blew out her breath. "I think I should file this away under 'painful lessons learned' and just go on like it never happened."

Will turned serious. "Good luck with that. Just don't wallow too much longer, okay?"

"Actually, I'm feeling a lot better now." Surprisingly enough, that wasn't a complete lie. "Wanna buy me dinner?"

"Sure, Squirt."

"Let me go freshen up. You can call Gwen and tell her I'm fine and she can put away the drums of war."

Will shook his head, but he had his phone out. She went to her bathroom to run a brush through her hair. Eying herself critically in the mirror, she realized she looked pale and a bit gaunt. No wonder Gwen and Will and Bennie were worried about her.

Her heart still hurt, but she didn't feel quite so hollow inside anymore. It was an improvement. She'd just have to settle for what she could get.

Ugh. She still hated that word.

Will had said that if she really wanted Nick, she'd have gone and gotten him by now. That's what Harrisons did, after all. He was only half-right. She wanted Nick, but she wanted him to want *her*, as well, and she couldn't swallow her pride enough to take that rejection again.

Painful lessons, indeed. There was no way she'd forget this one.

* * *

"Can I mention her name today, or will you bite my head off?" Lottie's head peeked around his office door as she asked the question.

"Mention who?" Nick laid the file he was reading on his desk. There was only one "her," but he was working hard to move on and outward appearances counted.

Lottie frowned. "Evie. Who else?"

His pulse accelerated, but he kept his voice even. "Of course you can mention her name. Why would I take your head off for it?"

"Kevin said…"

"Well, Kevin has really poor timing sometimes." In reality, Kevin was asking to get punched in the mouth for the way he kept talking about Evie, but he couldn't tell Lottie that.

"He did say she'd served you with divorce papers."

Kevin would be eating his teeth very soon. "She's not the first person in history to regret a quickie Vegas wedding."

Lottie's mouth twisted. "It seems so weird. Every time I saw her, she seemed so happy. And you guys really did seem like a good couple, right for each other somehow. I just don't understand." She shrugged. "I know, it's none of my business. I am sorry, by the way."

The knife that had permanent residence in his guts twisted a bit. "Is that why you brought her up? To tell me you're sorry we didn't work out?"

"No. I got something from Evie in today's mail that I wanted to ask you about."

"Evie's sending you letters?" *He* hadn't heard a word from Evie since she left for the airport. All communication had and would continue to be through her attorney.

"There was a note in there, thanking me for befriending her while she was here and inviting me to Dallas in the future. She's very polite, you know?"

"Her sister-in-law is some kind of manners guru. It's ingrained in her." And it must have rubbed off on him, otherwise he'd have stopped this conversation long before now. "So what else did she send you?" he prompted.

"Checks. Big, fat, massive checks for the Gleason Street Community Center."

He didn't need to hide his surprise. "Checks, plural?"

"One from something called HarCorp…"

"That's her family's company," he supplied.

"One from the Harrison Family Charitable Trust, and one from her personal account. There's a lot of zeros involved."

That he didn't doubt at all. "Evie can afford it. The checks will cash, don't worry about that."

"I'm not. I'm just wondering why she'd still bother. I mean, now that she's gone back to Texas."

"She likes giving money to projects that make a difference in people's lives. And she told you she'd help with the fundraising. Since she's not here anymore, I assume this is how she's fulfilling that promise." *Salving her conscience, maybe?* "Cash the checks and move on."

"If I cash these checks, we're going to have to name a wing of the building after her."

Now he knew why Lottie was so cautious about this. "That many zeros, huh?"

"*That* many zeros."

Good Lord. "Cash them." Something good could come of this debacle. He picked up the file he'd been looking at earlier, and Lottie took the hint to leave.

But Nick couldn't regain his earlier focus. Evie couldn't do *anything* halfway, could she? She got pregnant, so she had to get married. And she couldn't just get married; she had to move to Las Vegas. Into his house. Into his life. Into his heart.

He shook that thought off. The divorce papers delivered to him were an unwelcome reminder of how badly out of hand this whole situation had gotten because Evie couldn't go just halfway.

Well, she'd gone halfway on *one* thing. She hadn't fallen in love with him. Which sucked for him, since it was the one thing where he *had* gone all the way.

So he'd stalled on signing the divorce papers, when he should have just done it immediately and moved on. Prenups certainly made the divorce proceedings much quicker—if not easier.

Of course, when had anything with Evie been easy? From that first night, when his car had been broken into, up to now, *nothing* had been easy when it came to Evie. His whole life had been turned upside down.

And to prove how sick the whole situation really was, he actually *missed* it. Life seemed a little boring now without Evie and never knowing what she would throw at him next. He had learned a lot about himself recently, including a tendency toward masochism he didn't know he had in him. Why else would he want a woman so desperately when she did nothing but drive him crazy?

He even missed fighting with her—the snap and fire in her eyes, the way her skin turned pinker as her temper flared, how she could channel that heat in a completely different direction in a heartbeat. They fought, sure, but they fought fair and Evie never held a grudge. She had a short fuse and a big temper in that sinful body, and she was a yeller.

In more ways than one, he thought as a familiar heat spread over his skin like a painful memory.

Good thing he wasn't, or else every fight would have been a recreation of Evie and Will going toe-to-toe on the balcony, only with him playing her brother's role. Common sense should tell him this divorce was the right thing to do, because no relationship could handle *that* level...

He stopped that line of thought, confused. For all that yelling he witnessed, Evie and her brother were very close.

Tight, even. Even when Evie complained about him—which was frequently—there was no doubt she loved her brother. And Will, for all his glowering, seemed to adore her—even when she yelled at him.

He could relate to *that*. Adoring Evie, at least.

Evie *had* said that he reminded her of Will. Even called him the same epithet…

A thousand details hit him at once, and it led to clarity. Evie being so polite and gracious to everyone even though he knew it grated across her nerves at times. Evie guarding her tongue so she didn't end up in the papers. How she talked about "Evangeline Harrison" sometimes as if it was a different person.

That constant pressure had to build until it blew, and Evie was safe exploding at her brother. Because she loved her brother. Trusted him. Felt safe just being Evie.

Amateur armchair psychology was new for him—he didn't consider himself one for plumbing the depths of anyone's psyche—but this just might make sense. Did Evie only shout at the ones she loved?

Did that mean she might have feelings for *him?* Or was that just wishful thinking?

If she did, why did she leave without a fight? *Because I was very clear why I married her.* And he hadn't given her much reason to question that as circumstances changed.

Oh, he was an idiot, and he'd screwed up big time. He was a day late and a dollar short in this hellish mess. His wife had planned their divorce the day she married him, but now that she had moved to a different state and served him with divorce papers, all bets were off and he wanted to change the game.

He looked at the divorce papers and smiled. He happened to be quite good at games of chance. He'd anted up, and it was time to call her bluff and play the cards.

This was going to be interesting.

CHAPTER THIRTEEN

After surprising society—and her family, too, if reports are to be believed—with news of her nuptials and then disappearing for several weeks, Evangeline Harrison, now Rocco, is back in town, *sans* her new husband. While Dallas is glad to have her back, Evangeline is keeping a low profile these days, and hasn't been seen in society much, nor has she returned to her former position at HarCorp. This, of course, has led to much speculation about the situation. Is the honeymoon over? Is Evangeline back for good or only a visit? And where is her husband, Las Vegas nightclub owner Nick Rocco?

"IN LAS VEGAS, YOU NOSY witch," Evie answered with a scowl as she tossed today's issue of *Dallas Lifestyles* into the recycling bin. "Not that it's any of your damn business," she added as she closed the lid with a satisfying bang.

After much consulting with Gwen over shoe shopping and lattes, Evie knew there was no way she was going to be able to spin her divorce to make it less interesting for the gossiphounds. Not if her intentionally low-key return to town was already newsworthy of speculation.

She breathed the steam of her coffee deep into her lungs

as she leaned against the kitchen counter. *Hello, my life. How I haven't missed you at all.*

Of course, she would have to announce soon enough that she was getting divorced—those records would be public information once they were officially filed with the judge—and she knew the importance of preempting news like that. Not that she really cared anymore what people said about her. She was going through the motions out of habit more than anything else.

If she could manage to keep this under the radar, great. But she wasn't stressing over it, either.

The stress came from simply waiting. So far, there'd been no word from Nick or his attorney all week, so there was nothing to preempt for the gossips.

She still jumped every time the phone rang, both anticipating and dreading the call from Jackson that would end the suspense, but the limbo was killing her a little more each day. If Nick didn't make a move soon, she'd have to do *something* to break this stalemate. She couldn't go on like this. Nick haunted her dreams, even though she spent her days trying not to think about him or what life might have offered if things had worked out differently.

But she wasn't planning a return to her old life, either. Hell, she wasn't even sure how much longer she'd stay in Dallas. There wasn't *that* much keeping her here beyond her family, and she'd already reconciled herself to being away from them when she moved to Las Vegas. The offer of an interview from Circus Circus based on the resumé she'd sent had been a wake-up call, spurring her realization that she didn't have to stay in Dallas and be what everyone expected her to be. There was a whole world out there waiting to be conquered.

She'd turned down Circus Circus because Las Vegas— while tempting—wasn't on her short list of possible places.

California. New York. Chicago. Maybe even London. The choices were endless. But she couldn't explore *any* of those possibilities until she heard from Nick. Nick's *attorney,* she corrected herself.

And she had no idea when that would be.

She needed to finish getting ready. She and Gwen were going shopping this afternoon for the boys' birthday, and the symphony fundraiser was tonight. Without a good excuse, Evie needed to be there or else give everyone more fodder for *Lifestyles.*

Leaving her mug in the sink, she pushed through the swinging door, heading for her bedroom. As she passed through the living room, she heard the door *snick* as the knob turned and the lock tongue moved out of the frame. Stepping back toward the kitchen, where she'd left her phone, she mentally ran down the list of possibilities.... Will was at work; Bennie was at the beach; Gwen was meeting her at the mall. Anyway, the front desk would have called if she had a guest.... No one should be entering her apartment right now, and adrenaline rushed through her veins as the door started to open.

She was taking a deep breath to scream as a man stepped through the open door.

The scream died in her throat. *Nick.*

Her knees wobbled, and she couldn't say if it was from the adrenaline rush or the fact he looked so good she wanted to cry. Her heart still beat frantically in her chest, but that could be caused by either situation, as well.

"Evie? You look pale."

"Because you scared the living daylights out of me barging in like that. Don't you knock?"

"I did. No one answered."

"I was in the kitchen." *Driving myself insane thinking about you.*

Nick shook his head at her like a scold. "I told you not to leave your door unlocked. Anyone could just walk right in."

"I live in a manned building on a secured floor for a *reason.*

No one can just walk in here unless they live here." She stopped. "How'd you get in, anyway? No one at the desk called up."

"Howard and the gang don't seem aware that you filed for divorce. They just waved at me as I passed." He looked at her hands and frowned. "You're not wearing your ring, though."

She tugged the chain out of her shirt, letting the band dangle in front of her. "I wear it when I go out." It had been too painful to wear it on her finger, but it hurt to take it off altogether. "It seemed premature to quit wearing a ring when you hadn't signed the papers. It could lead to questions I don't want to answer." *And it would make it all real. Final.*

Nick cocked his head and looked as if she was an oddity in a sideshow. "So you haven't told people yet?"

This was embarrassing—to be caught like this. And she was completely unprepared to *talk* to Nick. Her stomach was turning over itself, and she didn't feel steady on her feet. "Just my family. And they know everything now, by the way. Well, Gwen and Will do, at least. I didn't see the sense in upsetting Uncle Marcus more than he already is by mentioning the baby."

"How are you feeling?"

Miserable. "I'm fine." *Pull your act together. You can get through this.* The muscles in her cheeks protested as she stretched them into a smile and tried to channel Gwen's calm coolness. "Perfectly healthy and back to normal. Thank you for asking. Would you like a seat? Something to drink? Coffee?" She was proud of herself; her voice didn't shake or crack, and this was very civilized.

She thought she saw Nick's mouth twitch briefly, but it must have been a trick of the light or her own scattered brain messing with her. "I'll sit, but nothing to drink, thank you."

Nick took one of the chairs, so she chose the opposite one to maximize the distance between them. She knew better than to get too close to him. Her dreams had been too vivid recently to risk proximity. *Be friendly and polite.* "So what brings you to Dallas?"

"You."

Her heart stuttered. "Me?" she squeaked. *So much for that earlier pride.* She cleared her throat.

"There's a problem with the papers you sent. I can't sign them."

Her heart soared. "Really? Why?"

"Nevada is a community-property state."

And now it crashed and burned. "Oh." She tried to keep the disappointment out of her voice. "But that shouldn't be a problem. We weren't married long enough to acquire anything."

"Technically, I bought The Zoo *after* we got married. That's community property now, and there's residency issues, plus the waiting period...."

Her head was spinning. "Jackson said..."

"Maybe Jackson isn't as up-to-date on Nevada law as he should be."

Surely Jackson looked into all of that... "The Zoo isn't a problem. I don't want it. I mean, I don't expect you to divide it. I'll sign off my share or sell it to you...."

Nick's eyes widened. "You want me to *buy* my own club from you?"

"I *said,* I'll just give it to you, but if that's not possible I'll sell it to you for a dollar or something...." Her disappointment over this "reunion" was quickly turning to frustration and confusion.

"And your prenup? That's a problem, too."

That jerked her back to the conversation. "What? The prenup? What are you...?" Nick wanted money from her? She stopped and took a deep breath. "Look. If there's a problem with anything, your lawyer can contact Jackson. I'm sure they can work around whatever the problems—"

"You can't just work around the law."

Evie felt her temper rising and fought to keep a lid on it.

"That's *not* what I'm saying. I'm just trying to get us out of this disaster with minimal damages to either of us. I don't want *anything* from you. Not money. Not your club. Nothing. An uncontested divorce shouldn't be this much trouble."

Nick nodded. "But my attorney has informed me that I have grounds for divorce, and that changes everything."

"What grounds?"

"Desertion."

What the…? "I didn't desert you."

Nick raised an eyebrow and indicated the room. "Looks like it to me. It'll probably look that way to the judge, too. That cracks that 'iron-clad' prenup of yours."

Now she was mad. "Son of a—"

"Language, Evie," Nick scolded. "Name-calling is not appropriate behavior for a lady."

That sent her to her feet, her blood boiling. "Don't try that with me. If you're spoiling for fight, bring it on."

Evie was mad. *Good.* It certainly beat that uncertain look from earlier that had led her to hide behind all that false politeness. He'd risked a lot, pushing her like that, but Nick was gambling here, and when the stakes were high, he knew he had to take the risks.

Of course, now Evie looked as if she'd like to remove his head from his body. "Big ugly battles end up in the papers. You sure you want that?"

Her chin went up a notch. "I don't care what people think anymore. I'm tired of living my life like that."

Good for her. "And your family?"

"Love me unconditionally. That knowledge…that's the one good thing to come out of this nightmare."

"At least *you* got something for your trouble, right?"

Eyes snapping, she turned on him. "Is *that* what this is about? You want something for *your* trouble?"

"You were the only trouble I had."

Instead of firing back, Evie seemed to deflate. She sighed and her shoulders dropped. "Yeah. I know. I've brought nothing but trouble to myself and everyone I love with this whole situation."

Did she include him in that group?

"I owe you an apology, Nick. For everything."

He hadn't been expecting that. "Such as?"

"I panicked, and I shouldn't have. I put you in a bad position and then did nothing but exacerbate it. I have a bad temper, and I tend to jump into things with both feet without thinking it all the way through. So I'm sorry about everything I put you through. Including the mess I seem to have made of our divorce." She shook her head sadly and a bitter laugh escaped. "After the mess I made of our marriage, I don't know why I'm surprised I messed this up. I certainly don't want part of The Zoo or any of that. If you'd like a cash settlement for your trouble, I'll talk to Jackson and have him work that out with you and your lawyer. You deserve at least that much."

What he deserved and what he wanted were two completely different things. He didn't deserve much of anything, but he *wanted* a hell of a lot. "That was quite a speech. When you decide to humble yourself, you certainly go all the way."

"It's not false humility. I can admit to my mistakes."

He wasn't sure he liked her tone. "And marrying me was a mistake?"

She smiled weakly. "I think we've proven that beyond a shadow of a doubt. I know money won't fix anything, but that's really all I have to offer."

She had a lot to offer him, but she didn't know that. "I didn't realize being married to me was such a burden that you'd be willing to *pay* to get out of it." Maybe he'd read this whole situation wrong. She certainly seemed resigned to her choice and determined to get it done as quickly as possible. He'd come to call her bluff; he'd never considered she might not be bluffing after all.

Evie ran her hands over her face and through her hair. "Being with you is many things. *Burden* isn't the word I'd choose." Then she turned to him and sighed. "It's definitely been an adventure. An eye-opening adventure for me, and though I know it has sucked for you, I'm actually very appreciative for that."

"Did I ever say it sucked for me?"

"You didn't have to." Her mouth twisted as she said it and he felt like that first-class bastard. "I'm sorry it turned out this way, but I would like to at least part as friends."

It had taken everything she had to get that speech out of her mouth, but she'd been careening from one emotion to the next and she just didn't have anything left in her.

Nick's eyes narrowed. "I don't think we can be friends."

Considering what she really wanted, hearing Nick say that was about the last blow her heart could take. "I'm sorry to hear that. I'll take you off my Christmas-card list."

"That's it? You just roll over? What's happened to you? Where's the Evie that charges in and goes for what she wants? The Evie who was willing to take me on over anything and everything?"

"She's tired of fighting. Look, I'm smart enough to know when I can't have what I want, and it's time to give up this fight."

There was that sideshow oddity look again. "Tell me the truth, Evie. What do you want?"

You. But she couldn't say that. "It doesn't matter."

"I think it does."

"Do you know what *you* want, Nick?"

"Yeah, I do."

"What's that?" When he hesitated, she tried to sweeten the

offer. "I just need this to be over with, so whatever it is, tell me, and if it's within my power, I'll happily give it to you."

Nick broke eye contact as he thought, and she knew she should be worried what he was going to ask for if it required that much thought. She'd put herself in a place of weakness for this negotiation, but she just needed this over with. Her heart couldn't break into any more pieces without killing her for real.

"I just want to ask you something."

"Okay."

"Were you happy in Las Vegas? At any time?"

It was an odd question, but she could answer it without hesitation. "Yeah, I was. Most of the time," she acknowledged.

"With me?"

"I know it sounds hard to believe, but I was—when I didn't want to strangle you, of course." He smiled, and that gave her a little courage. "Honestly, I thought for a little while there that we might be able to make it work. But we got married for all the wrong reasons, and it was just too much to overcome. Had I known the divorce would be this complicated, I wouldn't have asked you to marry me in the first place."

"There's actually a very simple solution to this divorce situation."

"Really?" She tried to inject some enthusiasm into her voice. "Tell me."

"We don't get one."

Her jaw fell open, and she couldn't manage to close it. It felt as if sunshine was pouring into the dark hollows of her chest, and her heart started to beat for the first time in ages. She stomped down the feelings; there was no way she heard that correctly. "I'm not following you."

Nick rubbed his palms against his thighs. "You're not making this easy on me. I've tried every way I can think of—including getting you mad at me—to break down that wall you're hiding behind." He laughed. "I should know better by now. So, I'm just going to have to bite the bullet."

She was teetering on a knifepoint, unsure if she should be hoping or praying. She swallowed hard and braced herself. "Um…okay."

"I don't want a divorce. There. I said it. I don't want a divorce, and I want you to come home. To Vegas."

That sunshine seemed to pump through her veins, filling her with hope. It was *cautious* hope, but without clarification… "Home? With you?"

Nick rolled his eyes in exasperation. "No, with Siegfried and Roy and the tigers. Of *course* with me. Jesus, Evie, how difficult are you going to make this for me?"

"But…"

Nick stepped closer to where she sat. "Do you really want a divorce? You just said you thought we might be able to make this work. Don't you want to try?"

She stood and crossed the room, not wanting Nick to get too close. She needed space—to think, to breathe. "What I *need* is to just get over you. And that's proving difficult enough—"

Nick interrupted her with a half grin. "Get over me? That rather implies…"

Me and my big mouth. "All right. Fine. You win." Nick just looked at her expectantly. "Do I really have to say it?"

Nick nodded and stood there, seeming to enjoy watching her die of embarrassment.

She crossed her arms over her chest and squared her shoulders. "I don't want a divorce, either, okay? For some reason known only to God and it's probably proof I'm truly insane, I'm in love with you." Nick's grin grew and she wanted to smack him. "I'm sure a good therapist will be able to help me sort this out."

Nick stalked toward her and she backed up a step. And then another.

"I'm probably confusing good sex with love or maybe all those pregnancy hormones messed my head up. Or something like that." Oh, *no;* she'd backed herself into a corner, and Nick closed in on her as she put her hands out to block his approach. "Um, Nick, I—"

He cut her off with a kiss. It was both sweet and hungry, sending happy shivers all the way to her toes at the same time it sparked her nerve endings to life. Nick leaned in, pressing his chest against her palms, and she could feel the heavy thump of his heart as it kicked up speed and he deepened the kiss.

She relaxed her hands and let them slide up his chest to his shoulders and finally clasp around his neck. Rubbing her thumbs against the muscles there, she heard his sigh as he broke the kiss and moved to nuzzle her temple.

"Missed you," he murmured against her hair.

"And...?" she prompted. Instead of answering, Nick's lips moved to her earlobe. She shivered, but she wouldn't be distracted by that. "Don't leave me out here on this ledge alone."

Nick pulled his head back and tilted her face up to his. "And I love you."

Peace settled on her shoulders, lightening her heart. "I've missed you, too."

"So you'll come home with me?"

She nodded, then gasped as Nick lifted her off her feet. Did he mean this very second? But no, the bedroom was the destination, and she wanted to shout with happiness when she saw the look in his eyes as he pressed her onto the mattress and lay at her side.

Propped on his elbow, he loomed over her, one hand tracing a lazy path up from her hip, over her waist and rib cage before stopping in her cleavage where her ring was nestled. Nick's eyes darkened again as he slid a finger over the thin gold chain. Then his fist closed around the ring, and one quick tug broke the chain.

He slid the ring back where it belonged with a tenderness that made her heart melt. "Much better," he told her. Then he frowned. "But still not right."

"Why? What's the problem?" She examined the ring, looking for a flaw.

"You need a rock. Some big, fancy bling to show off at your country club. And if we're going to do that, you might as well do the whole big white wedding thing. Give the paper that princess wedding they expected." Nick's fingers were working on the buttons of her blouse as he spoke, and a moment later it was on the floor.

"We can't do th-that." She stuttered when his mouth moved along the lace edge of her bra.

"Why not?" Now he was working the clasp of her jeans.

"It's against the r-rules. You only get one wedding. A do-over is tacky." He looked up at her, and she added, "Trust me on this. I know what I'm talking about. Gwen would have a cow…." She sat straight up as she remembered. "Oh, no! I'm supposed to meet Gwen."

"Now?" The disappointment in his voice amused her and aroused her at the same time.

"We were supposed to go shopping. Just don't move." She scrambled for the phone. "Let me call her and tell her… What *am* I going to tell her?"

Nick tugged on her arm, pulling her back onto the bed. "That you're very busy at the moment." He hooked his thumbs in the waistband of her jeans and panties and slid them down over her legs. Then he grinned wickedly at her. "And naked."

Fingers shaking from the kisses Nick placed on her inner thigh and the wet heat of his tongue moving against her, Evie barely managed to text Gwen with a message cancelling shopping. Whether it made any sense or not, she didn't know, and she didn't care as she dropped the phone and arched against Nick's mouth with a groan.

When she could think again, she tugged at his hair, pulling him up until they were eye level. "You are so bad."

"And here I thought I was pretty good." One quick thrust of his hips, and, *thank heaven,* he was buried inside her. "I can always try again and see if I can do better."

She was already trying to find a rhythm, rocking her hips against his. "Later."

Nick dropped his forehead to hers and held still. "Marry me, Evie. Again."

"I told you, it's tacky," she gasped, her fingers digging into his arms. She was going to die soon from wanting. "*Please,* Nick."

"I'm from Vegas. We invented tacky." He moved his hips just enough to send a shock wave through her. "Marry me."

She met his eyes. "Tell me you love me."

With a seriousness that healed every crack in her heart, Nick cupped her face and whispered, "I love you, Evangeline Rocco."

"Then I'll marry you. Again." She wanted to say more, but Nick was moving and she couldn't hold a thought in her head.

Two hours later, Nick asked, "Where do you want to go for our honeymoon?"

She thought for a minute. Just a few hours ago, she'd been examining all kinds of potential places to go. None of them seemed very tempting now, and Las Vegas, which hadn't even made her short list earlier, was the only place remotely interesting at the moment.

While Nick expressed surprise, it made perfect sense to her.

After all, she'd gotten very, *very* lucky in Vegas.

EPILOGUE

EVIE GROWLED LOW IN HER THROAT as pain creased her sweaty brow. He couldn't tell if she was growling at the actual pain or simply because she was in pain at all.

Nick smoothed her hair back from her forehead, only to have that growl redirected at him.

"Do not touch me," Evie gritted out. "This is all your fault, and you're not to touch me again as long as you live." She groaned and gripped the steel rails of the hospital bed. "And that might not be for too much longer," she snarled.

Sunny, the labor and delivery nurse whose attitude matched her name, patted his shoulder. "That's just the pain talking. She doesn't mean it."

He hesitated correcting her. Evie didn't make empty threats, and she was probably plotting his demise—his painful demise—during the moments of calm between contractions. Those moments were getting shorter, though, and he was feeling bad enough at this point to accept whatever painful torture Evie had in mind. She was in so much pain… "Can't you give her something? Anything?"

Sunny shook her head. "Not at this point. But we're getting close."

Another contraction gripped Evie, and his wife seemed to

channel that kid from *The Exorcist*. "This can't be normal," he complained.

"Evie didn't plan on doing this naturally, so she wasn't prepared for the pain. That's making it worse for her." Sunny checked a monitor and murmured encouraging words to Evie.

With the next contraction, Evie cursed a blue streak and threatened to remove a part of his anatomy she'd been rather fond of until her water broke.

"Language, Evie. You're going to be someone's mother." Will's dry tone contrasted with the lines etched on his face. Will was handling this only slightly better than Nick was.

"Bite me, Will. I don't know why Gwen didn't kill you after the twins were born."

"Because Gwen—unlike *some* people—was smart enough to get to the hospital before the window for her epidural closed."

"I was busy," she panted, "you butthead—" *pant, pant* "—how was I supposed to know…"

As Evie and Will bickered, Sunny frowned. She motioned him closer. "Do I need to get her brother out of here?"

"No. They're always like this. It's probably good for her—taking her mind off the contractions." And as long as Evie was sniping at Will, he himself wasn't in her crosshairs. Will had planned to come closer to Evie's due date anyway, so it was a nice coincidence he'd been in town for the dedication of the new Harrison-funded day-care center at Gleason Street when Evie went into labor two weeks earlier than expected. Gwen was still en route.

They'd waited over a year before trying to get pregnant again, and Evie had received the news they were successful with cautious optimism, unconvinced she wouldn't miscarry again and too scared to get her hopes up until after they crossed the three-month mark. After that milestone, Evie's entire outlook changed, and she'd become almost Madonna-like in her serenity during this last trimester. That had been a bit of a shock, but the feisty Evie he knew and loved was back now. With a vengeance.

Dr. Banks pushed through the door, his white coat flapping behind him. "Are you ready to do this, Evie?"

Evie smiled angelically at her doctor, relief written all over her face. "Yes. *Please.*"

"Then let's have a baby." Dr. Banks motioned to Will, who squeezed Evie's hand on his way out, and Sunny directed Nick into position as she helped Evie sit up.

Evie met his eyes then. "Wipe that smile off your face. I'm holding you *personally* responsible for this."

"The baby's crowning. Push, Evie!"

She squeezed his hand and smiled. "Thanks."

From page three of Dallas Lifestyles:

Evangeline Rocco, née Harrison, was spotted shopping with our own Miss Behavior and Sabine Wyndham last Saturday, while baby Charlotte spent the day with her doting father, Las Vegas nightclub magnate Nick Rocco, uncle, HarCorp's Will Harrison, and cousins in the HarCorp skybox watching the Rangers game. The newest addition to the Harrison-Rocco family empire then made her Dallas debut Sunday morning at St. Matthew's Cathedral in a beautiful hand-stitched christening gown reportedly imported from France for the occasion. No official photos of baby Charlotte have been released by the family yet, but casual snaps are surfacing as Evangeline introduces her daughter to the sights and society of her hometown.

Dallas society has suffered greatly from the loss of Evangeline to the lights of Las Vegas, but all reports indicate our Evangeline has taken Sin City by storm, as well....

ANOTHER WILD
WEDDING NIGHT
LESLIE KELLY

To Gina Hayes-McCann.
The greatest cousin anyone could ever ask for...
and my honorary 5th sister!

New York Times bestselling author **Leslie Kelly** has written dozens of books and novellas. Known for her sparkling dialogue, fun characters and steamy sensuality, she has been honoured with numerous awards, including a National Readers' Choice Award, a Colorado Award of Excellence, a Golden Quill and an *RT Book Reviews* Career Achievement Award in Series Romance. Leslie has also been nominated four times for the highest award in romance fiction, the RWA RITA® Award. Leslie lives in Maryland with her own romantic hero, Bruce, and their daughters.

Visit her online at www.lesliekelly.com or at her blog, www.plotmonkeys.com.

Prologue

AMANDA BAUER WASN'T VERY big on planning, nor was she too great on details. A big-picture person, she didn't technically fly by the seat of her pants—she was too good a pilot for that. But she usually only cared about crossing every T or dotting every I when those letters were part of a flight plan.

Still, there was one thing she *had* put a lot of thought and planning into: her wedding. So hearing about a screwup with the reservations at the country inn/resort where the members of her wedding party, and eighty guests, were supposed to be staying, didn't make her already-cloudy wedding day shine any brighter.

"Manda, it's not the end of the world," said Reese Campbell, the incredible man she would be marrying in two hours time. He sounded so calm and reasonable, as always. That was one reason he was her perfect man—he made home a place, not just a word, and was her very best friend. "It'll be okay."

"I can just hear my parents now. 'Anyone who would plan a Halloween wedding and expect their guests to come to a costume party afterward should expect nothing but trouble.'"

"Yeah, that sounds like them." He slid an arm around her waist and tugged her close. "But who cares what they think? What day could possibly be better for *us?*"

True. They'd met one year ago. Last Halloween had been the beginning of a wild holiday affair during which she and Reese had indulged in a lot of role-playing fantasy all over the country. They'd fallen in love in the process. So a Halloween-weekend wedding had sounded perfect, and an after-reception costume party even more so. Odd, yes. Unique. But absolutely right for *them* and the way they'd started out.

"Have I told you lately how beautiful you are?" he asked, tipping his head down to brush a soft kiss on her cheek.

"Thank you. But so much for not seeing me before the ceremony," she grumbled, thankful only for the fact that she hadn't been wearing her gown when she'd come down here to have a knock-down drag-out fight with the staff.

When she'd found out the inn had double-booked a quarter of their rooms, meaning several of her guests would be left sharing, or commuting back to the city, she'd almost had a full-on Bridezilla meltdown. Calling Reese had been the only way she could think of to occupy her hands so she wouldn't reach across the reception desk and strangle the chirpy little clerk who'd had the audacity to say it would be "neat" to have some Hollywood people around to lend some glamour to her big day.

She didn't want glamour. She wanted family and romance and fun and a big old party to cap off the night.

But no. A movie crew had invaded this small town an hour outside of Chicago. Here to film a sequence for an action flick, they had practically taken over. It didn't seem to matter that she'd booked the entire inn four months ago. Somebody had fouled up and the L.A. types were already here, ensconced in some of the cottages dotting the grounds, as well as a number of the rooms.

Including the damned bridal suite. Which was currently being occupied by a movie star. *Grr.*

"Mix-up my ass," she muttered. "I'll bet that ditzy clerk saw Ericson's name and sabotaged our reservations on purpose!"

Well, at least Drew Ericson was the leading man, and not a woman. No bride wanted to compete with Angelina Jolie or Megan Fox on her wedding day. Still, she might have trouble keeping her bridesmaids on the job if Ericson happened to come into sight.

"We'll just make the best of it," Reese said, drawing her away from the front desk. Because even Reese, with all his charm, hadn't been able to change the situation. At least he'd gotten a *huge* discount off the bill, though, and payment for rooms at an alternate location twenty miles away. "So a few guests won't get to stay here. You know some will be relieved to have an excuse not to come tonight. Not everybody is looking forward to it."

"Like my parents and the Mannings."

His nose wrinkled, thinking of Amanda's sister, Abby, and her soon-to-be in-laws. "Yeah, sorry, I just can't picture your poor sister's wedding. I'm not surprised she keeps putting it off. She might as well get married at the north pole—her fiancé's family is about that warm."

"Which is why they've become my mom and dad's best friends. The four of them could have been the Snow Miser's grandparents."

She frowned as she thought of Abby, who was engaged to marry a very handsome but aloof attorney. She and her sister hadn't been close for a long time—in fact, Amanda had asked her best friend, Jazz, to be maid of honor, rather than her only sibling. That had just about caused World War III with their mother, but Abby had understood.

In recent months, though, when Abby—who worked as an event planner—had been helping to plan for today, they had grown closer. So she could see that her sister was unhappy; anyone who wasn't totally blind could see it.

Which didn't say much for their parents' eyesight. Or her fiancé's, for that matter.

"Maybe we shouldn't tell Bonnie what's going on," he said.

"Why not?"

"It's a long story."

Bonnie was one of Reese's siblings—and a bridesmaid. Of his four sisters, she was the one with whom Amanda had become the closest. Bonnie had a huge heart. Unfortunately she hadn't found the right guy to share it with. Amanda sensed she wanted that very much, even if everyone else swore she'd had no interest in anything except her causes from the time she was little. A middle child, Bonnie had carved out her niche in the family by always playing peacemaker...but that shouldn't rule out a romantic life, as far as Amanda was concerned.

"I want to hear this story sometime."

"It involves Drew Ericson."

"Ooooh. Is she a rabid stalker-fan?" Amanda asked, not serious.

He snorted a laugh. "Hardly. Can you see Bonnie at a hand-grenade-flinging action flick?"

"Not a chance."

Bonnie had never met a tree she didn't want to hug, and was the most genuine person Amanda had ever met. It wasn't right that someone so beautiful and kind at heart spent her nights alone.

Unfortunately that spending-her-nights-alone thing had been pointed out last night, at the rehearsal dinner. While Bonnie was the peacemaker, the other middle child, Debbie, was a wise-ass, who'd made a snarky remark about her sister's nearly virginal state. Normally passive Bonnie had fried her sister with a glare.

"She was arrested for taking part in a peaceful protest when Drew Ericson was filming a movie last spring," Reese explained.

"Arrested for being *peaceful?*"

"I don't know the details. But she spent a night in jail." He shook his head, as if unable to visualize it any more than Amanda could. "Whatever happened, it left her hating his guts."

Now it was Amanda's turn to snort. "She's incapable of it."

"Okay," Reese conceded, "wrong word. Let's just say if she had to decide who to save from a burning building—Drew Ericson or a lab rat—she'd probably save the rat."

Amanda laughed, as she knew he'd wanted her to. Reese was trying to lighten her mood, and she loved him for it.

"Maybe we should see if Bonnie wants to switch hotels before she finds out he's here," he added.

"She can't. She's in the wedding party. Believe me, if I let Bonnie go, Jazz would be right out the door behind her. I think she'd be thrilled if she got to skip the party, considering I picked out her costume."

"Yeah, I can't wait to see her as a fairy-tale princess."

"Hey, it's her own fault for putting off doing it for so long. And, after all, she told me to just grab her something off-the-rack." And oh, grab she had.

Amanda figured her best friend would look gorgeous no matter what she wore, with her deep, violet eyes and jet-black hair. But since Jazz worked as the lead mechanic at Clear Blue Air, and usually wore either coveralls or jeans and engineer boots, the frilly, feminine costume would definitely be a change.

"So, you're okay? No more worrying?" Reese said.

Nodding, Amanda walked with him across the expansive foyer of the inn—its oak-planked floor gleaming, a faint scent of lemon rising from the freshly polished surface. The management might have fouled up her reservations, but she still loved this gorgeous old mansion, which seemed more like a Southern plantation than an Illinois country house.

"I'm fine," she promised, already moving past the disappointment and anticipating the rest of the day.

Suddenly a voice intruded from above. "What are you doing? You're not supposed to see each other before the wedding!"

Amanda and Reese exchanged a smile as his mother came jogging down the stairs, her curlers bouncing. The woman seemed to love her role as mother-of-the-groom.

"Now, you, scoot! Go put on your tux, then track down your groomsmen and make sure they're presentable," his mother said to Reese. "And you, come on. You've got some champagne to drink, some bridesmaids to giggle with and a beautiful gown to put on."

"I'd rather do that," Reese said. "Well, except the giggling part. And the gown."

"You crazy man." Amanda quickly kissed her groom. "I can't wait to marry you."

"Ditto," he said, his warm, loving smile sending warmth zinging throughout her entire body. "And please don't worry anymore about the rooms, sweetheart. I promise you, this is going to be a night nobody will ever forget."

First Kiss

1

BONNIE CAMPBELL WANTED that bouquet.

Everybody who knew her was aware she seldom asked for anything for herself. She would give the last dime out of her wallet to a stranger, would fight for the rights of the oppressed until she had no breath left in her body, and had, in fact, given the shirt off her back to a homeless person.

But she wanted that bouquet.

She'd never caught one. Actually she'd never tried. Not once in her twenty-five years had she gone elbow to elbow with a bunch of desperate women fighting to pluck the promise of marital bliss out of thin air. In fact, she'd felt a little embarrassed for them, sad that women were reduced to such desperate measures, all in the quest for romance.

And yet…she wanted that bouquet.

Which was why she stood in a crowded vestibule at the base of a sweeping staircase, watching her new sister-in-law, Amanda, fling the flowers over her shoulder from far above toward a crowd of single-but-don't-wannabe females.

"Watch out," a woman said, shoving her way to floral glory.

Bonnie watched the flowers arc through the air, heading directly for the bride's sister—who stood just a few feet away. Abby Bauer didn't look pleased about that. In fact, deer-in-headlights best described her expression, as if she hoped she *wouldn't* catch the bouquet as much as Bonnie hoped she *would*.

So she probably wouldn't mind if Bonnie stole it away.

Sending up a little mental apology, she lunged for the prize. Only at the last second, Abby swung her arm out and swatted it like a major league batter swinging at a fastball, sending it in the opposite direction.

"Missed it by that much," Bonnie whispered when the flowers landed in the hands of a bosomy blonde— the kind who'd probably had males flocking around her since she hit puberty.

Bonnie, on the other hand—quiet, petite, curly-haired Bonnie—well, she wasn't sure anybody noticed she'd hit puberty until after she'd graduated from high school.

"I got it!" the blonde shrieked, bouncing around joyfully.

"Hey, what was that all about? I thought you were far too enlightened to get down in the dirt with us competitive she-sharks," an amused voice said. "How much champagne have you had?"

Glancing over her shoulder, she saw her sister, Debbie. Her college-aged sibling had that devilish, I'm-just-waiting-to-find-a-reason-to-make-fun-of-you look on her face. Usually Debbie focused on stirring up everyone else, but last night, she'd turned her wicked sense of humor in Bonnie's direction.

Bonnie still hadn't quite forgiven her for the *almost-*

virgin remark. Not only because everybody at the re-hearsal dinner had heard, but because it wasn't too far from the truth.

Which sucked. Badly.

"I'm not drunk," Bonnie said. "I just happen to like tea roses."

"Yeah, right. 'Cause there's no other way to get a bunch of roses than a hair-pulling contest. Come on, what gives?"

"It's not every day our brother gets married," Bonnie said with a shrug, not about to explain *what gave*. Especially because she couldn't explain it without coming across like an idiot.

Debbie rolled her eyes. "Well, as far as I'm concerned, you shouldn't be worrying about catching a bouquet. You don't need to get married. You just need to get laid."

Bonnie frowned, not only at the mouthy comment, but because, again, Debbie was a little too perceptive. Frankly Bonnie hadn't been trying to catch that bouquet due to any white lace dreams. She'd had sexy, black-satin ones in mind, instead. And Debbie's virginal comment had put them there the previous night. Not that she was about to share that little tidbit.

"We'd better move so the guys can try to catch the garter."

She only hoped a certain groomsman didn't catch it.

"You mean so Tom can catch it," Debbie said with a grin.

Uh, yeah. *That* certain groomsman. He had been the reason she, for the first time ever, had almost involved herself in a catfight over a bunch of flowers.

Reese's friend Tom had a reputation as the most successful garter-catcher of his generation. In ancient times, epic poems would have been written about his triumphs in the garter wars.

He was also said to be an equally talented female-catcher. And while there had been no poetry, there were definitely some over-the-top tales circulating about his sexual prowess. Her older sister—divorced and angry—had long called him "the man whore." But Bonnie had only half believed the rumors.

She'd had a crush on him. He'd been every teenage girl's fantasy—the flirtatious older guy who'd teased her mercilessly. Their paths hadn't crossed in a few years, and she'd wondered if he was still as handsome and cocky as ever.

She'd found out at last night's rehearsal. Oh, yeah. Still handsome. Still single. Still cocky.

Still treating her like she was a kid.

That had bothered her. Then, after Debbie's comment, it had *really* bothered her.

God, did everyone in the family think that just because she cared about the environment and the needy, she didn't have a libido? Was she doomed to be Bonnie-the-*nice*-Campbell-girl forever? To always be Bonnie-the-peacemaker, Bonnie-the-bleeding-heart? Just because she'd carved out a place in her huge family by filling that role throughout her childhood didn't mean she hadn't grown up and have a woman's desires.

Okay, maybe she hadn't lived her adult life in a way that would change any opinions. She'd been busy with school, work and volunteering and hadn't had time for any long-term romantic entanglements. She'd never brought a man around to meet the family, never been engaged, never lived with anyone. As far as her family—Debbie—knew, she *could* still be a virgin.

She wasn't, though. Her first lover had been a long-haired guitarist she'd met in college. He'd been a crusader for the legalization of marijuana, for medicinal purposes, he'd said.

Uh…sure. They'd broken up after his third drug bust.

Since then, she'd had a four-month-long relationship with a grad student, before he left to join the Peace Corps. And something resembling a one-night stand.

Pathetic. But she hadn't really thought about *how* pathetic until Debbie's virgin crack.

That's why she'd thought of Tom. Sexy Tom. Tom who knew women, loved women, worshipped women, made pleasuring women his life's mission—or so "they" said.

Maybe he wasn't the dog everyone made him out to be—the stories might have come out of spite or jealousy. But if they were true, well, there were worse people to break a sexual dry spell with than one who was so interested in sex! Maybe the best way to shed her good-girl image was to have sex with a very bad boy.

Either way, getting a little closer to Tom hadn't seemed like such a bad idea. But after he'd done everything but give her noogies on her head last night, she'd realized she had to do something to make him see her as the adult she was now, not his friend's kid sister.

Which brought her to the bouquet. Whoever caught it would have some sexy fun, and share a dance, with whoever caught the garter. If he had to slide a bit of lace all the way up her thigh and couldn't see she had a woman's long legs and a woman's curves, he *never* would.

He never will.

Because she'd blown it. No bouquet. No sexy garter moment for her, just for the stacked blonde. No wedding night fling just to remind herself she was a sensual woman with normal wants, despite what her family, especially her snide little sister, might think.

Nope. Wasn't going to happen. How depressing.

"I'm tired. I'm going to find a place to sit down."

She didn't wait for Debbie to respond. She merely walked away, knowing her sister would be too interested in the garter-toss to follow. She also made a concerted effort to avoid bumping into any of her other siblings— tough since she had five.

Keeping her head down, she skirted the crowd, ignoring everyone, at least until she overheard a snippet of conversation between two of the other guests—both old friends of her mother.

"It is a shame we have to move to another hotel," said one.

"But it couldn't be helped," was the reply.

Bonnie stopped, eyeing the pair. "Excuse me, I couldn't help overhearing. Is there a problem with the rooms?"

"There was a mix-up and some of them were given out to those movie people," one explained.

"*Movie* people?"

The woman nodded.

Yuck. Of all the shallow people she'd ever met, those who lived in Hollywood were the worst. She couldn't believe how callously they treated vulnerable lands and habitats just to make the next blockbuster. From the fur they wore to the exotic animal dinner parties they hosted, she had no use for any of them. Especially since one particular actor had had her tossed into jail last spring, just because she'd tried to stop his crew from damaging the habitat for a rare species of bird.

"Didn't you hear?" the other woman asked. "They're

filming a movie nearby and the cast and crew are staying here." She tittered. "There's even a handsome movie star staying in the bridal suite."

Bonnie's eyes had begun to narrow as soon as she heard "movie people." When "movie star" and "bridal suite" entered the conversation, steam came out of her usually pacifistic ears.

"A spoiled, selfish actor is staying in the bridal suite where Reese and Amanda should be spending their wedding night?"

Nodding, the woman bit her lip, as if realizing that Bonnie—the nicest Campbell kid—was ready to go postal on someone.

Well, not quite that far. But a stern talking-to was definitely in the picture. "I'm going to find Abby, the bride's sister," she told the women, shaking with indignance. "She's the wedding coordinator. She'll do something about this."

And if Abby wouldn't? Bonnie would.

THOUGH THEY WEREN'T HIS favorite part of the job, Drew Ericson didn't usually mind location shoots. True, he hoped he'd never again have to set foot in the small Louisiana town where he'd spent eight hot, miserable weeks last summer shooting a movie about a bayou-born bounty hunter. But in general, since he was single and childless, being away from southern California for weeks at a time wasn't a big deal.

Until now. Because his stalker had followed him here.

"Are you sure it was her?" he asked, talking into his cell phone to one of the production assistants on the film *Grey Steele*—a movie in which he played the mysterious Mr. Steele.

"I'm sure, Mr. Ericson," the younger man said. "We were all given her mug shot so we could watch out for her."

"Hell." Drew glanced around the large suite, noting that the privacy curtains were firmly closed. Considering he had just gotten out of the shower, was still wet and wore only a towel slung around his hips, that was a good thing.

It wasn't that he feared Helen Jarvis. But damn, she was annoying. He was sick to death of feeling like he couldn't take a single step without being watched. The very thought that he now had to check the room every time he entered infuriated him.

The assistant continued. "I spotted her outside the shop where we were shooting today. When she saw me, she took off."

Of course she did. Considering he had a restraining order against her, Jarvis knew better than to stick around and get caught. "Did you let the guards know?"

"Yes, and the local police. Security will be tight."

Good. Though, honestly, he didn't hold out much hope that they'd catch her. The woman was as slippery as Jell-O. Security was tight on movie sets, too…yet she'd once managed to get on the lot and wait for him inside his trailer.

She'd done a lot of crazy things to get close to him— including showing up in his backyard during a private party. The woman even seemed ready to risk bodily injury to get his attention. Once she'd thrown herself in front of his car as he pulled out of his driveway—hoping he'd hit her, and have to stop.

Thank God he had good reflexes. And good brakes.

At first, everyone had laughed it off as part of the biz.

Then she'd shown up at a restaurant where he'd been meeting with his manager, posing as a waitress to take their order. Seeing her crazed desperation firsthand, his manager acknowledged the situation was serious. Like the-David-Letterman-stalker serious.

But the worst moment had been a call from his mother. A strange woman had followed her into a store and introduced herself as his girlfriend. When his mother had reacted with suspicion, the woman had gotten angry.

Harassing his sixty-year-old mother had been the straw that broke this camel's back. There was no more laughing Helen Jarvis off, so he'd brought in the authorities, had her charged with stalking and filed a restraining order. She wasn't supposed to get within five hundred feet of him, his family, or his property.

And yet, she'd still followed him to Illinois.

"Everybody's on alert," the assistant said, "though, maybe if she thinks she's been spotted, she'll get out of town."

Hopefully. But he doubted it—the woman didn't operate that way. Which meant he was again going to have to be on guard for her throughout the next few weeks. "Okay, please let me…"

He was interrupted by a sharp knock on the door to his room. Drew hesitated, the phone still at his ear.

"Sir? Everything okay?" the assistant asked.

"Yeah, sorry," he mumbled. "Keep me posted."

He ended the call and walked quietly toward the door.

Another knock. Harder this time. Sharp and impatient.

Jarvis had never been brazen enough to just knock before. It wasn't her slimy style. Then again, he hadn't seen her since the restraining order. Maybe it had pushed her over the edge. He just wished she would take no for an answer—because that's the one he'd given to her on the few occasions they'd come face-to-face. Then again, considering he suspected she was nuttier than a bag of trail mix, that was probably too much to expect.

"Hello? Would you please answer the door, I need to talk to you!" a woman said.

He hadn't listened closely enough to his stalker to know her voice, but it sure wasn't anyone else's he recognized. His tension increased, his eyes narrowing as he stared at the door.

"Look, I heard you talking, I know you're in there. Stop being such a jerk and open the door."

Jerk? He was a jerk for not wanting a crazy woman harassing his parents or breaking into his house?

This had gone beyond annoying to infuriating. He couldn't remember the last time he'd been so angry. Ignoring the advice he'd gotten from the police, he flipped the lock, grabbed the knob and yanked the door open.

"I've had enough of this! Who the hell do you think you are?" he snapped, glaring at the woman.

Who *wasn't* Helen Jarvis.

In fact, she looked absolutely nothing like the fortyish Helen Jarvis, who had bright red hair, bushy eyebrows and a crazy light in her eyes.

"Oh," he muttered, staring at the extremely attractive young woman, clad in a long, emerald-green gown.

She looked familiar for some reason, though he couldn't immediately say why. He just knew the thick, honey-gold hair tumbling in wavy curls halfway down her back framed an incredibly pretty face, complete with sparkling amber-brown eyes and lush lips. She wasn't very tall, but the formfitting dress revealed some impressive curves. He'd put her in her mid-twenties, a few years his junior. And she looked every bit as shocked that he'd yanked the door open so abruptly as he was at seeing someone other than the person he expected to find.

The shock quickly dissipated, though.

"Oh, for heaven's sake, it's *you?*" she said, her voice dripping with disdain. "You're the movie star? I can't believe this!"

Drew gaped. The woman who'd been banging on his door, calling him a jerk, was indignant that *he'd* been the one to open it. She'd apparently expected to tell off someone else.

"Go get dressed," she ordered. "I'm not some bimbo. That he-man, muscular look doesn't impress me."

Which was when Drew remembered he wasn't wearing any clothes. Just a white rectangle of terry cloth riding low on his hips, catching the rivulets of moisture that slowly streamed down his body from his wet hair. "Look, I think you have the wrong room," he said, tightening the knotted towel.

"No, *you're* the one who has the wrong room, Mr. Ericson," she shot back. "And if you had any decency, you'd get out of it."

"Who *are* you?"

Her eyes narrowed and her lips pursed in derision. "You don't know?"

"I haven't got a clue," he replied, even as that hint of memory teased his brain.

The answer seemed to annoy her even more. "Of course, you wouldn't, Mr. Movie Star."

Down the hall, the door to another room creaked open a few inches and a pair of nosy eyes peered out. Already on edge from the producer's call, and the stress of dealing with the stalker situation, not to mention this woman looking at him like she'd scraped him off the bottom of her shoe, he immediately stiffened.

He had no idea who those eyes belonged to. For all he knew, Helen Jarvis could be behind that door. Maybe she'd even arranged for this woman to serve as a distraction to get him to answer.

Whatever the case, standing out here wearing only a towel, within sight of Jarvis, or a tabloid reporter, or a member of his fan base, was a really bad idea.

He was just about to close the door in the strange woman's pretty face when she said, "I should have known it would be you. Who else would be arrogant enough to do this?"

"Do what?" he barked, almost shaking with frustration over a conversation that completely confused him.

"Ruin someone else's wedding, that's what!" She pointed an index finger at him, stepping closer, until the soft, satiny fabric of her dress brushed his bare calves, bringing a quick, surprising rush of awareness. He was also hit with a hint of a feminine perfume, soft and pretty. Like her.

Though, right now, she seemed anything but soft.

"I know you actor types are used to getting your own way, but would it have killed you to be unselfish for *once?* A regular room couldn't do for one night?"

The room. She was here to harass him about where he was staying, not to lay a trap, not to draw his attention away from any crazy stalker who might be lurking nearby, waiting to slip into his bed while he was distracted.

It was just about the damn room.

Both relieved and very curious, he said, "Sorry, lady,

I don't have private conversations in full view of anyone who wanders by."

Without warning, he reached for her arm and pulled her inside. Drew forced himself to ignore the softness of her skin, or think about how soft the *rest* of her might feel. It had obviously been way too long since he'd had sex if he couldn't stop thinking about how much he'd like to touch every inch of this woman, who'd been practically shouting in his face.

Her mouth had dropped open when he'd touched her, and she shook his hand off the minute she stepped over the threshold. "You can't just go grabbing people like that."

"I can if they're screeching unfair accusations at me in public," he said as he shut the door firmly behind her.

"Oh, yeah, I'm sure you're really concerned about your privacy considering you open doors to strangers when you're half-naked," she said with a definite eye-roll.

"You're a little hung up on me being half-naked," he said, just to egg her on. And, he had to admit, to see if she felt any hint of that spark he'd been feeling since the moment he'd opened the door.

She sputtered, a faint flush of color rising to her cheeks. "Wow, that's some ego. You should really get over yourself. You're not *that* interesting to look at."

People magazine would say differently, but, of course, he didn't point that out. That "Most Beautiful People" list was all kinds of embarrassing—not that he'd ever cracked the Top 10.

"Anyway, I don't care. Do what you want, get dressed or don't. I'm not intimidated."

Calling her bluff, he ignored the clothes strewn on

the bed, strolling over to casually lean against the back of the couch, which separated the sleeping and sitting areas of the suite. He didn't bother tightening up the towel, which had slipped so low, it was now just an inch or two above his groin—close to the money shot that would earn him an extra five mil if he ever went there in a motion picture.

She noticed. Her flush deepened a little; he could see that from several feet away. She parted her lips to suck in a deep, calming breath. Her low-cut dress revealed her slender, delicate throat and he'd swear he could see the flicker of her pulse pounding harder in her veins.

Or maybe he was just feeling his own.

Because oh, that dress *was* definitely low-cut, that throat *was* delicate, those curves *were* entirely too distracting. And the heat in her eyes, which she couldn't completely disguise, was arousing a response in him. Seriously arousing it.

Cool off, jackass.

He needed to bring down the temperature. Pronto. Getting hot and bothered about a complete stranger who'd just called him a selfish jerk and looked like she hated his guts was not a good way to start the evening.

"Would you like a drink?" he asked, gesturing toward the minibar.

"No, thank you."

"Suit yourself," he said, grabbing himself a bottle of water from the fridge.

"Oh. That kind of drink."

He had the feeling she thought he had intended to ply her with alcohol—him being the big, bad movie star and despoiler of innocents and all. Without a word, he reached in, grabbed another bottle and handed it to her.

Their hands brushed on the cold plastic, just a hint of connection, an air kiss of fingertips. But, just like when he'd grabbed her to haul her inside, he felt the sizzle from his hand all the way up his arm and throughout the rest of his body.

The woman was getting to him. Big-time.

She mumbled her thanks, opened it and took a drink as well. As she did, Drew found himself eyeing her left hand. Force of habit. Unfortunately married women didn't seem to mind cheating so much if it was with a celebrity.

She wore a small ring on the finger in question, but it looked like an opal or pearl. Not very married or engagedish, at least he hoped.

Good.

Though why he immediately thought that a good thing, he didn't know. He might be feeling some major attraction, but she didn't seem to be. He'd met the woman all of five minutes ago, and most of that time, she'd been glaring or snarling at him.

Which, actually, was kinda cute, contrasted to the sweetness of her lovely face and soft lips.

"Now, why don't you start over and tell me what it is I did that has you so furious." He lifted his mouth in a half smile, one that had worked on a lot of heroines in a bunch of movies.

She was either immune, or did a good impersonation of it. Swallowing hard and shaking her head, she said, "You're ruining my brother's wedding."

Wow. Big accusation, since he didn't know her, or her brother. "What do you mean?"

She began to explain the situation, her every word layered with reproach. When he realized the cast and crew of his movie had actually cost a bunch of people with reservations their rooms during someone else's big weekend celebration, he began to understand her anger. In fact, he probably would have felt exactly the same way.

"Look, I'm sorry, I didn't know there was a problem with the reservations. I don't handle these things."

She hesitated, staring hard as if gauging his sincerity. Then her jaw pushed out a little, suspicion and stubbornness quickly returning. "It's not just about the guests' rooms. The wedding actually took place *today.*"

"Well, I kinda figured that out. You are wearing a bridesmaid dress. And, unlike most I've seen, it's not an ugly one," he said with a wry grin.

Though, to be honest, the idea of taking that dress off her was looking better by the minute. Now that he knew she wasn't just loco, and had a reason for coming up here and telling him off, he was having a hard time thinking of much else.

Even if she hadn't been wearing the dress, he would have known the ceremony had taken place today. When he'd come back from the set this afternoon, he'd caught sight of an attractive bridal couple who looked blissfully happy.

Curious about that ring, he added, "So, were you the maid of honor? Or the *matron* of honor?"

Kind of a heavy-handed way to ask if she was married, but he was flying by the seat of his pants here.

"Neither," she replied, then tenaciously went back to her point, not answering his real, unasked question. "So, think about it. If the wedding was today, that means that tonight is the wedding night. You follow me?"

"Well, that would make sense." He refrained from making any lascivious wedding-night jokes, sensing that would only piss her off even more.

She waved an arm around, pointing to the silky sheers flowing down over the four-poster bed with its fluffy pillows and plush duvet. Then at the intimate café table with a vase of red roses, the fainting couch and, through the open bathroom door, the oversize bathtub complete with a tile inlaid swan on the wall above it.

"Tell me, did you happen to notice what room you're in?"

"Uh…a nice one?"

Gritting her teeth in visible frustration, she took a deep breath, as if to calm herself, then said, "You're in the honeymoon suite."

A lightbulb clicked on in his brain. "Oh, hell. Your brother and his wife were supposed to have this room for the night."

"Bingo. But they can't. Because a…"

"Don't say it," he said, holding his hand up, palm out. "I've been called a selfish movie star enough for one day, thank you very much."

"If the shoe fits…"

"Hey, I'm a guy, okay? Forgive me for not being smart enough to add bride and groom and honeymoon suite together and realize I needed to give up my room."

Her eyes widened a tiny bit, as if he'd caught her off guard at his willingness to give up his room. He didn't know why, though. It was, of course, exactly what he was going to do.

"You mean you…"

"I'm an actor, not royalty. Believe me, I really don't mind changing rooms. It's not a big deal."

Drew didn't give it another thought. He didn't feel prompted by her accusations or the heat in her eyes. He simply did the right thing. As he always tried to do.

Walking over to the antique desk, he picked up the

phone, called down to the front desk and told them he wanted to switch rooms with the newlyweds'.

And that, for the first time since he'd laid eyes on her, left the sexy stranger in the green dress utterly speechless.

2

AND TO THINK SHE'D ALWAYS considered movie stars predictable creatures. Well, hadn't she been proved wrong.

They were not supposed to be nice, thoughtful and generous unless there was a starving orphan to coo over, an impoverished nation laying laurels at their feet or a camera crew nearby to capture the moment. Nor did they just open their hotel room doors and yank strangers inside, while wearing nothing but a small—*oh, so small*—towel.

So when Drew Ericson—wearing that small, *oh, so small,* towel—called to request a room change, she honestly didn't know what to say. In fact, she couldn't say anything. She could only stare from a few feet away, feeling about as embarrassed as she'd ever felt in her life.

Bonnie—the *nice* Campbell girl—had come in here with a boatload of preconceptions and an attitude a mile wide. She'd called the man names, accused him of all kinds of things, because she was in a pissy mood after not catching a stupid wedding bouquet and facing down a sister who'd called her a virgin.

What was wrong with her? She had gone so far afield from her usual calm, gentle nature, she almost didn't recognize herself. She'd been spoiling for a fight—and Bonnie was the lover of the family, not the fighter.

Of course, part of the blame could probably be laid at the feet of the infamous Drew Ericson. After all, she did owe him a big heaping batch of payback for what he'd done to her last spring. And he didn't even remember!

That so hadn't improved her mood.

"Okay? Am I forgiven now?" the actor asked as he hung up the phone and turned around, a slight smile tickling those impossibly sexy lips.

She suspected his lips had launched the man's career. She didn't think any woman on earth—including already famous female movie stars who had some hand in casting—wouldn't want to sample them at least once.

His mouth wasn't his only devastatingly attractive feature. He had a strong, masculine, square-jawed face to go with it—emphasized by a pair of the bluest eyes she'd ever seen. When combined with his jet-black hair, the man had looks that would stop traffic, even if he weren't famous worldwide.

And then, of course, was the body... *Oh, God, the body.*

She'd lied when she said he wasn't interesting to look at. Because, frankly, only a woman without an ounce of estrogen would *not* want to look at him.

It was a bad thing that she'd had sex on her mind since last night. A very bad thing. Because this man was sex on a stick. Absolutely mouthwatering from his muscular shoulders, to his flexing arms, his broad chest, the muscles rippling across his flat stomach. And down to the edge of that towel. Even his legs and feet were perfect.

She'd seen him from a distance before, of course, as he'd driven by the protestors picketing his movie set last spring—the protestors *she'd* led. But she'd convinced herself he couldn't possibly be as good-looking up close as he was on airbrushed magazine covers, or in his movies—not that she'd ever seen one.

Now, she realized she'd been wrong. He was to die for. It had been all she could do to remain impassive when she'd let her eyes travel over those long ridges of muscle. She could have spent an hour staring at one errant drop of water that trickled from his hair onto his shoulder, sliding down, blazing a visible trail over the planes and valleys of his slick, hard body.

"Do you happen to know what room your brother and his wife are in tonight?" he asked, moving toward the bathroom. He scooped up a pair of jeans off the bed as he passed.

"Uh, yes. It's on the bottom floor, in the east wing, the very last room."

"Okay, thanks. Somebody from the staff is going to let them know, then clean out the room and move me down there," he said, not having shut the door all the way. He'd intentionally left it ajar so he could talk to her from inside the bathroom.

The bathroom with the mirror.

The bathroom with the mirror in which she—*oh, my*—could now see his amazing butt as he dropped the towel to the floor!

Holy crap. Movie star ass. Unbelievable movie star ass. The man could be a butt model, if there was such a thing.

Bonnie swung around to stare at the refrigerator, repeating, *I am not a letch* over and over in her mind just so she wouldn't turn back around for another peek. Of course, all the while, she wondered if *he* had turned around, presenting his other side to the mirror. That very interesting other side.

"Stop it," she told herself, sure the man hadn't just mirror-mooned her on purpose. If he wanted to embarrass her or show off his body, he could have dropped the towel right out here. She'd practically dared him to, saying she didn't find him interesting to look at.

Liar, liar, pants on fire. Well, she wasn't wearing pants, but beneath her gown, her underpants sure felt on the verge of exploding into flames.

"Did you want to do anything before they come up here?"

Do anything? Hmm. That was a loaded question.

Ericson emerged from the bathroom, shirtless, wearing just the jeans. She hadn't noticed whether or not he'd grabbed anything to wear under them.

Stop thinking about what he might be wearing under them.

"Hello?"

Trying to pull two thoughts together in her brain, she mumbled, "Huh?"

"After I pack up my stuff, the manager's going to send someone up to move it, then get the room ready for the newlyweds. But if you want to do anything, leave a note or some flowers or something, you could do that now."

Licking her lips, Bonnie said, "Yes, sure, that's a great idea. I'll talk to the wedding coordinator and have some champagne sent up for tonight after the party."

"Is the reception still going on?" he asked, sounding surprised. Then he tsked. "You snuck out of your own brother's wedding reception just to tell me off?"

"No, the official stuff is over. There's a big costume party tonight, though, out in the barn."

He shrugged. "Makes sense, I guess. Convenient that they got married the night before Halloween."

"You'd have to know Reese and Amanda. The party is perfect for them."

"Sounds like fun. Way better than the typical boring wedding reception with a smarmy deejay playing the 'Chicken Dance' and the 'Electric Slide.'"

Sighing, she admitted, "That was this afternoon."

He threw his head back and barked a laugh.

"Something tells me the Hollywood weddings you attend don't have quite the same level of entertainment," she said.

"No, they usually have some once-famous, now slightly has-been band that charges a quarter of a million bucks for a three-hour performance playing the 'Chicken Dance' and the 'Electric Slide.' With a cheesy rendition of 'Daddy's Little Girl' thrown in just for the hell of it."

She couldn't stop a tiny smile from widening her lips. So far, the man was so unlike the image she'd built him up to be in her mind for the past six months. Easy to talk to, quick to smile, laid-back and friendly. Not at all the monster she'd been imagining.

And hot. So damned hot. She wished he'd put a shirt on just so she could stop wondering how those ridges of muscle on his abdomen would feel pressed against her bare stomach.

Or, to be honest, how his bare anything would feel against her bare anything.

"I can't say going to weddings is my favorite thing," he admitted, "so I wasn't too heartbroken about not being invited to Charlie Sheen's latest walk down the aisle."

She chuckled, liking his down-to-earth manner.

Wrong. He's an actor. He could just be playing the role of nice guy. She knew better than most that he wasn't Mr. Friendly.

She stiffened her spine, determined not to be charmed by him. "Let's just say tonight's the real reception—the one that most suits the bride and groom," she said, thinking of how brazen and fun Amanda was—and how much Reese adored her. Then, remembering what he'd said earlier, she added, "And I didn't come up here to tell you off."

"You did a really good impersonation of it."

"Yeah. Sorry."

"What was that? I didn't quite hear you." A grin lingered on those lips and his eyes twinkled. The man was teasing her, knowing he'd firmly put her in her place and had kept her off balance throughout this whole conversation.

But he'd done something very nice that deserved a genuine expression of gratitude, not a grudging, mumbled one. "I'm sorry I was such a basket case. Thank you, Mr. Ericson. I'm sure Reese and Amanda will be truly grateful."

"Drew," he told her, retrieving a long-sleeved Henley shirt from the bed and pulling it on. "You never told me your name."

"It's Bonnie Campbell."

Now fully dressed—*thank God*—he stepped over and extended a hand. "Nice to meet you."

She should have taken the hand and left it at that. Instead she muttered, "We've met before."

His eyes narrowed as he studied her. "You do look

familiar, but I'm sorry, I can't remember why. Were you an extra or something?"

"A what?"

"I mean, did you appear in a scene in one of my movies?"

She snorted. "Definitely not. I would never watch one of your movies, and I most certainly would never appear in one."

The minute the words left her mouth, she realized how rude they sounded. Then again, considering he'd had her arrested, just because she'd wanted to save a bird habitat being damaged by one of his location shoots, he deserved a little rudeness.

But not after the nice thing he did for Reese and Amanda.

Almost stumbling over her words, she hurried to add, "I mean, I'm no actress."

He wasn't fooled. "I don't think not being an actress was your main objection. What's wrong with my movies?"

She couldn't imagine he cared, since he produced blockbuster after blockbuster. So she answered honestly. "They're just not my thing. Too violent, too bloody."

"You're a chick flick fan, huh?"

"Actually, I like nature films." She shrugged in self-deprecation. "And Disney movies. What can I say? I'm a wimp."

"Nature and Disney. Yeah, I can see how Bambi would appeal to someone who abhors violence," he said with a wry look.

Though she sensed he was teasing, she answered seriously. "I can't watch that one."

"Bet *The Lion King*'s not on your best-of list, either."

"Nope."

"Didn't Tarzan's parents get eaten by…"

"Enough!" she snapped. "I get the point."

"But we didn't even start on Cruella de Vil."

Seeing the twinkle in his eyes, she couldn't help chuckling. "Imagine what your adoring public would think if they knew you were such a dweeb."

As soon as the words left her mouth, she bit her lip, having no idea what had come over her. Bonnie had never in her life slung insults at a stranger like that. Though, to be honest, she hadn't been trying to be nasty.

It was just…he'd been very cute when exposing his thorough knowledge of kids movies. She didn't remember ever reading that he had any munchkins of his own, so maybe he was just a soft touch underneath all that rugged, tough-guy swagger. Considering he'd given up his opulent suite for a small, standard room, she suspected that was at least a little bit true.

He drew a hand to his chest. "I'm offended. I thought most guys would get points for being so well-versed on the important cartoon classics of the twentieth century."

She had to give it to him, the guy was charming. Not movie star, schmoozy charming, but genuine and almost boyish. It was an unexpected trait in a guy who made movies that featured weapons and fifteen-minute fight scenes with slow-mo close-ups of blood splattering, at least, so she'd heard. She could probably like this man, if she let herself.

She couldn't let herself, however. Because she was already too attracted to him. Liking might just shove her over the top and have her doing something crazy like asking him if he wanted to shove a lacy garter up her leg.

Or, um, shove something up something.

Stop it, idiot!

"Now, back to the point. Where have we met before?"

She was tempted to just leave without answering, but some part of her—probably the part that still smarted over the fact that she now had an arrest on her record—had to reply. "You probably saw my face through the bars as I was being hauled off your movie set in a paddy wagon."

Exaggeration. But he was an actor—they were used to it.

His impossibly blue eyes widened in shock. "What?"

"You remember the little problem on the set of the Civil War movie you made in Gettysburg last spring?"

He hesitated, then sucked in a shocked breath. Stepping closer, he lifted a hand to her chin and looked straight at her face. "I get it. You were one of those protestors, I definitely noticed you." He nodded slowly, almost smiling. "It took me a while to remember you without the signs. Still, I should have recognized the pissed-off expression, which always seemed so out of place on your beautiful face."

She jerked her chin away, also shoving away the flash of warmth that his words sent rushing through her. *Beautiful?* Hardly. She'd cop to pretty. But she was nowhere near as beautiful as the women he interacted with on a daily basis.

"I can't believe I didn't figure it out sooner."

"Maybe I should have shown up in my prison jumpsuit, that might have jogged your memory."

"Excuse me?"

She told herself to stop exaggerating; there had been

no jumpsuit. "The one they *could* have put me in once you had me hauled off to jail."

"What are you talking about?"

"It doesn't matter anymore, Mr. Ericson. I managed to survive my incarceration. Fortunately my cell-mate was just a tired old prostitute named Sally, not a huge, chain-wearing alpha-dog named Bertha looking to make me her bitch."

He started to laugh, shaking his head as if he thought she'd put one over on him. When she didn't join in his amusement, he said, "You're serious?"

"As if you didn't know."

"I *didn't* know."

Yeah, right. "Forget it. It doesn't matter. Now, if you'll excuse me, I should go."

He put a hand on her shoulder, stopping her from spinning around and walking out of the room. The warm pressure of his strong fingers against her bare skin set those banked sparks of awareness ablaze, until they roared through her. It was an innocent touch, not rough, not aggressive, certainly not sexual. Yet she felt utterly engulfed by the inferno of her own instinctive reaction.

There was power in those hands. Just as much as in the mouth, the face, the amazing body and that captivating personality.

But not a scary power. No, an utterly seductive, fascinating one. She could so easily see herself falling under his spell. And part of her wanted to. Desperately.

Maybe if he weren't a celebrity, if he were just a normal guy—if he hadn't had her tossed into jail—she'd have given in to her incredible reaction to him and taken a shot. But he was nowhere near a normal guy. He was totally out of her league. This wasn't like hoping to hook up with her brother's old friend. This guy was a super-stud who had women at his feet. No way would he be interested in her, and no way would she humiliate herself any more by making her interest known to him. She'd already had her fill of playing Bonnie-the-idiot for one weekend.

"Look, all I remember was there were some protestors who didn't want us filming in the battlefield, even after we'd gotten permission."

"Nobody was upset that you were filming in the battlefield," she clarified. "We were concerned about a rare species of bird that nests in one area of it, and your crew didn't much seem to care about disturbing them during mating season. When I went to try to talk to you about it, I got arrested."

He dropped his hand—*thank God, now breathe*—his frown deepening. "Did you sneak onto the set? Were you near my trailer?"

That made her try to mentally douse the fire. Indignant, she replied, "I didn't 'sneak' anywhere! I nicely asked a sympathetic staff member to take me to somebody in charge. He said you were a good guy and that you liked animals, so you might listen."

"I do," he mumbled. "I would have."

She continued as if he hadn't spoken. "Once I was inside, the guy went to find you, and the next thing you know, I'm grabbed by a guard and accused of being some kind of stalker."

"Uh-oh."

She rolled her eyes. "Jeez, it's not like we were causing any real problems, blocking the driveway or interrupting the filming. All we did was hold up some signs, and for that, I got a trip in the back of a squad car to the local jail."

He swiped a hand through his thick, still-damp hair, leaving it sticking up in jagged, sexy spikes. "Hell."

"Not quite, just a cell. But close enough, thanks." Another exaggeration. The jail actually hadn't been too horrid—it was the embarrassment that had lingered, not any discomfort. But keeping up the attitude helped to remind her she could not, under any circumstances, reach up and sink her own fingers into that messy hair to straighten it out.

Or to tug him close to any part of her body he'd care to sample.

"Bonnie, you have to understand…"

"Oh, I understand. You had a movie to make, and didn't want to deal with protestors trying to save the lives of some silly little birds. So you took care of the problem by having their leader hauled off in handcuffs."

He reached for her hands, lifting them and studying her wrists, as if the cuffs might have left a mark that lingered after all these months.

Bonnie shivered. God, this was almost worse than the touch on her shoulder. Because it was far too easy to imagine him encircling her wrists in those big hands, lifting her arms above her body so she was helpless to do anything but lie there, *loving* it as he made love to her.

"I am so sorry." Surprisingly he sounded truly remorseful.

Swallowing hard, she forced herself to focus, thinking about the words, not the *Penthouse* forum moment taking place in her mind.

"I mean it, I am genuinely sorry, Bonnie."

Well, maybe he was, now that she'd become a real person, not just a nameless protestor he'd been trying to get rid of. During her career in social work, and her volunteerism for social and environmental causes, she'd learned that most people would easily ignore an anonymous voice saying something they didn't want to hear. But when the words came from someone they knew, someone they could put a face and name to, they were more inclined to listen. Apparently she'd become human to the spoiled movie star.

Spoiled—but nice—movie star, she clarified.

"Please forgive me," he said. "And let me explain."

He continued to hold her wrists. That übersexy crazy awareness still sliding through her, Bonnie wondered if he felt her pulse race at the connection even as she pulled away.

"It's okay," she said with a forced shrug. "There's really no need." She began to edge toward the door, knowing she should get out of here, now, before she let herself be any further charmed by the man. Before she could ask him to move those hands somewhere else on her body.

This isn't some guy you can pick up for the night. You did what you came to do, now get out of here.

"You've made up for it by giving up the room to Reese and Amanda," she added, trying so hard to sound appreciative and not lustful. "Thank you."

"You don't understand. Please, sit down, talk to me. I think we've gotten off on the wrong foot here."

"Actually we got off on the wrong foot six months ago."

"So can we start over?"

She scrunched her brow, truly not understanding why he cared. He seemed to want to make things right.

But there was no need. They would never see each other again. She was a tiny little fly who would get splattered on the windshield of his life if she even thought about sticking around any longer. Because as nice as he seemed to be, there was no way he'd be interested in her the way she was becoming more and more interested in him. He could have sex with some of the most beautiful women of their generation. He sure wouldn't want a nearly virginal social worker from Pittsburgh.

"It doesn't matter anymore."

"But I want you to…"

Before he could continue, someone knocked on the door. "Mr. Ericson? I've come to move your bags."

The bags he hadn't even started to pack. They sure did hop to it around here when a superstar gave the orders.

Bonnie didn't mind, though, because the interruption gave her the chance to end this disturbing conversation. She'd come up here furious and righteously indignant at an arrogant actor, and had ended up becoming breathless and far too aware of Drew Ericson as a man. It was like sleeping with the enemy.

Don't even *go there.*

No, she couldn't possibly go there anymore, not even in the darkest, most wicked corners of her mind. Drew Ericson was totally and completely out of bounds. And needed to get totally and completely out of her mind.

Which meant it was definitely time to go.

OVER THE NEXT FEW HOURS, after he'd killed some time in the small lounge area, then moved to his new room, Drew couldn't stop thinking about Bonnie Campbell. If the beautiful young woman were to be believed, she had spent a night in jail, all because of him. Well, him and Helen Jarvis.

"Damn," he said aloud, not for the first time.

Last spring, when he'd gone to Pennsylvania to film

that movie, he'd been fresh off Jarvis's blitz attack in his trailer on the set in California. His manager had raised hell with the studio, and they'd been promised that security would be much tighter in the future, including on location.

It was easy to see what had happened. Bonnie— beautiful, passionate Bonnie—had been mistaken for Helen Jarvis, or someone like her, and had paid the price for the other woman's crimes.

He hadn't known, hadn't really been responsible, but he still felt guilty about it. If only she'd let him explain. But he wouldn't have that chance. She was only here for another day or two, at the most, and he'd be stuck for a few more weeks. Their paths would probably never cross again.

Funny how much that disappointed him, considering he'd only just met the woman. But the brief time he'd spent in her company had delighted him. Bonnie had no artifice—there wasn't a false bone in her body. Coming from a place where everything from smiles to teeth to breasts to personalities were fake, he found that incredibly refreshing. And aside from that, she was a damned beautiful woman. One who'd affected him so deeply, he couldn't stop thinking about her—the softness of her skin, the gleam of gold in her hair, the passion of her voice, the womanly curves of her body.

"The womanly curves you're never gonna see again," he reminded himself.

Disappointment weighing heavily on his shoulders, he finally thought about dinner and reached for the phone to call room service. But before he could dial, someone knocked on the door to his new room—which was smaller than his previous one, but still perfectly comfortable. Even for a spoiled movie star.

He hesitated, waiting to see if his visitor on the other side of the door accused him of being a selfish jerk, or gave any other sign that it was the one person he'd like to see right now.

Silence. Bummer.

This time, though fully dressed, he reacted cautiously as he approached the door. "Yes?"

"Mr. Ericson?"

A man's voice. Good on the one hand—it wasn't Helen Jarvis. Bad on the other—it wasn't Bonnie, either.

"Sorry to bother you. I'm the guy you gave your room to. My wife and I were wondering if we could have a word?"

He heard a feminine laugh at the word wife, and realized the bride and groom were paying him a visit. Not Bonnie—her brother.

Opening the door, he smiled at the couple. They had changed out of their wedding finery, but still shone with happiness that would scream "newlyweds" to anyone who looked at them.

"Hi," he said. "Did you forget something? Come on in."

Rather than responding, the bride—a pretty blonde—rose on tiptoe and kissed Drew's cheek. "Thank you so much."

Her husband smiled, not the least bit concerned. He was obviously confident in his new wife's feelings for him. "I'm Reese Campbell, this is my wife, Amanda. We really appreciate you giving us your room, especially since you've been in it all week, and you'll have to move again once we're gone. It was a nice thing to do."

Drew shrugged. "It's no big deal. I'm just glad I found out about it in time. I would have hated the thought of cheating you out of the bridal suite on your wedding night."

"How *did* you find out?" Reese Campbell asked.

"From your sister."

The other man sighed. "I have four. Care to narrow it down?"

Four? Four like Bonnie? Good God. "It was Bonnie. She came to my room and, uh…made her case."

Reese coughed into his fist, obviously taken by surprise.

His wife seemed even more so. *"Bonnie?"* She eyed her husband. "Lab rat, huh?"

"Excuse me?" Drew asked.

"He told me Bonnie preferred lab rats to you." As if suddenly remembering who she was talking to, she gasped. "I'm sorry. I think I've had a bit too much champagne."

So, Bonnie Campbell thought he was worse than a rat. Considering she believed he'd intentionally had her arrested, he could see why.

"That's okay," he said. "There was a misunderstanding the first time we met. But I think maybe today I went up in her estimation, at least as high as, I dunno…field mouse?"

"Well," said Amanda, her voice ringing with sincerity, "in our estimation, you went straight up to really nice guy."

"I'm glad to hear it. Hope you have a great time tonight."

That had sounded a little cheesy. *Have a great time having wild, steamy sex tonight.* So he quickly added, "I mean, at your costume party. It sounds like a lot of fun."

"I'm sure it will be," Reese said, a twinkle in his

eye saying he'd caught Drew's meaning the first time. "You're welcome to join us, if you'd like. You don't even have to wear a costume."

His wife looked at him like he'd grown two heads. "Yeah, right. The guy who goes to the *Vanity Fair* after-Oscar party wants to hang out with us and our friends and families."

Families. As in *sisters.* Hmm. "Actually I'd be delighted to go," he replied.

The bride's jaw fell open. "Uh...seriously?"

"Yeah. Bonnie will be there, right?"

Reece eyed Drew speculatively. "Of course. Why?"

"I don't know. Maybe I'd like the chance to go from field mouse all the way up to hamster or something."

His wife giggled, but Reese Campbell just continued to stare, his eyes assessing, curious. The protective older brother, wondering if big-bad-movie-star had designs on his sister.

Well, he did. But not in the way Reese Campbell might think. Drew wanted to spend some more time with Bonnie so he could convince her he wasn't the slimeball—er, what was lower than a lab rat?—she thought him to be. And, well, okay, maybe to see if she felt any of the same attraction he felt for her.

She does.

He knew women. He had seen the way her cheeks had pinkened, and how she kept moistening her lips. He'd heard her choppy breaths and felt her racing pulse. She definitely felt something.

Reese must not have seen any ulterior motives in Drew's expression, because he finally began to smile, too. "I tell you what. We'll warn everyone not to harass you, and we'll assign Bonnie to be your bodyguard to make sure of it, okay?"

Pretty Bonnie the bodyguard. He liked the idea. A lot.

Drew stuck out his hand, and Reese took it. As they exchanged a strong, solid shake, Bonnie's brother added, "Just be warned. My sister isn't always the sweet, quiet little bleeding heart she seems to be."

Drew barked a laugh. *Sweet? Quiet?* Yeah. Right. If this afternoon was Bonnie being sweet and quiet, he wondered what she would do when she was furious, or, when she was excited.

Frankly he was really looking forward to finding out…especially about the excited part.

3

"EXCUSE ME?" BONNIE ASKED, not sure she'd heard properly. Her brother *couldn't* have just said what she thought he had.

Reese explained it again. "Drew Ericson is coming to the party—he should be here soon. I told him you'd run interference between him and anybody who gets a little overzealous."

That's what she thought he'd said. "You must be kidding."

He ignored her shock. "Amanda and I have already been spreading the word to everyone to respect the man and let him enjoy himself. But just in case, we figured it would be good for somebody to stick close to him. Since you've already met…"

"Oh, yeah, we've met," she snapped.

"And you didn't like him?" her brother asked, looking curious. "Because I got the feeling he liked you."

"That's ridiculous," she said, even as warmth rose in her face at the very thought of it. Because she had more than liked him. She had wanted the man like she'd never wanted anything in her entire life. Liking hadn't even entered the equation—even if she had begun to suspect she could like him, if she'd allow herself to. "He had me tossed into jail."

One of his brows went up. "Really? He *personally* did that?"

"I think he set the whole thing up," she said, intentionally sticking to her long-held resentment of Drew Ericson. It was her only defense against sheer, utter attraction.

"The guy doesn't make his own hotel reservations. You really think he schemes to get people hauled off to jail?"

Bonnie hesitated, Reese's words sparking a few unexpected thoughts. She'd been angry—furious—for six months. She wasn't accustomed to feeling that way, and had almost needed someone to focus all that anger on. Drew Ericson had fit the bill.

She'd put it all together in her mind long ago, figuring Ericson had gotten someone to let her onto the lot in order to entrap her and get her arrested. No more leader, no more protest.

But what if that scenario wasn't true? As Reese had hinted, Ericson had handlers for everything. He hadn't even noticed he was in a honeymoon suite, for heaven's sake. He had been incredibly contrite, not to mention thoughtful and considerate…and, oh, yeah, just about the sexiest thing on two legs this afternoon.

Was it possible he really wasn't to blame, as she'd assumed all these months?

There was only one way to find out—she had to ask the man.

And when he walked into the party a short time later, and their eyes met across the room, she knew the time had come.

Ignoring the whispers, plus some dreamy sighs—only

a few of which were her own—Bonnie walked toward
the entrance. Drew was shaking hands with Amanda
and Reese, appearing relaxed and comfortable in the
crowd.

"I see you made it," she said.

"He even came up with a costume," said Amanda.
She waved at Ericson's clothes—khaki pants, a leather
bomber jacket and a brown, broad-brimmed hat.

He looked incredibly handsome, the outfit casually
sexy. Masculine. Her fingertips curling into the fabric
of her dress, she pictured rubbing them against the
soft, worn leather of the jacket, stroking those broad
shoulders.

Even more devastating, those intense blue eyes were
fixed totally on her. He swept a long, thorough stare over
her, from her head, down her long, flowing dress, to her
feet.

She was dressed as Mother Nature, and had made
the costume herself. Green vines wound through her
long hair, and she'd used face paint to draw more on her
skin—from her temple, down her cheek, all the way to
her neck. The long, low-cut dress was made of soft layers
of moss-green fabric that shifted and flowed with every
move she made. It whispered around her, like a breeze,
and made her feel utterly feminine.

"I like your costume," Drew said in a throaty voice.

Bonnie quivered. Never had she been more aware that
the beautiful green fabric she'd used to make the dress
was very thin. She'd wanted it wispy and fragile, and it
skimmed over her body hugging every bump, curve or
nipple it tried to cover.

*Nipple? For God's sake, don't think of your
nipples.*

Too late. It didn't matter if she thought of them or

not. She could already feel the way the material scraped over her puckered, sensitive skin. She told herself it was because she was standing by the door and there was a cool breeze. In truth, she knew she could be standing by a bonfire and her body would react the same way. Because the sexiest man she'd ever seen was staring at her with stark appreciation, and she couldn't have been more aware of him if he stroked her breast right here in front of everyone.

"You do look beautiful, Bonnie," said Amanda.

"Beautiful," Drew repeated.

"Thank you. Uh, your costume is great, too, especially on such short notice." True. He looked incredibly hot. But he *didn't* look like he'd come in costume. "I'm afraid I don't get it, though. Who are you supposed to be?"

Reese frowned at Drew. "Even *you've* heard of Indiana Jones."

"I doubt it," said Drew. "I don't think he's been immortalized in cartoon form yet."

"She might recognize the LEGO-video game version."

Oh, perfect. Her brother and a movie star were ganging up on her. "I know who Indiana Jones is," she said. "I just didn't make the connection."

"Knock it off," said her new sister-in-law. "No picking on Bonnie. The world needs more people like her—with huge, loving hearts." Amanda lifted her champagne glass in salute. "Here's to you, little sister."

"Sorry for making fun of you," said Reese, squeezing her arm. "Now, go play babysitter for Mr. Ericson here, and make sure Great-Aunt Jean doesn't plop down on his lap and ask him how he likes women with a little more experience."

That would be very funny, if it weren't such a pos-sibility. Or if Bonnie wasn't suddenly picturing *herself* plopping down on his lap and asking how he liked women with a little *less* experience.

"Shall we?" she asked.

"Absolutely."

He followed her, stopping every two feet to allow her to make brief introductions, hearing the same sentence again, and again…and again. *I just love your movies!*

A few of the single women tried to say more. That included the blonde who'd caught the bouquet. Strange, Bonnie had figured she would be in a dark corner with Tom by now. Instead she was right here, cooing and tugging at her French maid costume so it slipped a little lower on her more than ample breasts.

Funny, that was the first time she'd thought of Tom since she'd left the reception. Now she wasn't even in-terested enough to look around the barn and see if he was here, though she wasn't entirely sure why. A few hours ago, it had seemed so important to get his attention today. Now? Not even a little bit.

She didn't allow herself to think it was because of the man standing beside her, the man who charmed every person he met. That was a mental road she wasn't ready to go down. Normal girls from Pittsburgh did not end up with super-stud movie stars. Period.

To give him credit, Drew didn't seem the least bit bothered by the attention. Not a hint of impatience en-tered his voice as he spoke to person after person. Fi-nally, though, Bonnie's patience started to wear thin. Especially once her youngest sister, Molly, and two of her giggly teenage friends circled him. They resembled a trio of Girl Scouts around a campfire—eyeing him like he was a big marshmallow they wanted to smoosh between their graham crackers.

"I can't believe you're really here!" one of them said.

"Would you *please* say the line from that movie…"

"Okay, that's enough," Bonnie said with a weary sigh. "How about we let Mr. Ericson sit down and have a drink."

Molly wrinkled her nose. "Who made you his babysitter?"

"Actually the bride and groom did," said Drew with a self-deprecating shrug. "I gotta do what she tells me. What can I say? I'm completely at her mercy."

The words rolled off his tongue with the slightest hint of suggestion, and Bonnie watched all three of the girls melt at the thought.

"Let's go," she muttered, grabbing his arm. As she pulled him away, she added, "You'd better steer clear of that redhead. I've known her since she was four and let me tell you, if you're not careful, she'll soon be reenacting that movie *The Crush* with you playing the Cary Elwes part."

"Yikes," he said as they skirted through the room, heading for a table in a back corner. "Is that the creepy one with Alicia Silverstone stalking the single guy?"

"Uh-huh."

He cleared his throat, all wide-eyed innocence as he said, "Thought you only watched cartoons."

Oh, man. She had totally asked for that one. "What can I say? I was a moody adolescent."

Laughing, he replied, "I'm sorry, I was just teasing you again."

Bonnie suddenly stopped, realizing something. She liked this man's laugh. Liked his smile. Liked his sense of humor. Liked the tingle of excitement she felt when he teased her.

Hell, it was too late. She liked Drew Ericson. A *lot*.

This wasn't supposed to happen. How could she like a guy she'd so totally *dis*liked for the past six months? Especially one every other woman in the world had the hots for?

One you have the hots for, too. Admit it.

She might be a wimp when it came to movies, but Bonnie Campbell was not a liar. She could admit it…if only to herself. She did have the hots for this guy. The steamy, boiling hots. She'd gone back to her room after leaving him this afternoon and had seriously considered making friends with the showerhead, that's how hot he'd made her.

"Okay," he said, oblivious to her naughty self-evaluation as they sat at an empty table. "Who else should I worry about tonight?"

Forcing herself to put those crazy ideas out of her mind, Bonnie tapped her finger on her cheek, giving it some thought. "That blonde in the French maid costume caught the bouquet at the reception." *Grr.* "She's on the lookout for a husband tonight."

He grimaced. "That's enough to scare any man. What about this Great-Aunt Jean?"

Glancing around, Bonnie nodded toward her relative, who wore a Queen Elizabeth ensemble, compete with ruff and red wig. "That's her." The woman was holding court among the older guests, all of whom looked to be laughing and having a great time.

Frankly Bonnie hadn't been sure how this whole costume party thing would go over with that generation. She needn't have worried. They appeared to be loving it.

All in all, tonight had proven to be a great success.

The barn was huge, yet still felt bursting at the seams—as if more people were here now than had been at the reception earlier. Considering Reese and Amanda were so happy they'd invited every person they bumped into to come, that was probably not far from the truth.

"She's very imposing," Drew said.

"Aunt Jean? She's a pussycat. Just be warned, she is the nosiest person on the planet. If she gets you alone, she'll ask you all kinds of personal questions."

"Oh? Like what?"

She opened her mouth to respond before noticing his tone had been *too* innocent. The man was good. He'd almost gotten her to answer him, which would have caused her no end of embarrassment once she got started. Because knowing Aunt Jean, she'd ask things like, *What kind of women do you like? Are you seeing anyone? What's it like filming those naughty love scenes?*

The laughter lurking on his mouth confirmed he'd been trying to lead her into saying something she'd regret. "Forget I asked."

"Behave, or I'll abandon you to the marriage-minded maid."

Before he could respond, a man dressed all in black approached the table. Bonnie tried to do her job and say "No autographs," when he pointed out the coat on the back of Drew's chair.

"Oh, sorry," Drew said, standing and passing the coat over.

"Wow, guess he didn't recognize you," she said when they were again alone. "Is that an ego-killer?"

"Are you kidding? It's nice to be incognito for a while."

"Hi, Mr. Ericson! I'm a big fan," a voice said.

So much for incognito.

The fan turned out to be a waiter, dressed in a phantom costume. He was carrying a tray loaded with both champagne glasses and beer bottles. "Would you like something to drink?"

"I'd love a beer," Drew said. After accepting the bottle, he glanced at the label. "Campbell's Lager. Never heard of it."

"It's a family favorite," Bonnie said, not explaining why it was the only brew being served at this particular party.

After sipping, he nodded in appreciation. "Good stuff."

"Glad you like it," she said. "My family owns the brewery."

His brow shot up. "Seriously?"

She nodded. "My grandfather founded it and my father built it into a major East Coast operation." Feeling wistful, as she always did when thinking of her father, who'd died three years ago, she cleared her throat. "Reese is in charge now."

He held up the bottle, sipping again. "This is excellent."

"We're not on the West Coast yet, but give Reese time."

"I'm going to have to ship a few cases back home."

"I'm sure he'd be happy to send you some as a thank-you."

"Hey, I'll buy it by the truckload. Then I'll be the envy of my friends who will want to know where I found it. That'll get some word of mouth going before you break into the California market."

She saw by his expression that he meant it. It wasn't a casual promise, easily offered, easily forgotten. He was genuine and thoughtful. Considerate. And so unlike what she expected.

Which prompted her to finally broach the subject that had been bugging her all day. "So. About having me arrested…"

Drew reached across the table and dropped a hand over hers. Bonnie didn't draw away, surprised by the warm, casual possession of the gesture. Surprised, and also pleased.

"I am so sorry. I've been thinking it over and I think you were probably mistaken for a woman who's been stalking me."

"You mean *all* the women who stalk you?" she asked, enjoying the way that hand felt, heavy and strong on top of hers.

"No, I mean one in particular." His eyes narrowed and frown lines tugged at his brow. For the first time, the laid-back, casual good humor he'd displayed from the moment they'd met seemed to dissipate. "It's a long story."

"I'm listening."

"Okay," he said. "You asked for it."

Yes, she had. So Bonnie remained silent as he told her about this woman, Helen Jarvis, who had taken "crazed fan" up to a whole new level. She supposed it wasn't too surprising that male celebrities were stalked as much as female ones, but she hadn't given it much thought before. Drew was so strong, larger-than-life, it was difficult to imagine how hard it must be to feel helpless to protect his own privacy from someone determined to invade it.

Hearing that the woman had thrown herself in front of his car was bad enough. Then it just got worse.

She gasped. "You're serious? She confronted your mother?"

"Yeah. That was the line in the sand for me."

"I'm not surprised." She cast a quick look across the party toward her own mother, who stood laughing with Aunt Jean. Bonnie and all her siblings had been very protective of their mom since their father's untimely death. She couldn't think of anything they wouldn't do to protect her if she were being threatened.

"The rest was petty garbage—sneaking onto the set, breaking into my trailer, showing up at my house. Going after my family took things too far. That's when I got a restraining order."

Sucking in a breath, Bonnie zoned in on one key part of what he'd said. This crazed woman who'd made his life a nightmare for the past year had snuck onto one of his movie sets. "Oh, God, *that's* why security went nuts when I got on your set!"

"That's why. I wish I knew who it was who brought you in and then abandoned you to get accused of trespassing."

"You and me both," she said. Remembering the very nice young man, she mused, "I bet he was afraid for his job once he saw what had happened. That's probably why he didn't come forward."

"It was a coward's move," Drew said, his mouth tightening.

But even as his tension increased, her own completely disappeared. She suddenly felt as though someone had lifted an enormous weight off her shoulders. Bonnie hadn't really thought about how much the incident last spring had weighed on her, yet it obviously had. She'd felt not only abused and indignant, but actually offended at the thought that she'd been set up.

Now she knew she hadn't been. She had no doubt Drew was telling her the truth. That, more than anything, suddenly made her heart feel lighter than it had in ages. "Thanks for confiding in me," she said, smiling broadly at him, holding nothing back. It was the first real, heartfelt smile she'd offered the man.

Staring into her face for a long moment, he answered, "Thanks for listening. Now, do you think we could start over?"

"As in, pretend I didn't practically bang your door down and accuse you of all kinds of hateful things?" she whispered, overwhelmed with remorse for her own behavior.

He didn't answer. Instead he pushed his chair back and rose to his feet, extending his hand to her. "Will you dance with me?"

She didn't have to give it a second thought. "I'd love to."

HE WAS IN TROUBLE.

Drew had been highly interested in Bonnie Campbell when she'd been a pretty bridesmaid knocking on his door to tell him off. That interest had grown when they'd talked, when he'd learned more about her, heard her laugh, seen that smile.

Now, though, brushing up against her body on the dance floor—feeling the glide of her thigh against his, or the scrape of those perfect breasts against his chest—he had gone from interested to captivated.

He was surrounded by women daily. Most of the world thought those women were stunningly beautiful. Though makeup and camerawork could do amazing things for anyone, some of them really *were*.

But despite that, he couldn't remember the last time

he'd wanted to drag someone he'd just met to the nearest flat surface and make love to her in every way known to man. Until now.

Hot and damp with exertion, Bonnie swept her hair off the back of her neck with one hand. Holding it up, she looked so damned sultry, so feminine, every guy around paused to take a second look. She stole his breath, practically stopped his heart.

Drew stepped close. "You do know what you do to me, right?"

She blinked. "Excuse me?"

He let his stare answer, unable to look away from her full, pouty lips, her soft shoulders, and then at the green fabric molding the delicate curves of her body. The thin material did sinful things to the slopes of her breasts, outlining her pert nipples. No way was she wearing anything underneath, and he knew the brush of his lips there would feel *so* good—to both of them.

It had been a long time since he'd had his mouth on a woman. Too long. And he was suddenly starving, desperate for a taste.

"Stop," she ordered, her voice breathy and weak.

"Stop what?"

"Stop looking at me like…"

"Like I want you?"

She sucked in an audible breath. From a few inches away, he saw her pinken, as if all the blood in her body had gone to her skin to ready it for sensory input: his touch, his kiss, his tongue. He would be more than happy to give it to her. All that, and more.

"You can't," she whispered, dropping her hair.

"Can't want you, or can't have you?"

"Either. Both. I don't know."

"Which is it?"

She shook her head slowly. "Are you serious?"

"More serious than you can imagine."

"But I'm not…"

"Exactly," he said, knowing what she was going to say. "You're nothing like the women I know and work with."

"Right."

"Which, believe me, is a very good thing." Seeing her skepticism, he stepped closer. He slid one foot between hers, so their thighs tangled together as they moved to a slower, torchy song. Dropping one hand onto her hip, he stroked her lightly, wanting to fill both hands with those curves as he thrust into her.

"You are so far out of my league," she insisted, as if she really didn't know she was beyond beautiful and so sexy she would catch the attention of any man on earth.

"I can't help who I'm attracted to, Bonnie. Can you?"

She slowly shook her head, whispering, "No. And believe me, I've been trying."

"Why?" he asked, knowing instinctively what she meant. She'd been trying to hide her attraction to him.

"Because of who we are and where we are and how crazy the very idea of it is."

"Why is it crazy to want someone who you can't stop thinking about? Because I can't, you know. Can't stop thinking about you, picturing being with you." He intentionally brushed against her, knowing she had to feel the physical effect she had on him. She quivered in his arms and he whispered, "I want you, Bonnie. I want to make love to you."

She still hesitated, looking up at him with confusion, wonder. Snagging her bottom lip between her teeth, she was racked with indecision, he could see it in her eyes. She didn't know what to think; wasn't sure she could believe him. But chemistry didn't lie, and the desire between them was so thick he could bathe in it.

"If I can't have you, please say so. Otherwise I'm just going to keep thinking about it. If you're involved with someone else, or you don't feel the same way, tell me now."

"I'm not…" She half lowered her lashes. "…and I do."

He leaned in, breathing in the warm, spicy essence of her thick honey-gold hair. Catching a handful of it—soft, so incredibly soft—he held her tightly against his body, each of her curves softening in welcome to his angles. They lined up perfectly, top to bottom, as if they'd been made for each other. They just matched.

She shivered once, then softened, melted. Said yes, without saying a word.

"I know you came to my room thinking I was some big-bad-movie-star," he told her, wanting to get rid of any misconceptions before they took one more step.

"You are some big-bad-movie-star."

"Not bad," he promised. "At heart, I'm the guy who likes Disney movies and animals and would have cared about those little birds you were trying to protect last spring."

She tilted her head back and looked up at him. "Truly?"

"Yes. I'm just a small-town guy from Oregon who got really lucky and caught the eye of a director who was shooting a TV pilot in my hometown. I live in California now because I work there. But that *so* does not define who I really am."

He knew it sounded like a line, and wondered if she'd

believe it, but it was the truth. His address might have changed since he got his big break seven years ago. But he hadn't.

"No, you don't seem to be that type. Giving up your room, showing up here, putting up with this crowd… you really are a nice guy, aren't you?" She wasn't the first one to express surprise at that. It came with the territory.

"The friends I hang out with are old college buddies, not actors. And you don't see me in tabloids with actresses on my arms because the last time I dated one was in high school when I went out with the leading lady from *The Music Man*."

"You're not involved with anyone now?"

"No. I was until about a year ago, but since we broke up, I haven't had time to even think of meeting anyone for a drink."

A tiny smile appeared. "You and I had a drink together."

He squeezed her. "Does that count as our first date, then?"

Laughing lightly, she said, "A date? Do movie stars date?"

"They do if they want to show a woman she means more than a notch on a headboard." He tightened his hold on her hips. "I'm not looking to notch my headboard. If I wanted that, I could nod at Miss French Maid or someone like her."

She moved her mouth close to his neck, so that her warm exhalations brushed his throat. Then even closer, until it was her soft lips he felt there. "What are you looking for?"

"I'm not sure. A night with you? Or a thousand nights

with you? Whatever we want to do together between those nights?"

Bonnie shuddered against him, so he could feel the V of her thighs against his leg. A warm, womanly scent of desire arose from her, and her eyes were suddenly smoky with wanting as she looked up at him. "I think that first night is pretty close. As close as the last room in the east wing of the inn."

His room. "You're sure?"

"Oh, yes. I've wanted you since I met you. I just didn't think there was any way you could feel the same way."

"I do," he insisted. "Can we get out of here, now?"

She nodded, and without another word, they stopped dancing and headed for the exit. Her fingers laced in his, they crossed the gauntlet of cooing females and moviegoing males.

"You're leaving?" asked Amanda, the bride, who had just said good-night to another departing guest.

"Yes," Drew said. "Bonnie's going to make sure I get to my door."

Bonnie smiled at her sister-in-law, her eyes shining brightly. "Yep, you can count on me to do my duty."

Saying good-night, they stepped outside. The very second the door slid closed behind them, Drew had her in his arms. She melted against him, lifting her mouth for his kiss, parting her lips invitingly. Their tongues met and danced a slow tango, deep and sultry, and he knew their first time would be just like that. Hot and deep and slow.

"I want you so badly I could take you right here against the building," he admitted as he ended the kiss and scraped his mouth along her jaw.

"Ditto," she said with a soft moan. "But I want a lot of

privacy because I have absolutely no intention of being quiet or *nice* tonight."

"Mmm. Sounds good. Am I going to meet the wicked Bonnie?"

She looked up at him, her eyes heavy-lidded with desire. "You might be the first person to know the *real* me, Drew. God knows I'm tired of hiding what I really feel, what I truly want."

He knew what she meant. She wanted *him,* just as he wanted her. "Let's go," he said, needing that privacy more and more.

But with the very first step they took out from under the protective covering of the barn awning, they were hit with a light, misty rain. Her thin dress was no match for it, and instantly began to stick to her skin. Which looked sexy as hell, but couldn't feel very comfortable.

"Uh-oh," she said, then glanced back into the party. "I left my umbrella hanging on the coatrack. I'll go…"

No way did he want her walking back in there for any other guy to see the way that damp green material clung to her breasts, outlining the most perfect nipples he'd ever seen. His mouth was already watering for a taste.

"Let me," he whispered, meaning a lot more than just going to get her umbrella. But that would do for a start.

"Sure you can be without your babysitter?"

"I'm a big boy."

The look she gave him was wicked…lascivious. As if she were really looking forward to finding out.

"Hold that thought," he ordered.

"Deal. The umbrella's bright red, you can't miss it."

Nodding, he headed back inside, hoping to escape unnoticed to the coatrack. He should have known better, however. Every two feet, somebody stopped him to tell him how much they liked his movies or ask what he was doing in town.

It was a good ten minutes before he got back outside, an apology on his lips. "I'm so sorry, I…"

His words trailed off when he realized he was talking to air. Bonnie wasn't there. He peered into the shadows on either side of the door, seeing nothing.

"Damn."

He just couldn't believe it. She'd changed her mind, gotten cold feet. Yeah, they were moving pretty fast, but she wanted him, he knew that. He just wouldn't ever have imagined she would leave without talking to him about it first.

Frustrated, wondering how he could get her room number at this time of night, he suddenly caught sight of something several feet way. A splash of color lay in some rocks that led down a garden pathway. The color was familiar, and he walked over, growing a bit more uneasy with every step he took. When he reached it, bent down and saw that it was, indeed, a piece of Bonnie's dress, his uneasiness grew to concern.

When he saw its jagged edge, proof that it had been torn, his concern grew to worry. But he didn't really panic until he saw what was lying beside it: a sexy, high-heeled shoe.

Maybe the dress could have caught on the bushes by accident, but no way did the woman go walking off into the night without a shoe.

Which, he feared, meant she hadn't *voluntarily* walked off at all. She'd been taken.

4

BONNIE COULDN'T BELIEVE IT. She'd been on the verge of going back to the room of the sexiest man she'd ever met in her life to have wild sex…and she got kidnapped. Well, not *technically* kidnapped—she hadn't been thrown into the trunk of a car and driven far away—but she was definitely being kept against her will. Talk about bad luck.

"Let me out!" she ordered, pounding her fist against the door, still shocked by what had just happened.

One minute, she'd been waiting for Drew to come back with her umbrella. The next, she'd heard a woman's voice calling for help from the side of the barn. Worrying some mildly intoxicated party guest had fallen and couldn't get up, she'd headed toward the woman, and found herself grabbed by a bushy-haired redhead who outweighed her by a good fifty pounds. The woman had stuck something against her back, told Bonnie she had a gun, then marched her down a hill, over a tiny footbridge and right into this storage shed. Where she'd promptly locked Bonnie in.

It could have been worse, she supposed. Her assailant could have actually used the gun—*if* she'd really had one.

Something told Bonnie there had been no gun, but she hadn't taken any chances. Especially not once she figured out she was dealing with Drew's stalker. Helen Jarvis had made it clear that the only person going back to Drew Ericson's room with him tonight would be her.

On reflection, though, Bonnie had to admit, the woman had been more pathetic than scary. Changing tactics, she said, "Miss Jarvis? Please, just let me out. You know you can't do this. You're going to get into even more trouble."

"You're a home-wrecker!" a muffled voice said from outside.

As a social worker for the city of Pittsburgh, Bonnie worked on a daily basis with people who had mental disorders. So she knew better than to try to challenge the woman's delusions directly. "Keeping someone against their will is against the law. You don't want to get in trouble with the police, do you?"

Silence for a moment. Then, "I'm not keeping you. Just hiding you for a little while."

Bonnie didn't have to ask why. The woman was "hiding" her so she could get Drew alone.

"Now you just stay quiet and somebody will find you in the morning," the woman said.

"The morning? No! You have to let me out now." Coughing, she added, "There are chemicals in here. They're making me sick."

That was a bit of an exaggeration, but she feared it wouldn't be for long. There were lawn chemicals in the shed. It was too dark to see much, but she could certainly smell them. Fertilizer, weed killer, insect repellant, probably all kinds of poisonous stuff that put off fumes. She wasn't sick yet, but she had no doubt she would be if she were stuck in here for hours.

"Hold your breath," the woman said.

"*All* night?"

"Well…I guess I could call and have someone come and let you out after Drew and I leave."

"Leave to go where?"

"Home, of course. To our place in California. We live in a mansion in Beverly Hills with lots of bedrooms for when we start a family."

Oh, boy. This woman was cuckoo for Cocoa Puffs. And while Bonnie still felt sorry for her, she was also really getting annoyed. The burning smell of some kind of chlorine-based chemical was seeping into her nose and she now could make out the scent of gasoline, too.

"Look, you and Drew can leave," she said, trying to play into the woman's fantasy. "I won't get in your way, just please let me out of here."

Her captor didn't answer right away. Bonnie held her breath, hopeful. So far, the woman seemed sadly delusional, but Helen Jarvis didn't act as though she truly wanted to hurt her.

Then the answer came…and her hopes were dashed.

"No. Now I'm going, just try to take a nap or something and someone will let you out soon."

Take a nap? Fall asleep while breathing in gasoline and all these other nasty fumes? Sure. Right. Only if she wanted to risk not waking up.

Now angry again, Bonnie pounded on the door and yelled. But this time, there was no answer, not even the slightest brush of a hand against the outside of the shed. She knew, deep down, that Helen Jarvis was gone, leaving Bonnie trapped.

And nobody knew where she was.

She didn't panic. There were a hundred people in the barn less than thirty yards away. Her entire family, her friends. Surely somebody would hear her if she kept yelling.

Over that music? And the chatter?

"Maybe not. But Drew will be looking."

Unless he decided you changed your mind and ditched him.

Frankly, if she had come back out and found him gone, that's exactly what she would have surmised.

Hell.

She might actually be stuck in here for a couple of hours—at least until the party ended and the noise died down enough for any stragglers to hear her. As soon as the music stopped, she'd start screaming.

But as the fumes grew stronger, and her head grew lighter, another worry blossomed. What if she passed out? If she lost consciousness before she had a chance to make herself heard, she could really be trapped in here overnight.

Leaning toward the seam between door and jamb, she sucked in a breath, grateful for the hint of cool moisture from the fresh air she managed to inhale. Feeling her way along the seam, she found a wider spot farther down, at about knee level. Sinking to the floor, she focused on breathing through that opening, keeping her forehead resting against the door. Her heart was thudding now, her imagination taking her places she didn't want to go.

What if Helen forgot where she'd left her? What if

she ran from the police and never got a chance to tell anyone what she'd done? Or, what if she didn't get what she wanted from Drew—as she certainly would not—and was so angry, she intentionally let Bonnie rot? It was after midnight, on Sunday. The groundskeepers almost certainly would not be working in the morning, especially in this weather. So might she be stuck in here until Monday?

Her eyes had grown slightly accustomed to the shadowy darkness, and she looked around the small, ten-by-ten-foot structure. As she had suspected, bags of dried chemicals were stacked all around her; large containers of liquids with Poison markings, too.

"You can't stay here until Monday," she whispered, reaching for the door handle, jiggling it again, though she knew it was useless. As far as she could tell, Helen Jarvis had apparently put some kind of padlock on the outside. No way was she getting out of here without help.

They'll come looking. In the morning, when she didn't show up for the bridal breakfast, somebody would come looking for her, realize her bed hadn't been slept in and would start a search. So at the very worst, she just had to hold out until 9:00 or 10:00 a.m. Eight hours, tops. "You can do that."

Especially if she had no other choice.

Time seemed to be passing—the music played on—but Bonnie wasn't sure if it had been twenty minutes or an hour. She only knew that each breath she inhaled was a little more labored than the last. Her throat was hurting now, her nose burning, her eyes watering.

"Please," she whispered, "please find me."

She didn't add a name to the plea, but deep down,

she knew who she was talking to. He played a hero in his movies. Now she needed Drew Ericson to be one in real life.

"You're telling me Bonnie was grabbed by some crazy, jealous stalker?" Reese Campbell asked, glowering at Drew.

"I don't know," he said, remaining calm, not giving in to the deep worry that had gripped him from the minute he found Bonnie's shoe. "But can you see your sister just kicking off one of her high heels and traipsing away?"

"No," Reese said.

His wife, Amanda, who had walked outside for some fresh air a minute or two after Drew had found the shoe—then gone in and quietly gotten her husband—jumped in. "We'll call the police. Get everyone at the party to start searching."

Drew thought about it. "Listen, if it is Helen Jarvis, getting a hundred people out here hunting for her could make things worse. If she's panicked, and cornered, she…"

"Might hurt Bonnie?" Reese asked, his jaw rigid.

"She has no record of violence," Drew insisted, trying to keep himself calm. "But there's no point in putting her into a frenzy until we have to. You call the police, I'll call the head of security from the studio—they have pictures of her. Then you and I will start searching until they get here. Maybe we can find Bonnie without setting the woman off."

"All right," Reese said, reaching for his cell phone. "We'll do it your way. For now."

"Yes, we *all* will," said Amanda, glaring at her husband. "I'm searching, too."

Her husband pointed to her costume—a long, ragged

gown. Drew wasn't sure what she was supposed to be. "In that?"

"Just let me run to my room and change." She didn't even wait for him to answer before darting toward the inn, never looking back.

"Check Bonnie's room, just to be sure," Reese called after her.

"Already planning to," she replied, not slowing down.

"I'm sorry as hell about this," Drew said. "I should never have left her alone to go after that damned umbrella."

Reese nodded once, then turned his attention to his phone, talking to the police. Drew took the time to make his own call to the production assistant who'd phoned earlier. Telling him to get security out here, pronto, he then hung up.

"Okay, why don't we split up. You search from here to the west side of the lawn, toward the inn. I'll go to the other side, down toward the road," Drew said. Bending down, he picked up a brown paper bag, weighted with sand. Inside was a battery-operated electric candle, which, when removed from the luminary, produced a decent amount of light.

"Good idea," Reese said, doing the same thing. "Let's meet back here in ten minutes."

"Okay."

Without another word, Drew headed toward the road, skirting the barn. He passed the spot where he'd found Bonnie's shoe, and that ripped scrap of fabric. The grass was damp and slippery beneath his shoes and he half skidded down the slope. Today's rain had lifted the small, gurgling creek and it gushed powerfully beneath the pretty footbridge.

Reaching the wooden crossing, he spotted something, squatted down and shone the candle on the spot.

Footprints. One of which was bare.

His heart racing, he ran across the bridge, scanning wildly for anyplace she could be. None of the guest cabins were on this side of the property, just a few out-buildings, then a stand of woods separating the lawn from the road. He only hoped Helen Jarvis hadn't had a car waiting. If she'd whisked Bonnie off the property, God only knew where she was by now.

Refusing to think that way, he decided to call out, hoping if she was nearby, she'd be able to hear him. "Bonnie? Do you hear me?"

He heard nothing at first, nothing but the gurgle of the creek and the deejay working the party.

"Bonnie?"

A noise. Something thumped. He swung his head around, spying a maintenance shed not twenty feet away. Striding toward it, he hadn't taken more than a few steps when he heard her voice.

"Please help me—is somebody out there?"

"Bonnie!"

He charged to the door, seeing a padlock hooked through the latch. But Helen Jarvis had either been in a hurry, or she'd had some attack of conscience, because the lock wasn't snapped shut. It had kept Bonnie from getting out, but didn't prevent him from opening the door from the outside. As soon as he did, he saw a form crumpled on the floor. "Oh, God, Bonnie!"

"Drew?" she asked, turning her dirty, pale face up to him.

Drew dropped to his knees and pulled her into his arms. "It's okay, I've got you," he said, holding her tight, saying a little mental prayer of thanks that she didn't seem hurt.

Her face was buried in his neck, but he felt the sting of moisture from recently shed tears. She coughed weakly, her chest rattling. The air in the shed reeked of chemicals. His eyes stung after mere seconds, and she'd been trapped for almost an hour.

"We've got to get you outside," he said, rising to his feet, lifting her as he went. Holding her tightly in his arms, he stepped back out into the clear night.

She sucked in a few deep, grateful breaths. Keeping her arms curled around his neck, she stayed cuddled against him, as if not wanting to let go. Which was just fine. He had no intention of putting her down anytime soon. He wanted to keep her right where she was, safe in his embrace.

Though he needed to get her back up the hill so her brother would know she was all right, Drew gave her a minute to even out her breathing. Pressing soft kisses onto her temple, he whispered, "You're okay, it's over," again and again.

Finally she took a last deep, cleansing breath, then murmured, "How did you find me?"

"I saw your shoe on the ground, and a piece of your dress."

A pout tugged at her beautiful lips. "She made me rip my dress? I worked so hard on it."

"I know you did, sweetheart, and I'm so sorry." Already fairly certain he knew the answer, he asked, "Who took you? Was it a middle-aged woman with red hair?"

Bonnie nodded. "She told me she was Helen Jarvis. She saw me as some kind of floozy trying to steal 'her' man and was trying to get me out of the way."

His whole body tensed, his teeth clenching so hard he was surprised they didn't crack. "This has gone far enough!"

She ran the tips of her fingers up the tight cords of muscle in his neck. "I'm okay. She didn't hurt me and said she'd send someone back to find me."

He wasn't mollified. "Before or after you choked on fumes?"

Sighing, she admitted, "Yeah, that had me worried, too."

He squeezed her a little tighter. "I'm so sorry, Bonnie. Please forgive me. I can't believe you were exposed to that kind of danger because of me."

She shook her head. "I wasn't exposed to that kind of danger because of you—it was all because a mentally unstable woman took me. It is *not* your fault."

Maybe, but she wouldn't have drawn the attention of Helen Jarvis if it weren't for him. He'd brought one of the darkest parts of his crazy, frenetic world into the bright, happy sphere of this woman's, and couldn't feel much worse about that if he'd hurt her himself. "Thanks," he muttered. "But I think we both know my line of work invites this kind of bullshit. I should never have…"

She stared into his eyes. "Should never have what? Invited me to your room? Told me you wanted me?"

He didn't answer. Because, though that's what he meant, he just couldn't say it out loud. Deep down, he couldn't regret trying to make something happen with Bonnie. After just one kiss, he already knew she was someone special. Someone he wanted to spend a lot more time with. *One night? A thousand nights?*

"Don't you back out on me now, hotshot," she ordered. "If you think this gets you off the hook and you don't have to give me tonight or a thousand nights and everything that comes between them, you've got another think coming."

Smiling faintly as she echoed his thoughts, and his earlier words, he said, "Are you sure about that?"

She lifted her face, until her lips were a scant inch from his own, her sweet breath brushing his face, the warm scent of her perfume filling the night air, chasing away any remnants of the fumes. "I'm very sure," she whispered.

Then Bonnie removed that inch of space, brushing her mouth gently against his in a kiss that was as sweet as their first one had been passionate. Her mouth was soft and yielding. Tender.

He'd kissed many women in movies, and more than a few in real life. But he'd never quite gotten just how thrilling a simple kiss could be, until it was Bonnie Campbell's mouth, her hands around his neck, her breaths he shared, her soft hair brushing his face, her beautiful body enfolded in his arms.

Moaning a little, she tilted her head, parting her lips. Their tongues slid together in a soft exploration, slow and lazy. Against him, her heart pounded. His own sped up its pace, too. The beats seemed to find one another, to come together in unison as one hard, demanding thud.

But they were outside, and that misty rain was beginning to fall again. Her brother was worried sick about her. And a crazy woman who'd kidnapped her could still be lurking nearby. So, filled with regret, he ended the kiss.

Bonnie smiled lazily. "I liked that."

"Me, too."

"I want a lot more of those."

"Tonight?" he asked, making absolutely sure she hadn't had a change of heart.

"For a start."

Yeah. For a start. That sounded just fine to him.

As the rain started falling a little harder, Drew turned and walked back toward the footbridge. He trod carefully over it, and just as carefully up the hill, holding her still. She insisted she was okay and that he could put her down, but frankly, he wasn't ready to let her out of his arms.

Once they got back to the barn, he immediately looked for her brother, but didn't see him. He did, however, see the distinctive blue twirl of police lights up by the inn, as well as a number of people outside talking.

Heading that way, he let Bonnie down when Reese and Amanda appeared from within the crowd, spotted them and hurried over.

"Bonnie! Are you okay?" Reese asked, grabbing her and pulling her in for a tight hug.

"I'm fine. Just got locked in a storage shed."

Drew noticed she downplayed the incident, not wanting her brother to know just how dangerous the situation could have become had she been left there much longer.

"Well, it's over now, you're safe," said Amanda. "And that crazy woman is never going to bother you again."

Drew turned his attention to the bride, hearing a note of certainty in her voice. "They caught her?"

Amanda snagged her bottom lip between her teeth, slowly shaking her head. "Not exactly."

Reese, who had let Bonnie go, dropped an arm across his wife's shoulders. "Manda did."

Bonnie gasped and Drew raised a shocked brow.

"Apparently your admirer didn't do her research. She didn't know you'd moved out of the bridal suite," Amanda explained.

Drew, remembering that Amanda had been going back to the room to change, immediately understood. "Did she hurt you?"

Reese barked a laugh. "Uh, that'd be the other way around."

Amanda smirked. "And you thought I didn't need to take those kickboxing classes."

"Just remind me to never grab for you in the dark," Reese said. Then, with a "duh" look on his face, said, "Wait. Scratch that. What the hell am I thinking? It is our wedding night."

"One of the most exciting on record," she said with a laugh.

Turning to Bonnie and Drew, Reese explained, "The woman jumped out at her and my blushing bride starting swinging."

"It was purely reflex," Amanda said, sounding sheepish about having brawled on her wedding night. "She surprised me."

"Well, it should be no surprise to anyone that she's handcuffed in the back of a police car." His laughter fading, Reese sounded much more serious as he said, "She's facing charges for a lot more than stalking now. Kidnapping, assault and breaking and entering, to start with."

Good. If there was any justice in the world, the woman would be forced to get treatment for her mental issues. And if she didn't, prison was no more than she deserved for what could have happened to Bonnie if she'd been left to breathe in those chemicals all night long.

"The police are going to want to interview you, Bonnie," Amanda said. "We should let them know you're okay."

Bonnie nodded. "I am. Thanks to Drew." She smiled up at him. "I guess you really are a hero."

"Hardly."

"Well, you are in my book," she insisted. Then she rose on tiptoe and brushed a kiss across his cheek. Whispering so she wouldn't be overheard by her brother and his wife, she added, "And I'm looking forward to giving you a hero's welcome just as soon as I'm finished with the police."

5

Bonnie spent a half hour talking to the police before they left, taking a crying Helen Jarvis with them. Despite what she'd done, Bonnie felt a little sorry for the woman, who obviously had the faculties to realize she was in serious trouble. In fact, as soon as she'd been told she was being arrested, she'd started apologizing, saying she knew she'd crossed the line, she just wanted Drew so much she didn't know what else to do. She knew right from wrong, knew she had no real relationship with Drew.

Which, as a slightly more jaded Amanda pointed out, had probably shot any insanity defense.

It was well after 2:00 a.m. by the time they said their good-nights. They'd tried to leave earlier, but every time another person came back to the inn from the party down at the barn, the story had to be repeated and retold, and Bonnie had to assure yet another friend or family member that she was just fine.

Oh, and Drew had to stand there and be cooed and gushed over and called a hero again.

Finally, though, they managed to slip away. Fortunately Bonnie's room was just down the hall from Drew's, so she didn't think they raised too many eyebrows by walking off together. Frankly, though, even if they had, she didn't care. She'd been waiting for this—waiting to kiss him again, touch him, feel him, for hours.

They went by unspoken agreement to his room. Unlocking the door, he gestured for her to go in, then followed.

Alone with him at last, Bonnie waited for something—a flash of unease, of embarrassment, of awkwardness. But there was nothing. Just certainty of what she was doing, what she wanted. And him, watching her from a few feet away, staring at her like he wanted to memorize her every feature.

"You sure you're okay?" he asked. "Your throat's not sore?"

"I'm fine," she assured him.

Bonnie fell silent as he came closer, his body radiating warmth. When he was just a few inches away, she swayed toward him, drawn by his heat, his smell and the hunger in those clear blue eyes.

He smiled slowly in the semidarkness. "You take my breath away."

Before she realized his intention, he'd caught her in his arms, drawing her against his body. She wrapped her arms around his waist and tilted her head back, silently urging him to close that final few inch gap and kiss her.

She didn't have long to wait. In a moment shorter than a heartbeat his lips were on hers, and she sighed. His kiss was all she remembered, and all she imagined. Deep and wet and powerful. He slid the palms of his hands up and down on her back, then around to cup her arms, then finally down to wrap his fingers in hers.

"I am so glad I met you, Drew," she whispered as he

moved his lips to kiss her jaw. "Really met you this time, rather than just crossing paths, like we did six months ago."

"If we had really met six months ago," he told her, "we'd already have a hundred and eighty nights like this behind us."

He sounded so sure of it, as if he already knew this— tonight—wasn't possibly going to be enough for either of them. "I'd know exactly how to touch you," he whispered, kissing her earlobe, then her nape. "Where to kiss you, when to go slow and when to go wild."

Bonnie groaned, his words turning her on as much as his touch. "You're a fast learner," she told him, almost whimpering as he scraped the palm of his hand all the way down her arm, stroking so lightly she almost couldn't feel the connection of skin on skin. The barely there caress built her anticipation, leaving her wondering where he would touch next. Where that hand would go, which part of her body he'd kiss or taste.

Bonnie's breath came faster as Drew moved his fingers to her neck and gently began stroking the tender skin beneath her ear. Slowly, so slowly it nearly drove her insane, he trailed the tips of his fingers across her collarbone, then down to the deep V in the front of her dress. Pressing his mouth to her nape, he deftly tugged one sleeve down off her shoulder.

"Mmm," she moaned, wanting more. So much more. His fingers slipped down over the curve of her breast, teasing, tempting. She arched toward him. "Yes, there."

"We've got plenty of time."

She saw his smile just before he captured her mouth in another kiss. She shivered, from the pleasure, from the relief of giving in to arousal that had pounded inside her all evening. From pure, utter want.

"I want you more than I've ever wanting anything," he whispered against her lips as he drew her tighter in his arms.

Bonnie didn't say a word as he lifted her hands up to his mouth and pressed kisses on her fingers, slowly, with the patience of Job. She had the feeling he would be just this slow, just this deliberate, with every single step tonight. Every kiss would be a celebration, each stroke an exploration.

She could hardly wait.

"Are you cold?" he asked.

The room *was* cool with the October night air, but Bonnie didn't think she'd ever felt more hot. Her clothes stuck to her, annoying her sensitive flesh, and she nearly purred as Drew slid her dress from her other shoulder, pushing it to the floor until she stood there, wearing nothing but a tiny pair of panties.

"I'm just fine," she finally said, in answer to his question.

"You're much more than fine," he whispered as he looked down at her.

Bonnie felt no embarrassment as his eyes traveled over her body. The pure appreciation—the desire—was enough to give her a great deal of confidence. She saw the pulse in his temple pound and watched him part his lips and draw in a deep breath. Her skin tingled in reaction and she felt her nipples grow even harder under his gaze. As if he couldn't resist, he bent and pressed his mouth to the top curve of her breast.

"More," she begged.

He took his time, slowly kissing his way down her breast to the hard, sensitive tip. Even then, he didn't suckle her right away, as she wanted. Instead he brushed his lips across her, back and forth, so patient, so deliberate.

"Please!"

Only when she revealed her desperation did he comply, covering her nipple with his mouth and sucking deeply.

"God, yes," she groaned, twining her hands in his thick, black hair. She moaned. Her knees weakened.

Realizing it, Drew slid an arm around her waist, holding her up, fully supporting her weight. She was helpless to resist as he paid careful attention to both breasts. And she didn't even try to refuse when he lifted her into his arms and carried her over to the turned-down bed.

Placing her down upon it, Drew stood beside her and began to strip out of his clothes. When he lifted his shirt over his head and tossed it away, she hissed. She hadn't imagined it—the man did have the most perfect male body she had ever seen.

"You really shouldn't answer the door to your hotel room dressed only in a towel," she said with a throaty, hungry chuckle. "You have no idea of your effect on women. It can give them the wildest ideas."

"I like your wild ideas," he told her.

His smile gleamed in the near-darkness as he finished stripping off his clothes. For a moment, she simply had to stare at him, a gasp catching in the back of her throat at that proud, hard shaft rising from between his legs.

It had been a long time since she'd been with a man. And she'd never been with a man built like *him*. Yet she didn't feel the slightest tinge of worry. Instead she was flooded with a fresh river of lust.

They'd fit. Oh, yes, they would fit.

Before tossing his pants aside, Drew reached into the

pocket and drew out a condom. She didn't ask where he got it, just glad he had it. "Come here," she ordered.

He knelt on the bed, letting her reach up, put her arms around his neck and draw him down toward her. She couldn't stop touching him, running her hands across all that slick male skin. It amazed her that his flesh could feel so warm and pliant, yet cover the hard, rippling muscles of a perfectly toned male body. Her fingertips felt electrified, and her excitement grew until she could hear nothing but the pounding of her own heart pumping hot blood through her veins.

Restless, she shifted her legs, wrapping them around his strong, heavier one, tugging him close. Through the thin film of her panties she felt his thick erection, and her body's own rush of answering moisture.

Drew reached for the tiny swatch of fabric and began to tug it down her legs, his touch burning a path on her skin. Then he moved his hand back up, reaching for the tuft of curls over her sex. Sliding one finger between the folds of her body, he groaned, as if driven a little more crazy to find her so wet, so hot, so ready. His thumb dropped onto her clit and he toyed with it, even as he slid one finger into her.

"More," she ordered. "Please, Drew, I want you inside me. Make love to me."

"Gladly."

After donning the condom, he moved over her, and she parted her legs in welcome. She wrapped her arms around his neck, drawing him down for a deep, wet kiss. As he began to ease into her, Bonnie arched up, greedy for more, wondering how the man was capable of such restraint. But he seemed determined to keep it slow, to draw out every sensation, every emotion. She was almost sobbing both with how good it felt, and how desperate she was for even more.

"Please," she whispered.

And finally, he complied, driving in all the way, deep and hard. There was no pain, she was completely ready for him, her softness yielding instantly to him. Bonnie believed she'd never felt anything more delicious in her life. She closed her eyes, determined to savor every deep sensation. She loved the heaviness of his body on hers, the roughness of his hair on her skin, the smell of his sweat, and the steady strokes which filled her.

There were no more words as the rhythm caught them and Bonnie gave herself over to it. Lost in sensation, she couldn't form another coherent thought as he filled her again and again until she cried out in delight, and he answered with a final powerful thrust and a groan.

Afterward, she lay beside him, both of them gasping for breath. Her heart was pounding like crazy, as if she'd run a marathon. She knew it was more than the physical exertion. Emotionally, she'd had a complete workout.

Drew kept an arm across her, holding her tightly against his body, as if loath to let her go. Finally their breathing slowed, the heart rates calmed, stillness descended. But he didn't seem finished. He kept touching her, caressing her, keeping her senses on alert, the waves of pleasure threatening to roll over her again.

Drew Ericson was the kind of lover women dreamed of, but seldom ever had. He was totally and completely attentive, thoroughly in the moment, utterly in tune with his senses and her own responses. Honestly, she didn't know if she would ever get enough of him. Considering she liked him so much already, admired him, enjoyed being with him and now was rapidly growing addicted to his lovemaking, she greatly feared he was going to be one habit that would be very hard to break.

As if he'd read her thoughts, and was thinking the same thing, Drew mused, "One night? Or a thousand nights?"

"I don't know," she replied. "What do you think?"

He moved his mouth to hers, kissing her sweetly, softly, so tender and erotic at the same time. When he looked at her, his blue eyes gleamed. He made no effort to hide the raw emotion.

"What I think, in my gut, my intuition and in the very bottom of my heart, Bonnie Campbell, is that *ten thousand* nights is never going to be enough for us." He moved his mouth toward hers, and just before covering it in a kiss, added, "But it'll do for a start."

* * * * *

Halfway There

1

SERVING AS HER BEST friend Amanda's maid of honor, Jocelyn—Jazz—Wilkes knew exactly what her job entailed.

She was in charge of stuff like making sure the bride's veil was straight, or holding her dress up and out of the way if she had to pee. She'd straightened Amanda's train, held the bouquet during the exchange of rings, handed the bride a tissue when she started to cry during the groom's heartfelt recitation of the vows.

She'd seen to it that the flower girl didn't pick her nose throughout the ceremony, and, of course, she had a getaway car parked out back in case the bride got cold feet at the last minute—which, knowing how madly in love Amanda was with her groom, she doubted. In general, she'd been responsible for handling all the gal-pal stuff only the best of friends could ever depend on each other for.

She'd taken this maid of honor stuff seriously from day one. There wasn't a ribbon she hadn't tied, or a shower invitation she hadn't written or a dress fitting she hadn't attended.

Never having failed at anything—and loving

Amanda like the sister she'd never had—Jazz had been determined to do the job right. She'd been Thelma to Amanda's Louise for years, the two of them having become best friends when they'd realized they were so much alike—two strong females working in a male dominated industry. There was nothing she wouldn't do for the other woman.

Which was why she now dutifully stood with all the other horny single females, watching as the bouquet came sailing out of Amanda's hands, over her head, to the crowd waiting at the base of the staircase. Though Jazz was completely apathetic about it, maids of honor were all about tradition, and Jazz was gonna go down in history as the kick-assingest maid of honor ever.

"Outta my way, ladies!"

"It's mine!"

Ignoring the other women leaping into the air like brightly colored jack-in-the-boxes, Jazz remained quietly in her little section of floor space. She didn't lunge for the bouquet, didn't elbow anybody or do her impersonation of roller derby princess to get at it. Nor, however, did she leap out of the line of fire to avoid it.

She was there, a part of things, even if, frankly, in her opinion, the whole bouquet-toss was a silly tradition. She couldn't care less whether she caught the thing or not. She just had to do her bit and collect her green *Participant* ribbon.

It appeared right away that the green ribbon was the only one she'd be getting in this particular contest. The blue one appeared to be heading toward Abby, Amanda's sister, who, though she'd once seemed to have a major stick up her ass, was actually a pretty decent chick. She hadn't been at all bitchy about not having been chosen as maid of honor, despite being Amanda's only sibling.

And she'd done a great job as wedding planner. She'd even been a lot of fun at Manda's bachelorette party, letting down her hair and dancing her butt off with the rest of them.

Right now, though, Abby didn't look happy. In fact, as the bouquet came barreling toward her face, she looked like someone about to be swarmed by bees. That *hell-no* expression gave a one-second warning to her next move, so it really came as no surprise when Abby swung at the bouquet, flinging it away from herself like it was contaminated with cooties.

Interesting. Especially since she was engaged to be married to a hunk of stiff lawyer who stood watching the event from a few yards away.

Jazz glanced over at said lawyer, saw the shock—maybe even a flash of hurt—in his face, and realized Abby was gonna have some 'splaining to do. Considering both sets of parents were glowering, it would be a lot of 'splaining. Jazz was very happy not to be in that woman's shoes at the moment.

"Okay, everyone, let's make way for the guys to try for the garter!" someone called.

Checking the "stand there and pretend you give a crap about a bunch of flowers" thing off her mental list, Jazz drifted toward the ballroom, where the reception had been held. She intended to make a beeline for the open bar. Having laid off the alcohol today, wanting to be sharp and *on* for all her jazzy M.O.H. duties, she felt entitled to a little R & R—or Jack and Coke—now that the reception was winding down.

While the women squeezed away to make room for the men, who were sucked into the open space like dust bunnies into a vacuum, she again took stock of all the single guys present. She'd been on the lookout since last night, at the rehearsal, for an appropriate wedding flirtation candidate, but still hadn't found anyone who caught her interest.

As maid of honor, she would normally have first looked to the best man, but considering he was Reese's teenage brother, that was a no-go. But the other grooms-men were all single, as far as she knew. And there were lots of Campbell cousins and guys who worked for Reese at the brewery, not to mention some sexy young things from the airport where she and Amanda worked.

Funny thing was, none of them really rang her bell. The very cocky groomsman, Tom, who Amanda had warned her about, looked like a gigolo and would prob-ably have to be handled with venereal-disease-proof kid gloves. One of the other ushers was already drunk and sloppy, another appeared totally infatuated with one of Reese's many sisters. The guys from the airport were too familiar, the ones from the brewery too cozy with the Campbell family to hit up the bride's best friend.

There was, of course, one other option.

Nope. Not going there. Don't even think about it.

No, she couldn't let her thoughts go in that direc-tion, wouldn't allow herself to consider *him*. Blake Marshall.

The fact that the man had been on her mind so much was *completely* incidental. Because he was not her type. The two of them had about as much chance of hooking up as a stallion did with a beaver. *Don't think stallions and beavers. Especially not when you're thinking about him.*

She took in a deep, cleansing breath, acknowledging for the thousandth time that there was no way she was going to make a play for a guy who couldn't stand her.

Not even one she'd been having the most intense dreams about.

Not just sex dreams, either. Lately she'd been having strange, unusually sweet, romantic dreams about him, too.

Stop! If anything, those dreams just emphasized how wrong he was for her. Because romance hadn't been part of her repertoire for a long time. Not since she'd had her heart crushed under the heels of a couple of really heartless men.

"Hello, Jocelyn."

Closing her eyes briefly, she cringed, not even having to turn around to see who had spoken. She knew that voice. Knew that snobby tone. Knew the only person who refused to call her by her nickname. Knew that I'm-such-a-gentleman-nothing-you-can-do-will-ever-upset-me attitude.

It was her nemesis, the bane of her daily existence at O'Hare. The guy who could make her feel like something that had crawled out of the bottom of a garbage pit with one single, disapproving look. The guy she loved to hate and lived to shock. The one who was *so* not her type.

And who she couldn't stop thinking about. Fantasizing about. Dreaming about.

"Blake Marshall," she drawled, slowly turning around, forcing a casual smile to her face. "Fancy seeing you here."

Of course, she'd already seen him—he'd been around all day. Her stupid subconscious had probably made her walk in this direction.

"Nice wedding," he said.

"Very."

Inane, but about as much as she could manage right

now, until she figured out what else to say to Mr. Blake Marshall.

For some reason, Amanda had always really liked the guy. Jazz's first opinion of him, on the other hand, had been that he was a major pain in the ass. A drop-dead gorgeous one, yes, she'd always conceded that. But beyond his striking, boy-next-door good looks, she hadn't figured the man had much else to offer.

He was a customer relations manager, for heaven's sake, a yes-man who kissed corporate ass at the airport all day, calming angry passengers and smoothing over P.R. nightmares. He excelled at making nice and was so damned proper all the time, she'd sometimes been tempted to flash him just to see if he'd at least take a second look.

Only, lately, she was having a hard time remembering what she didn't like about him. And she was finding it much too easy to think about what she did.

"No luck with the bouquet, I see," he murmured, obviously having noticed that she'd participated in the so-not-Jazz-like event.

"Nope." Some wicked streak that always made her try to shock him had her adding, "Guess I'm just destined to sleep around rather than ever getting married."

"How fortunate for all the men in Chicago."

He said it so nicely, so evenly, she couldn't quite decide whether he was merely making conversation or had just totally insulted her. There was a hint of a smile on those really nice male lips, but whether it was because he almost always smiled or had just backhandedly called her a slut was anyone's guess.

"Why aren't you out there with all the other nerds trying to get a chance to cop a free feel on the blonde who caught the bouquet?"

Staring down at her, his handsome face absolutely expressionless, he replied, "I'm afraid she's not my type."

"Oh, 'cause she's female?"

Nothing. Not even the slightest flinch. The guy was uninsultable. Damn, that drove her nuts.

And, damn, why couldn't she bite her tongue? She just didn't seem to have a single bit of self-control around this man.

"She's a little too…blonde for my tastes."

She thought his gaze might have shifted to her own short, jet-black hair, but figured she had imagined it. Blake Marshall didn't like one single thing about her, she knew that much. Maybe that was why she always tried to get under his skin.

Blake Marshall. Even his name drove her nuts. It was a soap opera character name for God's sake. Just because he had the looks to match didn't make it any more acceptable. How could any guy be so damned perfect?

"Amanda and Reese seem like a great couple," he said, glancing out toward the stairway, where Reese was doing a sexy job of removing the garter from Manda's thigh.

"They are," she admitted with a faint smile. "Reese is a good guy. I think he might actually deserve her."

"I don't know him well, but he seems to make her happy."

"They're crazy about each other."

"I can tell."

Strange. She was having something resembling a normal conversation with Blake Marshall and wasn't yet tempted to do something totally inappropriate, if only to shock the man.

This simply wouldn't do.

"Are you enjoying yourself?" he asked, so polite, so proper, so frigging respectable.

"I was, but I'm not right at the moment," she admitted. Then, unable to help herself, added, "I can't seem to find the right lay for tonight."

His pleasant smile might have tightened the tiniest bit, the green eyes may have narrowed a smidge. Beyond that, nada. "Well, good luck with that."

"Thanks." Finally feeling like she'd made a teensy, weensy dent in his untarnished armor, she said, "Got any suggestions?"

"For?"

"For the traditional post-wedding hookup."

"Oh, is that a tradition, along with throwing birdseed and tying cans to the back of the groom's bumper?"

She shrugged. "It is in my book."

"Your book, huh?"

"What, you think just because I sling a hammer, I can't read?"

"No. I just think you're getting your books from the wrong library."

He sounded serious, not cool and snobby, as he usually did. That gave her pause for a second, and she had to wonder why he seemed to give a damn about anything she did, considering he didn't like her.

Then again, it was the wedding day of a mutual friend. If they couldn't call a truce today, they didn't deserve to be here.

"Want a drink? I was just about to have one to celebrate reaching the end of my maid of honor duties without any major incidents."

One brow lifted over a dark green eye, as if he didn't entirely trust her motives. Well, he did have reason. She had gone out of her way to annoy him whenever possible during the three years they'd worked together at the airport.

Amanda had once accused her of being Lucy to Blake's Charlie Brown. Like she delighted in antagonizing him because she secretly had a crush on the man.

Jazz had snorted with laughter at the time. Now, though? Well, she wasn't laughing anymore.

"Come on, let's call a truce today," she urged. "For Amanda's sake."

"A truce? I wasn't aware we were at war."

She snorted. "Gimme a break, you hate my guts."

That was the first thing she'd said that truly seemed to take him by surprise. His mouth fell open for a quick, shocked moment. Then he snapped it shut, slowly shaking his head. "You're wrong. You couldn't possibly be more wrong."

Jazz hesitated, hearing a note of sincerity there that genuinely surprised her. She'd been so sure this man couldn't stand her, yet his tone and his words said otherwise.

Maybe she'd been transferring her own feelings onto him.

Liar.

She had to concede, that wasn't it. She didn't hate Blake Marshall, not at all. He drove her absolutely crazy and managed to make her feel small with a single look, but she couldn't even pretend to dislike him anymore. In fact, she greatly feared Amanda was right. She did like him a little too much. On one particular occasion, she'd found him to be the most warm, sympathetic person she knew.

It had been at the airport several months ago. She'd been working late, alone in the hangar, and had looked up to see Blake there, watching her. He'd had such a look of sympathy and concern on his face, she'd immediately known something was wrong.

He'd told her the truth—one of her brothers, Danny, a Navy pilot stationed in the Middle East, was missing. Her own family didn't even know yet. The media had gotten wind of the story and contacted the airport, since Danny had worked for one of the major airlines before deciding to return to active duty.

Jazz's world had frozen in that moment. She knew she had to get to her parents' place, to stop her family from finding out from a stranger, yet she'd felt incapable of movement.

Blake had been right there, taking her in his arms, letting her sob and be weak and terrified for a few minutes. He'd said all the right things, given her strength and hope, then had insisted on driving her home.

Danny had ended up being fine. But on that night, when she'd been afraid she'd lost someone she dearly loved, Blake Marshall had been the one to hold her and keep the terror at bay. She'd allowed herself to forget how that had felt, how *he* had felt, holding her so tightly in his arms.

Now she remembered.

So, no. She didn't hate him. They might have gone back to their snarky relationship, but deep down, she'd known from that night on that he was one of the good guys. Even if he still drove her nuts.

Come on, you know it's more than that.

Maybe. It was at least possible that she found him attractive, but that didn't mean she would do anything about it. Because she knew he couldn't stand her.

Yet today, she found herself wanting to let down her

guard a little, relax and see if she could rediscover the man who'd held her in a rare moment of weakness. The man whose shoulders had been so incredibly broad, whose arms had been so very strong.

The man she liked. The man she dreamed of.

Licking her lips, she cast a quick, surreptitious look over his suit-clad form, noting again that the guy might have the mind of an executive, but he had the body of a porn star. All lean hips and broad chest and long legs. Yum.

What are you thinking? This is Blake Marshall!

Right. Blake Marshall. A man so totally unlike her, so out of her league that she'd never once considered trying to make a move on him, at least not when she was awake.

Why her thoughts were going that way now, she honestly couldn't say. She just knew that, suddenly— maybe because of the intense, vibrant way he'd said those words, *You couldn't possibly be more wrong,* she wanted to spend a little more time with the man. One-on-one time.

Naked one-on-one time.

If she'd already had a drink, she might have wondered if she was drunk even to think such a thing was really possible. But she was stone-cold sober. And *very* curious.

"So, if we're not at war, shall we just have a drink and toast to Amanda and Reese's happiness?" she asked, smiling brightly, hoping he didn't see how badly she wanted him to say yes.

He hesitated, staring at her for a long moment, then finally nodded. "All right then. One drink. For Amanda and Reese."

BLAKE DIDN'T WANT TO HAVE a drink with Jazz. He
didn't want to talk to Jazz. Didn't want to look at Jazz.
Didn't want to be anywhere near Jazz.

Because the closer to her he got, the closer he *wanted*
to get. And that was completely out of the question.

Desiring someone like Jazz Wilkes was like desiring
the worst, most painful, hug-the-toilet hangover of his
life. One incredible night of wild, crazy, addictive sex
followed by a day-after of sheer hell. Because he had no
doubt that's what would happen.

It wasn't that he hadn't been tempted to just go for
it. He had been, for a very long time. But he still had
some sense of self-preservation left, despite the way she
zapped his brain cells whenever she was in the same
room.

Jazz Wilkes was, without a doubt, the sexiest woman
he'd ever met. She was undoubtedly beautiful, with her
jet-black hair, her violet-blue eyes and her porcelain perfect skin. The body beneath her coveralls was distracting
enough on a daily basis. Now, dressed in a formfitting,
green bridesmaid gown that hugged every curve and ac-
centuated the full breasts and generous hips, she looked
luscious and feminine and downright sinful.

But it was more than her looks that appealed to Blake.
Jazz had more attitude than anyone he'd ever known, man
or woman. It was as if by choosing a male-dominated
profession, she'd decided to take on the sexual swagger
of a man. She was thoroughly in-your-face about her
sexuality, completely unrepentant about liking sex. A
lot. And having sex. A lot.

Part of him found that an incredible turn-on. He'd
thought about having sex with her in any number of
ways, in all kinds of places. From the floor of the han-

gar to the top of his desk to the biggest, softest bed he could find.

Another part, though—the part that wanted to punch the face of any man who was rumored to actually have had her—thoroughly disliked that side of her. He hated thinking of her with any other man, found the thought of some other guy's hand on her naked body infuriating.

He had no business feeling that way. No reason to be possessive, no excuse for jealousy. They'd never had anything other than a strict working relationship, except for the one night when he'd brought her news of her brother's disappearance.

Blake couldn't help it. He wanted her with a hunger that verged on sheer desperation. He wanted to touch her and taste her, to pound into her until the thought of every other man was driven out of her memory. Wanted to slowly make love to her until his touch was imprinted on her skin and she understood that nobody else could ever make her feel so good.

All of which was utterly impossible. Because no matter how sweet and smooth and potent it was going down, he'd still end up with one hell of a hangover once they both woke up.

Maybe when she realizes she's worth so much more....

Yeah. Maybe then. When she began to understand that she treated sex like it meant nothing because she had never cared about someone enough for it to mean anything, perhaps he could take a chance on loving her. But until then? No way in hell was he getting involved with Jazz Wilkes.

He kept that in mind as he followed her across the ballroom, trying to keep his eyes on the back of her head and not on the sway of her perfect ass beneath that formfitting satin dress.

"Jack and Coke," Jazz said as they reached the bar. Turning to him, she asked, "What's your poison?"

Blake glanced at the bartender. "The same."

"Oh, good! You didn't puss out and order white wine or something."

Damn, she was snarky. Utterly determined to unman him whenever possible. He only wondered if she had any idea why.

He knew, of course. Blake presented a challenge to her. The one man who actually wasn't interested. Or, at least, appeared not to be.

He had to keep her thinking that way. It was his only defense.

After they had their drinks, Jazz pointed to a quiet corner. He couldn't figure out what she was up to, but he knew it was something. No way had she just randomly decided to make nice with him for no reason.

Determined to keep his guard up, he followed her, until the two of them stood by a front window overlooking the veranda and front lawn. Not much of a view with the rain—although one couple had apparently decided to brave the elements. He saw a flash of emerald-green and realized one of the other bridesmaids was out there with some guy in a dark suit.

"Top shelf," Jazz said after she sipped her drink. "None of that cheap stuff. Pretty nice for an open bar."

He sipped his as well, wishing the icy-cold liquid would sluice into his veins and keep him chilled out. It was hard to stay that way when Jazz looked up at him, all moist-lipped and wide-eyed.

"So, Blake, you are staying for the costume party tonight, aren't you?"

"Yes, I plan to." He couldn't wait to see what kind of costume Jazz came up with. Knowing her, it would probably be thoroughly outrageous, driving him crazy with lust and frustration.

Hell. He should just say forget it and head back to Chicago now while he still had a brain cell left.

"You didn't get shoved over to the other hotel, did you? I mean, it would be a shame if you did—but maybe you could find somebody here with a double room you could share?"

Having heard about the mix-up with the rooms, he knew what she meant, though that twinkle in her violet eyes when she suggested *sharing* did give him pause. *What are you up to?*

"No, I actually have a room here, thanks," he said, eyeing her closely.

"Oh. Where is it?"

"Second floor."

She nodded. "I have a cottage. I guess Amanda didn't trust me in the main house. Maybe she thought I'd have wild sex and outscream her on her wedding night or something."

He sighed. "Must you?"

"Must I what, scream? Sorry, I'm a screamer. Can't help it."

"I meant, must you talk that way?"

"You criticizing my mouth?" she asked, looking both naughty and hurt all at the same time.

His mind went exactly where she wanted it to. Not that he was about to let her know that. "I'm saying you don't always have to go out of your way to be shocking.

You are capable of having just a normal conversation once in a while, aren't you?"

Jazz sucked in a quick breath, obviously surprised he'd yanked the rug out from under her. "I can when I want to," she said. Her chin went up. "I just don't happen to want to right now."

"Lucky me," he muttered.

"It could be lucky you." She licked her lips. "Like I said, I'm looking for somebody to spend the night with."

Jesus. It had finally happened. She'd stopped beating around the bush and just come out with it. He'd known she would, sooner or later. Jazz might think the way she constantly taunted and baited him was because of the way he seemed to disapprove of her. In reality, he knew it was because she felt the same sparks he did. She just didn't want to admit it—or couldn't see he returned the feeling. Heaven help him if she ever did.

"I'm not," he told her. That was true. He wasn't looking for a quick lay, as she'd put it. If and when the time came for him and Jazz, it would be about a lot more than that. Otherwise, it wasn't worth doing at all.

"Come on," she said with a small grin, "I know you're single. And so am I."

She moved a little closer, lifting a hand—so small and delicate for someone who did what she did. She brushed her fingertips across his throat, and he had to clench his teeth to avoid showing her how that slight touch affected him.

He felt it down to the soles of his feet.

"Jocelyn…"

"Look, Blake. I know we're opposites, but opposites attract, don't they? Haven't you fantasized about me, even a little?"

He was definitively pleading the fifth on that one.

"Because I've fantasized about you."

Swallowing hard, he closed his eyes briefly, then mumbled, "Knock it off, Jazz."

"Oooh, I am getting to you," she said with a grin. "You forgot to call me *Jocelyn* in that harsh, disapproving tone."

"I'm not harsh, and I don't disapprove of you," he snapped.

"Like hell."

How to explain? He couldn't. Not without telling her just how much more he wanted from her. And Jazz simply wasn't ready to hear that yet.

"I should go," he said. "The reception's breaking up."

"So how about coming back to my cottage with me for a little afternoon delight before the costume party?"

Shaking his head, he tsked. "You just don't quit."

"Not when I want something."

"Since when have you wanted me?"

She hesitated, her long, sooty lashes half lowering over her beautiful, amazing eyes. When she replied, her voice wasn't much more than a whisper. "Probably longer than I'd be willing to admit…even to myself."

She sounded serious, almost vulnerable, even. Blake's pulse pounded a little faster, his breathing hard. Because, for just a moment, he thought he was actually getting close to the real Jazz again. The woman who let her guard down once in a while, who didn't have to flaunt her sexuality because she knew she had a lot more to offer. The vulnerable girl who'd cried in his arms.

Then, just as quickly, that Jazz disappeared. Between one heartbeat and the next, that old, jaded half smile appeared on her sexy mouth and her shoulders stiffened in resolve. The moment of weakness evaporated, and it was the much more familiar Jazz who answered. "Come on, neither one of us has anything better to do. Admit it, Marshall, you know you're dying to bang me."

He let out a slow, even breath, unable to prevent a wave of disappointment from flooding over him. Jazz had disappeared behind that wall of oversexed bravado. She'd done what she always did—set out to shock and awe, never letting anybody actually get close enough to see the real woman underneath the sex-starved shell.

"Actually, Jazz, you're wrong."

She smirked. "Sure I am."

"I mean it," he said with a shrug. "Do I want to bang you? No. I don't. I really *don't*."

She stared at him, unblinking, not used to being turned down. He should have left it at that and walked away. But something—her closeness, the luminous eyes, the sweet scent rising off her skin, the warmth of her breath—made him step closer, instead. He slid one foot between hers, until their legs brushed. He could feel her thigh against his, even through her heavy dress and his pants. His arm scraped against her bare one, their chests so close he could almost feel the beating of her strong, vibrant heart.

Their mouths were just a few inches apart as he whispered, "Do I want to have sex with you? Yes."

He leaned closer, brushed his lips across her temple, rubbing his cheek in her soft hair. She said nothing, just stood there, frozen in shock.

"Do I want to make love to you? Absolutely."

This time, he heard a tiny whimper in her throat, felt her whole body sway toward him, as if the strength was running out of her legs.

"But *bang* you? Not a chance."

Blake took a step back. He immediately missed that warmth, that scent, that cocoon of wanting that had surrounded them, making him feel they were nearly invisible to the room full of people behind them.

"Come talk to me when you've grown up enough to understand the difference."

2

JAZZ WASN'T USED TO BEING turned down. Despite her reputation, she really didn't sleep around as much as some people might think, and she made a point to never approach someone she didn't already know would say yes. Having decided at a young age that love was not for her—considering most men found her a little too brash, too strong—she'd strictly set her sights on men who wanted her sexually but didn't expect anything the next morning.

At least, until today. She'd asked, and he had *not* said yes. She'd been firmly rejected.

Blake Marshall had not only said no, he'd done it in an incredibly cruel—if sensual—way. He'd given her a taste, just the tiniest glimmer of a hint of what she was missing, then insulted her by calling her immature, and walked away.

She wasn't sure which was worse. That he'd said no? Or that he'd aroused her so much first, just by moving close enough for her to get blasted by an incredible wave of testosterone.

Those lips on her forehead, the faint brush of his body—well, she had no doubt who she'd be dreaming about again tonight. Unless she had somebody else in her bed. And even then…

"Damn you," she muttered as she stared at her reflection in the mirror that evening.

Honestly, she wasn't quite sure who she was saying that to. Him, for humiliating her, and saying no? Herself, for asking in the first place?

Or Amanda—for picking out this stupid, ridiculous costume.

"A fairy-tale princess I am not," she mumbled. Stepping away from the mirror, she shook the dress, wishing she had a pair of scissors handy. She could cut off everything below the crotch and go as a pixie or something instead.

But no such luck. Not only did she have nothing with which to make any alterations, she also suspected Manda would kick her ass if she damaged this "masterpiece."

She could be on a float in the Disney Electric Light Parade. She'd pass as the offspring of lesbian lovers Snow White and Cinderella. All pale and black-haired, but wearing the most ridiculous, poofy, girly dress ever made.

It was a ball gown, pale blue, impossibly tight in the bodice, but with huge, hoop skirts at the bottom. The fabric was layered—blue satin and white lace. And the hoops were so big she would have to smooth them in every time she tried to walk through a doorway. Her four brothers—the ones who'd made her so tough and ballsy since childhood because it was the only way a tiny girl could hold her own against them—would howl with laughter if they could see her. Fortunately for her, none of them had been able to make it this weekend.

"I'll get you for this," she muttered, definitely talking to Amanda now.

Glancing at the crown, which had come with the costume, she drew the line. No way. The shoes—clear "glass" slippers made of plastic—were bad enough. No way was she wearing a freaking crown.

Actually, if she had her druthers, she would blow off this whole bash altogether. The wedding was over, as was the reception. She'd done her maid of honor bit to the best of her ability. What more could Amanda ask?

Except for her best friend to be there tonight, at what everyone knew was the *real* reception of Amanda and Reese's heart. This afternoon had been about ceremony and tradition. It had been about mollifying Amanda's uptight parents and playing the expected roles.

But tonight was about the real deal—the real couple and their life together. It was the meaningful part to anyone who really knew and loved the newlyweds.

Hell. There was no getting out of this.

Her only hope was that Blake had decided to check out and go back to the city, rather than face her again after his final crushing remark this afternoon.

Oh, she owed that man some payback. Seriously, who did he think he was talking to? Acting like he knew her better than she knew herself. As if he was absolutely sure that while she acted like she wanted wild, booty-rocking sex from any available hot body, she really wanted a great guy to give her regular, monogamous orgasms.

Like many "ogamies", monogamy was highly over-rated. She should know; she'd been there, done that, and had been on the wrong end of the teeter-totter when the guy had decided he wanted to play in another woman's playground.

Since then, Jazz had been quite happy playing the field. She'd never met a penis that wasn't just like any other, beyond size and skin tone. The bodies they were connected to were also pretty much interchangeable. Like that old movie actress—Mae West or Carole Lombard—used to say: cock-a-doodle-doo, any cock'll do.

You are such a liar.

Jazz closed her eyes, willing that voice in her head to shut up and leave her alone.

It didn't.

You know why you don't want to think of him, or any man, as anything other than a walking sex organ.

Maybe she did know. That didn't change things, though.

Jazz was just wired to have sex with men, not to actually be involved with them. Certainly not to ever be loved by them.

She'd been in love. Not once, but twice. And look where it had gotten her: Betrayed. Abused. Heartbroken. Crushed. Alone.

Never again.

Anonymous, meaningless hookups were just fine for her. And if snotty, stuck-up Blake Marshall didn't want to have one, well there would almost certainly be someone else at this party who would.

There was, of course, one problem.

Blake Marshall was the only man she wanted.

She didn't know why, didn't know how, but he had snuck up on her, worked his way in until he was all she could think about. Reflecting on it, she knew it had happened long before today. Finding him beside her this afternoon had been no accident, she'd subconsciously sought out the man. Just as she so often made excuses to go up to the front office at the airport, to happen to walk by his table when he was eating in the employees-only cafeteria. Something deep inside her had some masochistic need to get in his face. It was probably the same wicked streak that always made her try to shock him with a caustic comment or sexual jab.

Lucy to Charlie Brown. Blake, however, was not gullible enough to ever consider letting her hold the football.

God, did she hope he wasn't at the party. All this self-realization just wasn't good for her right now. And deep down, as much as she'd hated him at the time, part of her just couldn't help melting a little at the words he'd said to her this afternoon.

He wanted to have sex with her. He wanted to make love to her. He wanted more than a quick lay and a quicker goodbye.

"He does want me," she whispered, the truth of that finally hitting her, hours later.

She lowered herself to the bed, sitting quietly for a long moment, just letting herself absorb that fact.

He wanted her. Desired her. Was just as interested as she was.

But he wanted a lot more than she was ready to give right now.

Making love? She wasn't sure she even remembered how. Love hadn't been a part of her vocabulary for a good five years, and she hadn't missed it. Good riddance, in fact.

Jazz slowly shook her head, wondering when she was going to stop telling herself these wicked lies. Suddenly feeling more sad than anything else, she glanced at the clock and realized the party was already well underway. There was no more putting it off. Time to go and smile and be sassy and flirtatious and fun and never let anybody see what she was really thinking, feeling. Time to hide what she really wanted…but didn't actually hope to ever get.

Because as lovely as his words had been, at the end of the day, Blake Marshall was a man, just like every other man. Just like every other lying, betraying, heartbreaking man.

So it was better to forget he wanted her, forget she wanted him, and try to move on. Starting with the party.

Hopefully she could go in, be seen, spend an hour, then slip back out. She no longer wanted to find some anonymous guy to bring back with her, realizing that nobody she picked up would fill the empty part that had been gouged into her by Blake's impassioned words.

"Please don't be there," she whispered.

God, she hoped he wasn't. Because stiffening her resolve and reminding herself of all the reasons he was totally wrong for her would be a lot harder if she had to look into those green eyes and see the great guy she suspected was lurking inside the incredibly handsome package.

BLAKE SPOTTED JAZZ the minute she entered the room. In fact, she was impossible to miss. Studying her, he had to suck in a breath and put a steadying hand on the back of the closest chair.

Jazz was beautiful on any day of the week.

Tonight, though, she was heartbreakingly lovely.

There was a difference—subtle, maybe, but it was true. A thing could be beautiful, an object could exhibit beauty. But right now, Jazz almost glowed from within, taking his breath from his lungs and making him forget to replace it.

"Wow," said Amanda, who had been standing nearby, as happy and cheerful as only a blissful new bride could be.

"She actually wore it," said her husband, whistling a little.

Blake couldn't help asking, "Your doing?"

Amanda grinned. "Hey, she didn't make time to find a costume, so I found one for her."

"I can't believe she didn't just show up in her underwear and say she was coming as a Victoria's Secret model," Blake said, picturing it a little too easily.

Reese chuckled. "The night is still young."

"Don't give her any ideas!" said Amanda.

For the next half hour, Blake stayed on the far corner of the huge room, watching Jazz do her part to contribute to the party. She helped entertain, talked with just about everyone, danced a few times, had a few drinks. And, other than one single moment of eye contact, completely avoided *him*.

Eventually, though, fate, and an inebriated dance partner who gyrated her onto the opposite side of the dance floor, brought her right to his side. He'd been dancing with a woman from work, but immediately stiffened when he realized Jazz stood only a foot or two away, her oblivious partner still writhing against her like he intended to hump her right through her clothes.

"Hi," she said, her smile so forced he was surprised her face didn't crack.

He hated that he'd put that tension between them and wished he'd never said anything earlier. If only he'd walked away after she'd propositioned him. At least then she could still act like her normal, cocky self around him, continue flirting, not behaving as though he'd really hurt her—as if he had the power to do such a thing.

Unfortunately the tense body, too-bright smile and

too-wide eyes told him maybe he did have that power. Which shocked him. Damn.

"You look beautiful," he told her, not sure what else to say. Except, maybe, *I'm sorry I told you I want to make love with you. I should have just agreed to bang you and been done with it.*

That might have made her happy, might have given them both some sexual relief, but it would have crushed him. He knew it. He liked Jazz too much, wanted her too much, cared for her too much to go down that road.

"Thanks," she said. Then she raked a slow, thorough glance over him. She tried to remain jaded and sarcastic, but he saw the color rise in her cheeks. She was aware of him now, physically, sexually aware. It helped that his costume wasn't much like the stuffy, boring suits he usually wore at work.

When she spoke, her words lacked the sharpness she'd probably intended and her eyes continued to travel over him, as closely and intimately as a touch. "You look good, too. What are you supposed to be?"

He was wearing leather riding pants, chains, a black leather vest and fake tattoos. What the hell did she think he was supposed to be?

"He's a Hells Angel!" said Wanda, the woman he'd been dancing with. She giggled, the noise suddenly grating, though he'd always considered her a nice, if vapid thirtyish woman. "Isn't that the best? Can you imagine anybody coming in a costume more opposite than they are in real life?" Then she snickered again, this time, sounding a little less amused and a tiny bit spiteful. "Except, of course, for you, Jazz. You look positively… virginal!"

Jazz didn't so much as wince at the bitchy jab. Instead she smiled sweetly at Wanda, who wore a playboy bunny outfit that would have looked better on a woman ten years younger…and a few pounds lighter.

"I dunno, if they're handing out prizes for 'Most opposite from reality' your sexy centerfold costume has a real shot!" she said, her smile so bright and broad, Wanda didn't immediately realize she'd just been insulted.

It didn't take too long, though. A shaky smile appeared on the other woman's mouth, then it quickly faded. Her eyes hardened, even as Jazz's sparkled merrily.

Jerking her head back, Wanda looked up at Blake. "I'm so thirsty. Would you please be a sweetheart and get me a drink, honey?"

He stared at her, wondering why the hell she was acting like he was her date. He barely knew the woman. In fact, he'd only agreed to dance with her because he recognized her from work. Now she was behaving as though they'd come here together.

"Oh, don't let me interfere," Jazz said, waving a hand. She glanced over her shoulder at the inebriated dancing partner who'd been dancing behind her—a little too close behind her. "You want to go get some fresh air? It's really *stuffy* in here."

Blake tensed, watching her bat her eyes at the stranger, who couldn't take his eyes off her cleavage. She might be dressed like a sweet, virginal princess, but she also oozed sexuality. Any guy on the dance floor would see that look in her eyes as an invitation to do a lot more than get some fresh air.

Damn it, Jazz.

"You bet. I could definitely use some air. This costume is way too hot," the guy said, slurring his words a little. "Bet that dress is pretty hot, too."

In other words: *Let's get out of here and get naked.*

Jazz's smile tightened; she realized the dirty dancer might have taken her innocent invitation for a nastier one. But she didn't back down, not with Blake and Wanda standing right there. "Okay, let's go. Good to see you guys!"

Helpless to do anything else, Blake kept his eyes on Jazz as she and the guy scooted through the crowd, heading for the exit. He glanced at his watch, determined to go looking for her if she wasn't back in a few minutes. She was strong and tough and could take care of herself—but that stranger sounded like he intended to get lucky. Jazz, on the other hand, hadn't looked interested in doing anything except getting away. He wasn't sure if she had only been trying to make him jealous, or to show up Wanda. But now it looked as if she might find herself having to say no to a guy determined to hear the word yes.

Wanda, apparently remembering he was not her date, accepted another guy's invitation to dance, leaving Blake free to move closer to the door. He watched the second hand on his watch, saw it go around the dial several times.

"Five minutes," he muttered. "Time's up."

About to head outside, he stopped when he saw Jazz returning to the party…alone. Her mouth was tight, her brow furrowed. And her dress, he would swear, was slightly crooked.

His hands fisted at his sides and he strode toward her. "Are you all right?"

She glanced up, surprised. "Fine."

Looking past her, out the door, he did not see her dancing partner. "Where's your friend?"

She averted her gaze. "I don't think he was finished getting air."

"Did something happen?"

"What business is it of yours?"

"Damn it, Jazz." He grabbed her arm. "Did he hurt you?"

She shook her head. "I'm fine, Blake. Let it go. The guy's a loser."

Her voice held a hint of a tremor. Something *had* happened. Furious, he snapped, "You shouldn't have gone outside with him."

"Oh, I was asking for it, right?"

Hell, she could twist the words out of a sage's mouth. Running a frustrated hand through his hair, he said, "No. I meant, you and I both know you only went outside with him because Wanda was being catty and you still haven't forgiven me for what I said to you earlier."

Looking up at him, she licked her lips—those beautiful, kissable lips. "Are you asking me to forgive you?"

He moved closer, looking around to be sure they weren't being overheard. Jazz edged back, until she stood against the barn wall, and he followed. "Was what I said so unforgivable?"

"Only if it wasn't true."

"Then no, I can't ask for forgiveness, Jazz. Because I meant it." He lifted a hand to her face, brushed his fingertips across her soft cheek, rubbing the side of his thumb over her bottom lip. He wanted to kiss her more than he wanted to take another breath in this life. "I meant it," he repeated, his words little more than a whisper.

For a second, he thought she would wrap her arms

around his neck and draw him close for that kiss. But things were never that easy. Not with Jazz.

A deliberately cool expression crossed her face. "Well, then I feel sorry for you," she said, sliding sideways along the wall to scoot away from him. "Because you totally missed your shot and you are *never* getting another one."

3

THOUGH ALL SHE WANTED to do was leave, Jazz forced herself to remain at the party for another hour. She engaged in small talk, she had a drink, she nibbled on some Halloween-themed food. And she pretended to have a good time. But absolutely the only enjoyable thing about it was watching the way Amanda and Reese smiled and laughed and loved every minute of their big night.

For her, though, it was pure torture.

Torture, because, for the first time in years, she was second-guessing the choices she made. Earlier today, when Blake had made those outrageous comments about wanting to make love to her, she'd been caught unprepared, hadn't had time to react.

This time, though, when he'd admitted it was true, she'd done the one thing she didn't want to do. She'd turned him down flat and walked away.

It had been a grand and glorious exit, a great line, the kind of girl-power moment other chicks might share with their best friends.

And Jazz had regretted it one second after the words had left her mouth.

Because she *did* want Blake. She wanted to have

wild, hot sex with him, and had for a very long time. But today, after he'd turned her down so bluntly, she'd been forced to admit she wanted to make love with him, too.

It had been a long time since she'd made love with a man. A very long time. For the past several years, she'd made every effort to look at sex the same way men looked at it; the way her brothers looked at it. Hey, it worked for them, didn't it? Considering it a bodily function, an itch that could be scratched by the next available body seemed to work great for most guys she knew.

Including the two guys she'd loved. Not that she'd realized that at the time.

And it had worked for her. Or so she'd thought. At least, until lately…when it had *stopped* working for her.

It hadn't just been Blake's words. To be honest, she'd been feeling strange about her lifestyle for a few months. She'd chalked it up to not having sex for a while. A dry spell. In truth, though, she now wondered if the dry spell was the effect, not the cause. She'd stopped having sex because she'd realized it had stopped having meaning, rather than the other way around.

"I'm an idiot," she mumbled, sighing heavily over just how badly this day had gone.

Especially because, over the last hour, she'd had to watch from the other side of the room as sexy Blake Marshall danced and flirted and drank with half the other women at the party. It was as if she'd thrown a gauntlet at his feet and he'd decided to pick it up and swing it around at every horny female in the building.

It's your own fault, stupid. You should have just been honest, for once.

Honest about what she was thinking, about what she felt. Honest enough to tell him he'd been on her mind a lot lately, and that her thoughts weren't always just about having sex with him. Though, there was a lot of that.

But it was too late.

"Why are you an idiot?"

Amanda. Jazz hadn't even seen her standing close enough to overhear her crazy-person mumbling. "Just talking to myself."

"Talking to yourself, but definitely looking at someone else."

Jazz cast a quick glance at her friend, seeing that all-knowing smile. Manda was never snotty about it, and never rubbed it in, but she was almost always right. It was darned annoying. And right now, she looked like she'd just won the Final Jeopardy round with the question, "Who does Jazz want?" in response to the answer, "Blake Marshall."

"You want Blake," she said, confirming it.

"The hell you say." But the words lacked heat. Jazz couldn't even convince herself, and she sure couldn't convince her starry-eyed, love-is-in-the-air best friend.

"Oh, come on, do you really think I haven't noticed the way you've been acting around him for months? And him around you?"

"You're losing it."

Amanda crossed her arms and smirked. "Jazz, remember who you're talking to here."

She remembered. Miss-Always-Right.

"Why do you think I tried so hard to make sure he didn't get kicked to the other hotel tonight—I wanted to make sure you two had your shot."

Jazz felt her jaw drop open. "Seriously?"

"Yes, seriously." Amanda placed an arm across Jazz's

shoulders. "Look, I know you are the original man-eater, but honey, anyone who knows you at all can take one look at you and see your wandering eye has finally settled on someone at last."

She glanced across the room, saw Blake laughing with Wanda and a few others from work. She scowled. "Yeah. Someone who's not interested."

"Bullshit."

"Okay, he's interested," she admitted, "but not in the real me. He wants a nicer, gentler me."

"You are nice and gentle."

It was Jazz's turn to call bullshit.

"I mean it. You swagger and you swear and you have sex and you break hearts. But those are just things you do, not who you are."

Maybe. Perhaps Amanda was right, and there was more to her than she'd given herself credit for lately. Maybe there was even enough to deserve a guy like Blake. Maybe she'd actually grown up enough to appreciate a guy like Blake. Letting down her guard and inviting him into her real life, not just inviting him between her legs, might be the start of something special.

Or it could be the beginning of the end. The first step on a short journey to heartbreak. She just couldn't be sure.

The only thing she could be sure of was that being tough had worked for her for a long time. And old habits were hard to break.

"Would you mind terribly if I cut out for the night?" She lifted a hand to her forehead. "I really am tired and a little headachy."

Amanda looked disappointed.

"Look, I'm not saying never. Just not now," she promised. "Let me sleep on it. Hell, maybe I'll ask him to sit beside me at breakfast tomorrow."

"And at lunch, and dinner...and breakfast the next morning?"

She laughed, as Amanda had intended her to. "Who knows? I guess stranger things have happened."

Kissing the bride on the cheek, Jazz headed for the exit, keeping her stupid hoops pulled in so she wouldn't trip any poor hapless witches, devils or cheerleaders. Smiling at those she recognized, she pleaded a headache to anyone who tried to talk to her, and finally made it to the door. The on-again, off-again drizzle was on-again, but since her cottage was close, she didn't sweat it. It wasn't like she ever intended to wear this costume again, so she really didn't care if the rain ruined it.

She set off through the grass, her plastic heels slipping and sliding, then actually sinking. Tired of the costume, she stopped, bent down and pulled one shoe off.

It was probably a good thing she bent. Because stopping the way she had apparently threw off the balance of the guy who'd been following her.

The one she didn't even notice until he crashed into her and knocked her to the ground.

BLAKE HAD KEPT AN EYE on Jazz throughout the evening and had noticed immediately when she left. He hadn't tried to stop her. She looked weary and unsure, and he'd already hassled her enough for one day.

Besides, she'd made it pretty clear she wasn't interested. He'd missed his shot. Considering he hadn't wanted that shot on her terms, he really shouldn't feel so bad about it. And yet he did.

He was just about to go find Amanda and say goodnight as well when he spied the drunk guy who'd been dancing with Jazz earlier. The one she'd gone outside with and who'd come in long after she'd returned, looking more than a little annoyed. He'd been watching Jazz, moving through the crowd several feet behind her, though not speaking. And he followed her right to the door, watching from inside as she disappeared.

It might have been planned...but he didn't think so. Jazz had never been the type who needed to be sneaky about her affairs. She'd openly left with the guy earlier in the evening, so why would they need to be clandestine now?

The hairs on the back of his neck stood up. His blood surged a little harder in his veins, and he leaned forward, as if his body was warning him it was time to move. To go...somewhere.

The guy looked around the room, quickly, left then right, as if to see if anybody was watching. Then he slipped out into the night.

Son of a bitch. He was following her. Perhaps to force the issue, take what she hadn't been offering earlier tonight? Or to pay her back for turning him down—or for the way she'd turned him down?

Blake didn't know, and he didn't care. He only knew his gut was telling him Jazz was in trouble. So without a word to anyone, he strode through the crowd, moving people aside with a firm hand on a shoulder or a sharply barked word.

It was rude. He didn't care. Adrenaline pushed him onward and he was almost running by the time he got outside.

He hesitated, unsure which direction she'd gone, but only for a moment. Because, clear as a bell, he heard her voice.

"Stop it, get off me, you jerk! I said no!"

Blake swung around and took off at a run, heading toward the sound of her voice.

Ahead, he spied two figures, standing a few yards away from one of the guest cottages. He recognized Jazz instantly, the huge blue dress hard to miss. She looked like she was struggling—the guy wasn't too steady on his feet, but he had a tight grip on her. "I just want to walk you to your room," the man said, a lazy slur in his voice. "Come on, you know you want me to."

Blake didn't hesitate; he kept right on running. "Get off her, you bastard!" He plowed right into the man, sending him crashing to the wet, muddy ground. Blake landed on top of him.

"Dude, what the hell?" The guy struggled, trying to break free and rise to his feet.

Blake got there first. "You need to learn the meaning of the word no," he snarled, sending his fist in the direction of the other man's jaw. It connected with a crunch that hurt like hell but was still eminently satisfying.

"Blake, it's all right," Jazz said. "I'm all right, he didn't hurt me." She grabbed his arm, tugging him away. *"He didn't hurt me."*

"Not for lack of trying."

"He's drunk and he's stupid," she said, glaring at the other man, who was covered head to toe with mud and was now bleeding from the mouth. "Get out of here or I'll let him hit you again," she said to him.

The guy held up his hands, as if he were under arrest. "Don't, man, I'm sorry, I thought she was just playing hard to get."

"Hard to get would be a 'maybe.' A firm no, plus a knee to your groin should have clued you in to the fact that I was seriously not interested," Jazz snarled. "Now go."

The man obeyed, staggering back toward the barn. They watched him go, then Jazz whispered, "It's okay, I'm fine."

"Not for lack of trying," he shot back again, still keyed up and so on edge he felt the need to lash out.

"Excuse me?"

"Damn it, Jazz, you nearly got yourself raped all because you were mad at me."

Her eyes narrowed, practically shooting sparks. She looked furious, dangerous, with rain dripping down from her long eyelashes and her thick, black hair. "In case you didn't notice, I was taking care of him myself."

"That your way of saying thank you?"

"You…"

He shook his head, holding up a hand to stop her, then turned away. Blake needed to regain control before he said something he'd regret. Heaving in deep breaths, trying to calm his raging heart, he counted backward from a hundred.

He couldn't recall ever being so angry in his life. It had been driven purely by worry, of course—worry for Jazz. But still, he had a hard time forcing his muscles to unclench and his raging heartbeat to slow.

Finally, though, when he felt more in control, he realized he'd been way out of line. "I'm sorry," he muttered, turning back to face her. "I was afraid for you."

She didn't come back with a snappy remark, didn't cop an attitude because of the way he'd spoken to her. Instead, with quiet dignity, she murmured, "Thank you. I appreciate your help."

They stared at one another as the rain came down, harder, stinging and cold. Each drop landed on his skin, jabbing as if to punctuate that every second that ticked by was one less second he had Jazz in his arms. The night air was cold, rich with the smells of earth and autumn, but every breath he took was filled with nothing but her. Jazz's perfume. Jazz's breath. Jazz's skin. Jazz's womanly arousal.

He reached out a hand. She stepped toward it.

And melted right into his arms.

"I want you, Blake," she whispered before pressing her mouth to his in a warm, tender kiss.

He kissed her back, shocked at how good her mouth felt—better than he'd imagined, during the many times he'd imagined it. She parted her lips for him, licking at his tongue, not hard and desperate, not taking control as she so often tried to do with every part of her life. No, this was sweet, hungry, lazy desire, not wanton lust.

Oh, lust was there, too, sluicing through him, dripping down his body as steadily and surely as every drop of rain. But it was all wrapped up in desire and emotion and sensual awareness.

They kissed for a long time, rocking together, growing drenched and cold but not giving a damn.

Finally, though, she drew her mouth away from his, kissing his cheek, then his jaw. Blake kept his arms around her, holding her hips, filling his hands with her.

"I want you to make love to me," she admitted, her voice soft, small. "It's been a long time since I've wanted that with anyone. But it's true, I want it with you, Blake."

That was what he'd been waiting for, for so very long. And it was all he needed to hear.

4

JAZZ WASN'T THINKING, wasn't planning, couldn't make any other decision right now if her life depended on it. But she knew she wanted Blake with every fiber of her being.

Every other night, every other lover, every other man ceased to exist. There was only him, looking at her with desire in those green eyes, as if she were the most perfect woman he had ever seen.

She wasn't going to think about tomorrow or next week or being back at work or anything else. All she wanted, for this one night, was to feel wanted and adored. To be made love to, not to be banged. To exchange long, slow kisses and caresses, to savor every inch of physical connection she could get.

"I'm sorry I was so awful to you today," she whispered. "Well, every day."

"You weren't," he told her. "You've never been awful. You've always just been sexy, sassy you."

"I think the word you're looking for is snarky."

He shook his head. "No. Never. As for today, you made me open up and be honest with you for the first time."

"Really?"

He nodded. "I've wanted you for a very long time, Jazz. I just knew I had to wait until you were ready to handle that."

"Handle…"

"Being wanted by a real man. A man who could never be satisfied with a quick lay and an easy goodbye."

Covering her lips with his, he kissed her again, deeply, exploring all the recesses of her mouth. She tilted her head, pressing hard against him, but still needed more. Feeling the hot ridge of heat pressing against her thighs, she groaned, dying to see him—all of him.

Blake lifted her by the hips and held her as she wrapped her legs around him. She ground her sex into him, quivering and almost crying with utter need.

"That's my cabin right behind us," she said, before moving her mouth to his for another deep, lazy kiss. She tangled her tongue with his, loving the way he began to slowly move it in and out of her mouth, mimicking the way he would soon move his cock in and out of her body.

Blake carried her like that—her thighs open and welcoming, her sex warm against the seam of his pants— right to her door. He only let her down so she could get the key, then followed her inside.

She reached for a light switch, flicking it on. "I want to see you," she explained.

"Likewise."

Blake remained by the door, watching as she moved toward the bed. She turned toward him, smiling and feeling wanted, desired, even though she knew she must look like a drowned rat. Thick rivulets of water ran from her drenched hair down her face. But she didn't care. She felt beautiful and wet and radiant and happy.

Reaching behind her back, she unfastened her dress and shimmied out of it, letting it fall in a big blue heap to the floor. She carelessly kicked it away, seeing the way his eyes darkened with pure appreciation as he stared at her. She'd been looked at with lust before…but oh, this was something else entirely. This was a whole new level of sexual desire, something she'd never experienced— never even dreamed of experiencing.

"My God," he whispered.

Wearing just a black bra and matching panties, she felt like woman personified. And the desire in his face only reinforced that feeling.

She walked toward him, boldly, reaching up to cup his cheek. "Touch me, please."

He did, extending a hand and cupping her waist. His strong hands teased the top curves of her buttocks as he tugged her close. They kissed again, but this time, she reached between them to unsnap the silly leather vest he was wearing. Which, to be honest, didn't look so silly when wrapped around that incredibly broad chest. The man was so much stronger than she'd ever have imagined beneath his regular clothes. His arms were thick, flexing with rippling muscle.

His chest was the same way. As she pushed the vest off, she stepped back to look at him, fascinated by the swirl of dark hair surrounding his flat nipples. It thickened a little, then trailed down in a thin line over his flat belly, disappearing into his pants.

When she reached for those pants, he put his hand on hers. "Huh-uh."

She pouted.

"Slow and delicious," he told her, leaning down to kiss her again.

Yeah. Slow and delicious could work.

Blake unfastened his pants, letting them hang open, and she pressed hard against him. The man was huge and rock-hard. She didn't look down, wanting to keep her eyes closed like a kid on Christmas morning, knowing the surprise was going to be so much better than anything she could possibly imagine.

"Please," she whispered, rubbing her breasts against his chest, "I need…"

He understood. Blake reached around and unhooked her bra with a flick of his fingers, then stepped back enough for her to let it fall away from her breasts. He let out a low groan at the sight of her, then pushed her back until her legs hit the bed.

Spinning around, so he was the one sitting on it, he drew her close, then kissed the bottom curve of one breast. She shivered, arching toward his mouth, but he teased her, kissing everywhere but on the sensitive tip. Finally he took mercy and lifted his hand to her other breast, tracing the tips of his fingers over her nipple.

She gasped at the pleasure of it. But it still wasn't enough. Twining her hands in his hair, she silently begged him to taste her. To make her *feel*.

He seemed to sense her desperation and moved his mouth to her nipple, kissing her, licking, nibbling. Then finally, at last, sucking deeply.

Her legs gave way. She collapsed onto his lap, parting her legs to straddle him. He still wore his pants and boxer briefs, and she had her panties on, but that enormous cock fit delightfully against her sex. She stroked it, up and down, riding him through their clothes as he pleasured her breasts until she was sobbing.

"Please, Blake," she said, "let me touch you."

He didn't resist as she pulled away, standing up again and drawing him up before her. Biting her bottom lip, she reached for his pants, pushing them down over his lean hips. The boxer briefs strained to contain his cock, and she held her breath, reaching out to brush her fingers against a spot of moisture on the cotton fabric.

When she brought her finger to her mouth and tasted his essence, he sucked in a sharp breath. "Wicked."

"You have no idea how wicked I can be."

"You're wrong about that."

"Okay, I guess you have some idea."

But she intended to thoroughly prove it to him, to leave him with absolutely no doubt.

Jazz tugged the briefs out of the way, gasping as she saw that big, thick erection. All her feminine parts went even more soft and slick at the thought that she'd soon have all of that inside her.

He didn't let her push his clothes all the way off, as if not trusting himself to let her put her hands on him.

Hmm. She wondered how he'd feel about her mouth.

Deciding to find out, she pushed him back onto the bed as soon as his clothes hit the floor. "Lie down," she ordered.

He gave her a warning look, but she ignored it. Bending toward him, she kissed his flat abs, tasting the ridges of muscle, dipping her tongue into his belly button, then moving lower.

"Jazz," he groaned.

"Let me," she begged.

He didn't refuse her. Which she took as a yes.

Jazz had always liked oral sex. She liked getting it, and she liked the utter helplessness a man seemed to experience when he was getting it. But this was different. She wanted him in her mouth because she wanted to please him. His pleasure was foremost on her mind.

There was no calculation, no gamesmanship, no who's-on-top control issues.

She flicked her tongue out, licking at the thick head, tasting more of that moisture. He jerked when she blew on his skin, and cried out when she covered the tip of his cock with her lips.

Kissing, sucking lightly, she opened her mouth wider, taking a little more. Then a little more. He filled her, and she absolutely adored the fullness. Almost as much as she adored the taste—and the sound of his helpless pleasure.

"Jazz," he groaned, twining his hands in her hair.

She couldn't answer verbally, so she took more, swallowing as much of his cock as she could take. Then she pulled away, making slow, careful love to him with her mouth. He caught her rhythm and though he tried desperately to remain still, she knew by the instinctive thrusts of his hips that he was holding on by a thread.

"Enough!" he finally said, grabbing her shoulder and physically pulling her off.

She pouted. "I liked it."

"I liked it, too. But you know what I like better?"

She was almost afraid to ask—afraid it wouldn't be what she hoped it was.

"I like this," he snapped, flipping her onto her back. He reached for her panties, yanked them down, kissed his way up her thigh toward her aching core.

Oh, yes, it was what she'd hoped it was.

"Oh, please!" she cried when he moved close to the lips of her sex.

"Not yet," he told her, "I want to look at you first."

He sounded as if he'd never seen anything so pretty as her freshly waxed sex, bare but for the tiny tuft of curls at the very top. A painful process, but so worth it if only for the look on this man's face at this very minute.

"I somehow knew you'd look like this."

She writhed on the bed, arching toward his mouth. "Oh?"

"Uh-huh. Knew you'd be nice and smooth, just perfect against my lips and tongue."

"Prove it," she ordered, frustration welling up inside her.

He laughed softly, then kept kissing her thigh, letting his slightly roughened cheek brush against her, occasionally blowing out a low breath that made her shake.

Only when she was a writhing, begging mess did he give in and dip his mouth to her clit. When he sucked it between his lips, she bucked on the bed. "Yes!"

He ignored her, holding her hips with his big, strong hands as he licked her into insanity. He sucked and kissed her to the edge of orgasm, then moved down, slipping his tongue between the lips of her sex and licking all the way into her opening.

She couldn't help it. A low, quivery cry escaped her mouth and she began to shake. He moved again, going back to that throbbing nub, and this time, he didn't let up until she'd screamed out as a rollicking orgasm gripped her and thrashed her around on the bed.

She had barely stopped screaming when he moved up her body, kissing her tummy, her midriff, her breasts, the hollow of her throat and her neck. Finally he reached her face and pressed his mouth to hers. She wrapped her arms around his neck, holding him close, kissing him deeper.

Parting her thighs for him, she whispered, "I'm on birth control. And, uh, despite my reputation, I promise you have nothing else to worry about." Frankly

her reputation wasn't nearly as bad as some people—
Wanda—might think.

"Same here," he told her.

Then there was no more talking. He slid the tip of his
cock into her, easing in, making sure she was comfort-
ably taking every inch before he gave her another.

There were a lot of inches. So many she was gasping
by the time he buried himself to the hilt inside her.

"Okay?"

She nodded, unable to speak.

"You sure?"

"Hell, yes, I'm sure," she promised. Then she lifted
her legs higher, feeling him shift so deep he touched her
womb.

She cried out again in utter bliss.

Seeming to realize she was loving this, and in no way
in pain, Blake appeared to throw off his last restraints.
Grabbing one of her legs, he looped it over his shoulder
so he could drive even deeper. Jazz writhed, taking and
taking, then giving back, meeting thrust after thrust.

At some point, they rolled over and she was on top,
riding him hard and fast, loving the way he looked up
at her. He smiled broadly, playing with the wet hair that
stuck to her sweaty face. He appeared fascinated by
the way her breasts bounced with her every move. He
cupped them, tweaking, stroking, pinching a little, and
she was hit with another orgasm.

She straightened, cried out, feeling all her muscles
clench. Then, as soon as it released her, focused on
him—getting him there, too.

Seeing her like that seemed to have done the trick.
Blake's eyes were closed, he was panting and thrusting
wildly. But before he came, he turned her over again,

wrapping his arms tightly around her, burying his face in her hair.

"You're beautiful, Jazz," he told her. "So damned beautiful. And I've wanted you forever."

Then, with a final cry of pleasure, he came inside her, taking her over the top with him for a third and final time.

JAZZ HADN'T SPENT an entire night in bed with a man for a long time. In recent years, her bed-partners had not been the stay-the-night type, nor had she wanted them to be.

Last night, however, she hadn't minded. In fact, she'd loved it. If Blake had gotten up and started pulling on his clothes after making such amazing love to her—twice—she probably would have cried.

But he hadn't. He'd stayed curled up with her in the bed, throughout the long rainy, lovely night, whispering to her, touching her, making love to her, giving her more pleasure than she thought any person was capable of receiving.

Now, though, it was morning. Dawn's watery light was streaking through the window blinds. And with the dawn came day. With day, reality.

What that meant for them, she didn't know.

She'd done what he'd wanted. She'd let him make love to her. Now she wondered if she would live to regret it, as she had the only other times she'd truly let down her guard and opened her heart.

Oh, God, your heart? Are you kidding?

No, actually, she didn't think she was. She truly feared her heart had opened to Blake that night her brother had gone missing, when he'd been so strong and tender. And he'd sailed right into it sometime during yesterday and last night, when he'd made it so clear he thought she was worth a lot more than a quick lay and a quicker goodbye.

"What's wrong?" he asked, as if sensing she'd grown distracted.

She hesitated.

"Jazz?"

Not used to sharing her feelings or any of that gushy stuff, she considered making a flip remark, then seducing him again. That might get by the heavy moment, then they could go to breakfast, head back to the city, hopefully get together again soon and…what?

They'd burn out. He'd pull away. If she didn't let him all the way in, she knew that's what would happen.

She had to take a chance.

"You know what I said last night, about not being quite as experienced as some might think?"

He nodded.

"It's true," she said. "Not that I'm some wilting flower, believe me. But I don't sleep around quite as much as you might think."

"I don't think anything, Jazz. I don't really want to think anything about the past, who you've been with, who I've been with. I just want to move forward. With you."

She liked the sound of that. Moving forward together.

"I'd like that, too," she admitted. "But I don't know that it will happen unless I explain some things to you."

He curled his head under the pillow, so lazy-man-in-the-morning sexy, watching her with sleepy green eyes. "Like what?"

She licked her lips, twirling the bedsheet in her hands.

"It's okay," he told her, grabbing one hand. "You can say anything to me. It's not going to change how I feel about you."

How he felt about her? That was part of the problem—she didn't know how he felt about her. She knew he wanted her, knew he desired her, knew he intended for this to continue after they left this room. Emotionally, though, she just wasn't sure where he stood.

"I was a sweet, innocent little virgin once, you know." Seeing his brow shoot up, she added, "And I don't mean when I was fourteen."

"I didn't say a word."

She continued. "I have four older brothers and over-protective parents. Believe me, I was the textbook straight-and-narrow good girl until I went away to college."

"And then?"

"And then I fell in love," she admitted. "Madly in love with a guy named Chuck."

He rolled his eyes.

"Yeah, I know. Chuck. Yuck. The point is, I loved him with all of my nineteen-year-old heart."

"And he broke it."

"Oh, big-time."

He reached over and brushed a strand of hair off her face. "I'm sorry."

He was, she could see that. But every nineteen-year-old girl got her heart broken, she knew that. She hadn't quite made her point.

"After Chuck, I stayed single for a long time, then when I was twenty-two, I fell in love again. This time, I was sure it was the real deal. He proposed, I was wearing his ring, we moved in together, I was picturing the three-bedroom split level and babies. He was picturing…"

"Something else?"

"Every other woman he could get his hands on," she admitted, surprised that the admission still had the power to hurt her so many years later. Not that she pined for her ex-fiancé. Last time she'd heard a word about him, it had been that he was a used car salesman on his second marriage, paying child support to two different women. Loser with a capital L.

But thinking about the betrayal still stung. Thinking about walking into the apartment they'd shared and finding him in bed with another woman still ripped at her guts.

She didn't like talking about it, but finally, with Blake, she felt she could.

So she did. She told him the whole story. Told him how she'd felt at that moment, and how she'd reacted. Told him why she'd taken solace in the arms of a bunch of different men, until she'd begun to think every single one was just the same. This time, she was the one who loved 'em and left 'em, the one who really didn't care if the guy she was hooking up with was single or not. She'd been hurt and broken, now she did the hurting and the breaking.

Throughout her entire recitation, Blake watched her, quietly, only occasionally nodding or reaching out to touch her hand or her cheek.

Finally she was finished. She'd said all she had to say, revealed her deepest secrets, her darkest moments, her self-doubts. The only other person she'd ever told these things to was Amanda, and she'd had romantic problems of her own.

Once done, she felt drained, wrung-out, but glad to have laid things out on the table. Because if there really was something more here than desire, more than lust, more than a lay and a quick goodbye for them, now was the time to find out. And telling him the truth was the surefire way to see where she stood.

He didn't say anything for a while. He merely looked at her, touched her. Then, finally, he offered her a half smile and drew her closer, wrapping her in his arms.

"Jazz? Do you think you're finished with all that now?"

It wasn't what she had expected. She'd been prepared for questions, maybe even a judgmental glance. Not this casual acceptance. Not this…kindness.

"Yes," she told him, speaking truthfully, "I think I could be finished with it. It's not easy for me to trust, to let down my guard. But I think it's possible."

"You can trust me," he whispered. "I promise you, I will never do anything to hurt you, if it's within my power to avoid it."

That was about as much as any person could ever promise, wasn't it?

"I believe you."

He nodded once. "Okay then. It's done."

"Just like that?"

"Just like that."

Their stares met, locked, and she wondered if it could really be that easy. Could a bad reputation and a jaded attitude really be swept away by one passionate, loving night and the kindness of one single, amazing man?

He pulled her toward him and kissed her mouth, sweetly, tenderly.

And she began to suspect that yes, it could indeed.

LATER THAT MORNING, when they set out to walk to the inn for the wedding breakfast, Blake found himself marveling over how his life had changed in just eighteen hours. He'd driven out here from Chicago yesterday carrying a big torch for a woman who he'd hoped would one day get around to calming down and really seeing him as a man, rather than a conquest.

Now that woman was walking beside him, her hand clenched in his, wearing a smile so bright it rivaled the sun that had finally begun to peek out through the clouds.

He didn't fool himself that things would be easy, or perfect. But he already knew one thing: he was in love with Jocelyn Wilkes. Crazy in love. He had been for a long time; she'd just been too prickly to let him show it.

Now, honestly, he simply couldn't help himself.

He lifted her hand to his mouth and kissed it. "Do you have a ride back to Chicago?"

She nodded. "A limo is supposed to take everyone back."

"How about riding with me on my bike?"

She lifted a brow, looking up at him in surprise.

"You don't think I'd dress up as a biker if I didn't really have a bike, did you?"

"You? Seriously?"

"Come on, after last night, are you saying you still haven't shaken this picture you have of me as some boring P.R. guy?"

She smiled like a cat holding a canary. "Mmm. Nope, not boring. Not straitlaced. You have a very naughty side, Mr. Marshall."

"Well, that's only fair, considering you have a very *nice* one, Miss Wilkes."

Casting him a mock glare, she shook a finger at him. "Don't you dare tell anyone. That's one reputation I'll never live down."

"It'll be our secret, my love."

She stopped suddenly, freezing midstep on the lawn. Turning to face him, the laughter faded from her face and those violet eyes were searching, questioning. "What did you call me?"

He shouldn't say it. He knew it was too soon, that she wasn't ready, that he'd come across as crazy for being this sure, this soon.

But he couldn't lie to her. Couldn't look into that beautiful face without telling her how he really felt.

"I called you my love," he admitted.

She bit her lip.

Blake slid his arms around her waist and pulled her to him. "Don't chicken out on me now, Jazz."

"I'm not chickening out."

"Good. Because I love you."

He felt her stiffen for a moment, saw her mouth tremble. She stared wildly around, as if poised to flee.

"I love you. And you're okay with that," he insisted.

"I am?"

"Yeah. You are."

She hesitated for one more moment. Then, at last, nodded. A smile appeared, tiny, tentative, and she whispered, "I am."

Rising on tiptoe, she brushed her mouth against his. She didn't say the words back to him. He knew they wouldn't come easy to her lips. But as she looked into his face, her expression said it anyway.

She loved him. Someday, she'd say it.

And he was a patient enough guy to wait for her.

* * * * *

Last Call

_1_

PLEASE NOT ME, _please not me, please not me._

The mantra repeated in Abby Bauer's head, but it didn't help. Because, like an arrow shot from an expert marksman's bow, the bridal bouquet was headed straight for her. In fact, if Abby wasn't sure her sister didn't like Keith—Abby's fiancé—she'd suspect Amanda's over-the-shoulder aim had been intentional.

A bunch of other single women surrounded her at the base of the sweeping, curved staircase, a dozen steps below the bride. Each appeared ready to claw out someone's eyes in order to catch a stupid clump of tea roses cupped in baby's breath—like it was made out of diamonds or something. They elbowed each other, shrieking with laughter, jumping and reaching up so high a few in strapless dresses risked a wardrobe malfunction.

But no. The damn thing didn't so much as come close to another woman's updo. It was on a collision course with Abby Bauer's face.

She acted quickly, almost without thinking. Flinging up an arm, she backhanded the bouquet to the right, passing it like a volleyball player would set up a teammate's kill-shot.

"I got it!" shrieked a young woman Abby didn't know—one of the ones in a strapless dress. She hadn't popped a boob while clawing for the bouquet, but she was on the verge of doing so now, by jumping up and down. "I'm so excited!"

Yeah, and the men would be really excited if those Ds defied gravity and separated from her dress midleap. But maybe that wouldn't be such a bad thing. Because it would certainly provide a distraction from what she had just done.

She, a supposedly happily engaged woman, had batted a good-luck, next-to-be-married bridal bouquet like it was a giant flying cockroach.

"Maybe nobody noticed," she mumbled under her breath, almost scared to look around to see.

Maybe Keith had gone outside. To, uh, smoke. Only he didn't smoke. But maybe he'd wanted some air. Some cold air. Cold, wet, stormy air. And maybe his parents—and hers—had gone with him.

Because coldness suited every last one of them so very well.

Not Keith. At least, not the Keith she'd met and fallen in love with…the one so seldom in evidence these days.

Taking a deep breath, she shifted her gaze to the right. All the men, and the non-single females—or the simply non-desperate ones—had gathered in the reception room right off the foyer, to watch the standard wedding tradition through the arched doorway.

At the left edge of that archway stood Mrs. Manning, her future mother-in-law. The woman oozed disapproval. Her face seemed like it had been slathered with one of those facial mud-masks that had completely dried and was ready to crack apart into a million pieces. Tight. Hard. Brittle.

This wasn't good.

Next to Mrs. Manning stood her husband. The naturally deep frown on his brow had delved to crater depths, his pugnacious jaw thrust out and his chest even more so.

This *so* wasn't good.

Next to him? Abby's own prim, proper mother, whose eyes were saucer-size in her pale face. Upset didn't quite describe the expression. Scandalized was about as close as she could get.

Okay, this was bad.

Standing behind his wife, a hand on her shoulder, gripping her as he acknowledged how much Abby had just embarrassed him in front of the Mannings, was her father. He wore the fiery glare he usually reserved for Amanda, the "wild child" of the family.

Extremely bad.

But she didn't realize it was an utter calamity until she looked to the other end of the wide arch. Her stare immediately locked with the dark brown eyes she most didn't want to see.

Keith. Her fiancé. Looking a little stunned. And maybe, she realized with a twist of her heart, a bit hurt.

Oh, God, what have I done?

"Okay, it's time for the garter," someone shouted.

Abby quickly looked away, trying to calm her racing heart and smooth her choppy breaths. Thankful for the interruption, she turned her attention to the bride and groom. Reese, her new brother-in-law, was already on one knee on the stairs, lifting Amanda's dress with smooth, sexy determination.

All the women swooned a bit. Including her. Because the newlyweds were so erotically charged together, they made everyone else feel inadequate somehow.

"I want one," wailed the girl who'd caught the bouquet. Whether she meant a husband, or a man who could make stroking another woman's calf look absolutely orgasmic, Abby didn't know.

Funny, Abby wanted one, too. Oh, not a husband, at least, lately she hadn't. But a man who'd get on his knees and touch her with utter sensuality in front of a huge crowd of people, because he was so wildly in love with her and desired her that much. What woman *wouldn't* want that? Especially if she'd never had it—and feared she never would.

"Come on, big guy, you can do it. Take it off," Amanda purred, sultry laughter in her voice as Reese continued tugging the lacy garter down her leg. With his teeth.

Double swoon.

Once the garter was off Amanda's thigh and looped around her husband's finger, Reese stood and waved it at the crowd. The bouquet-hungry women moved away, making room for single men who would jockey to catch the frilly clump of lace. Abby trudged with them, finally working up the nerve to look at her fiancé again.

He stood in the same position. Silent. Still. Intense.

God, the man was handsome. Probably the handsomest one here. Everywhere they went, women's eyes were drawn to his dark brown hair, his sculpted face, full mouth, strong jaw. Tall and lean, he wore his expensive tailored suit as easily as most men wore jeans. Keith could be posing on magazine covers rather than working as a corporate lawyer. Her fiancé was everything a woman would want. And she'd wanted him, too. Desperately. Raised in a cold, passionless house, she'd held this secret, fairy-tale hope of someday falling wildly in love with her own Prince Charming. Despite the odds, despite her parents inattentiveness, she'd truly believed in happily-ever-after. Heck, it was why she'd become an event planner, because she so loved weddings, loved that moment when everything was shiny and beautiful and new and absolutely every couple was sure to make it.

That half of them didn't was something she wouldn't even contemplate. On that one day, anything was possible.

Yes, Abby Bauer, the "good" sister, the quiet, proper, nice one, was just a silly little romantic at heart. And Keith, handsome corporate attorney Keith Manning, had once seemed exactly like her perfect Prince Charming.

So what happened?

Good question. Honestly, she didn't know. Sometimes, he still seemed like that perfect man. When he let his guard down and stared at her with that wistful, tender expression, or when he whispered something sweet to her, when he dropped a possessive arm across her shoulders, she still felt certain he was madly in love with her.

Other times, though, she just wasn't so sure. And it was hard to fantasize about a happily-ever-after with even the most perfect of Prince Charmings if you weren't totally sure he was wildly, deeply in love with you, too.

Keith watched as she drew closer. Even from several feet away, Abby witnessed the moment his initial look of surprise—and hurt—gave way to a much more familiar cool, detached expression. He retreated behind the formal mask he almost always wore, except when they were alone. Which seldom happened anymore.

Where are you? Where did you go? Why won't you let me see the real you anymore?

She didn't know. So, with a sigh, she kept trudging.

Her parents and the Mannings bore down on her as soon as she reached the archway. "Abigail!" her mother snapped.

"What is *wrong* with you?" asked Mrs. Manning.

But before anyone could truly begin to berate her, Keith took her by the arm, holding firmly, staring down both sets of parents. "If you'll excuse us, Abby and I want to get a look at the grounds," he said, his tone even.

Mr. Manning and her father exchanged a glance. Then both nodded in approval, as if imagining Keith would take her outside to set her straight, ensuring she never embarrassed him in public again. She didn't suspect he would do any such thing, but the older generation obviously felt she deserved it. Lord, she felt like a fifteen-year-old schoolgirl caught between her parents and the school principal.

"Shall we?" Keith asked her.

She nodded, relieved, even though she'd just been thinking about how cold and rainy it was. "Great idea."

Keith led her away from the crowd, toward the French doors at the back of the reception hall—once a ballroom in the grand old house. With every step, she felt the weight of four pairs of angry eyes boring into her back.

Unable to help it, she cast a quick look back over her shoulder. Yep. Still staring. Still disapproving. Still so damned cold.

"Don't worry about them," he ordered in a low voice. "It's nobody else's business."

She had to wonder what he meant by "it." Them? Their relationship? Their engagement? Or the way she'd just reacted to a symbol that predicted a quick marriage for her.

They didn't say another word until they were outside on the veranda, alone. On a nicer day, the event would probably have spilled out here, but the drizzle and gusty winds kept everyone else indoors. Funny how much the grayness and the chill suddenly suited her mood.

"Cold?" he asked, obviously seeing her shiver a little.

"Yes, but that's not such a bad thing. I was starting to feel suffocated in there."

In so many ways.

"Me, too," he admitted. Then he slipped out of his suit jacket and draped it over her shoulders. "But it is pretty cool."

"Thank you," she murmured as his strong fingers brushed her skin. The heat of them was so stark against the cold day, she shivered again.

His hands didn't linger, not now, not when there was a chance someone could come outside. As usual when they weren't entirely alone, he remained impersonal. Whether carefully taking her arm when they walked, or dancing a few inches away at some social event, or greeting her with a chaste kiss on the cheek when they met for dinner, Keith always maintained that impeccable protocol. Not to mention a few inches of space. Not unkind, not unfriendly, but ever-so-proper.

Sometimes she found it hard to believe the same hands could do such amazing things to her body.

Not often. Not recently.

But oh, God, had he given her pleasure beyond imagining on occasion. With his intimate touch, the man had worked utter magic on her, nearly always without taking any for himself. As if he were addicted to the feel and taste of her body, he'd worshipped her for hours, only gaining his own satisfaction when she absolutely insisted on it. Even then, he had rarely wanted intercourse, swearing he was satisfied with her hand.

Well, she wasn't. Damn it, she *wasn't*. And if he was telling the truth, and that was really all he wanted, then she feared her fiancé was every bit as passionless as his parents—and hers. Which was too depressing to contemplate.

Wrapping the coat tightly around her body, she steeled herself against a rush of instinctive pleasure as his warm, masculine scent surrounded her. She didn't want to be vulnerable right now, sensing the conversation she was about to have would be a very important one—even though she had no idea what he was thinking. The man was so inscrutable, she couldn't tell if he was offended, angry, or amused.

Well, amusement was probably a stretch.

When he did speak, he sounded merely pragmatic. "You have cold feet."

She didn't even pretend to misunderstand, or joke that her toes were numbing up as moisture soaked into her shoes from the wet wood planking. "I suppose I do."

"Perhaps you could have said something, rather than taking it out on a poor bunch of flowers?"

That could have been teasing, if there'd been the least hint of humor. But his voice remained emotionless, his expression revealing absolutely nothing.

God, that passionless stoicism drove her absolutely crazy. It might be perfect for his job as a lawyer for a major international corporation, but here, between them, it was utterly maddening. "Maybe I *have* been by not wanting to name a date, or start planning anything," she snapped. "Maybe the problem is that none of you have heard me."

Keith frowned. *"None* of *us?* I thought I was the groom."

"Right. So when's the last time you looked at an invitation sample or checked out a photographer's work or anything having to do with a wedding?"

He shifted uncomfortably. "You know I'm not good at that stuff. It's what you do for a living, you're the expert."

Maybe it was a guy thing, and maybe he had a point. Still, she had been bothered that, lately, she and Keith never talked about their wedding, or their relationship, or anything personal at all. His aloof, self-controlled wall seemed to have grown with every month that passed, until they'd gotten into a two-dinners-a-week routine that was so bloody boring and predictable, she wanted to scream about it. "Yes, I'm the expert. But I would think you'd have a little interest."

"You're right, I'm sorry. I just figured it was a woman's thing."

"Spoken just like your father would say it," she said. *Or mine.*

"I'm sorry," he said, sounding as though he meant it.

She was in no mood to make up. "Or your mother. I mean, God knows, the wedding is all I ever hear about from her, and it's only gotten worse. I get a weekly phone call from her with a lecture demanding to know why I can find time to help Manda, or my clients, with their weddings and not plan mine." Frankly she'd always considered it a little like the cobbler's children going without shoes—there just didn't seem to be enough time in the day. Lately, though, she'd begun to wonder if, deep down, there wasn't more to it.

He was silent for a moment, then he turned and glanced at the grounds, his handsome, masculine profile still making her heart skip a beat. Though wet, the gold and orange autumn leaves provided a beautiful backdrop and the lawn still held a hint of summer lushness. He stared intently at it for the longest time. Then, finally, he cleared his throat, but he didn't look her way.

"Actually that's a good question, Abby. I think I'd like to know the answer myself. Why did you have so much time to devote to your sister's wedding, and none to ours?"

This time, there was something in the tone. Something that told her he'd been more bothered by what she'd done than his first response had indicated. As if she'd finally pierced that shell and was again speaking to at least the remnants of the man she'd fallen in love with. The one hidden beneath that withdrawn exterior—who she hadn't seen in so long she hardly remembered what he was like.

The one who deserved an honest answer.

"It *is* a good question, Keith," she said, her heart breaking as she admitted the truth, to both of them, for the very first time. "I suppose the answer is because I don't really want to marry you."

HEARING HER ADMIT IT, hearing the woman he loved with every ounce of his being say she didn't want to marry him, was easily the worst moment of Keith Manning's life. Feeling as though she'd kicked his legs out from under him, he had to clutch the railing, holding so tightly, wet splinters of wood dug into his palms.

He'd lost her. He'd lost, *period*. For the first time, ever.

The enormity of that stunned him into silence.

He'd never failed to get something he truly wanted. And he'd wanted Abby from the day they'd met—when she'd come to plan a fund-raising event for the law firm where he worked. Only after he'd gotten to know her did he realize she was every bit as beautiful inside as she was outwardly.

He'd fallen so hard it had scared the hell out of him. Keith had never felt anything like it, had never been a slave to his emotions. He'd always figured he'd meet a decent woman who fit into his lifestyle and shared his goals, and they'd settle down into a convenient partnership with respect and mutual admiration. That was the way every other marriage he'd ever seen—from his parents to his colleagues—had been.

But Abby? Abby made his blood boil.

She made him wild with lust, with her almost exotic, dark eyes, her long, silky brown hair, her lithe body and her subtle laugh. She made him so crazy with wanting he had to fight a constant inner battle not to back her into the nearest corner and take her in rough, animalistic passion.

He'd never done it. Abby was gentle and quiet, not very experienced. She came from a reserved background. She had this belief in a happily-ever-after, wanted a Prince Charming who'd treat her with respect. That's exactly what he wanted to be to her. And Prince Charming, as far as he recalled, had never dragged Cinderella into the nearest broom closet and screwed the glass slippers right off her feet.

He'd always respected women, of course, but those he'd had affairs with had seemed fine with the kind of steamy sex he was into. But he'd been raised to believe a wife was different, and he damn well *knew* Abby was. So he'd restrained himself, kept his basest desires in check, because the last thing he'd ever want to do is hurt her, or repulse her. He'd been what had been drilled into his head for his entire life, and given her exactly what he'd thought she wanted at the same time: a complete gentleman.

Apparently for nothing. He'd somehow managed to scare her off, anyway. "You're serious?"

"Yes."

It was all he could do to control the roiling emotions surging through him as he heard the finality in her voice and realized it was over, that he'd never have her the way he'd always wanted to. That she wouldn't be his wife. His lover. Or the mother of his children.

He'd lost. And for the life of him, he didn't know why. How could he lose when he'd played the game by every single one of her romantic rules?

Only a lifetime's worth of training at the hands of two rigid, emotionless parents and the presence of a hundred people in the room just beyond the closed doors kept him from dropping to his knees and begging her to tell him what he'd done wrong, to give him the chance to make it right. Instead he released the rail, dropped his hands to his sides and turned again to face her.

Abby's beautiful face was tear-streaked, her mouth trembling the slightest bit. Yet there was resolution there. He saw it in the squared shoulders, the uplifted jaw. She meant it.

Still, he had to ask, "You're not in love with me anymore?"

She sucked in an audible breath, and her throat

quivered as she swallowed. "I don't want to marry you, Keith."

She'd avoided the question. Not that it seemed to matter since the end result was the same: no Abby in his life. "So this is it? It's over? We're finished?"

A brief hesitation, a searching glance, then she nodded. "Yes. I think we are."

"Just like that."

"It's been building to this for a long time," she said softly, "and I think we both know it."

He managed not to laugh at himself. Because, no, he had not known it. Sure he had sensed Abby's distraction, maybe a little withdrawal. But he'd figured it was work, or stress, her obnoxious parents—or his. He'd never imagined she'd changed her mind about him...
them.

She reached for the sparkling engagement ring he'd flown to New York to buy for her. But Keith waved a hand. "Keep it."

It had been specially made for her. No other woman could ever wear it. That would break his heart beyond all repair.

"I can't do that," she insisted. "It wouldn't be right."

"I don't want it," he said, staring at her from three feet away, feeling like it was three thousand. His openhearted Abby had suddenly become a stranger—an aloof, distant stranger.

"It's the principle..."

"Look, if you don't want to wear it, fine. But I have no use for it. Donate it to charity or something, I don't care." He glanced toward the reception hall. "Though, actually, you should keep it on for a while. I'm sure you don't want to spoil your sister's day. If everybody finds out, an argument could break out. My parents will be angry, yours will be put in the position of having to defend you."

"They wouldn't," she said quietly. "Defend me, I mean. They certainly never have before. I have no doubt they'll find this indefensible."

He stared, unable to read her, but certain of one thing: Abby had changed. She had never said anything disloyal about her family, which had always shocked him, to be honest. Because, as parents went, hers were almost as crappy as his.

"I'll break it to them after the reception and we'll go," he offered. "I'm sure you don't want us sticking around for the party, anyway."

"I somehow doubt they were looking forward to it."

Maybe not. But he had been. Very much.

Yes, she'd picked out a stupid Roman warrior type costume for him. But seeing her as a Grecian goddess would have made it worthwhile. He'd looked forward to dancing with her, holding her in his arms—even though he couldn't hold her tightly for fear he'd lose his head, do or say something to reveal his wild need, to offend or frighten her. To somehow fall off that princely pedestal and let her see that he was just a guy, just an average, normal, horny guy who was so racked with hunger for her, he had a hard time keeping a sane thought in his head.

The realization that he'd never hold her again had him ready to throw back his head and howl.

"All right. Thank you." Then she turned toward the door. "I should go. The reception will be ending soon."

He almost let her, was about to watch her walk away,

with quiet dignity, which, he knew, was what a real man *should* do.

Be strong, be stoic, never show your emotions. Words he'd learned to live by from a very young age. Words that had been reinforced throughout his law school days and his legal career.

But he just couldn't let her go without some kind of explanation. Maybe it would be hurtful, but he still had to know. So he stepped closer, lifted his hand and pressed it flat on the closed door.

Swallowing hard, knowing he was going to sound too damn needy but unable to help it, he simply asked, "Why?"

She tilted her head to look up at him, surprise widening her brown eyes a tiny bit. Then, shaking her head in visible sadness, she answered. "Because I don't want the kind of life I can see spread out before me. I want what Amanda has with Reese—freedom, excitement. Pure passion."

He sucked in a breath, so shocked, he dropped his hand.

"You're a good man, Keith," she said. "A wonderful man. But the truth is, I want someone who'd have no problem falling to his knees and tugging a garter off my leg in front of a hundred people without a second thought. One who would actually kiss me in public. One who'd fly to Vegas and play hooker-and-john with me, no matter who found out."

His head spun and he had trouble focusing. He'd heard the story about her sister Amanda's embarrassing YouTube incident, when she and her fiancé had gotten caught on camera playing a sexy game in Las Vegas. In fact, he'd heard it from Abby's shocked mother, and had naturally assumed Abby had been just as shocked.

Even though he, himself, had found it funny as hell. Not to mention exciting.

She went on. "You're gorgeous and you're charming and you're everything a woman could want. But, I'm sorry, I want a husband who doesn't consider me part of his regular, daily routine. Who isn't content to provide me with an occasional orgasm just so he can check them off his to-do list, and then go back to work."

Keith's heart raced and he actually staggered back.

"I want to marry a man who desires me, who wants me desperately. Not one who can just as easily live without me." She shrugged sadly. "And judging by how you've reacted to this conversation, I was right. You're not that man."

The whole world had just turned upside down, his blood pounding wildly through his veins.

Jesus, she thought he didn't *want* her?

He lifted a hand, reached for her, not knowing exactly what to say, only knowing he had to tell her she was wrong. *So* wrong.

"Abby, wait, you don't…"

But before he could say another word, the door opened from inside and a trio of giggling teenage girls peered out. Abby took their intrusion as a chance to end the conversation, saying, "Goodbye, Keith," before ducking around them through the door.

Ignoring the girls, he stared after her, frozen into place.

She thought he didn't desire her. Thought he wasn't passionate enough for her. Thought he hadn't had sex with her more than a few times because he wasn't interested…when, in truth, he had to stop himself before he took a lot more than she was ready for.

Even the most basic, vanilla sex he'd had with Abby

had surpassed anything he'd experienced with anyone else. But it had left him so hungry, so desperately aroused, he feared he'd scare the hell out of her with all the wild, sexy things he wanted to do with her. Honorable, noble heroic types weren't supposed to be that way, right? So he'd stayed away, indulged his need by giving her pleasure, but holding back from his own, until they were married, certain that, deep down, Abby would be every bit as passionate once they were man and wife.

He'd thought he would be teaching a shy pupil the basics, when it appeared she was already ready for the expert class.

He'd misread her, hadn't understood her, hadn't taken the time to find out what she really wanted. When it came to sex, he'd seen only what was on the surface—the lady, the happily-ever-after dreamer. He'd missed seeing the woman.

In short: he'd blown it.

"Idiot," he muttered, mentally calling himself worse names.

But not for long. Soon, the conversation began to take another shape in his mind. His beautiful fiancée had bared her heart, voiced her deepest needs, thinking she was talking to someone who could never fulfill them.

She was wrong. So wrong. And while she had broken their engagement, the woman he loved had also given him hope.

This wasn't over. Not by a long shot. Though she didn't know it, Abby already had exactly the kind of man she wanted.

He just needed to prove it to her.

2

"ABBY? WHERE ARE YOU? Has anyone seen Abby?"

Hearing Bonnie Campbell, one of the other bridesmaids, Abby slid lower in the leather chair in which she'd been hiding. Abby wasn't in a partying mood. Or a talking one. So she kept quiet.

After the scene with Keith, Abby had skulked off and found a quiet corner in the library to be alone. Deep in thought, she'd barely registered the murmurs as the reception broke up, people going to their rooms to relax between social events.

She hadn't cried. She'd simply felt…numb.

Her life had changed so drastically. Turned on a dime, or, in her case, on a bridal bouquet. If someone had asked her this morning if she would break her engagement today—to a man she'd been convinced was her one true love—she would have laughed hysterically. Part of her—probably a bigger part than she'd care to admit—was sure she'd made the biggest mistake of her life.

"He didn't try to stop you," she whispered.

No. He hadn't. He'd been stoic and calm, as always, except when she'd talked about their sex life—or lack thereof. Then he'd looked shocked. But that was probably a male ego thing.

It wasn't as if Keith couldn't please her in bed. Far from it. But she wanted someone who was interested in doing it more than once every few months, and who really wanted to participate!

She just didn't understand. Keith was passionate in so many other ways. He worked hard at his job, yet made time to do a lot of pro bono work, and volunteered with a program for at-risk teens. He wasn't a workaholic, he played hard, too—never missing a weekly basketball game with his friends. He even had a creative streak, sometimes picking up the saxophone he'd once thought of playing professionally—before his dream-killing parents had convinced him he was wasting his time.

She *knew* the man was capable of a lot of passion.

Just not with *her.*

"Abby, are you in here?" Reese's sister must have been part bloodhound, because the library doors were suddenly flung wide.

Sighing, Abby peeked over the chair. "I'm here. What is it?"

Bonnie rushed in. "Did you know about the movie people?"

"Yes." Frankly she was grateful for them. When Amanda and Reese had asked for volunteers to go to the other hotel, the Mannings had stepped right up. She doubted they'd be back.

"What are we going to do about it?"

"It's already done," she said as she rose from the seat. "Those who left were fine with moving to the other hotel."

"I'm talking about the bridal suite. Some *Neanderthal* is staying in it," Bonnie snapped, sounding furious.

"I know. But the inn is discounting all the other rooms, and comping tonight's party. Plus, Reese and Amanda can come back and stay in the honeymoon suite anytime, on the house."

"Anytime *except* their wedding night."

In her line of work, snafus were common. This one was a biggie—but the concessions the inn was making had been expensive. And it wasn't like Amanda and Reese required a traditional wedding night—they'd been living together for months.

Abby, on the other hand, might, indeed have had more of a white-sheets event, considering she wasn't far past the virgin state. If she were getting married. Which she wasn't.

I'm not getting married. It still hadn't sunk in.

"This is unacceptable!"

"Amanda and Reese seem to be okay with it."

"Well, I am not okay with it. And I'm going to do something about it." Then, her eyes flashing, Bonnie spun around and left.

Once Bonnie was gone, Abby glanced at the clock. After five. The party would be starting in a few hours, and she needed to get her act together and put on a happy face, for Amanda's benefit.

Tomorrow morning would be soon enough to let everyone know what she'd done. Soon enough to slide the beautiful ring off her left hand and think about a life far different from the one she'd been planning for the past two years.

Soon enough to let herself grieve for the fact that Keith Manning would not be part of that life.

UNLIKE THE RECEPTION, which had been held in the ballroom, the Halloween costume party was taking place in an old barn on the grounds of the inn. As lovely as the mansion had been for the daytime events, the barn was just as perfect for tonight. Unused except for storage, the place was cavernous, with plenty of room for the live band, a bar, a dance floor and dozens of tables.

Though Abby had been looking forward to tonight, now she was in no mood to attend. She couldn't, however, bail on her sister. So, dressed in a slinky Grecian Goddess costume—which she'd chosen because she'd wanted her fiancé to see her as sexy and alluring instead of steady and reliable—she set out across the grounds.

The path between house and barn was lit by an army of glowing jack-o'-lanterns, and the day's rain had left behind a mist that heightened the atmosphere. Fresh bales of hay and scarecrows flanked the sliding barn door. Wood-carved witches flew in silhouette against a cloudy sky broken by beams of watery moonlight. Hand-lettered signs warned visitors to turn back, and threatened danger ahead.

Huh. The only danger Abby would land in tonight would be if her parents came and decided to confront her about her colossal stupidity—at least, that's the term she assumed they would use. Well, one of them, anyway.

Though she'd hoped to evade notice, Abby hadn't even gotten her damp coat off before she was spotted. "There you are," said Amanda, looking radiantly happy. "It's about time."

Seeing her sister's heavy makeup and attire, Abby laughed out loud. No wonder Amanda had kept her costume under wraps. "The Corpse Bride? Seriously?"

Amanda twirled in her tattered gown, sending up puffs of what looked like dust but was probably powder. "Isn't it great?"

For Amanda? "It's perfect. Though I doubt the folks agree."

Amanda shrugged. "They'll never see it. They called, saying this was a young person's thing and they'll come by tomorrow."

Hiding her own relief, Abby looked for any sign of hurt in her sister's face, but saw none. Amanda had moved past years' worth of neglect and disapproval from their parents, living her own life, to hell with the consequences. Abby envied her that. A lot. And today, for the first time, she had to wonder if she was more like her sibling than she'd always believed.

"Now, go. Find that handsome man of yours and have some fun!"

Abby was saved from having to admit Keith wouldn't be here by the arrival of more guests. Slipping away, she headed for an empty table, determined to sit out the party. Accepting a glass of champagne from a passing waiter dressed as a vampire, she settled in a corner, trying to remain unobtrusive.

It didn't work. Because, after congratulating herself on having come in unnoticed by anyone except Amanda, she got that funny, almost indescribable feeling of being watched. Her skin prickled, and a vague sense of aware-ness had her sitting straighter in the chair. Confused by the unusual sensation, she glanced around to see if someone really *was* staring at her. At first, she noticed nothing—just standard Halloween revelers dressed as fairies, witches and devils, all having a great time.

Then her gaze landed on one partygoer standing near the bar, and stopped dead.

Abby sucked in a quick, surprised breath. Not because the man in black was staring at her—he wasn't—but because of his costume. He was literally, the Man in

Black. The Dread Pirate Roberts, aka Westley, from her *favorite* movie of all time, *The Princess Bride*.

Her heart fluttered a little, as it had the first time she'd seen the movie as a closeted-romantic teenager. She'd loved the story, the romance, the "perfect" kiss, the grandeur, the excitement, the happily-ever-after. Most of all, she'd loved the mysterious man-in-black—an ultimate Prince Charming who'd literally climbed mountains and fought giants for the one he loved. And now, for the first time in her life, she was seeing him in person. Well, sort of.

"Hot, isn't he?" someone murmured.

Abby glanced up to see Jazz, her sister's best friend. The maid of honor looked incredibly uncomfortable in a fluffy, frilly blue ball gown with big, hoop skirts. Nobody would ever mistake Jazz Wilkes for Cinderella, but somehow, she still managed to look absolutely stunning in a costume that she clearly disliked.

"Beyond hot," she agreed, seeing the other woman's eyes locked on the stranger, too.

"The Spanish guy was always my favorite in that movie, but this dude definitely has me reconsidering."

Completely understandable. With the billowing, lace-front pirate shirt, tight black pants, knee-high boots, gloves, the scarf and mask covering most of his face, he had totally nailed the costume. But the most breath-stopping part was that he wore the clothes like they'd been made just for him—like he *was* the character. The outfit fit his incredible body to a T, showcasing the rock-solid form. He was lean, broad-shouldered, slim-hipped. The pants verged on indecent and she, the "good girl," cast a few discreet glances there. Frankly there was a lot to look at. A whole lot.

As if that weren't enough, he also had an incredibly

sensuous mouth, which was emphasized by the mask that covered everything down to his nose. Eminently kissable.

Utterly dazzling.

"Wonder where Buttercup's hiding," Jazz mused. "I bet I could take her."

"I'm quite sure you could. Still, she's probably around here somewhere," Abby said with a smile. Jazz was definitely a ballsy one. "I can't see a guy coming in *that* without a girlfriend having forced it on him."

"Or the bride," Jazz grumbled, carelessly fluffing her own dress, with its layers of blue satin and white netting.

Suddenly Jazz whistled. "Stick out your chest, he's coming over!"

The other woman was right. The stranger was weaving through the crowd, skirting the dance floor, headed this way. Abby turned and quickly looked around—definitely *not* sticking out her chest—wondering if his missing princess bride was sitting nearby.

It honestly didn't occur to her that he was heading for her table until he stopped right beside it.

"Dance?"

His voice was mysterious—a whisper, low, throaty, supersexy. The one-word invitation was as much a command as a request, and Abby quivered a little in her seat, wondering why Jazz hadn't yet dragged the guy out onto the dance floor.

When the maid of honor nudged her not-so-gently in the shoulder, she realized the man *hadn't* been talking to Jazz.

"Me?" she squeaked.

His dark eyes glittering behind the mask as he stared down at her, he nodded.

Abby's heart was racing; she hadn't come here to dance or actually have a good time. She'd broken her engagement less than six hours ago for heaven's sake. This man couldn't know that, obviously, but she still wore a big rock on her left hand, and it hadn't deterred him one bit.

"Come on."

No. No way was she ready to get next to another man—even one who seemed to have stepped out of her deepest fantasies. She instinctively shook her head. "No, thanks."

"Pull up your big girl panties and go dance with the man," Jazz snapped, nudging her again, this time harder.

"I'm sorry…"

"Please," he urged, extending a gloved hand.

Abby looked at it, then up at him, then at Jazz—who was more attractive. Drop-dead gorgeous, in fact. Why this incredibly sexy stranger would have chosen *her*, she simply didn't know.

One thing she did know—he wasn't going to *let* her refuse. Without another word, he lifted her hand into his and tugged her to her feet. She allowed it, helpless to do anything but follow—silent, breathless—as he led her into the crowd of dancers.

The band had been playing standard Halloween stuff—the "Time Warp," the "Monster Mash." But suddenly, as the man in black stopped walking and turned to face her for the dance, the music segued into something slow. A torchy old blues song about black magic.

Black magic. Yes, that fit. Because it was as if he'd cast a spell on her, pulling every lucid thought from her brain and every word of refusal from her tongue. She couldn't think, couldn't speak. And when he stepped close, she was sure her heart would stop dead in her chest.

"Okay?" he whispered, the word riding a warm exhalation.

"Um…"

"Relax." He laced their fingers together, then twisted his arm around hers, bent both of them, and lifted their clenched hands between their chests. It wasn't a standard dance position, but rather intimate. Personal. Familiar.

The way they stood also put the side of his silk-covered arm against the outer curve of her breast. Abby trembled, shocked to her core by the waves of excitement rolling through her.

Beneath her flowing white gown, her breasts tightened. Not abundantly curved, she didn't always wear a bra, and the cut of this costume made it difficult. So the only thing separating her sensitive skin from his hard, hot chest were two silky layers of fabric—her dress, and his shirt. The material didn't offer protection, merely heightened the extreme intimacy of their embrace, bringing erotic whispers of sensation to her nipples.

He made a sound—something like a groan, and she knew he was aware of it, that he could feel the pebbled tips of her breasts brushing against him. Embarrassed, she considered pulling away, leaving the party before this got too crazy. But something stopped her. Her own instincts? Or the certainty that he wouldn't let her go? Both?

As if knowing she wanted to flee, he slid his other arm possessively around her waist, a big, strong hand flattening against the small of her back. The tips of the stranger's fingers rested so close to the curves of her bottom, she instinctively jerked away. Which meant she arched *toward* something else: his groin. Her reactive movement had slammed their already close hips into a hot, wanton connection.

She gasped. Tried to pull back.

He kept her still, not letting her ease away. Not seeming to care that his hips ground into hers, that she could feel his hot, male sex pressing into the juncture of her thighs—and getting bigger by the second.

Good Lord.

If not for their clothes, they could be having sex, right here on the dance floor surrounded by other people. There was absolutely no way he would be able to hide his physical reaction if she was to walk away. And he didn't seem to give a damn.

"You're beautiful," he whispered.

She shook her head.

"I mean it. You're the most beautiful woman here."

"I think your vision's been impaired—either that or your mask has slipped down too far over your eyes."

"Do you always react to those kinds of compliments with sarcasm?"

"Do you always offer those kinds of compliments to complete strangers?"

"What can I say? You're just so damn sexy, I can't help myself. I can't stop thinking about those big girl panties."

Abby swallowed hard, shocked at the intimacies in his voice. An image flashed through her mind—this man, lifting her dress, inch by inch, making his way toward the so-not-for-little-girls thong she wore underneath.

"I can't take my eyes off you."

"You don't even know me," she said, confused, on edge, knowing something crazy was going on and not sure why she didn't much care. Her heart was racing,

her breaths shallow and raspy and all she could think
was— _What is happening to me?_

Though he had been speaking in a low whisper, they
were still surrounded by people, and somebody dancing too close could probably overhear them. Still, she
remained in his arms, not wanting the strange interlude
to end just yet.

"I mean it. I want you so badly I can barely stand up
straight."

She tried to pull away. Again, he wouldn't give her
as much as an inch.

"Breathe," he ordered.

"I don't think I can."

He moved his face closer, until his scarf-covered
cheek brushed hers, and every inch of their bodies
touched, from face to calf. Holding her breath, Abby
melted against him, sure of absolutely nothing except
this felt so good, she couldn't resist. Slowly they began
to sway, moving to the music, each tilt of their bodies
giving a little, taking a little, building the tension yet
also feeling so incredibly right.

Finally she relaxed enough to do as he'd ordered, and
breathed deeply. His warm, masculine scent filled her
nostrils, and sense memory finally filled in the rest, answering all the questions. Somehow, she couldn't muster
surprise as she acknowledged the truth. The costume
had thrown her for a few minutes, since it was _so_ out of
character, so unexpected. As was the incredibly sexy,
suggestive conversation.

But oh, yes, she knew him.

She knew that scent. She knew the voice hidden behind the raspy whisper. She knew that body. She knew the sensations he was bringing forth in her.

The only thing she didn't know was what Keith Manning—her ex-fiancé—was up to.

3

KEITH'S INTENTION hadn't been to trick Abby. He hadn't worn the costume to try to disguise himself, or changed his voice with the intention of seducing her as a stranger. No. The whole point of tonight was to show her that he, Keith Manning, was absolutely the man she wanted. He didn't want to entice her to cheat...not even if she did it with *him!*

But he'd also known getting her into his arms, on the dance floor—getting her to *listen*—wouldn't be easy if he showed up in the costume she'd chosen for him. She'd take one look at him and put her guard up. Her emotions were still tangled, she'd be defensive and wary.

Besides, it wasn't something he could tell her. He needed to show her, prove the point, make the grand gesture. She deserved it.

Hence his costume: the Man in Black. He had decided to become the idealized, romanticized hero from the movie she so loved. And now he had her right where he wanted her, right where she belonged. In his arms.

He felt the moment she fully relaxed, and suspected she'd finally figured out who she was dancing with. But he wasn't sure, not entirely. So he couldn't give up the game just yet.

"Better now?"

"Better. I like your costume," she whispered.

"I like yours, too."

"I take it there's no Buttercup lurking around?"

"Who's that?"

"The Man in Black's true love." She huffed a little. "Have you never paid attention to the movie?"

He couldn't help chuckling. The only thing he remembered about the movie was that Abby loved it, and there was a dude dressed all in black who was damned good with a sword.

"How on earth did you get it so quickly?"

Ah. Confirmation. She definitely knew. "A client of mine is married to the director of a theater company in Chicago. I called, she had something she thought would work, so I went and picked it up."

She nibbled her bottom lip. "You drove all the way to Chicago and back just to get a costume?"

He nodded.

"Why? If you wanted to come to the party, you could have worn the one I got you."

"Let's just say I wanted to find something I knew would get your attention," he admitted.

"It definitely worked. You got it."

"Good."

They were silent for a moment, swaying a little, then she said, "I do like this one better than the one I bought."

"Yeah, I know. But I could never figure out why. This character wasn't the Prince Charming you told me you always wanted."

"When I was twelve," she said with a chuckle.

Keith sighed, wondering how he could be considered smart when he'd been so utterly stupid about this woman.

"Besides, the prince was a creep in that movie," she told him. "Westley was much more exciting."

"You like that he was a mystery man, then?"

She shook her head slowly, tilting it back to look up at him. Her brown eyes were wide as she studied his face, her gaze resting long on his mouth, as if she were thinking what it would be like to kiss a masked man—even one she'd kissed a thousand times before.

"Not necessarily," she finally replied.

"Swordsman?"

"Not that, either."

"Pirate?"

At last she laughed softly. "No." Though she probably didn't know it, she pressed against him even harder, relaxed and so naturally seductive every one of his senses went into hyperdrive. "Well, okay, maybe a little. Pirates are very sexy these days. I think I was ahead of the trend on that one, having such a mad crush on you…er, I mean, on that character."

"But he wasn't all pirate," he added, trying to remember more of the details from the film, which Abby watched at least once every year—and had suckered him into watching once, too.

"No, he wasn't. There was a very tender, but passionate lover underneath all that black."

Passionate. She'd said that earlier, that she wanted passion. He'd had it to spare, he'd just never trusted himself—or their relationship—enough to share it with her.

Well, that was done. Finished. He knew some of what she wanted, and intended to find out the rest. Then he would go about giving it to her for all the days of their lives, if she'd only let him.

"Passionate, huh?" he asked. "How do you know? I think that film was rated PG at most."

"I had to use my imagination." She licked her lips, staring up at him, her expression so guileless, he was caught totally unprepared when she added, "Though, I would have preferred some graphic, X-rated scenes."

Keith paused midstep, letting his mind wrap around that. Abby—kind, friendly, sweet-natured, inexperienced Abby—fantasized about watching porn? God, how much did he not know about this woman he'd planned to marry?

"You like to watch other people have sex?" he asked, the words almost choking him.

"I don't know. Maybe. There's so much I haven't done, I don't know what I'd like."

"That's a crime against nature," he growled.

"Not knowing what I'd like?"

"Never having the chance to find out." He brushed his lips against her ear, hearing her sigh at the contact. "Why don't you tell me what you want to try, in your quest to find out what you might like?"

She hesitated. "I'm not used to talking about things like that."

"Another crime against nature," he admitted, mentally kicking himself all over again. "Please, Abby," he added, "please talk to me. Give me a chance."

"A chance to do what?"

He answered with his heart. "To save us."

"It's…"

"Don't say it's too late," he ordered. "Don't say everything went wrong without at least giving me a chance to show you why you and I are so right."

She stared up at him, searchingly, as if trying to see the real man behind the mask. Hell, maybe she'd never seen him. Maybe he'd never *let* her see him.

He knew he'd never let her see the man who'd wanted her so desperately. "Please," he urged. "Open up. Share your fantasies with me. Tell me what you want. You can trust me."

There could be no more hesitation, no more holding back. Abby did trust him, in every other way, he knew that. Now he was asking her to take a gamble and trust him with her most erotic longings.

Her eyes drifted closed. She fell silent. Then, maybe it was the mask, or the music, or the plea in his voice or the fact that she'd dumped his ass today, something made her open up about things they'd never discussed. Her voice sounding almost dreamy, she said, "I want everything. Just everything."

He wanted to know more. He needed to know more.

"Specifics."

She hesitated for a second. Licking her lips, she admitted, "I want to be tied up."

Holy shit. He missed a step in the dance and almost landed a boot-clad foot on her toes.

"I'm not into serious bondage or S&M—at least, I don't think I am…."

Thank God for that.

"But I think I could like being gently restrained, unable to do anything except feel every sensation and accept every bit of intimacy I can get."

Keith's teeth clenched and he hissed each breath between them. The woman was killing him here. Absolutely killing him.

"I see," he finally mumbled. "Go on."

She did, without any hesitation, as if now that she'd opened the floodgates, she couldn't hold back against the current of her feelings. "I want to have sex in a public place, where there's a risk of exposure."

He almost tripped again. Exhibitionism. Abby. Unreal. "Anyplace in particular?"

"It doesn't matter. The fear of discovery is the key part."

Catching the vision himself, he said, "During a game at Wrigley."

She let out a sound like a purr, deep in her beautiful throat. "In the backseat of your car while it's parked at the stadium."

"I'm liking this idea," he told her. "And I also liked the first one. So far, we're two for two."

"I also want…"

A couple dressed as Fred and Wilma Flintstone danced a little too close, and she snapped her mouth closed. He suspected that whatever she'd been about to say, it was very naughty.

He could hardly wait. Drawing her closer to the edge of the floor, as far away from the cave-couple as he could get, he said, "Go on. What else?"

Her voice low, she replied, "I want oral sex to be only foreplay—an appetizer rather than an entire meal."

Wow. Direct hit. That hadn't just been a fantasy, it had been an accusation, aimed right at him. And he couldn't deny that it stung. "I thought you liked…"

"I do like it," she insisted, nodding as she stared into his eyes. "I love it. I love getting it, but I'd like to be on the giving side, too." Her throat quivered as she swallowed and her voice fell to a sultry whisper. "I'd also love to both give and get at the same time."

"God," he muttered, his mind flooding with those

images. The idea of Abby's perfect mouth wrapped around his cock as he licked her into insanity almost had him exploding in his stupid pirate pants. "I never thought you'd be into that."

"You never asked."

"My mistake. And believe me, I regret it." He definitely did, especially now when those images continued to play in full Technicolor glory in his brain. Not to mention engorging his cock.

"The point is," she told him, "it needs to be about arousing each other till we're out of our minds. Then we have sex." She sounded earnest. Serious. "I might come, but I'm still left almost desperate with wanting you inside me."

She thought he didn't feel the same way. Thought he hadn't felt like his heart would rupture every time he'd pleasured her and then walked away to a lonely shower and a tight fist.

"I want sweet sex, like we've had, Keith. It's been wonderful. But I also want it wild and hot and intense."

"Again, I didn't know," he whispered.

"Would it have mattered if you did?"

"Of course!"

She shrugged, looking almost helpless and her eyes were moist. "Well, I didn't know if you were even interested, if you were holding back, if you had to force yourself to do as much as you did, if there was someone else…"

"No. Not once. Not ever."

She nodded in acknowledgment of that. "Okay. Still, I'm just telling you what I've been thinking. I never *knew* and I was so damned frustrated. I actually had to buy myself a battery-operated boyfriend and read the hottest romance novels I could find just to get some relief, and it still wasn't enough. Because I wanted *you*."

He closed his eyes, both incredibly turned on, but also feeling like utter shit for having left her so desperate.

"I'm sorry." Keith was barely moving, not even really pretending to dance anymore. Neither was Abby. She seemed completely intent on her every word. All around them the dancers continued; the music changed, the tempo sped up, but they slowed, and slowed, until they were utterly still. "You can't imagine how sorry, Abs."

"Let me put it bluntly."

"You mean you haven't been so far?" he asked, still mystified and shocked at the way they'd been at such cross-purposes, both wanting the same thing, neither opening up enough to admit it. And his head continued to swim with incredibly vivid sexual images—all the things he'd wanted to do with her for so long… She'd wanted them, too.

She didn't laugh. "The truth is, I like being who I am in public, and I can even stand to have a man who won't flirt with me or give me deep, wet French kisses when anybody else is around."

Yeah. That'd be him. Though, not for the reasons she might think.

"But in private, in my bed, I want to be someone's sexual obsession." She pressed her lips into the nape of his neck, licking, nipping a little. "I want sex that lasts for hour after hour, in all kinds of positions. Sex that feels so good it's almost painful. Rough and sweaty and intense and possibly illegal in some states."

He let out a sound, half laugh, half groan, so incredibly turned on he didn't know if he'd be able to remain on his feet for much longer.

"I want it in every way it's possible for a man and a woman to have it," she said. "And then I want it all again."

He nodded, unable to speak.

"Most of all," she said, "I want the man I'm with to be just as desperate for all those things as I am. To want me with every ounce of his being."

"I do," he said, the words torn from deep inside him, an admission he'd been holding back for far too long. "I swear to you, I do."

She shook her head sadly. "How could a man who wanted me that much be able to strip my clothes off and give me pleasure and then just walk out the door?"

"Like checking an orgasm off a to-do list?" he asked, remembering what she'd said earlier.

"Yes."

"Only a very stupid man who couldn't see what was right in front of him would do that." He lifted a hand to the back of her head, twining his fingers in her silky brown hair that she'd curled into long, goddesslike ringlets. Tugging it slightly so she had to tilt her head and look up at him, he admitted in a hoarse voice, "You and I have got a lot to talk about. A lot to clear up."

He bent down and brushed his lips across hers, sliding his tongue between them, sharing a breath, a heartbeat, a silent promise.

"I thought we were talking," she whispered against his mouth.

"It's a start. But there are some things you need to know. And I intend to tell you. Only, right now, Abs, if I don't get you alone somewhere and fuck you until neither one of us can move, I'm going to embarrass myself right here in the middle of your sister's party."

ABBY'S HEART WAS POUNDING so hard, it was a wonder she could remain standing. Her legs had grown as weak as sticks of warm butter and her sex throbbed with sheer desire. She was desperate for him. Inflamed. Their sexy conversation about what she wanted was wild enough—she'd just never imagined what a turn-on raw, graphic language could be. Keith had never spoken to her like that. Nobody had. And right now, at this moment, she was more excited than she had ever been in her entire life.

He was obviously in the same boat, at least judging by the huge erection pressed against her groin. Getting out of here with *that* would be a trick.

"Follow me," she said, pulling away and spinning around so her back was toward him. They were at the edge of the dance floor, unnoticed by most of the other partygoers, who were all gyrating and laughing. Apparently nobody had noticed the erotic-romance-novel-worthy moment taking place a few feet away.

That's how she felt. Like the sexually charged heroine of one of those novels she so loved to read. She would never have dreamed of saying such intimate, sexual things a few years ago. Now, she was different…no longer unsure of who she was, or how she would act. No longer determined to play the good girl role just because her big sister had the bad one all sewn up.

She wasn't good. She wasn't bad. She was just a woman who finally had the guts to admit what she really wanted.

Like one of those heroines in the books, she knew just what to do to get it. Reaching for one of his hands, she tugged him after her and headed not for the big sliding door at the front, through which she'd entered—it was way too crowded over there and they'd have to say good-night. Instead she went the other way.

She'd toured this place a few months back, when planning the party, and remembered the layout. From this big, open area, a dark hallway extended back through a maze of long-unused stalls. At the end was an office… and another exit that would put them within twenty feet of the inn.

And her room. And her bed.

"Where are we going?"

"Back way out," she told him, speaking over her shoulder. She couldn't turn around and look at him, couldn't see the raw hunger in his face, not if she wanted to stay focused on moving forward until they could get somewhere private.

Within a dozen strides, they were out of the well-lit party area, disappearing into the back half of the barn. They had no sooner been swallowed by the shadows when Keith stopped her.

"I have to touch you," he muttered. "Please." Moving closer behind her, he slipped an arm around her waist and pulled her back against him. Abby sighed, awash with pleasure as he moved his warm mouth to her neck. Kissing, biting lightly, he whispered more of those crazy-erotic words, telling her what he intended to do to her.

Wild things. Wicked things. Dangerous things. Things she'd dreamed and fantasized about doing with him but had never thought would actually happen.

Her already damp sex grew slick and swollen against her tiny panties. Unable to help it, she had to grind back against him, desperate for some relief. That thick ridge pressed hard against her, and she writhed, feeling the silk-encased heat edge between the curves of her bottom.

Keith continued exploring her neck and the vulnerable spot at its nape, nipping, sucking, kissing. She was whimpering by the time his hand dropped down to the juncture of her thighs. Cupping her, he pulled her more firmly against him, using his fingers to toy with her sex while his member nestled ever tighter against her backside.

The position was wicked. Hinted at all kinds of wild sexual things they could do, and the ways in which they could do them.

Abby wanted to try them all.

"I want you like this," he growled, as if reading her thoughts. "Want to lift you up and slide you down on me, just…like…*this*."

"Yes, yes." The idea of being taken from behind, or while standing up, or *anything* other than basic man-on-top excited her beyond belief.

Lifting his other hand, he pushed the strap of her dress—a filmy strip of fabric—off her shoulder and let it fall, baring her breast to the cool night air. He stroked her, toyed with her nipple—tweaking, pinching lightly—until she felt a moan rise up in her throat.

They were no more than twenty feet from the crowd. Lost in shadows, but still easily visible should anyone venture down this way. Keith was already fulfilling one of her fantasies.

It was dangerous. And incredibly erotic. And pretty dumb. This wasn't a baseball field where they'd be anonymous—her sister's big new family, and a lot of friends, were the ones who would catch them if they got any crazier.

Yes, she was dying to continue. But letting this go

any further would just make it more painful when they finally did stop to get somewhere more private. "Come on, we should get out of here before I refuse to let you stop."

He stepped back, let her shift her dress back into place, then took her hand again as they headed for the exit. Their footsteps clicked on the floor, creating a rapid tattoo that matched her heartbeat, their anxiousness and desperation audible and thick as the night itself.

When they reached the door, Keith threw his arm out, prepared to open it without even slowing down.

Suddenly realizing something, though, Abby grabbed his hand and stopped him. "Don't!" Shaking in utter disappointment, she pointed to the red Emergency sign. The door was equipped with an alarm. If they went through it, everybody back at the party would be forced to leave to make sure there was no fire, or else come investigate.

"You've gotta be kidding me," Keith groaned.

"I know." Frustration made her whole body quiver as she imagined having to go back into the party, back through the crowd, smiling, making small-talk, saying good-night, hiding the fact that she was dripping wet and so aroused she thought she might die if she didn't get him inside her soon. "I can't…"

"Neither can I," he snapped.

And then her sexy ex-fiancé—God, had she really jilted this man, thinking he wasn't *passionate?*—lifted her into his arms and strode toward the nearest abandoned stall. He kicked open the swinging door with one booted foot and carried her inside.

The place had been converted years ago, the floor was bare, the air a bit musty with disuse. But it was dark. And semiprivate. "Good enough," she said.

He didn't reply. Instead he was already grabbing the sleeves of her dress and pushing them down, tearing the fabric, not that she cared. The dress fell in a wispy heap, puddling around her high-heel-clad feet, leaving her wearing nothing but a lacy thong.

They both completely ignored the party going on in the front of the building, though the music and voices were audible from back here. They could be discovered by anyone who decided to do some exploring. It wasn't like the swinging stall door actually gave them any real privacy.

I don't care. I so *don't care.*

"You are the sexiest thing I have ever seen," he muttered, devouring her with a long, desperate stare. Keith looked like a man trying to decide which dish to try first at a banquet table. "Did you really think I didn't want you?"

"You gave a pretty good impression of it."

"I'm sorry, Abby. You can't imagine how sorry," he said, pressing a warm kiss on her lips. Their tongues slid together, tasting deeply. Each breath was shared; even their heartbeats seemed to fall into sync.

They'd kissed a thousand times. And at first, this kiss held a hint of that same gentleness. But it soon changed as pure, unbridled lust took over. They devoured each other's mouths—she wanted to memorize the taste of him, the scrape of his teeth, the slide of his tongue.

When the kiss finally ended, Keith immediately dropped to his knees, pressing his mouth into her middle and breathing her in like he could imprint her very essence onto his lungs. She reached for the mask and scarf, tugging them off and tossing them away, revealing his handsome face striped with shadow. The desperate desire she saw there was enough to stop her heart.

It was true. This man was dying for her. Keith Manning wanted her beyond all rational thought. Just as she'd always hoped he would. He was her dream man again, the one she'd wanted, the one she loved. The one she'd intended to marry.

What had changed, she didn't know. If she'd misread him, missed the signals, just been too inexperienced to understand...well, that was all in the past. Now there was only this. This gorgeous, sexy, amazing man—the man she loved—on his knees. Loving her. *Wanting* her.

As she wanted him. Not just now...always.

She hadn't yet taken off the ring. She only hoped he didn't want her to.

Twining her fingers in his thick, dark hair, she watched as Keith pressed hot, openmouthed kisses on her stomach, then slowly rose to explore her breasts. He covered one taut tip, sucking hard—deep and shocking—then went to the other. The night was cold against her damp skin and her nipples tightened even more. Sensation flooded her—the air against her body, his spicy masculine scent heady and intoxicating, his mouth doing such incredible things to her breast, his hands warm and heavy against her hips.

"This! I've wanted this for so long," she whispered, almost wonderingly.

"Not as long as I have," he said, kissing his way back down her body. This time, he didn't stop at her stomach. He tasted her hip, then lower, to the hollow just above her pelvic bone. His lips tracing the line where the thin stripe of elastic rode above the small thatch of curls covering her sex. Sweeping the thong off with a scrape of one fingertip, he bared her for a more intimate caress.

This time, when he licked and nibbled her sensitive clit—bringing a yelp of pure satisfaction to her mouth—Abby didn't wonder if the amazing oral sex would be the end of their evening. Tonight, she knew, it would be only the beginning.

Almost as if the knowledge of that was enough to inspire it, an orgasm washed over her, sudden, hot, intense. Crying out, she sobbed his name. Her hips jerked, and he squeezed his hands around them, his fingers digging into her backside as he continued devouring her as she came against his mouth.

"Appetizer," he muttered against her when she'd finally stopped shaking.

"Yeah."

He rose quickly, as if knowing her patience for slow, sweet caresses was absolutely gone. She wanted power. Desperation.

Possession.

Reaching for his shirt, she didn't waste time with buttons. Instead she tugged it up and helped him yank it over his head. He tossed it on the ground, then went for the waistband of his pants. Abby stroked his chest, rubbing the tips of her fingers across the long ridges of muscle, twining them in the crisp hair.

He unfastened the pants and shoved them down his hips. Neither of them could wait long enough for him to get them all the way off. She simply reached for him, wrapping her hand around the rock-hard shaft, so desperate she knew she would beg if she had to.

"Abby," he groaned, thrusting into her hand. "I've got to be in you."

"Do it!"

Pressing her back into a corner, he grabbed one of her thighs and lifted it over his hip. Abby arched toward him, gasping when he thrust into her, hard and deep.

This was no slow, quiet lovemaking. It was everything

she'd told him she wanted. And far better than she'd ever dreamed.

They remained very still for a moment, and Abby savored his powerful intrusion into her body. She squeezed him, deep inside, and felt him shudder in response.

Buried to the hilt, Keith pressed his face in her hair and breathed deeply. "Okay?"

She twined her arms around his shoulders, digging her nails lightly into his muscles. "More than."

"Hold on."

She held on.

Reaching for her other thigh, Keith picked her up and wrapped both her legs around his waist, cupping her bottom in his big, strong hands to support her weight. He drew out, then thrust again. Harder. Faster. Each time digging a little deeper, carving out more of a place for himself inside her. She felt like he was claiming her as his own, planting his flag.

His breathing grew more rapid, as did hers. Keith pressed her back against the wall; the wood planks dug into her skin, but she barely noticed it. All she could feel was the fullness, the pounding of all that heat against her womb, his mouth on her neck, his heart beating against hers.

All she could feel was absolutely glorious.

And most of all, *wanted*.

4

HE'D RIPPED HER DRESS.

Not just ripped it, he'd torn the thing beyond repair.

Funny, though, Abby didn't seem to mind one bit. In fact, the look on her face was pure feminine satisfaction, as if she loved the fact that she'd driven him to such lengths.

Hell, she *did* love it. Every word she'd said to him today proved that much.

She just hadn't anticipated that he'd love it even more.

God, they had been running in circles around each other for so long, it was no wonder they'd almost lost what they had. If he hadn't had the sense to come here tonight—to show her how much he desired her and what he'd do for her—they likely really would have remained apart. He'd have gone back to Chicago and buried himself in work to get over her, to bury the pain. And Abby would have done the same. Both always wondering, neither reaching for the phone.

They'd come close...so close. He never wanted to be that close to losing everything he'd ever wanted again. Which meant he'd do whatever he had to to make sure she never doubted his feelings—and his desire—for her again.

He'd shown her the truth—taken her the way he'd always wanted to. Now it was time to talk to the woman… to let her know tonight wasn't a fluke. Abby needed to understand that he'd felt this way about her since the first time he'd set eyes on her.

But not here, not in a stall. Not when anybody could walk back here and spy her with her dress torn to shreds—and his back equally shredded by her sharp nails.

"Maybe if I tie it like a halter?" she mumbled, trying to shimmy her costume around and use two undamaged straps to tie around her neck.

"Sorry, beautiful, you still look like somebody ripped your clothes off and ravaged you."

"Mmm. Ravaged. By the Dread Pirate Roberts."

Keith laughed, pressing another kiss against her lips. "Or the Dread Lawyer Manning."

She giggled, so adorably sweet and so irresistibly hot he wanted to have her all over again.

Soon. Conversation first.

"Uh, why don't you just tie it around your waist and put my shirt on. You can say you spilled something on yourself.

"So I get to look like a klutz rather than a sex goddess?"

He lifted a hand to her cheek, scraping the side of his thumb across her lips. "You *are* my sex goddess, Abs."

"Well, it's about time you worshipped at my altar, then," she quipped, raising a brow in challenge.

"Yeah. It is. Now let's get out of here and find a

private place so I can make another sacrifice to your sexiness."

"What are you going to sacrifice this time?"

"I dunno," he said, wagging his brows, "you definitely drew blood on my back. What more do you want?"

Gasping, she bit her lip. "I'm so sorry."

"I'm not. Now, let's get out of here. I think it's time for our talk."

"I'm all ears."

He glanced down at her naked body. "Actually you're all breasts right now, at least as far as I can see. And while I'm not complaining, I would hate to have to stop on the way out of here to beat the crap out of some guy who got to see you like this, too. So let me grab that shirt for you."

"Yeah, right. So you can walk through the party with that gorgeous body half-naked and my claw marks on your back? Then I'd be the one beating somebody up."

"The scratches would show I'm taken," he pointed out. "Very thoroughly."

She playfully smacked his upper arm. "I have a better idea. I left my coat draped over the back of my chair. If you go get it, I'll just put it on and button it up. Nobody will ever know what I'm wearing—or not wearing— underneath. And that way I won't have to scratch out another woman's eyes for ogling you in all your bare-chested glory."

She sounded a tiny bit jealous, something he'd never heard from her before. He liked it. He liked everything about this new Abby…on top of loving her with all his heart.

"Okay, wait here," he said, kissing her one more time, then donning his shirt. He didn't bother tucking it in, or putting the mask back on. The party was in full swing—loud, with lots of champagne and beer being consumed. He doubted anybody would even notice him.

A dress-ripped-off-her Abby? Yes. But not a slightly disheveled pirate.

When he reached the party, he blinked a few times to allow his eyes to adjust to the bright light. Then he made his way through the crowd, trying to remember which table Abby had been sitting at. It took a couple of minutes, and when he finally did locate it, he realized someone else had taken a seat in the chair.

He blinked again. Because that looked a whole lot like Drew Ericson, an actor who'd made his name synonymous with shoot-'em-up-action-flicks. "Excuse me," he said. "Do you mind…"

"Yes. He minds," someone interjected with a sigh. "He's a guest of honor and I've been ordered by the bride and groom to babysit him and make sure he has a good time. So, sorry, no autographs."

That, surprisingly, came from one of the other bridesmaids. The one with curly hair—the groom's sister, he believed. He'd first thought she was a quiet little thing, but she sounded pretty annoyed now. Ericson rolled his eyes and shrugged good-naturedly, seemingly amused by his "babysitter."

"Actually I just need to get the coat he's sitting on," Keith said. "It's Abby's."

The actor immediately rose. "Sorry, man."

"Oh, I'm so sorry, too," said the bridesmaid, flushing a little. "It's been a…strange day."

Keith couldn't help smiling, thinking his had been absolutely fantastic. "Hope it gets better for you," he said, grabbing the coat. Then he headed back for the hallway, skirting the wall so he wouldn't be too obvious when he turned down it. Fortunately he wasn't spotted, and got back to a pacing Abby no more than five minutes after he'd left.

"You found it?"

"Underneath a movie star, no less."

Her eyes widened.

"Doesn't matter," he said, helping her slip the coat on. He carefully buttoned it, then stepped back to inspect her.

"Do I look okay?"

Other than the fact that her thick, beautiful hair had fallen out of its curls and hung in sexy disarray around her face, her lips were swollen and red, she had a few abrasions on her neck from his roughened cheek, and her eyes were sparkling with secretive pleasure?

"You look like someone who's just been thoroughly shagged."

She laughed. "Well, then, let's hope nobody looks too closely."

Nobody did, and within ten minutes, they had made their escape from the party and headed across the grounds to the inn. The full moon above had brightened, the day's rain clouds having finally drifted away. Dried leaves crunched beneath their feet and the air smelled wet and earthy. They didn't usually experience nights like this in the city, and he found himself liking it a lot.

Abby seemed to, as well. Because instead of heading toward the front door, she suddenly veered right, tugging him along with her. Further down the lawn stood a pretty gazebo, and he realized right away that was where she was headed.

"Is this okay?" she asked as she stepped up into it.

"Very."

They sat down on a bench, and for the longest time, said nothing, merely soaking up the evening. And thinking about what would happen now. Then Abby made a tiny sound, like a throat-clearing, that told him she was ready to talk. Turning to look at her, he saw the way she bit the corner of her lip. She appeared tight and tense, averting her gaze, and, the biggest tell of all, twisted the ring on her left hand.

"Don't," he ordered, knowing exactly what she was about to say.

"Don't what?"

"Don't kick yourself for dumping my sorry ass."

"I didn't really…"

"Yeah, babe. You did."

She turned her stricken face toward him, staring him in the eye. "I am so sorry."

Keith slid an arm across her shoulder. "I'm the one who's sorry. I wasn't honest with you. Or with myself. You had every reason to doubt me and more reason to bail out." He gently kissed her temple. "The thing is, I was operating under this delusion that you were too good."

"Too good for you? That's ridiculous."

He shook his head. Then, wanting her in his arms, he pulled her off the bench and into his lap, taking one of her hands in his, the other resting on the small of her back.

"Actually I thought you were too good, too pure, for the kind of sex I wanted to have with you."

Her jaw dropped open. "You wanna repeat that?"

He sighed heavily. "I guess it sounds crazy. Maybe it was. I had this whole idea of how a man is supposed to act around his fiancée—or his wife. What he should do, and what he shouldn't. I wanted you like crazy. God,

Abby, I took so many cold showers and jerked-off so often it's a wonder I didn't break my dick."

She couldn't hide a smile, obviously liking that he'd been so desperate.

"But the things I fantasized about *doing* with you—to you—just didn't seem like the kinds of thoughts I should be having about the woman I wanted to marry. The one who would bear my children." He frowned. "The one who seemed so romantic, so sure of the possibility of Prince Charming and happily-ever-after. I wanted to be that for you, Abby. Wanted you to see that white knight I sense you've been looking for since you were a little kid being raised in a cold, loveless house."

Tears rose in her eyes and he suspected he'd hit the nail on the head with that one. It wasn't hard to see why Abby had held on to those fantasies, especially once her sister had left and she'd been alone in the mausoleum, hoping for a way out, too used to being the good daughter to dream of breaking free for herself.

"You were," she told him. "Honestly, you were. I just realized very early on that I wanted the real man, not the noble prince."

"You've got him," he told her. "I know you didn't before—I never let on, never let you see. I treated you like…well, like a goddess. But a stone one, not a warm, flesh and blood one."

She reached up and unbuttoned her coat, then drew his hand to her chest, whispering, "I'm warm, flesh and blood."

He bent down and brushed his mouth across the top curve of her lovely breast, above her steadily beating heart. "I know. I'm sorry I put you on a pedestal."

She nodded, accepting his apology. "Let me guess… leaving aside the idea that you had to be some noble being in order to deserve me, and that my view of love and relationships came from one too many fairy tales, *yours* came from your parents?"

Shifting uncomfortably, he admitted to both of them, "Probably."

"I have to be honest," she said, a frown tugging at her brow. "I don't really like your parents. But if it helps, I don't like mine very much, either. Love them. But don't like them."

He laughed, delighted by her honesty, her openness. Abby had always been warm and funny, at least when she wasn't around her family or others who had certain expectations of her. Now, though, with all the barriers down, he really liked the way she wasn't pulling any punches.

"I'm not offended one bit, because I feel the same way about them, too. Yours and mine."

She let out a relieved breath, as if she'd really worried that she had said something unforgivable. "Hey, maybe we'll get lucky. Maybe they'll be better grandparents than they were parents. I've heard that can happen."

He held his breath, hearing what she hadn't yet said out loud, grasping the lifeline she'd just thrown him.

She continued. "In the meantime, though, will you understand if I say I'd like for us to give up your house and my apartment, and move to another part of town, away from all of them?"

He didn't answer the question, focused entirely on what it meant. "Does that mean you're going to marry me, Abby?"

She didn't laugh it off or call him silly. Instead she nodded, solemn, sincere. "If you'll still have me."

He bent to brush his mouth against hers. "I'll have

you. I'll have you and take you and want you and love you every day for the rest of my life."

Slipping out from under her, he dropped to the floor of the gazebo, getting on one knee. The first time he'd proposed to her had been over an elegant dinner in a fancy restaurant. He hadn't been on his knees. Now, he wanted her to see just how much he wanted this. Her. *Them.*

"Abigail Bauer, will you do me the honor of becoming my wife?"

She nodded without hesitation, her eyes sparkling with moisture. Tugging the engagement ring off her finger, she dropped it into his hand, then extended her own so he could slide it on all over again.

This time, it felt like more than an engagement. It was a lifelong promise, the first moment of their marriage.

"For richer, for poorer, in sickness and in health," she said.

"In wild, crazy passion and in tenderness, to have and to hold from this day forward," he told her, sealing the deal with a soft kiss.

She tightened her arms around his neck. "You got a deal. Just be warned, I'm going to be insatiable. I think I might be a bit of a nymphomaniac."

"Sounds good to me. I plan to jump your bones every night of the week and twice on Sundays once we're married."

She wagged her eyebrows. "It's Sunday."

Oh, how he liked this new, naughty Abby. "But we're not officially married yet."

Shrugging, she lifted her hand to her coat and slipped the rest of the buttons open. "I think we could make an exception just this once."

The moonlight shining through the slats in the side

of the gazebo danced across her skin—she was luminescent, like one with the night. A mysterious moon goddess meant only for him.

Keith helped her with the final buttons, pushing the coat open, then off, so he could press warm kisses on her bare middle. He moved his mouth to her breasts—kissing her nipple, moistening it until the night air hardened it to a tight, sensitive point of sensation. She shivered, and he covered her with his mouth again, sucking gently, loving the roll of that soft flesh against his tongue.

She twined her fingers in his hair, quivering, sighing. "Do you have any idea how you make me feel? You do realize I was so angry and hurt because I *wanted* you so badly, don't you?"

"I know."

"I want to do this with you forever," she told him, sounding dreamy and tender. "I want us to still do this together when we're old and gray."

He laughed softly. "Even if I have to get my knees replaced, honey, I am so up for that."

She leaned down and caught his mouth in a deep, slow kiss, their tongues tangling in sweet desire. Kissing Abby was one of his favorite things to do on this earth. And now, knowing they were right, and fine, and good, it was even better.

Dying to have her again—slow and hot and sultry this time, rather than fast and frantic—he unfastened his pants. Abby slid forward on the seat, parting her thighs invitingly, the silky dress falling over them. In their frenzy, he'd torn her thong, and she was completely bare beneath the fabric. Bare, soft, wet. He slid his fingertips across her slick sex, glad to see she was every bit as aroused now as he was—even though they'd just had wild sex in the barn.

He hoped it would always be like this. That they'd always desire each other so intensely. And that they never let misunderstandings come between them again.

"Please, Keith," she whispered, leaning closer, until her warm channel brushed against the tip of his cock.

He didn't need any further coaxing. Kissing her again, and twining his hands in her hair, he slid into her slowly, inch by inch, savoring the warmth and the tightness and the sensation that was uniquely Abby.

"I love you so much," she whispered against his mouth.

"I love you, too, Abs."

After just a few strokes, Abby began to take control. While they were still joined, she gently pushed him onto his back, until he lay flat on the floor, then straddled him. Her long hair fell in a brown curtain around them, drops of moonlight sending glimmers of gold dancing through it. He reached up to cup her breast, certain he'd never seen anything more beautiful, more desirable in his life than this woman on top of him.

Though slower this time, it was in no way vanilla sex. Abby took him, rode him, setting the pace and the tone and the depth. She knew what he wanted and he gave her what she needed and together they acknowledged everything that had turned out so right about this very difficult day.

They were right. They were, in fact, just perfect.

BY THE TIME THEY PULLED their clothes into some semblance of order and headed inside, it was very late. The party was still going on full swing, and those who weren't in attendance were probably already asleep, because the inn was silent and still as they entered.

Abby led Keith to her room, unable to keep the smile

off her face. Tiny bubbles of laughter tried to spill from her lips. She couldn't remember any moment when she'd ever been happier—not even the first time Keith had proposed to her, when she'd been younger, starry-eyed, never dreaming that someday sex might be a problem between them.

Now she knew what it was to have an adult relationship, to truly be a woman. To demand what she wanted and make sure her lover knew how much she wanted him, too.

Once inside her room, she locked the door, then dropped her coat and torn dress to the floor. Her shoes, which had been hanging by the straps on one finger, joined them there.

The light was on, and Keith stared at her, as if he'd never seen her before—as if they hadn't just made love by moonlight.

"Three times on Sunday?" she asked, lifting a brow and chuckling.

"Maybe we should write this down so we don't forget by the time we get around to getting married."

Though there was humor in his voice, the words suddenly made her feel both selfish and a little sad. Swallowing, she whispered, "I really don't want it to be too long before we get around to it."

He held her stare. "How soon would you like to do it?"

"Um…tomorrow?"

Keith nodded slowly, not laughing outright as she'd half expected him to. "I'm liking this idea."

"Our families would be upset."

"Even more reason to like it," he said with a boyish grin. "Are you sure you wouldn't mind missing the big, fancy wedding?"

"I just had Amanda's," she said with a shrug. "Honestly, I couldn't imagine anything more wonderful than running away and marrying you right this very minute."

He gave it about ten seconds thought, then leaped to his feet, grabbed her suitcase and started throwing her clothes into it. "Vegas?"

Laughing joyously, she pulled a pair of jeans and a sweater off the bed and shimmied into them. "Absolutely." Then she took his hand and smiled at him, happiness filling her every molecule.

"I love you, Keith. Tomorrow just doesn't seem soon enough to become your wife."

Stepping close, he drew her into his arms. "I love you, too, Abs. We're going to have a great time."

"In Vegas?"

"In our whole marriage."

She nodded, agreeing.

Then, together, they threw the rest of her things in the bag, crept out of the room and down the stairs.

Ten minutes later they were in his rental car, heading back to Chicago. And less than twelve hours after that—one day after she'd broken their engagement, Abby Bauer became Mrs. Keith Manning.

Or, in his words, the goddess of his heart for the rest of his life.

* * * * *

Epilogue

THERE WAS SOMETHING TO BE said for hotel sex.

Reese and Amanda had been lovers for a year, but last night—their wedding night—had been one for the record books.

Funny thing was, it had included no playacting, no props, no naughty games. Just pure heartfelt passion and deep, true love. She knew not every night of their marriage would be as glorious as the first, but oh, had they set the bar pretty damned high.

"Almost ready to go, Mrs. Campbell?" her handsome husband asked, watching her from the other room as she finished putting on her makeup in the bathroom.

"Do we have to?"

"Post-wedding breakfast and we're the main attraction. Sorry, I think we have to."

"Can't we run away like Abby and Keith did?"

Wow, had that been a surprise. Her baby sister had left a note for her at the front desk, saying that she and her fiancée—who had *so* not looked boring in his incredibly sexy costume last night—had eloped.

"I wish we could," Reese said, "considering you're going to have to be the one to break the news to your parents."

She snorted. "Are you kidding? That's one of the few things that could drag me out of this room—getting to see their faces when they find out that Abby is a little more like me than they'd ever thought...or feared!"

Reese understood; he always understood. "I just hope I'm not the one who has to explain if Bonnie forgets to go back to her own room this morning and my mother goes looking for her."

Amanda, who wasn't sure how her husband would feel about his little sister getting lucky with a movie star, turned to stare at him, one brow raised.

"Oh, come on," he said, "you don't *really* think she was going back to her own room, alone, last night, do you?"

"Well, judging by the way they were looking at each other, no, I don't. I just wasn't sure how you'd feel about it."

"I'm not sure yet. Ask me tomorrow, after we find out whether there's more to this than one wild wedding night."

She liked the sound of that. Their wedding, being a wild one, not just for them, but for their friends.

"I guess we weren't the only ones who got lucky."

"Judging by the way Jazz and that guy you work with at the airport were hanging all over each other, I suspect not."

She liked that idea—Jazz and Blake. Stranger things had happened. They said opposites attract. Whether opposites stayed together in the long-term was anyone's guess. But knowing Jazz—and Blake—she suddenly had the feeling they were just what the other needed.

Reese walked into the opulent bathroom and stood behind her, meeting her stare in the window. His hands on her hips, he pulled her back against him, then bent to kiss her neck.

"Last night was amazing," he whispered.

"You mean the part where I beat up some crazy, kid-napping stalker?"

Chuckling, he nibbled her earlobe. "Uh, no, the other part." Wagging his brows he added, "But you being all violent and badass is pretty hot. Maybe we'll have to play tough boxer-chick and hapless trainer."

She giggled, turned in his arms and wrapped her own around his neck. "Are you still going to want to play naughty games with me when we're senior citizens?"

"Absolutely." He kissed her forehead, kissed the tip of her nose, then lightly kissed her lips. "I love you, Mrs. Campbell."

Amanda liked the sound of that—Mrs. Campbell. She knew she was going to like it all the rest of her days.

"Okay, husband, let's go see what craziness every-body else got up to last night."

He smiled down at her. "Or we could stay here awhile longer and get up to a little more craziness ourselves. It is our anniversary, after all."

Hmm. Breakfast, loud family, friends, noise, depar-tures, hugs, complaints, congratulations?

Or hot sex with her brand-new hubby?

What an absolute no-brainer.

"I like the way you think, Reese Campbell, and I can't wait to hear what you have in mind."

He laughed, tugged her tighter, then whispered some-thing extremely naughty in her ear.

"Scratch that. I *really* like the way you think."

Then Amanda and her husband, Reese, proceeded to celebrate the one year anniversary of the day they met… by being just as wild and passionate as they'd been from the very start.

* * * * *

MILLS & BOON®

The Chatsfield Collection!

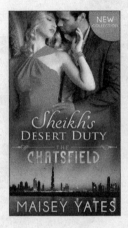 

Style, spectacle, scandal...!

With the eight Chatsfield siblings happily married and settling down, it's time for a new generation of Chatsfields to shine, in this brand-new 8-book collection! The prospect of a merger with the Harrington family's boutique hotels will shape the future forever. But who will come out on top?

Find out at
www.millsandboon.co.uk/TheChatsfield2